S0-AXR-417

## THE SEER

"*You will cross the sea, young miss. But you will be taken away by those you do not know to a country across all the seas of the world. You will never return here. Someday you will be more than an empress and those who have wronged you will spill their blood over all your city.*"

"*But why will I never come home? This is my home and I love it. I don't want to cross the sea or live anywhere but on Flower Island.*"

"*What you want is not important. I have seen what will be—I can tell you no more.*"

**UNABLE TO FIND FAWCETT PAPERBACKS AT
YOUR LOCAL BOOKSTORE OR NEWSSTAND?**

If you are unable to locate a book published by Fawcett, or, if you wish to see a list of all available Fawcett Crest, Gold Medal and Popular Library titles, write for our FREE Order Form. Just send us your name and address and 35¢ to help defray postage and handling costs. Mail to:

**FAWCETT BOOKS GROUP**
**P.O. Box C730**
**524 Myrtle Ave.**
**Pratt Station, Brooklyn, N.Y. 11205**

(Orders for less than 5 books must include 75¢ for the first book and 25¢ for each additional book to cover postage and handling.)

# MISTRESS FROM MARTINIQUE

Helene Thornton

FAWCETT GOLD MEDAL • NEW YORK

*MISTRESS FROM MARTINIQUE*

© 1979 Helene Thornton

All rights reserved

Published by Fawcett Gold Medal Books, a unit of
CBS Publications, the Consumer Publishing Division of
CBS Inc.

All the characters in this book are fictitious, and any
resemblance to actual persons living or dead is
purely coincidental.

ISBN: 0-449-14195-0

Printed in the United States of America

10  9  8  7  6  5  4  3  2  1

The author would like to acknowledge the help of the French Tourist Board in providing invaluable assistance into her research on Martinique, also the Turkish Tourist Board and staff of the Topkapi Serai Museum for showing so charmingly the astonishing treasures of the former Sultan's palace.

. . . *Son teint est pâle et chaud; la brume enchanteress*
*A dans le col des airs noblement maniérés;*
*Grande et svelte en marchant comme une chasseresse,*
*Son sourire est tranquille et ses yeux assurés* . . .

"The Creole"
BAUDELAIRE

# BOOK I

*The Island
of Flowers*

# Chapter 1

*The year, 1768. The place, Martinique, a small* island of jagged blue peaks surrounded by emerald sea and silver sand. Natives call this island Madinina, the island of flowers, and over the years, visiting French sailors have adoringly nicknamed the women of the island *les femmes du paradis.*

On a tree-lined hillside, in the heart of the island, there is a *manoir*, built in the traditional French style. Below it, on the plantation, sugarcane sways like pale green sea in trade winds blowing from seaward. The house is called La Maison du Midi. Its windows are shuttered in white, its granite walls covered in ivy, pink-tongued orchids and fronds of swaying wistaria. In the cupola of a conservatory, which adjoins the house, tropical flowers can be seen pushing their way through its windows like exotic animals.

Inside the conservatory, a child plays with her kitten. She is Aimee Dubuq de Rivery, daughter of a French settler. Aimee is five years old, a great beauty with wide turquoise eyes and clouds of silvery blond hair. She is a charmer, quietly clever with a steely will and a sparkling smile that dazzles all who meet her. Upstairs in a silk-hung bedroom, the owner of the estate, Aimee's father, lies slowly, reluctantly dying.

Near the child, on a reed bench, a huge mulatto woman sits sewing. From time to time, she eyes Aimee lovingly. The woman is a giantess who stands over six feet tall and weighs more than two strong men. She is thirty years old and has been with the family for almost twenty years. Her father was a French seaman, her mother a descendant of Carib warriors who once occupied flower island. This is Aimee's Da or nanny. As such, she is a respected member of the Dubuq de Rivery household. Damama, as the child calls her, would willingly die for her charge or at least commit murder for her. She watches Aimee, whose head is bowed, silver hair tickling the kitten as she feeds it sugared rose leaves.

"How many time do I have to tell you if you give that cat rose leaves it'll get worms, you hear me, w-o-r-m-s!"

Aimee feeds the kitten another rose leaf, all the while watching Damama with wide turquoise eyes full of laughter.

"If it gets worms it goes and *dies!* Then you'll cry like a banshee cos you can't play with it."

"It won't die."

"Sure as hell will!"

"Don't say he'll die, Damama. Bijou is my little beauty and you're bad to talk like that."

"And you, little miss, are dis-*o*-bedient. You hear me? If you have a pet you have to be its parents, mother *and* father. It's a *big* responsibility, I'm tellin' you."

"All right, I won't give him any more rose leaves."

"Good girl, that's my good girl."

Aimee sat, quietly considering what Damama had said.

"Don't look at me with a face long as a boiled cow's tongue! What's wrong with you, little miss?"

"I'm sick of being quiet. Why couldn't Cousin Rose stay for dinner like she usually does and why *can't* I play my trumpet?"

"Cos your papa's ill, that's why."

"He's ill every day but you always let me play my trumpet. So why can't I play it today?"

"Madame says you can play the piano or your violin."

"I hate them. Why can't I play my trumpet?"

Damama sighed. One thing was sure, that little girl was a very determined character! Monsieur Dubuq de Rivery owned all the land as far as the eye could see, the beach far below, the sugar plantation, slaves, forest, cottages and barracoons of French and native workers. His daughter was used to having her way. Only Damama, with love and patience, can control Aimee's autocratic gaze, her demanding presence, her youthful joie de vivre and impatience.

A basking turtle swims out to sea toward the lighthouse on the point. It is six o'clock on a summer's evening. The scarlet tropical sunset comes suddenly, fiery fierce and full of promise. Inside the house silence reigns, the silence of those awaiting death. In surrounding silk-cotton trees, frogs croak and insects chirp, and far below on the plantation, slaves sing a Sunday hymn of supplication for the recovery of their kind seigneur.

"Why are you looking so sad, Damama?"

"Sad? I'm never sad, I'm just thinkin'."

Damama shifted on one foot then the other as Aimee watched, uncomprehendingly. Touché, the houseman, came in, whispered in Damama's ear and left, silently, head bowed, face gray as a phantom. Damama looked hard out of the window as the sun slipped over the horizon. Then she went round the room lighting the lamps and giving herself time to think. How could she tell the child? Why must *she* tell the child? Why did Madame spend all her days simpering in her damned mirror trying to convince herself she was still good-looking when everyone mistook her for a skeleton! Ha! It was not funny, it was decidedly not funny.

Aimee watched Damama admiringly, awaiting her chance to leap into the woman's arms. Finally, she snuggled, contentedly, against shiny brown cheeks, coaxing a smile from Damama's long face.

"Take me to bed, I'm so sleepy. Tonight you must tell me the story of the lady who lived under the sea with Thomas Turtle."

"You sit right there on my back, little miss, and I'll have you in bed before you can say 'when'."

Carrying Aimee, Damama charged upstairs. Aimee hung

on to her neck, legs gripping her sides, squealing excitedly at the nightly thrill of a high-speed ascent.

Damama bathed Aimee, slipped a fine cambric night-dress over her head and lifted her into bed. Then the woman opened the curtains and stared out to sea at moon-lit palm trees and green waves. How best to tell the child? How best to say what had to be said without hurting the little angel?

"Damama?"

"Yes, little miss?"

"Why did Papa not come to say goodnight to me. He always comes to say goodnight even when he's very ill."

"You remember the story about the lady who lived under the sea?"

"With Thomas Turtle?"

"That's the one. You remember I told you she had a sister who lived up in the clouds?"

"With the angels and all her friends who had died?"

"That's right, little miss. Well, your papa's gone to live up there now. He died tonight cos he was just *too tired* to live till tomorrow mornin'."

Aimee looked out of the window for a brief moment. Then she tucked the kitten into bed and took Damama's brown hand. The tiny face was pale and earnest, the big blue eyes wide and troubled.

"If Papa is dead who will look after Mama and me and you and all the plantation people?"

"Your Uncle Theo, I reckon. He's a good man, a *real* good man."

"And what if Mama dies *and* Uncle Theo?"

"Then Monsieur Charles'll come and see to everyone and I'll be here to look after you. I'll *always* be here, little miss. I'm your very own Damama and I'll look after you forever! So don't you go worryin' your head about things."

"But what if *you* die?"

"Die! I'm sure as hell not gonna die till you're a big girl, not till you're as big as me and maybe not even then."

"Am I going to be as big as you someday, Damama?" asked Aimee.

"Bigger, most likely, providin' you aren't too dis-*o*-bedient."

"That's good news."

"Why?"

"Because when I'm as big as you I'm going to fight Richard Le Brun. He's a horrible boy from Grosse Pointe."

"Why's he horrible then?"

"He told Cousin Rose she wasn't pretty and she cried."

"Cousin Rose always cries. She's a little Madame, that one, she gets her way through cryin' like a waterfall."

"But she is pretty, Rose is *very* pretty, isn't she, Damama?"

"Sure she is, but not as pretty as you."

"Will I be as big as you soon?"

"No, I don't reckon you will."

"Why not?"

"Cos you don't eat enough, that's why."

"I'll eat more tomorrow, you'll see."

Damama lit the candle and tucked the silk spread round the tiny body. She turned out the lamp and kissed Aimee goodnight.

"You all right now, little miss?"

"Yes, Damama."

"Not worryin' about your papa?"

"No, not now."

"I'm off to bed right now, this heat's killin' me. If you want somethin' call, the door's open, like always."

"Goodnight, Damama."

"Goodnight, little miss."

Damama went to bed, wondering what Madame would say if she saw the kitten in Aimee's bed. Madame hated cats, dogs and just about everything in the animal kingdom. The great lady liked pretty clothes, pretty jewels and seeing Aimee for a few minutes after lunch each day. Damama tossed and turned in the humidity of the night, slapping mosquitoes and cursing armies of fireflies that danced a frenzied fandango on her ceiling.

At three, she woke, hungry as a gravedigger. She ambled down to the kitchen and grabbing a leg of pork on a plate, returned to her room. She covered the meat with hot chili pickle and ate till the bone shone clean. Then she slept until the sun rose over the horizon and a child in pink cambric kissed her resoundingly on the ear.

The smell in the kitchen was beautiful. Monsieur Armande, the chef, had lived on the island for many years. He had a mulatto wife, and the food they concocted combined the best of two very different cuisines. One of Aimee's favorite games was touring the cold pantry with Damama, trying to guess what all the magnificent concoctions were and sampling them without letting Monsieur Armande suspect what they were doing. Sometimes, Damama got carried away by the game and ate a salver of land crabs or a loaf of banana bread. Damama loved banana bread. Each morning, she had it for breakfast with a bowl of coconut milk, but Monsieur Armande gave her only two slices and Damama had a two-loaf capacity.

Aimee squealed in delight as a large capon disappeared into the pocket of Damama's apron. Perhaps they would eat it on a picnic in the garden later in the day. Picnics were a much-favored occupation on the island. Aimee loved them almost as much as she loved Damama.

The funeral took place the following day. Madame Dubuq de Rivery wore her best black with a ship draped in matching tulle suspended miraculously from her new coiffure. Halfway through the long service, she grew tired and her head leaned, imperceptibly, as she dozed. Ominously, the ship developed a list to starboard and had to be adjusted sharply by the wife of the military governor of the island. Damama, who was watching from the rear of the small chapel, tried to keep from laughing. Another few days with that fancy hairdo and mice would start running in the larded tresses. Then Madame would scream for Toby in the middle of the night, to chase them out of her room.

Later, as Aimee sat by the graveside arranging flowers neatly over freshly dug earth, the girl wondered if her papa had already gone to the place above the clouds. If not, he would be feeling terribly hot under all that heavy soil. She resolved to ask Patou, the gardener, to plant a tamarind tree to shade the spot where he lay.

Cousin Rose's mother, Madame Tascher, had come to pay her last respects. Rose had been left at home with her father, who was indisposed. Damama snorted loudly at the word. She knew all about Gaspard Tascher, who got drunk.

14

as a lord four times a week and ran around waving his manhood at any female who looked likely to be interested! No wonder little Rose cried like a waterfall three times a day. Her young life had been overshadowed by the constant threat of Gaspard's leaving the family for some fancy lady from the city. Damama knew only too well that Rose was the only person who could control her erring father with tears, curtsies and tiny bunches of violets. At five, Rose was already a coquette but Damama was not optimistic that she would succeed in holding her father's affection for much longer.

As time passed, the household adjusted to the loss of its seigneur. Monsieur Theo, Aimee's uncle, ran the estate efficiently and visited the house often to entertain them with stories of events in the capital and his travels to nearby islands. Madame grew pale and ever thinner till Damama began to worry. It wasn't natural to be that thin! Lord, it seemed as though Madame could walk between raindrops and sideways she was almost invisible. Damama decided to speak to Madame about her eating habits but the lady refused politely to discuss the matter.

Damama pondered the problem for a few days, then she tackled Monsieur Theo on the same subject. Monsieur Theo sat watching the ceiling for a considerable time, then he surprised Damama with his frankness.

"I know I can trust your discretion, Da."

"Yes, sir!"

"It's probably best if I inform you of the true facts of Madame's illness."

"Sir?"

"Madeleine—Madame—has an illness from which she will not recover."

*"Oh, Lord!"*

"She has known for some time, indeed since before my brother died, that she was not long for this world. The illness takes its victims very slowly, but Dr. Fauchon makes sure she does not suffer by giving her enough opium to keep her out of pain. He says she has less than two years to live."

"God help us, sir!"

"You must speak of this to no one. I am telling you only because it affects you more than any of the other members of the household. Before long, you will be solely responsible for Aimee. Her education and financial requirements are my responsibility, of course, but you will be the only female person on whom she can rely."

"Yes, *sir!*"

"Aimee has many female relatives in France and indeed on this island. But we are scattered about and she sees most of them only at festivities and holidays except for Cousin Rose."

"I shall do my best, sir. I shall defend little miss with my life!"

"Let's hope that will never be necessary, Da."

"Yes, *sir.*"

"That's all now; thank you for your concern. I hear you're having a picnic this afternoon?"

"We're off to Trinity Beach, sir."

"Who's driving?"

"Toby, sir."

"Best not be too late home; my bones tell me there'll be a storm tonight."

"We'll be back by four-thirty, sir, I promise."

"Da?"

"Yes, sir."

"Michael Leyritz and his wife have invited Aimee to the birthday of André, their son, on Sunday week. Do you think she would like to go?"

"I'm sure she would, sir."

"I'll arrange it then."

Damama walked on and sat down on the veranda, wiping her sweating face, surprised to hear her heart beating loudly in her ears. Dammit! What a family they were, dying off before they were thirty! Looking up, she saw Aimee running across the lawn toward her, arms full of yellow allamanda. How lovely the child was, a perfect golden sight. Damama ran to meet her, scooping the girl in the air and covering her with kisses. She would be the best mother in the world to Aimee Dubuq de Rivery. Damama closed her eyes, praying for the strength to do all that would be necessary.

16

At two, coachmen arrived, and Monsieur Armand delivered the picnic basket.

"You made plenty of red beans, Monsieur Armande?"

"Enough for an army!"

"And *chou palmiste*?"

"Of course, madame."

"And suckling pig?"

"*Two* because last time you told me you 'lost' one on the way!"

"Stop scowlin', Monsieur Armande. Perhaps I'll bring you back an iguana and that'll make you smile."

"Madame, every time you go on a picnic you tell me you'll bring me back an iguana, and do you? Of course you don't! You're *méchante, très, très méchante!*"

"This time, maybe I will."

Monsieur Armande walked slowly back to the house.

"Monsieur Armande?"

"What now?"

"You put in some fruits and a little flask of punch for Damama?"

"I have put everything you ever asked for in that basket, madame. What more could you possibly want? If you continue to eat as you do we'll have to employ boys to carry you in a chair before you're forty!"

"That sounds just right, Monsieur Armande. I could do with a couple of strong boys to attend to my female appetites. I get a little lonely in this big house all on my own."

"Madame, you're impossible!"

Monsieur Armande fled, red-faced, back to his kitchen. Damama threw her head back and laughed out loud as she ran into the house to call Aimee. The child appeared in a dress of fine blue lawn tied at sleeve and hem with posies of forget-me-nots. Two boys in livery took their places on the postilion and the coachman drove them at a sedate canter down the drive.

Aimee was happy. She sat, clutching Bijou, the kitten, eyes searching surrounding green foliage for favorite tiny monkeys and bright yellow macaws. On a dusty road, they passed a goat and her newborn kid and native women carrying baskets on their heads as they walked back from market. The sun shone, hot as Monsieur Armande's oven, and Damama covered them with her red silk parasol. Aimee held her hand, sniffing the smell of clove and coriander that clung to Damama's clothing. She smiled as she thought of the picnic basket. Damama would eat like a hungry mule and drink rum and syrup punch till she sang out of tune. And on their return, Monsieur Armande would marvel that one woman and a small girl could eat such a vast repast.

Aimee closed her eyes. How beautiful it was on flower island. The sun always shone, warm and golden, and flowers burst forth into bloom on houses, hedgerows and hillsides. Flower island was the best place in the whole world to be.

Toby left the victoria under a clump of coconut trees as they made their way to the beach. First he spread heavy oiled cloth on the sand, then soft mohair rugs. After he unpacked silver dishes, he had the other two grooms carry the food. When the meal was ready to eat, Damama dismissed the coachmen and they waited under the trees, playing *boule* and swapping stories of fish they had almost caught and women they had almost loved.

Aimee ate cherries, strawberries, watermelon and a piece of her favorite, lampling pie. Damama ate most of the rest. After a brief rest, they went along the beach searching for pirate treasure and jewels washed up from wrecks along the coast. The procedure was always the same. Damama bent low, searching, while Aimee proffered colored stones, broken glass, metal cask-binders and seaweed for her nurse's approval. Once, they had found a tiny gold ring with ruby stones clustered at its center and Damama had chortled with delight all the way home. The incident had given them endless enjoyment and every excursion since had held the promise of another find, another treasure, another lovely surprise. Aimee wore the tiny ring on her little finger, showing it to everyone she met.

Today, they found nothing but a fish skeleton and some pretty conch shells. They returned to the picnic table and Damama drank the punch as Aimee refreshed her thirst with sweet lime cordial. Then Damama called the men over to finish the remains of the meal and asked Toby to lend her his penny whistle. He handed her the whistle and

18

Damama disappeared at a fast pace among the bamboo trees, closely followed by Aimee. Through green parasol ferns, plumiera bushes and campeachy trees, Damama strode on, parting heavy vegetation with her big strong arms.

"Where are we going, Damama?"

"I'm intendin' to catch me a iguana."

"An iguana!"

"That's right, little miss."

"Monsieur Armande will be *very* surprised."

"Today, I'm gonna make that Frenchman eat his big starched hat!"

Damama stood for a few minutes listening to thrushes chirping, wood pigeons cooing and the scratchy scuttling of red land crabs galloping sideways into dense bamboo. In the distance, they saw women washing clothes under a waterfall. Damama continued to listen, then she motioned Aimee to silence and took her place under a soursop tree. She produced Toby's whistle and rendered a lively version of *"Auprès de ma blonde."* Aimee sat at her side, wide-eyed at this unexpected performance.

One tune followed another, from sprightly ditties to sad, melodious songs of sea, sand and sailors in love. After an hour, Aimee's eyes began to close. The air was warm and slumberous, and she fell gently asleep at Damama's side.

Suddenly, there was a great thud and Aimee woke to see Damama leaping with a triumphant cry on an iguana she had managed to lasso. Skirts flew skyward, exposing voluminous white frills and red satin drawers. Damama, grunting and cursing like a wily mariner, applauded her own expertise.

"By jingoes, I got discipline!"

"What happened?"

"What happened? I caught me a iguana, that's what happened."

"But *how* did you catch it, Damama, where was it?"

"It was up there in that tree, takin' a rest after lunch and dreamin' of happy times lovin' lady iguanas and eatin' passion fruits. When I played Toby's whistle, Mr. Iguana listens and listens till he falls in a trance and slips off his branch onto the ground. Then I lasso him and that's that! Oh Lord, I can't wait to see Monsieur Armande's face."

"Mama doesn't eat iguana. She told Monsieur Armande he wasn't to have one in the house!"

"She loves it, little miss. Monsieur Armande tells your mama it's turkey meat cos ladies are generally a bit scared of reptiles. Now you run and bring Toby. Tell him to hurry cos I promised Monsieur Theo we'd be home by half hour past four, and home by half hour past four we *must* be."

Aimee ran, eyes dazzled by what she had seen. She returned, minutes later, with the carriage, three sleepy-eyed mén and an empty picnic basket. They dragged the lizard through the undergrowth and deposited it in the rear of the victoria. Toby drove home in fine style.

Damama and Aimee sang as they passed the old fortune-teller's shack. Aimee peered into the overgrown garden, full of curiosity about the lady some said could foretell the future. She had often asked Damama about Euphemia the seer but Damama didn't approve of knowing the future . . . "might find out I'm gonna fall down a hole next week and think how much worryin' that would give me." So Aimee's questions were never answered. She had secretly decided to bring Cousin Rose to Euphemia's shack once they were old enough to walk out alone. It would be marvelous to know all the lovely things that would happen when they grew up to be French miladies of Martinique.

Monsieur Armande blushed as Damama presented him with her offering. He staggered under the animal's weight and disappeared toward the cold store beaming at the prospect of the luscious dishes he could make from the fine meat.

"Madame, I congratulate you, you are truly astonishing! I am most grateful for your gift. Allow me to give you this as a token of my esteem."

He presented Damama with a circle of banana bread, a foot thick and two feet in diameter. Damama's eyes widened with delight at her reward. She beamed wickedly at Monsieur Armande, grabbed her prize and disappeared upstairs with Aimee. Monsieur Armande sighed. What a woman! Who else would catch a four-foot iguana and cart it all the way from Trinity Beach? He was sorely tempted to explore Damama's other talents but he found himself being watched by Lulu, his wife. Lulu was even jealous of mosquitoes that bit Monsieur Armande's ears, and so he decided that discretion was the best policy. Discretion was an excellent protection against Lulu's passion for fidelity. That night, he dreamed of being trussed up by Damama and boiled in champagne for her supper!

# Chapter 2

*Aimee's seventh birthday was spent at her cousin's* mill, La Pagerie, near Trois-Ilets. Her eighth was celebrated at home with Damama, Uncle Theo and Mama, who now lived in bed every day all day and had for many weeks past. Madame made a great effort to come downstairs for an hour to present Aimee with her gift, a necklace of turquoise set in gold with a matching pin for her hair. Aimee hugged her mother and rushed away to show Damama the new treasures.

Madame sat, quietly looking out into the garden, smiling sadly as she watched Aimee and Damama jumping up and down in delight at the splendid gifts. Madame turned to Monsieur Theo and asked him to take her back to her room.

"I'm so tired, Theo; as the hours pass I feel no pain, only exhaustion. Soon, I believe, I shall fall asleep forever."

"My dear, I wish I could help you."

"You have helped me. You came to live here and you look after us all so beautifully. I'm *so* grateful for all you have done."

"Aimee has had a lovely day thanks to you."

"I did the right thing, didn't I, Theo?"

"You have always done the right thing, Madeleine."

"It's not been easy for me to allow my own child to grow up without really knowing her mother. But this way is best for Aimee. She loves her nurse, to Aimee Da is her Mama. When I die, I'm sure she will barely notice my passing."

"She will notice, Madeleine. She loves you dearly and longs to please you. I believe Aimee has great wisdom for one so young. She knows you are ill and tired, so she tries not to trouble you with her demands. She plays with Da and relies on her strength."

"Do you really believe she loves me, Theo?"

"I know she does, Madeleine."

Before Aimee's ninth birthday, Madame died peacefully in her sleep. She was buried next to her husband in the far reaches of the garden of La Maison du Midi.

Aimee was very sad in the weeks that followed. Mama had stayed in her room and rarely spoken to anyone, yet her presence filled the house with pretty feminine things. The silver bowls of jasmine, potted primroses, jardinieres overflowing verbena and rare orchid flowers had been Mama's way of filling the house with perfume. Mama's wardrobe of rich lace, satin, georgette and crepe de chine, all imported from France, was enough to send any girl-child wild with joy. Mama had let her play in the ribbon drawers and sometimes permitted her to rummage in the jewel cases and trinket boxes. An afternoon in Mama's pink silk bedroom had been something very special, and Aimee missed it terribly.

Alone, she cried bitterly. Death was horrible. Why did people have to die and leave those they loved alone and unhappy? Damama found her red-eyed and trembling, covered in soil from sitting on the dirty steps of the conservatory.

"If you cry much more Bijou'll cry too."

"Cats can't cry, can they?"

"I don't rightly know. But if Bijou and you cry then I'll cry as well, and you never saw anythin' like that in your whole life!"

"Oh, Damama, funerals are miserable and death is horrible. I hate it!"

"*French* funerals are miserable, little miss. Creole funerals are real jolly, somethin' like carnival time."

"How can a funeral be jolly?"

"Someday, I'll show you, I promise. Now, wipe your eyes and give Damama a *big* smile. Your mama's up in the clouds right now, keepin' a eye on you. If she sees you weepin' what's she gonna think of us both?"

"What shall we do tomorrow, Damama?"

"After you finish your lessons, we'll go for a picnic or we could try a bit of river fishin'. Yesterday, Monsieur Armande asked me if I knew how to catch rainbow fish. I told him I'd bring him some next time we go on a expedition."

"Let's go tomorrow then."

"Tomorrow it is, little miss."

In the morning, Damama carried a long-pronged fork and Aimee a willow pannier to hold the catch, as they walked down toward the river. Monsier Armande watched them hurry through the silk cotton trees until they were out of sight. He shook his head wonderingly. He had never cared to venture into the jungle. He had a great fear of snakes, a terror of raccoons, and every parrot on the island bit him when he passed. He sat down on the big kitchen rocker and thought of his wife, Lulu, far away in the south visiting her sisters. Then, he thought of Damama and temptation flushed his cheeks. He rushed to the cold store to calm himself with a glass of camomile and lime.

An hour later, Damama and Aimee returned, delightedly waving a stick on which five rainbow fish hung. Monsieur Armande was ecstatic and Damama noted the pink flush on his neck. Her teeth began to chatter from long immersion in cold crystal water and she pulled her wrap around her, patting Monsieur Armande on the back mischievously.

"I swear, Monsieur Armande, I'm cold enough to die; you got somethin' you could warm Damama with?"

Monsieur Armande's eyes rolled and he loosened his collar and fumbled with a bottle of rum.

"I'll make you a hot toddy if you like, madame."

25

"You got anythin' else locked away in that pantry that'd make me warm real quick?"

Damama gave Monsieur Armande a push and led him into the pantry. Aimee sat on a stool waiting, patiently, for them to return. She ate some strawberries and a coconut cake, wondering what Monsieur Armande had in his pantry that Damama needed so urgently. Probably it was a banana bread loaf. Aimee smiled as she heard Damama roaring with laughter and Monsieur Armande gasping, "My God, madame, not again!" After a long pause, Damama emerged beaming like a contented cat. She was carrying a plate of cold guinea fowl and a loaf of her favorite bread. Monsieur Armande's face was bright pink, his eyes shining like twin beacons. Aimee wondered why his hands were trembling so.

"You sure know how to start a woman's female appetites, Monsieur Armande. I reckon I shall get hungry again round ten so you make good and sure you're ready with somethin' to tempt me. Come on, little miss, I'm gonna tell you a story. Lord help us! I'm a powerful happy woman today!"

Monsieur Armande collapsed into his rocker, fanning himself with his apron. Ten o'clock! At ten o'clock Damama would return to devour him. He smiled and closed his eyes, thinking of the power of her great brown body and the fun in her knowing brown eyes. Lulu, his loving but jealous wife, would be away for another week. Monsieur Armande wondered, ruefully, if he would still be alive to greet her on her return. He fell asleep for an hour snoring gently. Then he went to his room to prepare himself for Damama's arrival.

The next day, Cousin Rose arrived for lunch and stayed until early evening. She chattered happily with Aimee as they played in the conservatory and planted a special kind of violet she had brought as a gift for her so adored cousin. Before she left, Rose gave strict instructions on how the violets should be watered.

Aimee watched, admiring Rose's beauty. Her cousin was taller by far than she and was growing much more quickly though they were almost the same age. Rose knew all about France and talked of her longing to live in Paris. Aimee wondered why anyone would think of leaving flower island but she listened, patiently, politely, to all her cousin said. She had a great sense of responsibility toward Cousin Rose because the Tascher family were much poorer than her own.

As the sun began to fall toward the horizon, the two girls sat on a velvet sofa in Aimee's room, looking out to sea, enjoying tall glasses of lemonade and cinnamon toast made by Monsieur Armande. Coral luminescence filled the room, lighting Rose's dark hair with a fiery red glow. Her wide green eyes were suddenly sad and Aimee kissed her to make her happy again. Rose took her hand, stroking it gently.

"Can you keep a secret, Aimee?"

"Yes, but not from Damama."

"Damama doesn't matter, she's good and kind."

"What is the secret? Tell me quickly, I can't *wait* to know."

"I think Papa is going to leave us and go off with Madame Ellene."

"Leave you! But who will care for you and Aunt Tascher?"

"No one, we shall be all alone in the world."

"Who is Madame Ellene?"

"She owns a shop where lots of pretty girls work in Trois-Ilets."

"But what makes you think Uncle Gaspard will go away?"

"I just know he will, that's all. Mama told me to be specially nice to Papa so he would love me *so* much he *couldn't* go away and leave us. I've been lovely every minute of every day. I even planted violets and angel flowers under his window so he called me his beautiful little lady. But it didn't mean *anything!* He's going to leave us and go to *her*. Oh, I could die!"

Cousin Rose burst into tears and sobbed violently until Damama appeared to calm her.

"Now what? Come on, Miss Rose, no waterfalls! Let me hug you and make you feel better. Go fetch some cocoa sugar cakes, little miss. I asked Monsieur Armande to make some specially for Cousin Rose."

Aimee ran to fetch the treat, appalled that Rose should

have to suffer such torment. She returned to the bedroom to hear Rose talking to Damama, tears banished, childish fury taking its place.

"Mama said if I was nice to Papa and loved him dearly and gave him flowers he would never leave us, and now he's going to go despite everything! Men are bad, and I *hate* them!"

"Some men are bad and some are good, Miss Rose. You can't hate all of them, that's for sure."

"When I'm a great lady in Paris, I shall beat them and treat them like alligators! That will make them try to please me, won't it, Damama?"

"I don't rightly know. Perhaps they'll just up and run away from you."

"Well, I shan't be nice and give them flowers because they'll leave me like Papa's going to leave me. And I do *so* love him. Oh, I wish I could sit down and *die!*"

Aimee rushed to offer the cocoa cakes before Rose could start weeping again. The child dried her eyes, hugging Aimee as she ate the sugary sweets till a glow of pleasure suffused her face.

At six the carriage arrived to take Rose home. As the girl left with a wistful wave and grateful thanks for their kindness, Damama wiped her eyes and blew her nose loudly.

"Damned if I don't wish that child could come and live here. She's a very troubled soul, that's for sure, and no good'll come of it. You just wait and see."

# Chapter 3

*By the time Aimee was ten years old, she was* already an accomplished young lady. Her days were filled with lessons from a French tutor, Monsieur Maurice, who instructed her in reading, writing and simple calculation. She also had an English teacher, Mr. Carrington, a charming young man who was employed as a manager at the Maritime Station. Damama told her that Mr. Carrington was a gentleman who lived far away from his Irish home, because he had fought a duel and severely wounded someone. His father had sent him away to Martinique to avoid trouble with the Irish law. The other tutor employed by Uncle Theo was Madame Sylvie, a gentlewoman of thirty, recently widowed, who was teaching Aimee dancing and the social graces.

Aimee had already learned the intricacies of the minuet, the coranto and various *danses rondes*. Next, she would learn the complications of the cotillion. Damama snorted at formal dancing. She loved the calenda and the beguine because they started her female appetites and that was a pretty good feeling.

One night, Damama took Aimee to a slave wedding on the sugar plantation below. Aimee was delighted at the prospect of staying up long after the moon rose high in the sky. She had slept all afternoon in preparation for this special treat. Uncle Theo was away in St. Pierre so he would never know she had visited the plantation compound at such a late hour.

Arriving with Damama, Aimee was wide-eyed as she looked over the tidy outlines of the granary, drying tower, waterwheel and distillery. She was placed on a stool near a wooden table loaded with food. Damama rushed away to find plates, which she piled high with canary, crabs and cassava bread, sweet potatoes and conch shells full of lamb. They drank lime and nutmeg punch and bowls of coconut milk. Aimee watched as slave men and women formed separate lines in preparation for dancing the notorious calenda. Sitting stiffly upright, fingering the folds of her new pink dress, Aimee was unaware of a young black boy watching wide-eyed in admiration of the tiny silver goddess.

The sound of drums gripped between the knees of black musicians filled the night with a leisurely beat and a song lazily sung. Dancers and spectators joined in the song, hands clapping, feet tapping, faces wreathed in smiles. After a while, the beat increased to a faster pace and two lines of dancers pranced back and forth, together then apart, together then apart, continuing the original movement without touching the person in the opposite line. Finally, the drummers drummed a fevered beat, the signal for suggestive gestures, invitations, loud cries and the frenzied beating of bodies.

Aimee was hypnotized as she watched the two lines draw apart and then unrelentingly together. As they drew close, men and women thrust their lower regions forward hard against one another, grinding, pulsing, beating, searching, sweating as they threw their heads back in an ecstasy of simulated sexual largesse. Aimee felt hot and vaguely disquieted. She looked for her nurse, but Damama had disappeared. She was far away in her own private paradise, quivering, shivering, shimmying her lower regions against those of a slave Aimee had never seen. The young man was blacker than the others with big white teeth and rippling muscles. He wore a pair of raggy pink trousers and shouted encouragement to Damama as the lines oscillated to a finale of spent bodies. .

Aimee felt sweat gathering on her face and a strange weakness took her limbs so she could barely move. The young boy who had been watching her ran for a gourd of papaya juice, and bowing, handed it to her. Aimee drank gratefully, eyeing the young man with wonder. The boy was at least twelve, perhaps more. He was not African, despite his color, and Aimee wondered if he was a descendant of Carib warriors like Damama. She thanked him politely, watching as he ran back to the table with the empty gourd.

A feast followed of lobster and turtle boucanned over a slow smoky fire. Aimee tasted food she had never seen before, relishing breadfruit, charcoal-broiled plantains and a sensational syrup of tangerine, passion fruit and nutmeg. As time passed, the bridal couple disappeared to their hut and the noisy celebrations continued. Damama danced without a pause, as dark blue night sky turned green, then yellow with the dawn of a new day.

Aimee began to feel sleepy. The young boy approached and beckoned her. He led her down a narrow path to a spot within inches of the sea and piled gray moss and ferns from the undergrowth into a makeshift mattress on the sand. Then he motioned her to lie down. He took a bamboo stick and tapped away land crabs and tiny sand spiders as Aimee watched, uncertainly. She wondered where Damama was and if she ought to return to the compound. The young boy smiled encouragingly.

"I am Peter; your Da is my aunt. You look tired, Miss Aimee. Please try to sleep, and I will guard you."

Aimee crept onto the soft moss bed and curled up, covering herself with her shawl.

"You're very kind, Peter."

Closing her eyes, she drifted into a jumble of thoughts and imaginings, picturing the natives dancing and reviewing her own strange feelings as she had watched them. She almost slept but the unusual circumstances prevented her from truly relaxing.

After a while, she felt the welcome warm glow of sunrise. She lay still, wondering if Peter was still there. She felt his hand on her hair and she froze, barely breathing, as he lightly kissed her shoulder. She wanted to throw her arms round him and smother him with affection. But instinctively she knew that it would be wrong. So she stayed, silently feigning sleep. Within minutes, she turned and opened her eyes. He was still sitting, on guard, stick in hand looking out to sea.

"What are you thinking, Peter?"

"I'm thinking that when I'm a man I shall sail far away from Madinina and make my fortune."

"How will you make a fortune?"

"I'll find treasure on the far island."

"How do you know there's treasure there?"

"My father told me before he died."

"My papa died a long time ago."

"I know."

"Did Damama tell you?"

"Yes, she comes to see me every Sunday. My father was her brother. He was headman at your father's distillery. He died of the spotted fever two years ago and I work in his place."

Damama appeared at that moment, accompanied by the handsome young man. Her face glowed with happiness and she appeared almost beautiful. Aimee studied the vast frame and the shiny brown taffeta dress with its scarlet undergarments. She fondled the fluffy hair curled in corkscrew ringlets and bunched around Damama's ears. Damama was truly a lovely lady. Aimee took her hand proudly as they walked away from the party.

"Peter made me a bed and guarded me."

"Peter's a good boy, a very good boy."

"Can he come and live at our house?"

"I don't rightly know, little miss. Peter has his own room over the distillery because he has a job lookin' after Monsieur Theo's donkeys."

"But he could live in our house and guard us all the time, couldn't he?"

"We'll see about that. Perhaps someday I'll go ask Monsieur Theo if he'll give his permission."

Aimee slept late the next day. She lay in her silken bed thinking again and again of the wedding party and how watching the forbidden dance had made her feel so weak. She thought of Peter who had wanted to guard her and keep her safe and she wondered if Damama had asked Uncle Theo about his coming to stay. If Peter lived at La Maison du Midi, they could all go fishing and she would have someone to fight and chase around the lawn. Damama was too big to fight, and Cousin Rose didn't care for rough play, and neither of them liked being chased around the lawn. She waited to have news of Peter's arrival but nothing happened and Damama never mentioned the matter again. But soon Aimee forgot all about him in the excitement of the news that Damama brought one sunny morning.

"Cousin Rose is coming to stay!"

As Damama burst in with the welcome information, Aimee was so delighted she jumped up and down on the bed until Bijou ran and hid under the armoire, meowing pitifully at the loud noise.

They decided to go to St. Pierre to buy material so Damama could make Rose new underwear and a new dress for her birthday. They would buy her a scented box of velvet hair ribbons and a basket to hold flowers from the garden and perhaps a music box as well. Cousin Rose loved flowers and spent every daylight hour in the conservatory and surrounding gardens. She loved music and already had learned to play the piano, violin and dulcimer. Damama thought Rose a clever little girl even if she was something of a flirt.

A visit to St. Pierre was a grand occasion. Toby and the two grooms wore their best olive serge and hats with turkey feather crests. Damama always wore brown. When Aimee asked why, Damama replied, "Brown is the color of the earth and I'm a woman who *loves* the earth, little miss." For everyday use Damama wore brown cotton or voile, on special occasions the rustling brown taffeta, but for visits to St. Pierre she wore her best brown wool, bought by Monsieur Theo as a Christmas present. Aimee was dressed in voile with a bonnet of bright green silk and yellow daisies. They embarked in strong sunlight, shielded by Damama's red silk parasol and chattering happily of all they would do in the big city.

From time to time, throughout its history, the island of Martinique had been occupied by the French. The invaders had built harbors and warehouses for food and trading

33

supplies, barracks for soldiers and a vast slave market for one of their most profitable cargoes. Chandlers and dockers were employed year-round to service the French fleet while paymasters, harbor masters and a resident garrison kept business and private life on the island functioning as nearly as possible in the French style. Slowly, the elite landowning colonists from France had imprinted Gallic panache on the lazy, languorous dreamers of flower island.

As their victoria passed houses belonging to native workers on the nearby banana plantation, they watched a man making fire in a tinder socket. Far away, on a deserted headland, they saw the house of two lepers and baskets of food left by villagers at the outcasts' gate. They continued through a small town, where Damama roared with laughter at the coffin maker's sign "Bargain Prices, Coffins Made to Measure."

Within minutes, the heavens opened and a sudden deluge nearly drowned them. Toby screamed that the carriage wheels were stuck in the mud and Damama beat him with her parasol to make him do something about their predicament. But Toby sat, stupefied by the storm, mutely staring up at the sky long after the rain had ceased. Damama cursed loud and long. Then she took off her boots, hoisted up her skirts and roared to the two grooms to assist her.

"You two better get your fat asses off that damned seat and push like your life depends on it."

Aimee watched as the two men pushed, but the carriage did not move an inch. Then Damama stepped alongside and the three heaved till their faces turned red with effort. Finally, the carriage moved on down the road and Toby had to call the horses to a halt while the others caught up.

Damama was furious at the sight of mud on her best brown wool. "Dammit, I'll have the skin off that Toby's back, just see if I won't," she cried. She continued to mutter under her breath for half an hour until Aimee remembered the picnic Monsieur Armande had made. Damama beamed, suddenly delighted, telling Aimee confidentially that Monsieur Armande was something of a fellow. She swigged sugar syrup and sweet rum and ate a hefty slab of suckling pig. Then she tried the pigeon pie and took a helping of Aimee's lampling. Peaceful again, Damama leaned back contentedly, as the sun came out on fresh green landscape. Aimee watched Damama, wondering what she was thinking.

"Are you happy, Damama?"

"Sure am, little miss."

"Isn't the sun warm?"

"Beautiful, the best sun in the *whole* world. You know, little miss, some places don't hardly get to see the sun so we should be real grateful that we're so lucky."

"Do you know if they have sun in France?"

"Not much, I reckon."

"Monsieur Maurice was telling me about Paris. He says I should go to school in France."

"Stupid fellow; this is your home and nowhere else!"

"Monsieur Maurice says Paris is very beautiful."

"I expect it is, but it's cold enough to make your bones ache permanent. It doesn't just rain for five minutes in France, it rains for *five days*! I know because a ship's captain I met once told me so. He was a *Français* from Paris not a *française créole* so I reckon he knew what he was talkin' about."

"How could it rain for five *days*, Damama?"

"I don't know, but this sea captain said the rain there is somethin' terrible. They only have summer in the months of July and August and sometimes it forgets to arrive! Rest of the year, I reckon it rains just about every day. If I went to France I'd freeze to death in all that shiverin' weather."

Aimee digested the information as they passed a wayside fruit vendor with wooden bowls overflowing melon, papaya, pineapple, guava and big green coconuts. On the outskirts of the city, they saw convicts in white uniforms working with hand plows under the strict eye of an overseer with a bullwhip. And soon the road grew busy with women carrying heavy baskets of sweet potatoes, lemons, lobsters and ortolan for city markets. Damama snorted indignantly.

"Women on this island are treated worse than donkeys! If I had my way the men would all be made to work instead of sittin' outside their houses smokin' their pipes and playin' silly tunes on their tin whistles!"

Aimee listened intently.

"Men that expect women to act like beasts of burden

35

don't deserve what women have to offer. They don't understand that give-and-take is mightily important in life."

Damama heated to her subject. "Monsieur Armande give me a big banana bread loaf and I give him some rainbow fish in return. Monsieur Theo gives me a good home and I give him my loyalty forever! But men who give you nothin' and expect somethin' in return, they need their gizzards slittin', that's for sure."

Aimee listened, nodding quietly in agreement with Damama's sentiments. Houses on the edge of town were shanties made of boxwood and strengthened paper with tin roofs and no windows. The smell from the shanties made Aimee feel sick and Damama covered her nose with a scented silk handkerchief. Farther on, houses of wealthy planters were surrounded by campeachy trees and had verandas shaded with rush matting hung on long bamboo poles. But it was the houses of the city center that pleased Aimee most. Shaded from midday heat by sandbox and tamarind, they were prettily colored and extravagantly designed. Some were made of wood painted pink, turquoise, terra-cotta and *pistache*. They stood by the side of shops colored green and yellow, red and blue with scarlet geraniums hung from first-floor balconies. The most expensive ladies' shop in town had turquoise scalloped shutters on a pristine white facade and a gold bell to be rung to gain admittance to its exclusive interior.

Yellow painted horse buses crowded the streets, colliding with handcarts and gentlemen's carriages. The scene was one of great color, immense disorder and incomparable excitement. Damama ordered Toby to wait in a shady square while she and Aimee did their errands. They passed street vendors selling fruit, ribbons, seeds and giant tissue paper flowers. Damama guided them across the disorder of the road past her favorite grocer's shop and a store selling chandlery. Finally, they stood outside the ladies' shop with the golden bell. Aimee rang it enthusiastically and a sober-faced assistant in dove gray serge opened the door and asked them to come in.

Aimee chose velvet ribbons in blue, gray and violet and a music box hand-painted with wild roses. They bought expensive lawn and lilac silk for the dresses that Damama

36

planned to make for Cousin Rose. Finally, they selected two tiny bonnets covered in rosebuds with satin ribbons and tulle surrounds, one in saffron and cinnamon for Aimee and one in violet and fuchsia for Rose. The goods were placed in gold-striped white boxes and handed to a delivery boy to be taken to the waiting carriage. Damama and Aimee were well pleased with their purchases. Rose would have quite a birthday.

Fishermen sat near the quayside mending green nets with long wooden needles and pet parrots screamed raucous greetings as they passed by. Aimee thought the warehouses near the harbor were squat and ugly but Damama had friends in a bar near the port and whenever they came to St. Pierre she called on them. Today, she was anxious to get the mud off her best brown wool and to dry out her undergarments.

Damama handed Aimee over to her Aunt Beeka so the old lady could give the child a real Creole lunch, and then she proceeded upstairs to the attic where her friends lived. They had a line on the roof for drying washing and a big flat iron to take creases out of her precious clothing. Damama stripped and covered herself with a cotton sheet, watching as they rinsed her dress hem and red satin drawers. She relaxed happily with a glass of rum punch as they hung her things in the wind that blew like a cold slap from the open ocean. Then they gossiped for an hour until her friends left her to join Aimee and Aunt B. for lunch.

A waiter from the cafe below took Damama's lunch upstairs on a tray. It was midafternoon before he returned with a sheepish grin and a ruffled shirt. Aimee observed him closely, noting that he looked just like Monsieur Armande had looked after his visit to the larder with Damama. Perhaps her nurse had had one of her attacks of female appetite. Aimee began to be curious about just what happened when that occurred.

They drove home past cotton plantations and sugar mills covered in ivy. Night came with the sunset that never failed to surprise by its suddenness and in the distance they heard insistent drumbeats that spoke of celebrations and slaves dancing the calenda. Aimee sat perfectly still, cheeks burning at the remembrance of that night when she had first seen the dance. Damama seemed unusually quiet, eyes half closed, body sleepy and satiated by her experiences in the city.

In a village square, they saw girls wearing colorful *douillettes* tripping back and forth to the tune of a black fiddler. Heads covered in bright foulards, legs exposed under half-raised skirts, black hair lustrous and flowing, they presented an unforgettably sensuous picture. Damama called Toby to halt the carriage for a moment.

She jumped out and approached an old peasant woman wearing a wide cartwheel straw hat who sat at the side of the road leaning over a glowing charcoal brazier. Damama bought black puddings made of turtle meat and hot chili sauce and they ate gleefully, wiping their hands on a cloth she kept in the carriage in case hunger took her during journeys to and from the city. As they ate, they watched a native girl dressed in red, dancing the beguine, arms wrapped tightly around her man's neck, bottom switching back and forth against his tight red trousers. Damama closed her eyes briefly and told Toby to drive on. Aimee closed her eyes too and wondered why she felt so strange, so often, lately.

Far behind, in the dancing village, a pickaninny watched the girl in red as she danced so languorously. The baby took the rhythm, mimicking the steps. On flower island, everyone danced.

# Chapter 4

*When Cousin Rose arrived after lunch, Aimee* was shocked to see how thin she had grown since their last meeting. She stared in alarm at Rose's threadbare shawl and shabby bonnet. Rose appeared quite unaware of her cousin's attentions, rushing upstairs, immensely relieved to have arrived for a holiday in the luxurious bonhomie of La Maison du Midi.

Damama, too, noticed the split leather of Rose's boots and the cheap cotton of her underpinnings. She clucked in alarm at the pallor of Rose's face and the brittle thinness of her wrists. She resolved to feed her till her seams burst and ask Monsieur Theo if Rose could stay a while longer till she was able to recover from the obvious privations of the months since her father's desertion.

Once upstairs, Rose sat on Aimee's bed dabbing her eyes with trembling fingers.

"Oh, Aimee, I wish Mama and I could always live with you and Damama. But who would look after our slaves? They're so kind and good and they stay even when Mama cannot pay them."

"Where has Uncle Gaspard gone?"

"Papa went away for many months with Madame Ellene. Elias, Mama's headman, says they went to the far island. But now he is back and he stays in Madame Ellene's villa near Diamant. Sometimes, Mama says she's going to burn it down, and I shall help her. When she talks of Papa her face goes red and my knees tremble so I can't stand."

"Don't think about it, Rose, you'll be happy here and Damama and I are taking you to St. Pierre to the carnival next Saturday," Aimee insisted. "Now, you're not to cry, because Damama gets upset when you cry. She told me if *she* ever cried the whole house might fall down!"

Rose laughed a silver laugh and the two ran outside to inspect the garden, the glasshouse and Aimee's new pony. Rose clapped her hands delightedly at the violet plants she had brought on her last visit. Their purple flowers covered the shelves with deep fragrant petals and it was obvious the gardener had paid them most careful attention.

"Rose?"

"Yes, Aimee."

"Will you come with me on an expedition?"

"An expedition?" Rose asked. "What exactly is that? I never heard of such a thing. I don't wish to go hunting in the jungle if that's what you mean."

"No, only for a walk along the road a little way. We can be there and back in ten minutes."

"But my boots are full of holes, Aimee."

"I'll give you some of mine. I'm going to take you to see Euphemia the seer. People round here say she can tell the future."

Rose's eyes widened and she sat down on the terrace, dropping her flowers and staring vacantly out to sea.

"Could she tell me if Papa will ever come home to Mama and me?"

"I don't know, perhaps she could if she saw it in the future."

"Could she say if I will ever live in Paris?"

"I'm sure she could if you are going to go. They say she knows from just looking at you what will happen in your life and even when you'll die."

"Oh, I don't want to know when I'll die, that would frighten me."

40

"Don't be afraid, I'll look after you, Rose, I truly will. Even when we're grown up, I promise to protect you."

"I love you, Aimee. You're my best friend in the whole world."

"Perhaps we'd better go another day when you've settled down a bit and are not so tired."

For months, until the pineapple-picking time began, Monsieur Theo's workers had been preparing for the great carnival before Lent, the Vaval. Now they were ready, costumes sewn, masks decorated, floats enlivened by flowers and fruit. Aimee was happy to be able to go to St. Pierre with Damama and Cousin Rose. It was her first big carnival and Rose had seen only village carnivals before. And lately, Rose had rarely been out of La Pagerie, for Madame Tascher had to spend every day working in the sugar mill or the distillery, urging her workers to ever greater effort. Rose had stayed with her mother, comforting and consoling her and growing daily wiser in the ways of the world.

Damama began to sew Rose's new petticoats, chemises, drawers and nightdresses. Monsieur Theo had ordered that the child be re-equipped, at his expense, in a style suitable for a young lady of good breeding. Cousin Rose tried everything on and then tried them on again, impatient for her new wardrobe to be ready, stroking pretty ribbons Damama threaded through crisp white starched petticoats and soft cambric body tops. She grew so excited when she saw the lilac silk and the champagne crepe that Damama insisted she lie down for a while in case she faint, or worse, burst into tears.

A week passed and Damama finished most of the sewing. Rose tried on the new bonnet of violet and fuchsia flowers and the silk dresses bedecked with posies of pink petunia. She turned in front of a long mirror, entranced by her reflection. Then she clung to Damama, kissing her and thanking her profusely. She ran to show Monsieur Theo and Monsieur Armande and the others belowstairs, whirling and twirling as they admired her. That night, she slept fitfully, rising twice to tiptoe to the velvet sofa to see if her new clothes were safe. Then she sat on the bed, stroking Aimee's hair and looking out on the dark sea.

Rose thought of her mother at home in La Pagerie.

Mama had had no new clothes for almost two years. She lay, wondering if Damama could be persuaded to make Madame Tascher something out of the leftover silk from Rose's new dresses. She fell asleep, uncertain how best to ask.

The next morning Rose sat on Damama's knee and put her arms round the black woman's neck lovingly.

"Now, Miss Rose, what are you after?"

"I was wondering."

"Wonderin' what?"

"I was wondering if you could make Mama a new petticoat from the silk you have left from my new dresses?"

"Well, I'll be darned, you want me to go on sewin' for a year!"

"Mama has had nothing new for almost two years. She has holes in all her skirts and her lace sleeves are tattered, and I *hate* her to look so poor!"

Rose burst into clouds of tears, her body shaking with sadness and chagrin. Damama struggled to speak.

"No waterfalls please! You hear me, today is your birthday and I'll have no cryin'."

Rose cried louder than ever.

"Damned if you aren't more disobedient than your cousin ever was! What a life I have with you two little madames."

Aimee, who had been listening to all this, thought for a moment, then she whispered in Damama's ear. Delighted by her suggestion, Damama grabbed Cousin Rose, lifting her up under her arm as she followed Aimee out of the room. Aimee unlocked the pink silk room where Mama's clothes remained, unused and unwanted like graceful reminders of their owner's absence. Damama dropped Rose on the floor, drew herself to her full height and announced in a loud voice, "Miss Rose, you are privileged to come in here. Usually, little miss comes in her mama's room on her own and no one but me is allowed to come in with her. Now you say thank you like a good girl."

"Thank you, Aimee, thank you very much for letting me come in Madame's room."

Aimee opened the wardrobe doors proudly and exclaimed, "Look, Rose!"

"Oh, Aimee, I never saw so many beautiful things."

"These are Mama's clothes, and sometimes I come here to play with them."

As Rose stared with shining eyes at rows of luxurious lace, lawn and heavy shimmering satin, Aimee continued, "Damama is going to pack a trunk with some of Mama's things for you to take home with you. Aunt Tascher is almost the same size as Mama was before she was ill so they should fit very nicely. Now don't cry, Rose, or I shall be very angry!"

Rose's eyes filled with tears as she struggled to speak.

But Aimee said, "Don't say anything, just help me choose which dresses Aunt Tascher will like best. Then we'll go and find petticoats and bodices to match. Mama had a hundred pairs of shoes, just wait till you see."

The smell of jasmine still lingered. Madame had used its oil to scent her body and dried jasmine flowers to perfume her cupboards. Aimee inhaled the sweet smell, remembering the frail pale face, the soft voice, the thin fingers that had played Papa's harpsichord in the salon. She shrugged, trying hard to forget her sadness as she followed Rose through ceiling-high wardrobes in the adjoining dressing room.

They chose a blue silk, a violet ninon, two cambrics sprigged with muguet and a splendid deep wine velvet. They laid tea gowns of lawn and muted silk on the pile for Damama to load into the trunk. Then they found boots to match every outfit. After an hour, they adjourned to a carved armoire and selected delicately stitched bodices, nightdresses, negligees and underskirts, piling them up until Damama had to sit on the big leather trunk to close it.

Cousin Rose stood, quietly looking around the room. Pink hibiscus flowers had been arranged in cut crystal vases on the table and writing desk. There was no dust on the dressing mirror or the chiffon-draped bed. Rose wondered how often Aimee came here to play and pretend her mama was still alive scenting the air with sweet perfume. As they prepared to leave, Aimee paused and handed Rose a blue velvet box.

"This is for you, Rose, for your birthday. We have lots of other gifts for you but this one is very special."

Rose opened the box and saw a velvet neck ribbon in deep sapphire blue with a fine gold cameo wreathed in pearls. She recalled seeing her aunt wear it in happier days.

"Thank you, Aimee, thank you so much. It's a beautiful present, the loveliest I ever had."

Rose vanished after they returned to Aimee's room. Damama was frantic at the suddenness of her disappearance. She searched every room in the house but she still could not find their guest. She called Monsieur Theo and explained her predicament. Then Aimee had an idea and ran off in search of Rose.

Rose was sitting under the jacaranda tree weeping as though her heart would break. She was furious with herself for crying. Damama and Cousin Aimee would grow sick of her in a few days if she did not try to be more cheerful. Tears came because her heart was heavy with sadness and she felt if she did not cry she would burst! All this kindness and charity touched her so she dissolved into showers of pent-up emotion. She wiped her eyes, praying to be calm again. Then Aimee appeared with a glass of mulberry-leaf tisane and a piece of peach and sugar pie.

"Damama's very worried about you, we've been searching everywhere in the house trying to find you, Rose. You'd better eat this and then come back and tell her you're safe."

Damama threw her hands up and cursed loud and long when the two girls appeared, timidly, in the hallway. But she was pleased to see Cousin Rose wearing the splendid new cameo carefully tied under her tear-stained chin.

"Now, miss, where have you been?"

Rose swallowed hard and tried to speak.

"Rose was sitting under the jacaranda tree, Damama—thinking."

"Cryin', more like it! Good job I'm takin' us to the carnival tomorrow or we'd all be weepin' for a month."

Later that day Monsieur Theo called the two girls into his study. His face was unusually stern. Aimee put her arm round Cousin Rose as they stood together before him. Monsieur Theo sat at a rosewood desk which was surrounded by crystal display cabinets containing his collection of rare china and tropical shells. Rose looked about her wonderingly, sniffing the smell of beeswax, starch and polish from ornate fire irons in the grate. Monsieur Theo poured himself a glass of wine and handed smaller glasses to each child.

"Cousin Rose, I am almost angry with you."

"I'm deeply sorry, sir."

"When you stay with us at La Maison du Midi you must not disappear."

"I won't ever do it again, sir."

"If someone disappears we all have to search for her and if we love the someone who disappears we become frantic. Do you understand, child?"

"Yes, sir, I do."

"If you are sad and want to be alone you may have the Blue Room as your own private study."

"Thank you kindly, sir."

"If you are worried and want advice come and talk to me, I shall help, if I can. Now, here's a gold louis for you, Aimee, and one for you, Cousin Rose. Spend them tomorrow in St. Pierre when you go to the carnival."

"Thank you, sir," they chorused.

"I'm having a dinner party tonight. We shall celebrate your birthday, Cousin Rose, and you will be guest of honor."

Aimee ran to kiss her uncle.

"I want to see if Madame Sylvie's lessons have been worth all the time and expense! We shall dance the cotillion together, Aimee."

Chandeliers glittered with wax candles over tables loaded with silver dishes piled high with delicacies prepared by Monsieur Armande. A dozen ladies and gentlemen arrived, expensively bewigged and ostentatiously dressed, most of them from neighboring plantations.

After dinner, an orchestra took its place in the garden room and guests formed pairings for the cotillion. Rose watched, admiringly, as Aimee joined in the elaborate dance, changing places and bestowing flowers and tapers on her final partner, Uncle Theo. As the evening wore on, candles flickered, the ladies' jewels glittered and both girls thought it was the most exciting evening they could remember. The last waltz was announced and Aimee, partnered by the son of another plantation owner, whirled around the luxurious silk-walled room. Rose was led to the floor by Jean-Paul, youngest son of the Marquis de Porte-Maillot.

The young man, overwhelmed by her beauty, danced, back rigid, almost afraid to touch her. Rose smiled sweetly, fluttering long black eyelashes seductively till he trod on her toe and apologized profusely.

She gripped his hand more tightly to steady him and asked in a husky voice, "Do you know what color my eyes are, Monsieur Jean-Paul? Damama says they are green but Cousin Aimee swears they are gold. What is your opinion?"

The young man leaned forward and Rose raised her chin toward him as they glided out onto the moonlit balcony.

"I think they are gold *and* green, Mademoiselle Rose. I have heard of rare folk whose eyes change color. Perhaps you are one of those lucky individuals."

"Perhaps I am . . . And what color are your eyes?"

"Mine?"

"Let me see, I think they are blue, navy blue like a *matelot*'s coat."

Rose moved very close for a brief moment and he smelled the sandalwood scent of her body. Then she danced away past the arcaded pillars of the veranda and back into the garden room for a final curtsy before vanishing.

The young man wiped his brow and sat down abruptly. Jean-Paul de Porte-Maillot, aged eighteen, flushed and flustered by a young girl just eleven years old. He watched for Rose's return but she had disappeared. He smiled, affectionately. The *françaises créoles* were special women, doubly exciting, or so it seemed. His uncle, the governor, had warned him to stay away from them lest he be ensnared by their hot-blooded sensuality and find himself unable to leave flower island without leaving his heart behind. He vowed to find Rose again someday when she was just a little older.

Aimee walked out into cool evening air, happy to be away from the noisy bustle of the crowded room. Dressed in silver lace with exotic poinsettias in her shimmering hair, she reflected that soon she too would be eleven. Native girls married when they were ten, many younger. *Françaises créoles* usually married at fourteen or fifteen. Aimee wondered if she too would marry and become mistress of a great mansion on the island. She was determined to go with her cousin to see Euphemia the seer to find out what was in the future.

She heard a rustle in the undergrowth. For a moment, she stood silently listening. Peter, Damama's nephew, emerged from the bushes carrying his pet parrot. Aimee had not seen him since the night of the native wedding. Suddenly he was a man and she realized that he was much older than she had originally thought.

"Peter! I'm so pleased to see you. I've been dancing and I was so warm I thought I would walk a little in the cool air. Isn't the night beautiful? Where have you been?"

"I was in the kitchen helping Monsieur Armande. Damama arranged it because I'm very strong. I carry potato and pineapple sacks for him."

"Are you well? Why did you never come to live with us in La Maison du Midi?" Aimee inquired.

"Perhaps your uncle didn't like the idea."

"I liked it."

"It was your childish fancy, that's what Damama says."

"Shall I tell you a secret, Peter?"

"Yes."

"You remember when I went to sleep and you guarded me on the beach?"

"Yes, I remember it."

"Well, when I was asleep you kissed me. I know because I was only pretending to be asleep."

Aimee laughed as the young man blushed furiously. He looked almost angry with her.

"I didn't tell anyone, not even Damama."

Peter walked on, looking at his shoes and scowling.

"Why did you kiss me, Peter?"

"I kissed you because you smelled so pretty and looked like an angel and I wanted to know how you felt from very close."

Aimee paused, thoughtfully. The parrot flew from his shoulder to a hut far away and Peter stood looking down at her, hearing his heart beating and wishing he dared do what he wanted to do. Aimee suddenly felt hot and uncertain. Then she heard herself saying something she knew she should not say. "Kiss me again, Peter."

He picked her up touching her lips, briefly, then put her

47

down against the tree almost angrily. He said, "I have to go now, Miss Aimee."

"Why? Why must you go?"

"You're too young to understand my feelings. A man has his appetites and I'm old enough to need things you can't provide."

"Monsieur Armande has plenty of food if you're hungry."

"I'm not hungry for food, it's not that kind of hunger," he said.

"How are you hungry then?"

"I'm hungry for kissing and loving and hugging and doing things you don't even know about. Now go in before I'm in a heap of trouble."

Peter ran away through the woods, but Aimee lingered awhile, picking jasmine and night-scented stocks, aware for the first time that Damama's hunger and her female appetites were not for banana bread and lampling pie. She smiled and ran back to the house. Kissing and hugging and doing things she didn't even know about! She would ask Damama all about those things in the morning.

But in the morning, Aimee forgot, because the sun came out warm and wonderfully golden and it was carnival.

They drove to St. Pierre in Monsieur Theo's best carriage. All along the route villagers danced the beguine and even in the early hours of the morning, streets were bedecked with flowers and bright pink paper flags. A pet-seller tried to halt their progress, proffering parrots, canaries, monkeys and tiny dogs that had no bark. Damama boomed that they were not interested in starting a zoo and the carriage drove on past poison trees and prickly pear hedges to the main road for St. Pierre. Progress was slow because everyone was enroute to the city.

In the city, French colonists, landowners and bourgeoisie mingled with African slaves, freedmen and the cinnamon-cheeked natives of flower island to celebrate. The governor surveyed the scene from the balcony of his residence with military leaders and personal friends from the *gratin* of Martinican society. Drumbeats and cannon fire heralded the start of the parade. Steel bands, brass bands and the French Navy ensemble led the way for natives in brightly colored masks and gaudy straw hats, painted ladies flaunting flashy satin crinolines and undulating dancers who coaxed watchers to a brief beguine. "Skeletons" in black body coverings painted with white "bones" leapt by, frightening all the children. Favorite legends, depicted in flowers and balanced precariously on horse-drawn platforms, followed. Cows, goats, dogs and parrots passed by in wreaths and brightly painted collars. Fiddlers, horn blowers and tom-tom drummers mixed with the marchers, encouraging abandoned dancing and cheering those who threw off their clothes, rolling their moving parts with vivaciousness. Demons, dragons, tigers and princesses passed by prancing happily in merry masquerade.

Aimee was entranced. Cousin Rose blushed and giggled at things she felt but could not understand. Damama shouted encouragement to all her friends and someone covered her head with a wreath of garish gold flowers.

Children passed, dancing a lively samba. Lords and ladies of the colonial commission joined in, masked and spectacularly bewigged, their inhibitions lost in unaccustomed anonymity. They formed lines and danced the forbidden calenda, bumping, thrusting, grinding, pushing with all the abandon of slaves at a midnight celebration.

After the parade had passed by, stalls and booths appeared, as if by magic, and cockfights became the order of the day. *Tombola* stalls were erected next to gambling and shooting booths as the crowd jostled to compete for a chance to win precious currency. Damama pushed through, shielding her two charges from the crush. She made a sudden sharp turn away from the main square. There had been a hanging in St. Pierre the previous week and Damama had seen enough, from the distance, to know that the bodies were still blackening in the sun as an example to all who passed.

The two girls saw nothing as Damama led them to the cafe near the harbor that she always visited on trips to St. Pierre. They were surprised to find the doors closed, the shutters secured. Loud music, shouting, cheers and the sound of jubilation reached their ears from inside as Damama hammered on the wall and shouted to be admitted.

"What's goin' on in there?" Damama yelled. "Sounds

like they're having themselves a party. Why do you reckon they locked the door?"

A man appeared and asked what they wanted.

"Never mind what we want, you go tell Aunt Beeka that I'm here and me and my two young ladies are in need of some liquid refreshment."

"Tell her yourself, she's in there."

The man grinned, indicating a small side room. Damama passed him by, walking quickly through to Aunt Beeka's quarters.

Aunt B. was lying in her coffin, covered with flowers and dead as sweet Jesus. Damama noted that the woman had her favorite clay pipe in her mouth and a bottle of good whisky on the side of the coffin, in case she felt like a swig. She nodded approvingly. The two girls stared in amazement, unsure whether to be afraid or to laugh out loud.

Damama turned to them and made an announcement. "This is my Aunt Beeka, young ladies. She's gone and died by the looks of things though you never can be sure on that subject. It's always best to wait awhile and make sure she's in the clouds before you go shovin' her under the earth."

Aimee and Rose listened in amazement.

"You remember, little miss, I once promised you I'd show you a Creole funeral. Well, this is it. It's really a party and not a bit miserable like those of the *françaises de la métropole*."

"But if Aunt B. is dead why is everyone laughing?" Aimee asked.

"They're laughin' cos they drunk too much rum punch and they drunk too much rum punch cos they don't want her goin' to meet her maker lookin' miserable. They know she loved parties best of anythin' so they're givin' her one to see her on her way. Now, come and meet all my friends and let's have ourselves a fine time."

The two girls met all Damama's relatives and most of her friends. They were lifted onto marble-topped tables by the waiters and applauded by the assembly as they danced, like tiny revolving dolls. They drank pomegranate punch and ate lamb stuffed with pine cones and fish from the high mountain lakes. Damama disappeared for an hour

50

with her waiter friend and Aimee concluded that they had been filling Damama's feminine appetite with hugs and kisses and things she must remember to ask about.

In the early evening, the storytelling began with irreverent tales of plantation owners who grew too fond of their female slaves. The law of the island said owners who begat mulatto children must pay penalties to the crown of valuable sugar. Slaves so used were confiscated and given to the monks of La Charité.

Damama laughed loud and long at the very idea. "Those monkmen have a pretty good time consolin' young girls, I reckon. They say they don't use their masculinities but I hear tell they use them pretty good and pretty often!"

She sat back, fanning herself with a banana leaf, and everyone listened as her friend, the waiter, told the story of a colonial wife well known for her jealousy of her husband's favorite slaves. The lady went regularly to the monks of La Charité to accuse her husband of fathering new children. This way she got rid of her rivals and the monks enjoyed the new arrivals.

The punch was passed round and the waiter warmed to his theme. "Last week she did it again and accused her man, like always, of fatherin' another child. But the slave goes and accuses the monkman of bein' the father and everyone believed her. Lord, was there a fight! They were real glad to let her go home after that!"

Damama laughed like a gong, slapping her thighs and roaring irreverently.

"I hope I never go near any of those holy men and women. If they promise the Lord not to think about their natural appetites, I reckon they're all plumb crazy!"

At dusk, Damama and the girls left the bar and drove out of town as the sun set on the far horizon. Rose fell asleep where she sat and Damama covered her with a woolen blanket. Aimee stroked Damama's arm as she watched the sky turn yellow, green and deep blue with the approach of night. She thought happily of the carnival, the strident color, noise and cacophony of delicious excess. But she was thankful to be going home. At Pointe Royale there was only peace, silence and sunshine.

Damama hummed a lilting lullaby and talked about what they would do tomorrow. "Tomorrow, the sun's

51

gonna shine like it always does and we'll be real happy like we always are. You and Cousin Rose can pick flowers so I can fill all the bowls in the house just like your mama used to."

"Monsieur Armande's making lobster for lunch tomorrow."

"He's a good man, Aimee, a real good man. Maybe we'll ask him for a picnic so we can go see the waterfall at Moulin Soleil. How's that for a good idea?"

But there was no reply. Aimee was already asleep, her head resting on Da's arm. Damama kissed the silver hair and covered her with a rug, humming softly, happily all the way home.

The day dawned, finally, when Rose was due to return to La Pagerie. In the morning, she was unusually quiet, pale and withdrawn. Damama reminded her that her mama would be thrilled with all the new clothes and everyone would be pleased to see her. Rose had been with them a month and Monsieur Theo had given permission for her to return for the hottest weeks of late summer.

Rose looked up at Damama and kissed her cheeks. "I want to go home because I love Mama and miss her very much when I'm away. But I don't want to leave you and Cousin Aimee. I'm so happy when I'm here and I'm so sad at home. It isn't Mama's fault, it's just that she always looks so unhappy, and I feel sad since Papa went away."

"Things'll change, Miss Rose, you'll see. In a while she'll feel a whole lot better. Time is all your mama needs."

Aimee called from the garden and Rose ran to meet her. Damama watched as they ran through tall tree ferns to the dusty road beyond.

"Now don't go wanderin', you two!"

"We won't, Damama, we'll be back in a few minutes."

Aimee's face was pink with excitement.

"Are you ready to come to see Euphemia the seer?"

"If you like, Aimee," Rose answered.

They ran down a narrow lane bordered by thorn hedge. As they drew near the seer's shanty, Cousin Rose remembered that tellers of the future had to be paid. Aimee gave her a silver penny to give to the old woman and Rose thought how clever her cousin was always to remember everything.

The house, almost hidden from the road by leaves of overgrown giant hydrangea and massed parasol pines, was built of boxwood and tin. They crept cautiously through winding pathways and saw the old crone sitting under a mango tree smoking a clay pipe. She was covered in a ragged cotton smock that had once been green, gray hair plaited in a hundred tiny plaits and oiled with goose grease. Her eyes, clear, young and vibrant and greatly at odds with the lined face that seemed older than time, pierced theirs as they approached her.

Cousin Rose began to tremble and dropped her silver penny. But Aimee stepped forward, handed it with her own to the old woman and curtsied.

"Madame Euphemia, we would like to know our future. Is it true that you can tell us?" Aimee asked in a clear voice.

"Perhaps . . ."

"And will you tell us?"

The woman looked intently at Aimee then at Cousin Rose standing close behind. She puffed her pipe, thought awhile, then told them to sit down. Rose saw that around the house the seer had collected earthenware pots of dead poisonous snakes, frogs and water beetles. Butterflies and moths impaled on pins decorated the pastewood walls fluttering in the warm, dry breeze. Rose shuddered as she held Aimee's hand. Aimee had noticed the dead animals, too, but she ignored them, watching the old lady breathlessly.

The woman took a handful of silver sand and poured it into Aimee's cupped hands. She told the child to drop it on the ground. Then she caught Aimee's wrist and pressed her palm onto the sand. Finally, she plucked a hair from her head and examined it intently. Then she repeated the procedure with Cousin Rose. After a while, she closed her eyes and let her head fall on her chest. The two watchers wondered if Euphemia had fallen asleep. Aimee grew impatient at the charade and nudged the seer with a sharp tap.

"Madame Euphemia! Tell us what you see, please."

The old woman turned to Rose, smiling sadly. "You will cross the sea and marry a fair man who will be taken from you. After a while, you will marry again and someday you will be an empress."

Rose was so amazed, she immediately forgot all the questions she had intended to ask the seer.

The old woman turned to Aimee thoughtfully. "And you also will cross the sea, young miss. But you will be taken away by those you do not know to a country across all the seas of the world. You will never return to Madinina. Someday you will be more than an empress and those who have wronged you will spill their blood over all your city."

"But why will I never come home? This is my home and I love it. I don't want to cross the sea or live anywhere but on flower island."

"What you want is not important. What will be will be, I can tell you no more." The old woman left them, closing the door and drawing the torn blinds.

The girls returned to La Maison du Midi as a sudden downpour turned the roads to mud, the garden to moist green profusion. Then, it was time for Rose to depart. There was little opportunity to discuss what they had been told, though they spent a few precious minutes in the conservatory as Rose waited for the carriage to arrive.

"Aimee, did you believe Madame Euphemia?"

"No, I thought she was stupid!"

"I don't really know whether I believe her or not."

"I don't ever wish to leave La Maison du Midi, and Uncle Theo told me I can always stay here. I don't even have to go away to school if I don't want to."

"Mama can't afford to send me to France, so I shall never cross the sea either," Rose sighed.

"She was silly and we wasted our silver pennies. Damama told me seers tell lies. I should have believed her."

"I still have the money Uncle Theo gave me to spend at the carnival. I'm going to give it to Mama when I get home."

"When you come next time we'll go to Marigot and watch the skiff races."

"Thank you for being so kind, Aimee. I do so love you. I love you almost as much as I love Mama."

"And I love you, Cousin Rose."

# Chapter 5

*It happened one week after Aimee's twelfth* birthday. Damama remembered it in years to come as the moment when the peaceful, sunny life they had always known ended.

Monsieur Theo had been away for a long visit to the far island. He returned pale, wan and trembling with a fierce ague. His skin had turned gray and his pains increased. Dr. Fauchon was called to his bedside. But it was futile. Monsieur Theo died just as the good doctor arrived. Some said he had been poisoned, unwittingly, by the primitive food of the far islanders. But no one knew for sure.

The inhabitants of La Maison du Midi were stunned into the apathy of sudden despair. Even Damama sat, silently, in her room, wondering what would happen to them now that wise, kind Monsieur Theo had gone to his maker. She had never met Monsieur Charles, the man who would now take over the estate. But her nephew, Peter, had seen him once when he had gone with Monsieur Theo to the far north of the island to visit Monsieur Charles's plantation at Macouba.

Peter had taken a profound dislike to Monsieur Charles and reported him to be nothing like Aimee's father or his beloved Monsieur Theo. Damama recalled Peter's innocent words. "He had blond hair and a pink face and he made strange gestures and laughed loudly all the time. He has two or three ladies who sit near him and they were very pretty with lips that shone like the sunset and silver paint on their eyelids. One of them tried to caress me while Monsieur Charles was watching and he laughed very loud when I ran away."

Damama wondered what kind of games Monsieur Charles really played and why Monsieur Theo and his brother had never visited or been visited by this mysterious black sheep from the wrong side of the blanket.

She did not have to wait long for her fears to be confirmed. Monsieur Charles arrived before the funeral to inspect the property. He came with three pretty ladies and a smooth-skinned mulatto boy. He stroked the child in a familiar fashion as he spoke and the three painted ladies watched and giggled, encouraging his explorations. Monsieur Charles's ashen gray face was enlivened by rice powder, rouge and lip stain. Damama's eyes widened at the prospect of what little miss would say when she saw this he-whore waiting in her father's study!

In the afternoon, Monsieur Charles toured the grounds, gardens and plantation compound. He smiled indulgently at Peter, who blushed at the shock of seeing him again.

"Dear boy, you must come to the house this evening and bring some of those special passion fruits for my friend Lucinda. You remember my little *poupée*, no doubt, from your visit to Macouba?"

Peter stared at Lucinda with her bright red hair and her bright red mouth and intense blue eyes that made him feel dizzy as a snake facing a mongoose. Monsieur Charles laughed a high-pitched giggle, fanning himself with a scented lace handkerchief.

"*Ma petite*, I swear you've sent the dear boy quite dumb. He keeps falling over his feet! Young fellow, come at ten and don't be late. We shall all be waiting for you, do you hear what I say?"

Peter nodded, mind numb from shock at the astonishing encounter. He was seventeen years old and much wiser than on his first meeting with the strange quartet. He watched as they returned to the house, shaking his head, wonderingly. Perhaps Monsieur Charles selected his ladies because they were so very different or because they refused to be separated. He stared after them in total confusion.

Lucinda, all in red to match her hair, linked arms with Louise, so pale and blond she looked like death in a flimsy shroudlike dress. Only the gleaming green of her lizard eyes showed that Louise was alive and aware of her surroundings. The other woman, La Verne, was tall and broad-shouldered with dark skin like Damama's and long black hair extravagantly curled. She wore men's clothing and affected a monocle. Peter was convinced she was a witch. He heard their laughter from the distant silk-cotton tree path as he returned to his room over the distillery. He wondered, ruefully, what Damama would say if she knew of the invitation.

Aimee was stunned by the bizarre visitors. She curtsied to Monsieur Charles and to the three ladies, staring at his powdered face and debating whether he was really a gentleman or if he could be a lady in disguise. The three ladies were beautiful and dressed astonishingly with wondrous coiffures. One of them appeared to have forgotten her clothes and been forced to borrow from Monsieur Charles.

Damama led Aimee away, as soon as she could, to their own quarters.

"Shall I not eat lunch with Monsieur Charles and the ladies?" Aimee asked.

"No, little miss, you will not."

"Why not?"

"Cos he wants us to eat in our room."

"Does he not like us, Damama?"

"I don't rightly know, little miss. I don't know at all what that gentleman likes."

"Which of the ladies is his wife?"

"None of them, that's for sure! What would *he* do with a wife?"

"But they live in his house at Macouba."

"They're his mistresses or somethin' like it, that's why."

"What is a mistress?"

"A mistress is nearly the same as a wife only she doesn't get a weddin' ring."

"Why not?" Aimee inquired.

"Oh Lord! How many more questions? You can only have one wife, little miss, but you can have any number of mistresses providin' you have enough money to keep them in pretty clothes and jewels."

"Does Monsieur Charles have lots of money?"

"I don't know. I reckon he must have."

"What is he doing here?"

"He's come to see the house and the plantation."

"Why?"

"Cos he's got to decide what he wants to do with them."

"*Do* with them? Is he not going to live here and look after us like Uncle Theo did after Papa died?"

"It's not the same, little 'miss. Uncle Theo was your father's real kin. Monsieur Charles is not really family at all. His mother was a native woman and his daddy was related to your papa's family."

"Then why is he here?" Aimee was thoroughly confused.

"He's here cos all your real kin are dead and your papa's will said that only a member of the family, however distant, could take responsibility for the estate. You're not old enough to do that yet, and Monsieur Charles is the only one left cos your family die so young. Your papa's will said if Monsieur Charles ever took over, you were to go away to school."

Aimee began to cry and said, "I don't want to go away, Damama."

"I know you don't, little miss. Let's just wait and see what develops."

"But what will Monsieur Charles do?"

"I reckon he'll sell the place and go back up north. Macouba's his home; he has all his house people and slaves there."

"Oh no, don't let him sell La Maison du Midi!"

"Don't fret, little miss. I could be wrong, but I got a feelin' that's what he'll want. Best to be prepared."

That night Damama slept soundly, snoring gently, exhausted by the excitement of the new arrivals. But Aimee lay awake, wondering, praying and hoping desperately that Damama was wrong about Monsieur Charles's intentions. If he sold the house they would have no home except his home in Macouba, and she had once overheard

58

Uncle Theo talking about it to his headman. Uncle Theo had said the wind blew and a volcano smoked, killing grass and flowers, and all the crops were flattened by gales that came up suddenly, wreaking havoc on the estate. Uncle Theo had been tired and weary on his return and had never ventured again to Macouba. She had overheard Mama arguing with Uncle Theo about his habit of giving money to Monsieur Charles. Perhaps he had given money to keep Monsieur Charles away! Aimee shuddered at the very thought.

Now Uncle Theo was dead, the money to keep Monsieur Charles's estate running could only come from the sale of the Midi plantation. A tear rolled down Aimee's cheek, then another, as she buried her head under the pillow and sobbed. She began to feel thirsty. Unused to being awake so late, she also felt hungry and longed for some of Monsieur Armande's cold fowl. She heard the landing clock strike ten and wondered if she dare wake Damama to ask her to bring food from the kitchen. Tiptoeing to Damama's room, she saw that her nurse was fast asleep. Aimee smiled, lovingly. Damama had been very upset at Monsieur Charles's arrival. Perhaps it would be best to let her sleep.

Putting on slippers and a warm wrap, Aimee tiptoed downstairs. She was passing Monsieur Charles's bedroom when she saw Peter being led upstairs by two of the mistresses from Macouba. Lucinda and Louise were laughing gaily, each holding one of Peter's arms, as they swayed up the stairs. Monsieur Charles followed with La Verne, who was holding a silver candelabra in one hand and the sleeve of his coat with the other. Aimee slipped out of sight behind a heavy door curtain. They did not see her as they passed.

Quietly, she ran down to the kitchen and found a jug of lime juice and some cold chicken in the pantry. She drank the clear fresh liquid and ate the meat. Then she crept silently back upstairs. The landing was very dark because there was no moon. As she felt her way along the balustrade, she heard the sound of voices in the room adjacent to her own. Overcome by curiosity because one of the voices was Peter's, she crept through a trapdoor in the paneling and emerged behind a heavy velvet curtain in the alcove of the bedroom next to her own. Aimee smiled gleefully, excited by the adventure. Damama had shown her all the trapdoors and secret corridors of the house and sometimes they played in them and ran all the way to the kitchen to give Monsieur Armande a shock by emerging from the panel in the pantry.

As Aimee parted the curtains carefully, she caught her breath sharply at the scene before her. Monsieur Charles and the man-dressed mistress were sitting together on a chaise longue, toying with gammon knacks and drinking long glasses of champagne. Lucinda was naked on the bed, caressing her own breasts and writhing back and forth as though unaware that she was not alone. Louise was undressing in front of a cheval mirror. Soon, Peter was being unbuttoned by the two on the sofa. Monsieur Charles exclaimed at Peter's body and offered him a prize if he could beat the "wager."

Although Aimee had no idea what the wager might be, she felt herself turn hot and cold and more breathless by the minute. Lucinda let her hair down so it covered her shoulders like bright orange silk, glowing in the lamplight. Her breasts were large and heavy and her thighs had dimples like those in her cheeks. Monsieur Charles led Peter to the bed. He spread Lucinda's legs wide apart and pushed the boy toward her.

"Did you ever see such a pretty sight? She is yours to do with as you will. Come along, young fellow, *do* something. It's not often a man gets such an opportunity, and we're all waiting to applaud you!"

The other girl, Louise, joined Lucinda on the bed. Her body was as pale as the other was rosy, as slim as the other was round. She leaned eagerly forward and kissed her conspirator passionately, moaning and muttering with delight as Lucinda provoked her to mischievous ecstasy. Excited by their own wantonness, they pulled Peter toward them, tugging at his remaining clothing, titillating his tender places and touching, tasting and tickling his manhood till he began to cry out in wild abandon.

Aimee trembled violently. Peter's body was very different from hers and she began to understand, at last, what Damama had meant when she talked of men with swollen masculinities. She held on to the heavy curtain as dizziness overwhelmed her. Nervously, she leaned heavily on the rail and it shifted with a metallic scraping sound. Monsieur Charles, who had heard the noise, approached to investigate. The three people on the bed heard nothing. First one woman, then the other, took what she needed, laughing wildly and groaning ecstatically. The splendid masculinity oscillated back and forth between one and the other, untiring, making them vie for its thrusting attentions.

Aimee stood rooted to the spot until Monsieur Charles took her by the hand and led her into the room. He presented her, delightedly, to La Verne.

"Look who I found."

"Where was she, for heaven's sake?" asked La Verne.

"Behind the curtain, my dear, behind the curtain. How old are you, Aimee?"

"Almost thirteen, sir."

"Old enough to know what is happening here?"

Aimee blushed furiously, aware that he was watching her but that the three people on the bed had not even heard her entrance. Monsieur Charles led her to the bedside and held a candle near the three writhing bodies to give her a better view, but Aimee shuddered and turned her head away from the throbbing ensemble.

"They are enjoying their carnal appetites, child. Now you know what is in store for you before very long. Do you think she's old enough for a first taste, La Verne?"

The dark woman shrugged as Monsieur Charles untied Aimee's bodice and bared her budding breasts. He fondled them disinterestedly without taking his eyes from the trio on the bed.

"She has breasts like little peaches. Perhaps I should eat them, or perhaps you should! Ladies of tender years are your specialty, are they not?"

Dazed, Aimee was led toward the dark woman as the sounds from the trio grew more frenzied. Candles flickered and Monsieur Charles held a lamp near her body so La Verne could examine her minutely. La Verne slipped the cambric nightdress down and Aimee stood naked before her. Fingers plucked at her, twisting and turning and then pulling far away from her body. Aimee felt a strange, hot, pleasing sunburst in her very core and fainted clean away.

Monsieur Charles was spellbound. "She loved it! She'll be useful when she's a bit older and we get her away from that giantess! Look at her body! I've a mind to give her to the boy."

"Best to wait awhile. We'll have fun with her in Macouba once she's away from the associations of her home."

Aimee awoke in her own room with golden sunshine warming her face. Damama was leaning over her exclaiming that she had slept till long past ten.

"You feelin' all right, little miss? You usually wake at seven."

Aimee looked at Damama, relieved that she seemed unaware of the happenings of the previous night. Aimee stared out of the window and to the door of the next bedroom.

"You been havin' bad dreams, or somethin'? Well, never mind. Here's your breakfast; you'll feel better when you've eaten. There's soursop and fresh rolls and fried prawns."

Aimee sat, silently wondering if Damama could see any difference in her as a result of the night's experiences.

"You're pretty quiet, that's for sure. Somethin' botherin' you, little miss?"

"No, I'm just hungry, Damama."

After breakfast, while Damama removed the tray to the kitchen, Aimee sat staring out the window. At first, she was unsure whether she had dreamed the happenings of the night. But on reflection, she knew it was real. She opened her nightdress and surveyed her breasts, shuddering as she recalled the touch that had made the breath vanish from her body. She touched herself wonderingly, aware that she was feeling the same chest-constricting cramp first felt on the night of the native wedding. It was a good feeling and she longed to feel it again and again.

Suddenly, she understood that she had developed female appetites just like Damama. She buried her head in her arms and prayed that Monsieur Charles would have departed before she went downstairs. She felt certain he would know from looking at her that the events of the night had thrilled as much as displeased.

But he had not departed. He was sitting in the library with the three ladies when Aimee passed by on her way to the garden with Damama.

He called out, mockingly, "I trust you slept well, Aimee?"

"Yes, sir, thank you kindly." She blushed furiously at the lie, wobbling uncertainly and staring at the ground.

"You must join us for lunch at one. Don't be late."

"No, sir."

She curtsied and ran out to join Damama. Behind her, Monsieur Charles laughed outrageously.

"What did *he* want, little miss?"

"He asked how I slept and said I must join him for lunch."

"Ha! That gentleman had best watch his behavior!"

"Is he going home soon, Damama?"

"I reckon he'll go tomorrow. I heard Toby talkin' to his coachman."

"When do you think we'll know what is going to happen to us?"

"We'll probably know tomorrow. Now don't fret, little miss. I'm takin' you to Flamingo Lake this afternoon for a grand picnic, so you just cheer up."

Aimee ate lunch in the garden room with Monsieur Charles and the three mistresses. He looked deathly pale and his hands shook with an ague that never left him. Aimee deplored the way he ate his food, dribbling down his jacket and spitting bones to the floor for his dog to eat. The three ladies chattered and laughed and made jokes and the dark one watched her with hungry eyes that made Aimee's face turn scarlet with confusion.

"Are you going to join us again this evening, Aimee?"

"Sir?"

"In the green room as you did last night?"

"No, sir, thank you kindly."

She sat, staring at her plate, longing to run away as Monsieur Charles turned to the ladies, laughing loud.

"That boy was strong, was he not? Two ladies until dawn and barely a pause for breath. *Mon dieu!* He deserved his wages."

Lucinda fluttered her lashes, giggling excitedly.

"I have another one for you tonight, my dear little

*poupées.* His name is Jacques and he comes from the same plantation. Jacques is bringing his brother so we shall have quite a celebration. I can promise you a very jovial time."

"May I return to my Da now, sir?" Aimee said as she slipped from her seat and curtsied politely.

"Why? Are you tired of us already? Your cheeks are flushed like a sunset. Does my talking excite you?"

"Sir?"

"I think you're ready for breaking in, young lady, and I for one shall enjoy the watching."

Aimee looked longingly out to the garden.

"Are you happy here, Aimee?"

"Yes, sir, very happy; this is my home."

"You know I intend to sell the place?"

"Oh, no! Please don't. Where shall Damama and I live?"

Monsieur Charles sniffed his scented handkerchief disdainfully.

"Uncle Theo told me I could always stay here."

"Well, Theo had no right to say that!"

"Please, sir, *please* don't sell the house."

"I have no option, my dear child. I cannot keep traveling from Macouba to look after the property, and I cannot afford to pay a manager to do so. Macouba is my home and I like it there. It's far enough away from all those inquisitive do-gooders of Fort-Royal."

"But where shall I live after you sell La Maison du Midi?"

"You will have a choice, Aimee. Either you can go to school in France, as your father wished, or you can come to live with me. I shall get La Verne to teach you interesting ways, and when I'm tired of watching you entertain me and my friends, I shall marry you off to a rich landowner."

Aimee struggled to speak as tears filled her eyes.

"We'll have grand times, don't be tearful. I shall teach you that pleasure is everything. Pleasure is my god, dear child, and I've spent a lifetime pursuing it."

"Sir, may I go to Damama?"

"Before you leave us, would you deny that you enjoyed what happened to you last night?"

Aimee tried to run from the room but La Verne caught her and brought her back.

"Answer me," he growled.

"I don't know, sir. I'm very confused."

"You fainted from ecstasy! Are you such an idiot that you don't know the joy your body can bring you and those with whom you share it?"

Aimee looked at her feet, conscious that her heart was beating very loudly.

"I intend to teach you to please me and my mistresses and my dogs and my servants and slaves and all our friends. I shall show you how they can please you. But it will be your choice, Aimee, dear. Macouba or the convent in France. You won't get much enjoyment there, I can assure you!"

Aimee wiped her eyes and looked at the white powdery face with its sagging skin and wrinkled neck. Monsieur Charles smelled of rosewater and eau de cologne but his breath smelled of mangrove swamp. She lowered her eyes, uncertain what to say.

"One other thing, Aimee."

"Yes, sir."

"Your Da, does she know what happened to you last night?"

"No, sir."

"That's a wise child, because if she did I would have no option but to send her away to the far island. I shall be seeing her at four this afternoon, and I shall inform her of the conditions I have just told you."

"When would I have to go to France to the convent, sir?"

"As soon as the house and plantation are sold, of course. I would have no objection to you and your Da staying here till then, though there would be no staff to look after you so it would be a little . . . lonely, shall we say."

"Yes, sir."

"Away with you then and think about what I have told you."

Aimee ran to the garden and disappeared into the bushes. She heard Damama calling and waved to show where she was. Damama's face was like thunder.

"I heard some of what that yellow-faced he-whore said. Me and Monsieur Armande were just comin' in from the garden at the end of the conversation. I caught Monsieur Armande another iguana and he come to admire it."

Aimee sat, frozen with fear and apprehension.

"If Monsieur Charles thinks he's sendin' you off on your own to school in France he can think again. You're too young to go anywhere without me. That man is plain ignorant of how young ladies live!"

"Oh, Damama, what ever can we do?"

"Don't you worry, little miss. I've been asked to see Monsieur Charles at four this afternoon and I intend to give him a ultimatum, that's for sure."

They walked back to the house and sat in the kitchen with Monsieur Armande, drinking lemon barley cordial and consoling each other as Damama gave her opinion of Monsieur Charles.

"I reckon he's a bad man, a real bad man. He's got the squintin' eyes and folk with the squintin' eyes always have the devil in them. He's not got a good bone in his body. Just wait till they bring folk round to buy this place. I'll make good and sure no one does anythin' of the kind."

At four, Monsieur Charles sat alone in the study. Damama entered, curtsied and stood facing him, feet planted firmly apart on the silk carpet.

"Madame, I intend to sell this house as soon as I am able, and I wish Aimee to come to live with me in Macouba. Naturally, she will have no further need of your services after that time."

Damama glowered in silence.

"Did you hear me, madame?"

"I heard you—sir."

"If she does not wish to live in Macouba, I shall place her in the Convent of Our Lady of Nantes. She would, of course, have no need of your services there either. So, you had best make arrangements to leave this house as soon as it is sold."

Damama remained silent and impassive.

"My dear lady, are you listening?"

"Yes, I am listenin' but I am takin' no notice of what you say cos what you say is bullshit—sir."

"Be silent! Damn your impertinence. I'll have you

66

flogged! Or better still, I'll have you sold at the auction next week."

"You'll do nothin' of the kind, you lily-faced he-whore!"

"Lucinda! La Verne! Come quickly and bring my salts."

"Now you listen and make sure you listen good, Monsieur Charles. I am Miss Aimee's Da, always was and always will be. Her mama charged me to look after that child and look after her I sure as hell will till I'm good and dead."

"You'll be sold before the week, I promise you."

"Sold! Go pull your dangler! I'm a freedwoman, you can't sell me. I'm no slave to be threatened and ordered around. I have money of my own that Madame gave me in case of disaster, and you, sir, are a real big disaster!"

"Be quiet, you fat pig!"

"You can call me names, you mangy little pisser, but it won't do no good cos I'm deaf to your insults. Now you listen real good because if you touch that child or harm her or try to take her to your charnel house in Macouba I'll slit your throat and eat your black heart for breakfast —sir!"

Damama's voice echoed like thunder till the chandeliers tinkled and Monsieur Charles began to sweat through his rice powder.

"I could barely avoid listening, madame."

"If and when this house is sold and you arrange for little miss to get sent off to France to freeze in all that fallin' rain, I go with her to protect her from folk like you. Now you agree right now or I'm gonna make sure you die before the week's out."

"I agree, madame, I agree," Monsieur Charles replied meekly.

"From now on, little miss and me can get by pretty well without you. You just go home and stay home, but before you leave make sure I have enough money to pay Monsieur Armande and his lady wife and the house staff."

"I have no money."

"Then I'll take this . . . and this . . . and this . . . Sit down!"

Monsieur Charles tried in vain to escape as Damama

plucked the ruby tiepin from his neck, the gold watch from his waistcoat and the jeweled rings from his fingers.

"That's all I have to say. I trust you understand my feelin's in the matter."

As Damama marched out, Monsieur Armande, who was hiding outside listening to the conversation, wiped his sweating brow and stole softly back down the back stairway to the kitchen. He put the meat cleaver back on its hook and gave himself a glass of brandy. *Sacre bleu!* What a woman! He washed his sweating face and fanned his burning body and went off to tell Lulu what had happened.

Monsieur Charles prepared to depart soon after his interview with Damama. He gave a triumphant smirk to the sad-eyed staff grouped on the steps to watch his departure. Then he climbed into his carriage and addressed himself to Monsieur Armande, who was temporarily in charge of the household.

"I shall return soon. The sale of this house has been arranged. But I do hope I shall not have to come back before two months because the journey tires my little *poupées* so."

"Of course, sir."

"See that no one remains who has been ordered to leave and remember that the auctioneer will be here on Tuesday for those slaves who are to be sold."

"Yes, sir. May I ask a question?"

"If you must . . . if you must."

"What will happen to the plantation if all the slaves are sold? The harvest will soon be ready and they are needed here."

"I've arranged for temporary workers to come in to see to all that. They can manage what has to be done, no doubt."

"Yes, sir."

"And Monsieur Armande, do see that Aimee does not wander too far from home. I should have preferred her to come with me . . . but perhaps she will change her mind once she realizes that life at La Maison du Midi can no longer be as splendid as it was in dear Theo's day."

Monsieur Armande bowed his head, clenching his fists to control his anger. Damama put her arms around Aimee.

"Good day to you, Aimee."

Aimee hung her head, refusing to speak as tears gathered in her eyes.

"How prettily you cry. I adore little *poupées* who cry so sweetly."

Then, he was gone. Damama watched the carriage till it was a speck on the far horizon.

# Chapter 6

*The weeks passed slowly as summer humidity* rendered the tempo of life languorously lazy. Monsieur Armande was alone in the vast kitchen because Lulu no longer had time to assist his endeavours. She had had no option but to take over the household cleaning and general housekeeping with all the other staff gone. Monsieur Charles had dismissed the living-in workers and sold all the slaves, even Toby, the coachman, whose elderly mother still lived alone in a hut on the adjacent plantation. Toby's mother had cried for weeks after his departure and the rest of the servants had gone sadly on their way to other homes or almshouses.

Damama had to drive the coach whenever she and Aimee wished to visit the town or go for a picnic to Trinity Beach. She remained stoic and cheerful, determined to keep the child calm in the uncertain days of waiting.

A month later, they were informed that buyers would visit the house the following weekend. Damama rushed about making preparations to receive them, laughing aloud at her own thoughts and enlisting Aimee's help in her devious designs. In the kitchen, Monsieur Armande sang for the first time in many months at the prospect of watching his good friend frighten off those who wanted to take over their home.

Aimee was astonished to see Damama politely greet the agent and two wealthy French landowners who came with their wives. The party arrived on a dull gray afternoon in the wettest month of the year. Damama was pleased, for if the visitors tried to inspect the plantation they would get soaked to the skin. She led them into the salon and asked if they wished to take some refreshments. Aimee curtsied politely and went to the kitchen with Damama, giggling excitedly and waiting for the bell to ring. Minutes later it sounded frantically and Damama tripped upstairs, feet resounding loudly, eyes shining with anticipation. The land agent was furious, the two ladies wide-eyed and greatly perturbed.

"Madame, may I ask what this is?"

"Yes, sir, that's a rattrap."

"And what is it doing in the salon?"

"We keep rattraps in all the rooms, sir. Late master's orders. Ever since a black rat ate Miss Aimee's sister when she was a little baby in the cradle, master was crazy to kill every rat in the area! But they love comin' inside, they just *never* seem to learn."

One of the ladies fainted with a sharp cry. The other leaned over her frantically waving spirits of ammonia under her nose. Damama bobbed politely, delighted with the effect of her words.

"I'll go fetch tea now, sir, and a glass of brandy for the lady. She'll be just fine when she's eaten somethin' substantial."

Damama disappeared to the kitchen, returning discreetly to lay a loaded silver tray before the silent party. She withdrew and stood outside the door listening as the two ladies pleaded to leave immediately. But their husbands were adamant, they must see the land and the plantation before departing. Damama thought for a moment, then she ran outside to the garden and returned chuckling quietly. Opening the salon door a fraction, she pushed in a fat gecko found in the undergrowth. Then she opened the door and asked politely if the guests required anything more from the kitchen.

The steel trap snapped shut with a great clatter and Damama rushed to take it out of the room before anyone could see that a lizard, not a big black rat, had released the spring. She covered the trap with her foulard, apologizing profusely to the company that their tea had been so disturbed. She was delighted to note that both ladies were unconscious as she closed the door.

After a while, Monsieur Armande watched the party leave. One of the ladies had to be carried to the carriage. The other was leaning heavily on her husband's arm. Damama sat at the kitchen table eating a loaf of banana bread.

Monsieur Armande patted her on the back proudly. "Madame, you have saved us from disaster. Let's hope they never return."

Aimee laughed excitedly at the story and Damama repeated it often till it became a favorite joke. They began to settle into the new, simple routine of life and, as time passed, to feel hopeful that La Maison du Midi was perhaps too expensive a property to be easily sold.

Their hopes were shattered by the news that yet another prospective purchaser would visit the property within a few days. This time, the visitors were a family newly returned from Africa. Damama's eyes widened and she racked her brain to know how to frighten them away. She knew from a friend that Africa was full of snakes and rats as big as rabbits. It would need more than a rattrap to frighten settlers from the Black Continent!

Aimee watched as Damama paced the floor.

"What are you thinking of, Damama?"

"I'm tryin' to figure out how to scare off these new folk."

"I could hide in the secret panel and make scratching noises like a rat."

"Rats no good for these folk, little miss. They'll be used to rats cos rats run all over the damn place in Africa."

"I could be a skeleton like the one that frightened Cousin Rose at carnival?"

"Skeleton's no good either. Everyone knows an old bag of bones can't do much harm."

Aimee sat silently trying to work out what would frighten a grown man and his lady wife. Then she sprang up, eyes shining joyfully.

"Ghosts, Damama!"

"Ghosts? You clever child! We'll tell them this house has got evil spirits. That'll frighten them clean to death. Folk in Africa are terrible afraid of evil spirits."

Damama spent the next few days in elaborate preparation. She visited a niece at Trinity Beach and another who lived near the seer's shack just down the road. On the day of the buyers' arrival, Aimee sat in the garden under the jacaranda tree watching white butterflies flit on scarlet poinsettia flowers. She smiled happily. Today was going to be a special day. Damama had promised. Aimee tied a ribbon round Bijou's neck and led him into the house.

The new land agent arrived in a gilded carriage with a hard-faced man and his pale gray wife. The woman was thin, tired and nervous-looking. Her husband had a pig's face and Damama decided it was very likely he had a pig's nature to match. She seated them in the salon, withdrawing quietly to bring a tray of tea. The agent stopped her as she was about to leave the room.

"Madame, a word please."

"Yes, sir."

"How long have you been in this house?"

"Nearly thirty years, sir. I came here when I was ten."

"Is the harvest a good one this year?"

"One of the best, sir, but it's always good."

"And the house, is it strong and good to live in?" the agent continued.

"Perfect, sir. I reckon this is the best house in the whole area."

"Thank you. You can bring tea now."

The agent beamed at her comments and Damama disappeared to the kitchen. Aimee was waiting, wide-eyed with expectation, to play her part in the charade. She repeated all Damama had taught her during the week and ran to the salon, delighted to be part of the conspiracy. The pale lady kissed her cheeks and asked her to sit beside her on the sofa.

"What is your name, child?"

"Aimee, madame."

74

"And how old are you?"

"I am almost thirteen, madame."

"Are your parents away?"

"No, madame, they are both dead and so is my Uncle Theo, Papa's brother. He died six months ago."

"Dear me, how very sad," the pale woman exclaimed.

"Damama says everyone who comes to live here dies young, but that's not true because Damama hasn't died and she's quite old."

The lady smiled and looked at her husband, but he was deep in discussion with the agent.

"And what do you do here all day on your own?"

"I'm not alone, madame. Damama is here and Monsieur Armande the chef and his wife Lulu."

"Are you really never lonely?"

"Never, madame. Mama often comes to talk to me and we go to her room and play with her jewel box."

The lady started, violently. Then, eyes wide, hands fluttering, she begged an explanation of the strange statement. Aimee looked at her shoes, then she curtsied and begged leave to return to the kitchen.

"But my dear, explain what you have just said."

"I cannot, madame. Damama will be very angry if I do."

"Your Da is a servant and servants do as they are told, do they not?"

Aimee tried hard not to laugh out loud. She continued to stare at the ground as Damama had taught her.

"Now, what did you mean when you said your mama comes to talk to you?" she persisted.

"Damama and Monsieur Armande have seen her. Monsieur Charles said we were not to tell anyone about the spirits in the house or about the banshee that wails outside in the woods. He thinks no one will ever buy the house if they find out! I shall be in trouble for telling you!"

Aimee tried hard to cry but she lacked Cousin Rose's ability to turn on tears, so she dabbed her eyes with a lace kerchief and sniffed sadly. The lady, trembling with alarm, called to her husband to pay attention as Aimee slipped quietly out of the room. On cue, Damama entered with a tray. The woman was whispering frantically to her husband. The agent began to fidget uncomfortably. The prospective purchaser asked Damama if she could spare him a moment.

"That girl, is she all there, madame?"

"Miss Aimee is very clever and bright, sir."

"She has just told my wife that her mama comes back from the dead to see her."

Damama pretended to look confused.

"She's just imaginin' it, sir, I assure you."

"And she says there are bad spirits in the woods and a banshee who wails outside. Have you ever heard such a thing?"

"Never, sir! I have *never* heard a thing. Little miss must be jokin'. She loves to joke when visitors come to the house."

As Damama began to pour the tea and to hand out tiny chocolate cakes with orange wings, a fearful, pitiful cry echoed in the distance. It was followed by another high-pitched, eerie and horrendously haunting lament. The lady cried out and grasped her husband's arm. He clenched his fists and ran to the window, frantically searching the woodland for the source of the terrifying disturbance. Damama continued to pour the tea without appearing to have noticed anything unusual.

"Will that be all, sir?"

"What in God's name was that cry?"

"Cry?"

"That wailing or screaming or whatever you wish to call it."

"I heard nothin', sir. Most likely it was the wind. We get powerful strong winds in this area."

Exasperated, the man turned to the agent, who had gone deathly pale, and asked, "Did *you* hear that cry, sir?"

"I must confess I did not, sir. Now let's have some of this excellent tea and then I'll show you the plantation."

The visitor struggled to speak. He turned to his wife, took her by the arm and proceeded to the door saying, "Time to go, my dear. It's obvious to me that this man has paid the servant to pretend she doesn't hear that infernal creature. We know all about the power of evil from our days in Africa and we want no more of it! Good day to you, sir, madame."

The pair went off in their carriage at a gallop, leaving

the exhausted land agent behind. After tea, Damama drove him back into town, apologizing profusely for the hideous scream.

"Happens often, sir, and scares the hell out of visitors!"

"My dear lady, it nearly stopped my heart."

"I figured I best pretend I heard nothin'."

"You did your best, madame, and I'm most grateful to you for your excellent account of the property."

"Thank you, sir. If ever you come again I'll do the same."

He handed her a gold livre and walked stiffly back to his office. Damama roared joyfully to the horses as they galloped all the way home.

Monsieur Armande made a celebration supper of lobster stuffed with coconut and succulent pork in sweet sauce. The kitchen was lit with a display of colored candles and Damama wore her best dress. The "banshees" laughed riotously at their aunt's exploits and Aimee decided that Damama's relatives were the best "ghosts" she was ever likely to meet. They all toasted Aimee with champagne and everyone agreed that she who never lied had, for the love of her home and friends, lied most royally that afternoon.

A few days later, Damama decided they would pay Cousin Rose a visit. Monsieur Armande needed a rest and Lulu had been ill. The couple would visit Lulu's relatives in the south of the island and rest until Lulu had recovered. Damama packed a trunk for Aimee and a cardboard case for herself. She picked pineapples, custard apples, alligator pears and luscious passion fruit from the conservatory. Monsieur Armande made boxes of banana bread, brioche, sugar biscuits and cinnamon buns to augment Madame Tascher's meager larder. Finally, with a heavily loaded carriage, they departed for La Pagerie.

The sun shone hot as an oven, birds sang in blue branch trees and lizards darted like small green shadows along the pathway.

Snuggling near Damama, Aimee asked how long they would be staying.

"Week maybe, depends."

"What does it depend on?"

"It depends on how things are. If everyone keeps weepin' we'll come home day after tomorrow."

In midafternoon, they paused for a rest and a picnic by Flamingo Lake. Aimee was entranced, as always, by the colorful spectacle of flower island. The water of the lake was sapphire blue, dotted with the white and pink of a hundred spindly-legged birds. The sky was deep gold with approaching sunset. Aimee picked hibiscus flowers to make a wreath for Damama's head while they talked of La Maison du Midi and what would happen when it was sold. Aimee still dreamed and hoped to remain living there. But Damama was gravely worried. If the house were sold, they would be sent to France because they were no longer wanted. If it were not sold they would still be sent to France because the larders would soon be empty, the cavernous cellars bereft of supplies. Da sighed, sadly. Determination to make Aimee's last months on flower island the happiest of her young life grew.

The horses cantered to the coast road that led to Trois-Ilets, the village nearest to the Tascher home. Flying fish leapt in the ocean and silver dolphins played near off-shore islands. Aimee was happy as she watched a coral glow fill the sky making the landscape dreamlike and wonderfully warm. Damama's face glowed cinnamon red and the horses shone like lithe bronze statues.

The village had a row of brick houses around a square with a pump, stocks, shops and a small church. La Pagerie, the Tascher house and compound, was nearby in the depth of the forest. The carriage rolled downhill into a humid green, gloomy clearing buried from sight, lit only by meager sunlight that reached through cottonwood trees, dappling the lawn and making shadows on windows and walls. Aimee ran through a massive stone archway into the house to greet her Aunt Tascher and Rose. Damama carried the supplies in, walking back and forth, back and forth, with tins, kegs, bottles and pies till the kitchen looked ready for a party.

Madame Tascher was delighted to see them. She sent a woman to prepare their room, and handed out glasses with the prune brandy she made every year during harvest. Damama listened as they talked happily together.

78

"Ma Chère Aimée, you're so grown-up I hardly know you."

"I look just like Mama, don't I?"

"Exactly like your mama, except your hair is much lighter, it's like spun silver. Have you been well?"

"Very well, and Bijou, my cat, is also well although he's very old."

"Did she ever have kittens?" Cousin Rose asked.

"No, Bijou's a boy and Damama says boys don't have kittens."

"My goodness, *ma chère*, how grown-up you are! Tell me all about Monsieur Charles."

"He wears rice powder and paints his cheeks with ocher. He has three lady mistresses who laugh at everything he says," Aimee explained to her aunt.

*"Mon dieu!"*

"One of the ladies pretends to be a gentleman, and she wears clothes just like Monsieur Charles and takes snuff till she sneezes like a sailor!"

"Dear me, what is happening in the world?"

"Monsieur Charles sold all the slaves and sent the house servants away. We only have Monsieur Armande and his wife Lulu. Now Damama and I have to look after *everything*!"

Aimee launched into an account of the visiting purchasers and how Damama had dispatched them till Aunt Tascher laughed so much she had to loosen her stays. Damama walked to the window, noting that ladders leading to the vast rum vats were broken, the roof leaking, the barracoons shabby and uncared for. She smiled at Madame Tascher, admiring the woman's courage and her cheerful bonhomie. There was no doubt that La Pagerie needed a man's presence to restore it to order and good condition. She listened as Aimee explained what had happened to them since the death of Uncle Theo.

"Monsieur Charles says I must go to live with him in Macouba when the house is sold. If I don't go to Macouba, I shall be sent to France to a convent."

"Oh, no, Aimee!" cried Rose. "You can't go away, I shall never see you again."

"Don't cry, Rose, perhaps it won't happen."

"But you can't go and live in Macouba, it's horrible

79

there. I know because Papa once went to the north and the wind blew so hard that he fell over and broke his ribs!"

Madame Tascher passed sweetmeats round and poured everyone more brandy. Rose sobbed till her eyes grew red and Damama felt compelled to comfort her.

"Don't worry, Miss Rose, whatever happens I'm here to look after little miss."

"But can you go with her if she goes to the convent in France?"

"Of course I can. I'm stayin' with her forever."

They chatted for hours, until night fell and a cool breeze replaced the steamy heat of afternoon. After dinner they sang songs and Madame Tascher told the tale of what had happened when her headman had won a prize at the *tombola* in Fort-Royal.

"He bought himself two bottles of French brandy and drank them both, so he fell in the sea and floated clean out to Diamant. If Papa Latour hadn't been fishing, I would be without a headman today!"

Damama watched Aimee laughing happily. Wistfully, she dreamed that this happy moment could continue forever.

That night, Damama lay awake, thinking how hungry she was and how it was no fun to go stealing cold fowl from the kitchen if Monsieur Armande was not there to chastise her. She thought of Aimee and Rose and the future and what it would hold for all of them. She tossed and turned, unable to settle down as the sounds of the unfamiliar house besieged her ears. Cicadas twittered relentlessly in casuarina trees, monkeys screeched in the forest and the sunken depth of the location increased the noise till it was almost deafening. By morning, Damama was homesick and cursing that she had ever thought of leaving La Maison du Midi.

Days passed and time dragged slowly on. Rose took them on a tour of the estate, pointing out favorite mules and goats in nearby fields and picking armfuls of amaryllis to give to her cousin.

Aimee sat under a flambeau tree, threading fallen red petals into a necklace to match her dress and wondering if they would soon go home. She loved Rose intensely but she was homesick and nothing helped the hollow feeling that came when she thought of La Maison du Midi. The heady scent of honeysuckle and hibiscus reminded her of Mama's room. What would become of the jewels, the clothes and all the pretty trinkets if the house were sold? She walked back to the clearing behind Damama and Rose, knowing in the depths of her heart that she would soon have no home. The thought made her want to spend every precious last moment at Pointe Royale. She decided to ask Damama if they could return the following morning.

Later that night, Aimee lay awake, listening to Damama snoring through the open door. She sat up, impatient for the dawn. After a while, she walked to the window and called to a bullfinch, croaking in an aloe tree. Toward dawn, she became aware of a scarlet glow in the far distant sky. When she ran to the veranda, she was astonished to see night sky in the north of the island lit by what looked like flames. She called to Damama and asked what was happening.

"Oh, Lord! That damned volcano's havin' itself a burn," Damama exclaimed.

"What must we do? Shall I wake Cousin Rose and Aunt Tascher?"

"No, no need to do a thing. We're miles and miles away from all that trouble. You just go back to bed before you catch yourself a chill."

Damama's heart pounded as her mind wrestled with the problem of the burning mountain. They were safe, far away from the lava flow. La Maison du Midi was also safe. Monsieur Theo had once told her that they had nothing to fear on that score. She smiled, remembering his words . . . "Only a hurricane could destroy this house and it would have to be a very great one." But Monsieur Charles's house and plantation at Macouba would not be safe, because they were in the direct path of the lava. Damama tossed and turned, uncertain whether to wish him dead or pray that he would never descend again on Pointe Royale.

She decided they had better leave in the morning. Aimee had told her about her homesickness, and Damama felt sure if Monsieur Charles arrived in their absence there was no telling what mischief might result.

The next day, they learned from messengers that the

81

eruption had not been a grave one. A banana plantation at Prêcheur had been destroyed and some others at Macouba and Basse-Pointe, but the flow had not reached St. Pierre because the lava had ceased as suddenly as it had begun. Damama packed their bags after explaining her fears to Madame Tascher. Then they departed at a gallop for the welcoming vistas of Pointe Royale.

# Chapter 7

*They approached the house in the early evening.*
Aimee's eyes widened as she saw smoke coming out of the tall chimneys.

"Look, Damama, someone is in the house!"

"My goodness, now what?"

"I think Monsieur Charles has already arrived or at least his servants have."

"Let's hope he's left all those popsies and popinjays behind in Macouba!"

But he had not. As they neared the house, they saw the three mistresses and Monsieur Charles dismounting from their carriage and a dozen servants unloading trunks, cases and boxes from horse-drawn carts. Damama rushed to see what was happening, bumping into Monsieur Charles in her haste.

"What are you doin' back so soon? Your home's in Macouba, you said so yourself."

"My home *was* in Macouba, madame, but last night the volcano erupted and inflicted damage so severe that it will be many weeks, perhaps months, before we can return.

My little *poupées* and I are homeless and heartbroken at the calamity," he said as he ran inside.

"Ha! Heartbroke he says. Got to have a heart to be heartbroke, that's for sure. That fellow needs murderin', little miss. I wish Monsieur Armande would come home. He knows all about poisonin' folk and he's gonna be needed here before long!"

Aimee was waiting for Damama to bring her some lime cordial from the kitchen when she heard the sound of voices in Mama's bedroom. She crept to the door and listened. Quietly opening the door, she saw Lucinda and Louise trying on Mama's jewels. Aimee felt a great pain in her chest and a wave of rage that gave her a strength she had never known. She snatched the necklace from one girl and the pair of opal earrings from the other.

"These belong to my mama and you may *not* touch them!"

"Fiddlededee! Look how angry she is. Now run along and play, little girl, before you have one of your fainting spells."

"This is Mama's room and only Damama and I can come here."

"You mama is dead, little girl, dead and gone, so run and play before we get very angry."

Aimee looked round, appalled to see Mama's clothes on the silken bed, her furs on the chaise longue and beautiful jewelry carelessly scattered on dressing table and floor. A black houseman appeared at the door, struggling with a velvet-bound trunk.

"Where'd you want this, milady?"

"Over there, in the corner, and hurry."

"Yes, milady."

Appalled, Aimee cried out, "This is my mama's room and *you* may not use it."

The black servant paused, uncertain of what to do.

"Get her out of here, Lucinda, she's beginning to aggravate me."

The redhead picked Aimee up and tried to carry her to her room, but she struggled and bit Lucinda's wrist clean through. The woman screamed and fell on the floor, sucking her arm and cursing like a sailor. Aimee ran to Damama's room, snatched up the red silk parasol and ran back. She hit Louise resoundingly on the head, then hit the black houseman and the two boys who had arrived with suitcases. Screaming like a dervish, she kicked Lucinda till the woman ran away, cursing her. Aimee drew the bolts on the door and windows. Then she tried to move the trunk, but it was too heavy and cumbersome for her to stir. She gave up and sat exhausted on the floor.

Damama found Aimee putting Mama's jewelry neatly back where it belonged. She helped the girl return everything to the armoires and wardrobes and then asked what on earth had happened. Aimee could barely speak for fury.

"Lucinda and Louise were trying on Mama's jewels!"

"Lord help us! I wondered what on earth was happenin'. I ran clean up the secret stairway from the pantry cos I figured someone was murderin' you!"

"They want to put their clothes in Mama's armoire and use her room as their own!"

"Well, they can't," Da insisted.

"I kicked Lucinda and bit her arm, and I hit everyone with your parasol."

"You did? Well, I never!"

"Then I shouted and made them all go away."

"That's my girl. Best to let them know where they stand. Now, just one more thing left to do."

"What's that, Damama?"

"Just this, little miss, just this." Damama flexed her arms a few times. Then she opened the window wide, picked up the trunk and threw it far into the garden. The suitcases followed and a box of cheap trinkets found on the dressing table. She closed the window, drew the blinds and scooped Aimee into her arms, covering her with kisses.

They played snapdragon for an hour and drank jasmine tea as Damama waited for Aimee's face to return to its normal creamy paleness. She felt very proud of her charge. A lady she may be but she was a true Carib warrior when it came to trouble! She kissed Aimee a dozen times and told her all her favorite stories as a special treat. At seven, she decided that Aimee was calm enough to eat supper. She was about to leave the room when she found the door locked.

"Door's locked!"

"How can it be locked?"

"I don't rightly know but I can't open it."

"Perhaps Monsieur Charles is angry about what I did. He'll probably try to starve us to death as a punishment."

Damama battered on the door but nothing happened. After a while, she sat down, glowering at it as though it were personally responsible for their problems.

One hour later, Monsieur Charles called to Aimee and Damama almost choked as she heard the three mistresses giggling outside.

"When you are ready to apologize, Aimee dear, you may come out. I shall keep your door locked for many days if necessary. You will be very hungry, I'm afraid."

"I shall not apologize, Monsieur Charles." Aimee was in a rage.

"My dear child, I assure you, you will, and when you have apologized you will give the key of Lucinda's room back to her."

"Never!"

"Don't try my patience, stupid girl."

"That is Mama's room and no one else can use it."

"*That*, my dear child, is Lucinda's room and you may not enter it ever again. And now goodnight and sweet dreams. Perhaps we shall see you in the morning."

Damama threw her head back, laughing outrageously. Aimee stared anxiously at her, fearful that all the problems of the last few weeks had sent Damama out of her mind. But the big woman was slapping her thighs and chuckling fit to burst and Aimee began to laugh with her.

"Why are we laughing, Damama?"

"I'm laughin' cos that old he-whore's so stupid he deserves to fall down a hole!"

"Why is he stupid?"

"He's stupid cos Monsieur Armande gave *me* his keys to the pantry and the wine cellar before he went. You can't get into the wine cellar 'cept through the pantry and you can't get into the pantry without goin' through either the panel from our room or through the kitchen."

"Then Monsieur Charles will go through the kitchen."

"It'll take him a long time, little miss. A long, long time."

"Why?"

"Monsieur Armande has taken his keys with him and the doors leadin' to the kitchen are all locked. When I heard all that rumbustin' earlier on I thought maybe we had robbers in the house and I locked the larder and cellar doors before I came back up the passageway. The only way Monsieur Charles can get in the kitchen is through four big oak doors set in solid stone that your papa had specially made and builded to withstand a earthquake!"

Aimee began to smile.

"That houseman's so frail I figure if he tries to break the door he'll break his damned neck. Oh, Lord! This is funny, it's too damned funny."

Damama laughed and slapped her sides till her ribs ached. Then she crept to her room and let herself into the panel that led to the larder of Monsieur Armande's kitchen.

"What shall we have for dinner, little miss?"

"Whatever looks good. I'm very hungry."

"Monsieur Armande boucanned loads of turtle and partridge before he went away and there's fruit and pumpkin soup. I'll bring us a bit of everythin'."

Damama disappeared laughing all the way and Aimee sat, pensively looking out toward the beach. Fishermen were çooking lobsters on a low fire in the distance. She shuddered as they hit their catch and cut it in half with thin steel wires. She looked away to avoid seeing the thin legs moving as the body cooked slowly over glowing embers. Pigeons cooed in jacaranda trees and glyceria bushes glimmered in the defiant fire of a tropical sunset. For a brief moment, everything turned fiery coral, then, as always, darkness fell like a secret curtain. Aimee heard Damama's heavy feet on the stair and ran to welcome her.

"Look what a feast I brought, and there's champagne to celebrate!"

"What are we celebrating, Damama?"

"We're celebratin' your fightin' victory, little miss. Not many young ladies your age know how to defend their rights. Now see here, I got eggplant and red beans and a piece of turkey *boucané*. I sure hope Monsieur Armande comes back tomorrow. I reckon he'll kill himself laughin' when he sees what's goin' on."

Monsieur Armande did return, but he was not laughing. He stood, dejectedly, outside the locked kitchen staring at Monsieur Charles. Finally he asked, "Why are the doors locked, sir?"

"Have you a key, Monsieur Armande?"

Something in the urgency of Monsieur Charles's manner made the chef lie. "My keys are inside the kitchen, sir. I expected to find the spare keys hung in the hall."

Monsieur Charles sighed weakly. He had had no supper, no breakfast and Lucinda was roaring like a dervish in fury at their plight. But he was adamant that he would not approach Damama for assistance. They could all starve first! He looked imploringly at Monsieur Armande.

Monsieur Armande was amused. Only Damama would have locked everyone out of the kitchen, and she must have had a very good reason for her action. He turned to Monsieur Charles and inquired politely what had happened.

"There was trouble with that bitch of a giantess, and she locked us out of the kitchen."

"Well, bring her down immediately and force her to give up the keys!"

Monsieur Charles looked uncomfortable.

"She and the girl are locked in their rooms. I had to discipline them rather sharply last evening. They will do without food and drink until Aimee apologizes for her monstrous behavior to my little *poupée*, Lucinda. She *must* be made to give up the key to her mama's room! Lucinda and Louise need it immediately."

Monsieur Armande understood at last.

"But monsieur, with respect, Aimee will never give you the key. She holds her dead mother in great reverence and she will die if necessary for her belief."

"Then she will die and the giantess with her!"

"I doubt that they will die for quite some time, monsieur."

"And why not, may I ask?"

"Because if Damama has the keys to the kitchen they will eat all the contents of the shelves and the cellar and the pantry first."

"Their rooms are locked, they cannot get out."

"There is a passage from Damama's room to the larder,

88

sir. This house is full of concealed corridors. Damama often uses hers to startle me almost to death."

"Where are my salts? . . . Dear me! . . . I suppose I must capitulate. That infernal child has the devil on her side and who can fight the devil?" Monsieur Charles nearly fainted. He sat down, cheeks dropping, yellowed eyes wearily surveying the scene. Eventually, he dispatched a houseboy to run upstairs to unlock the door. The boy tried to open the door but found it bolted on the inside. He returned to report the situation to his master. Monsieur Charles burst into tears and had to be taken to lie down in the salon.

"How I suffer! First I almost lose my home in that inferno and now I have to live with a slave who rules the household and a girl who looks like an angel but who has the temper of a fiend incarnate. I suffer, Monsieur Armande, believe me."

The three ladies gathered round, patting his head, scenting his handkerchief with eau de cologne and reassuring him that all would be well.

Monsieur Armande ventured an opinion. "Perhaps Damama wants something, monsieur?"

"Give it to her, give her any damn thing! Send the boy to ask what diabolical designs she has for us all."

The boy returned with a request that Monsieur Charles should write a paper stating that the room of Madame Dubuq de Rivery would remain as it was, untouched and unoccupied, and that Miss Aimee would suffer no further punishment for her behavior of the previous afternoon.

Monsieur Charles held his head despairingly as he wrote the paper. "How does she know of such things? She's a slave, not a lawyer!"

"Damama has many friends, monsieur, lawyers, shipowners, captains, doctors, waiters . . ."

"And chefs, no doubt!"

"Chefs also, monsieur. She learns from all her friends and so has become very clever. Sometimes I think she is cleverer than all of us."

Damama and Aimee descended in style. Aimee gave Monsieur Armande a kiss and hugged him happily. Damama saw that Monsieur Armande's hands were trembling, his face wan. Troubled by his silence, she crept down later that night to talk with him.

"Where's Lulu?"

"My wife is dead. She died two days after we left here."

"Dead! How can she be dead?"

"As you know, she had the concretion. When we arrived at St. Anne it grew worse and her mother insisted on calling a native doctor to advise what should be done. He gave Lulu a draught of gunpowder and it burst her stomach. She died the following day. A terrible spectacle, madame. I shall never forget it."

Damama's eyes widened in alarm. She made a rum punch and warmed it on the fire. In the still of the night, she took Monsieur Armande's head on her knee like a sick child, stroking his hair till he fell fitfully asleep. Then she covered him with a blanket and crept back to her room.

Weeks passed quickly with sunny days full of color and warmth. Rose arrived for the skiff races but returned home the next day because she was terrified of Monsieur Charles. From time to time, agents brought prospective purchasers round the house and plantation but no one bought because La Maison du Midi was too expensive for all but the richest investor.

By mid-August the island was bathed in deep gold light from dawn to dusk. Over the summer, Aimee had grown taller, her figure fuller. Monsieur Armande observed that she seemed more reticent with strangers and was sometimes secretive. Damama thought only that Aimee was more beautiful every day and more modest than was good for her. The child's skin had the creamy texture of a magnolia petal, her hair a hundred silver ringlets. Her eyes were clear and direct and thickly fringed with black lashes. She was neither tall nor short, simply beautiful in every way. Damama's hands could encircle the tiny waist and she frequently marveled at Aimee's tiny feet and delicate hands. The girl's slimness made her appear light and insubstantial, but Damama knew that her body was strong and her mind fearfully determined. When they went to St. Pierre, Aimee's beauty drew gasps of admiration and her smile made everyone adore her.

Monsieur Charles and the three mistresses did not adore

her, however, and it was to their enormous relief that the house was unexpectedly sold one afternoon to a purchaser from South America. The man requested possession at their earliest convenience and Monsieur Charles promised it within the month. Damama eavesdropped on subsequent conversations till she was sure what Monsieur Charles was up to, then, cautiously, carefully, with great sympathy, she began to prepare Aimee for her departure for France.

Damama was sad. Soon, Monsieur Armande would be alone, slaving away in the kitchen with no one to make him laugh and no one to provoke his masculine appetites. And she would be in France, shivering in the rain and dying of boredom with a group of holy women. Damama looked up to heaven and pulled her tongue out at God. If he was looking, she hoped it would remind him of her existence and start him caring for her again.

Monsieur Charles was transformed. He beamed at the servants and threw a ball for Aimee's birthday, inviting all his hard-drinking, dissolute, depraved intimates to regular lunch and dinner parties that lasted for hours and ended in strange exhibitions and decadent displays. Neighbors no longer called and La Maison du Midi became synonymous with the sins of its temporary master.

Aimee remained aloof from Monsieur Charles's degeneracy. She was happy with Damama and impervious to the lustful glances of La Verne. But she was not without curiosity. Sometimes, when Damama was asleep, Aimee crept to the top of the stairs and watched the strange happenings taking place in the great hall. Men dressed as as women, women as men, with Monsieur Charles presiding over the scene, watching gleefully without ever taking part.

One night, Aimee sat on the top stair to watch as Lucinda and Louise enacted strange fables for the other guests. The two ladies were quite naked except for velvet throat ribbons and black silken stockings. After a while, men from the guest group ran to join them; Aimee watched, fascinated, as the two girls, lying back to back, serviced queues of rampant male admirers. She heard Lucinda laughing and calling for them to hurry and she saw Monsieur Charles standing over the redhaired mistress encouraging her to drain every drop from the waiting band. Aimee grew breathless at the astonishing sight, her hands began to tremble and she felt a strange glow spread over her cheeks and through her body.

She was leaning against the banister when she heard her name softly called from somewhere along the landing. She gathered up her robe and turned to find herself face to face with the son of Admiral Dieudonne. The admiral was below, displaying his masculinity for all to see. His son stood, eyes shining, watching Aimee.

"I am Emile-Bernard Dieudonne."

"Sir, I am Aimee Dubuq de Rivery."

"I know, I've seen you in the house when I came to visit. Are you going downstairs to join in the fun?"

"No!"

"Why not?"

"I don't like such things."

"Then why do you watch them so avidly?"

Aimee blushed furiously, biting her lip in embarrassment.

"They excite you, no doubt. You're very young and very pretty."

"I'm to be sent to school in France soon."

"You'll have a grand time in France."

"I'm to attend a convent school."

"You'll still have a fine time! They let you out to visit the towns and churches and worthy monuments. I've had some of my best times with convent girls out on the loose! You'll soon find yourself a lover and start enjoying life."

"I'm not yet old enough for such things, sir. I'm a virgin and expect to remain so," Aimee said as she turned away.

"Being a virgin brings no enjoyment; a virtue perhaps but a bore."

Aimee struggled to pass him in the corridor, but her legs felt weak as he caught her and drew her into the doorway. He cupped her face in his hands and kissed her, exploring her mouth and stroking her silvery silk hair. Bemused, aware only of her longing for him and the scent of cigar smoke and lavender on his body, Aimee did not struggle. Dieudonne slipped his hands inside the thin cambric of her robe, lifting the heavy softness of her breasts and exposing them to his scrutiny. He bit her nipples and Aimee cried out softly in her excitement. Then she pushed him away and tried again to run to her room, but he was too strong. He carried her into the bedroom next to her own where she had seen Peter and the two mistresses on that exciting night so long ago.

Aimee knew she ought to cry out or scream but she could not. Deep inside, she longed for what he could make her feel. He lifted her nightdress and bent to kiss her body from head to toe and back, soothing her trembling limbs and reassuring her with pretty phrases. She thought of Damama, asleep in her room, snoring and dreaming of men she had loved and men she hoped to love, and she prayed that Monsieur Charles would not appear round the door.

Her eyes widened as she saw Dieudonne's body, sunbronzed and strong with a thick, rampant masculinity that approached the place it was made to fit. She felt such longing for him that she broke into a fierce flood of perspiration that drenched her hair and made her face wet with dew. Suddenly, in a brief flash of lucidity, she looked round and panicked at her situation. She leapt from the bed, grasping her nightdress, and ran like the wind to her room.

She heard Dieudonne's exasperated voice following her. "You bitch! You teasing little bitch!"

Locking the door, she flung herself on her bed and lay burning with the feverish cramp of longing. She touched her body gently, willing it to be still, but nothing calmed the beating of her heart. The need inside her welled repeatedly like oncoming waves of torment. She drank cooling lemonade from her bedside carafe and thought of Dieudonne's body and the breathtaking touch of his hands. As she thought, she imitated what he had done until violent shudders racked her body and she knew she was pacified.

After a while, Aimee looked in the mirror, holding a candle against the glow of her cheek and smiling at her trembling hands. Then she prayed for forgiveness for being as sinful as Lucinda and Louise. As an afterthought, she also prayed that Damama would not find out and chastise her for what she had done. Damama never mentioned men and what they could do but Aimee knew she enjoyed her female appetites whenever she could. Aunt Tascher condemned ladies who needed what men could do, but Cousin Rose said she had not yet decided about such matters. Aimee wondered if she would dare tell Rose what had happened when they met again. She began to feel fearful that she was ill. Of late, her body seemed to have a mind of its own and to be needing and longing and demanding things she barely understood. She drank another glass of cool liquid and, finally, she slept.

Aimee and Damama had their last picnic a few days before they were due to leave the island. Monsieur Armande accompanied them to Trinity Beach on a hot, humid afternoon. When the meal was over, Damama drove home while Monsieur Armande sat next to Aimee, holding a string of boxfish that they had caught together. He was so depressed that even the sun and the smell of salt sea air could not cheer him. Aimee smiled encouragingly and Monsieur Armande realized, with something of a shock, that she was no longer a little child. Something knowing twinkled in her eyes and he wondered if she knew more than Damama imagined.

"What will you do when we are gone, Monsieur Armande?"

"I am leaving La Maison du Midi, mademoiselle."

"But we are going on Thursday next."

"I shall come with you to the port to see you on your way. Afterward I shall not return."

"But where will you work? Have you already found other employment?"

"I applied to the maritime director for a post as his personal chef, and he has been kind enough to engage me."

"And where will you live?"

"I shall have quarters in his house at Anses-d'Arlets near La Pagerie. I intend to visit your cousin to ask for news of you every month, mademoiselle."

"I shall write very often and send you gifts, Monsieur Armande."

"Perhaps someday I also shall return to France."

"If you do, you'll come to see us, won't you?"

"Of course."

"Damama, did you hear what Monsieur Armande just said?"

"I heard it and I hope it's true."

"This is where we shall be, Monsieur Armande. I've written the address on my calling card. I shall never forget you, you know," Aimee announced.

"And I shall never forget either of you two great ladies."

Damama wiped tears that rolled down her face and urged the horses to a gallop. Clouds, dark and threatening, loomed overhead and a white spiral rose in the sky dancing around and about in ever increasing circles.

"What's that, for heaven's sake? Looks like a ghost jumpin' around the heavens."

Monsieur Armande, looking grim as they drove up the drive, said, "I believe it is a hurricane, madame. Listen to the wind and look at those birds. They are trying to fly into the house! Hurry, we must lock all the doors and secure the windows. Run inside, mademoiselle, there's no time to lose."

Monsieur Charles was away in the capital securing the sale of the property. The three ladies had accompanied him to shop in the city. The house was empty and unlit. Aimee and Damama ran upstairs and closed all open windows and the shutters that covered them. Damama drew the curtains and lit candles and completed their packing to take her mind off the howling wind. Aimee took Mama's jewelry and some of her most beautiful clothes and packed them with her own belongings ready for the great journey.

Outside, they heard a loud resounding crash and the tempest roaring like an angry Valkyrie. A chimney clattered down the roof, falling to the ground and shattering the glass cupola of the conservatory. Aimee began to wonder if her sins of the previous evening had caught up with her. Perhaps God was angry and intended to punish her for all she had done. She kneeled down and asked his forgiveness for her erring ways. Damama listened in amazement to the detailed confession.

"Lord help us, what are you talkin' about, little miss?"

"It's true. Oh, it's true, Damama."

"Well, if it is, it's not a almighty disaster!"

"I did it and I'll probably be killed for being sinful like Louise and Lucinda."

"Nonsense! You're just developin' your female appetites. You're old enough to get wed and if you're old enough to be a wife you're old enough to think overheatin' thoughts!"

They sat down and Damama gave her a lecture on the problems and pitfalls of lovemaking, ending on a stern note: "Now! No givin' fellers the glad eye, not till you're good and married anyway. I don't want to be Da to a rich man's mistress!"

Then Damama dissolved into peals of laughter and hugged Aimee tightly to reassure her. Aimee thought of all she had learned about men and love and how babies came into the world. Babies, Damama had said, must have fathers. Aimee nodded in agreement, relief flooding through her that Damama was not too angry. Damama tried not to tremble. Lord, what a shock! Her little baby developing lustfulness at thirteen and nearly doing something they might have regretted! Secretly she laughed at young Dieudonne's chagrin. But she said a prayer that poor dead Madame had not been watching from her heavenly scented boudoir.

As night fell, the storm worsened and the forest reverberated with sounds of uprooted trees and flying debris. Monsieur Armande made dinner in the kitchen and instructed them to sleep in the cellar. Aimee was delighted at the prospect of such a novel experience. She helped carry small objects to their sanctuary as Damama brought the trunks downstairs for safety. Monsieur Armande found mattresses for each of them, a pile of woolen blankets and enough candles to last the night. Damama grumbled all the way upstairs and all the way back that Monsieur Armande was a fearful pessimistic fool, but she obeyed because she had never heard such a tumult before. She looked out of the window and saw the sea rising like a mountain to reach halfway up the plantation.

They spent the whole evening drinking champagne and eating lobster patties while Monsieur Armande told stories of his youth in Paris and of his first wife, Alouette. They lit dozens of candles to take away the chill of the solid rock walls. Aimee tried to ignore ominous crashes that punctuated the conversation, but she held Damama's hand. In the early hours, as Damama sang songs of the island, learned in childhood, Monsieur Armande realized, with something of a shock, that he loved the giant black woman.

Aimee slept, unaware that outside fishes leapt from sea to river seeking safety, birds sheltered with men in flimsy cottages on the shoreline and shanties disappeared into the sky like tiny paper boxes. Out at sea, eighty ships sank and a thousand lives were lost in the darkness of the deep. The sound of hurtling stone and breaking wood reached a crescendo just before dawn. Damama leaned against Monsieur Armande for comfort.

"Monsieur Charles is in St. Pierre with those girls. I reckon he'll be scared clean out of his liver!"

"Nowhere will be safe from this, madame. It is a disaster."

"We're safe, thanks to you," Damama said softly.

"Shall we open some more champagne?"

"I'll miss you, Monsieur Armande."

"And I shall miss you, madame. More than you'll ever know."

"What's happenin' upstairs, d'you reckon? Sounds like the house is fallin' down."

"The house won't fall down. It was built of solid granite. But I doubt if we shall find things as we left them last night."

"What's your new employer like?"

"He's very Parisian. He vomits at the thought of eating iguana or turtle meat."

"They're all the same, in the beginning. Listen, Monsieur Armande, just listen . . ."

Suddenly, there was silence. Deathly, peaceful silence. Monsieur Armande unlocked the cellar door and walked down the rocky passage to the kitchen. He paused, appalled at the sight before him. Damama held his hand and they stepped over broken timbers, shattered glass and the remains of the kitchen furniture into devastation.

Every cup, plate, glass and pot lay broken in a thousand pieces. Dead seabirds bled down the walls from where they had flown in panic, jamming the kitchen windows with their bodies. No glass remained in the tall panes and the black iron stove had been lifted by the force of the hurricane so it leaned, drunkenly, against the kitchen door. Monsieur Armande took Damama's arm and led her through the house. He paused in the hall, sitting on the stairway, near to tears at the horror of the damage.

Velvet curtains hung in shreds blowing in the warm wind from seaward. Armoires of rosewood and mahogany lay defaced by debris, and seaweed stained fine velvet sofas now bereft of legs and armrests. Silken walls and crystal chandeliers were covered in ugly brown mud and smashed glass littered the carpets. In Aimee's bedroom the four-poster remained intact, bedecked by shards of organzine from tattered frills and counterpane. In Madame's room the smell of jasmine alone remained to remind the onlooker that this unholy disorder had once been a dainty boudoir. Damama picked up a piece of fur, laying it down on a shattered gilt chair. Then she ran downstairs to prevent Aimee from seeing, too suddenly, what they had so narrowly escaped.

Monsieur Charles never returned to the house. He remained, entombed with his three mistresses, under an expensive restaurant in the center of Fort-Royal. They had laughed and lusted and drunk a toast before the building collapsed, burying five hundred people. Rescue squads formed to aid the injured, doctors arrived from the far island and the rich began to mend their shattered mansions. The poor slept in the streets, in makeshift tents or on the beaches. Eventually, order rose from chaos and those who could tried to forget the calamity.

La Maison du Midi stood empty and broken, granite walls firm but the strong, elegant interior devastated. The family lawyer, Monsieur Lautrec, took over Aimee's guardianship and the matter of the sale of the estate. Aimee was bewildered by the suddenness of her loss. She wandered through once elegant interiors weeping for the grandeur of times past.

On the evening before their departure Madame Tascher and Cousin Rose arrived, pale-faced and agitated by the traumas of the past week. Their house, La Pagerie, had been destroyed by the hurricane. Only the granite mill remained solid and invincible.

During tea, Cousin Rose explained their situation.

"We've all moved to the mill, Aimee, and I have a bedroom upstairs where Mr. Jim used to sleep. It's very comfortable, and I have all the things we have left from my old room which weren't broken."

"And what of the future?" Aimee asked.

"We'll stay in the mill because Mama has no money to rebuild the house and, anyway, she feels safer in the mill. Old George was killed when a tree fell on him and we had him buried near the beach. Mama cried because everything is going wrong! We don't know what to do. Oh, I wish I could come with you to France."

"I'm not going to Paris, you know. I'm only going to a convent in Nantes and that won't be very nice."

"But why did Monsieur Charles not send you to Paris?"

"I don't know. I think he chose Nantes because it's where the ship docks and he knew a lot of the gentlemen in that city who run the ebony trade and the spice run."

"Aimee?"

"Yes, Rose."

"Say you won't forget me. Promise to write and send me news of the latest styles and Paris bonnets."

"I promise," replied Aimee as she sipped her tea.

After a while Aimee whispered to Damama and they went upstairs with Mason, Aunt Tascher's boy, and brought all that remained intact of Madame's clothing and jewels.

"This is for you, Aunt Tascher," Aimee said, handing the things to her aunt.

"*Ma chère*, I can't take all that!"

"Yes, you must. Sell the jewels so you can rebuild the refinery. They're mine now, Aunt Tascher, and I want you to have them."

Cousin Rose cried silently and clutched Aimee's hand.

"I've taken Mama's pearl hair brooches and her diamond necklace and pink diamond clusters. Damama has packed them safely for the journey. I shall always treasure them and when I'm grown up I shall wear them as Mama did. But the rest of the jewelry is needed here."

"I don't know what to say, *ma chère*."

"Promise me something?"

"Anything."

"Promise you'll write and tell me all that is happening.

Promise you'll invite Monsieur Armande to tea and make him write to Damama."

Madame Tascher solemnly promised. Rose wiped her eyes and said she would keep a diary of everything that happened on the island and send it each month so Aimee would not be so homesick.

All too soon, their visit was over. They kissed goodbye and ran to the coach. Rose bit her lip till it bled in an effort not to weep. She sat, tiny heart face sad and full of longing, waving till her carriage disappeared into the forest.

As they reached the bend, Rose called out, "Don't forget me, Cousin Aimee, I don't want you to forget me!"

A last wave, then she was gone. Aimee dissolved into tears. "I shall never see her again, Damama."

"Nonsense! You're only goin' to school till you're sixteen, not till you're sixty!"

"I shall never see Rose again, you'll see. Oh God, I wish I could die!"

Aimee ran inside and hid in the kitchen, sobbing till night fell and Monsieur Armande carried her upstairs. She remembered the seer's words: "What you want is not important. What will be will be." She cried herself into a fiftul sleep.

In the morning, Aimee walked alone around the wrecked barracoons of the plantation, through the woods where bright-plumed birds sang a merry welcome and hot golden sunshine warmed the soil in perfumed clearings of exotic vegetation. She heard Damama call that it was time to go and ran toward the house, pausing for a brief second to pick red bougainvillea to press as a reminder of home.

Soon they were in the carriage on the way to the port. Monsieur Armande cleared his throat a dozen times and even Damama was numb, staring hard ahead as though her eyes were trying to remember every cactus flower, every honeybee, every colorful detail of her beloved island. At the headland, near Trinité, they paused to look back, briefly, and Aimee held Damama's hand tightly. Deep in her heart, Aimee knew that she must remember, forever, what she now saw. Bright green sea lapping a silver beach, jade lizards dancing on frangipani leaves and a little boy eating watermelon were recorded, never to be forgotten.

Far behind, the great house lay desolate among surrounding silk-cotton trees.

Gulls screamed overhead and a brig, *La Celeste*, stood in the harbor waiting to take them away. Monsieur Armande carried their trunks on board. He kissed Aimee on both cheeks and handed her a tiny present. She opened the parcel and saw a charm made of silver and mother-of-pearl in the shape of an angel's face. Monsieur kissed Damama formally and handed her a basket of food and a slip of paper folded neatly and covered in red ribbon.

"This is my last picnic for you, madame. I have done my best in the difficult condition of the kitchen."

"Goodbye, Monsieur Armande. If that new employer of yours ever comes to France, see you come with him."

Damama's cheeks grew wet and she blew her nose loudly, saying, "Damned if I'm not upset. My heart feels big as my stomach and my stomach feels pretty miserable too. Goodbye, Monsieur Armande. God bless you, sir."

Monsieur Armande walked stiffly down the gangplank and it was heaved aboard as the captain shouted his orders from the bridge. Native girls in colorful foulards danced on the quayside, blowing kisses to departing sailor lovers and singing the traditional farewell of flower island . . ."*adieu madras, adieu foulard.*" The sun shone, high in a deep gold sky, and they waved frantically till grape-blue mountains on the skyline disappeared and they were surrounded by high rolling waves.

Aimee felt strangely empty. She sat with Damama on deck, watching as her faithful friend read Monsieur Armande's letter. Damama sighed and hugged her close.

"Monsieur Armande's given me a note for money case we ever need it. It's his savings, little miss. I don't know how we could ever thank him for all he's done."

"We can send him a present when we get to France."

Damama looked sad enough to die.

"Damama?"

"Yes, little miss?"

"Now Monsieur Charles is dead, who will pay for my schooling and our food and journeying?"

"Monsieur Lautrec, the lawyer, is gonna take care of all that. He was a good friend of Monsieur Theo's and he'll

101

do what has to be done a sight better than that he-whore ever would have."

"And when I finish at the convent, where shall we go?"

"I don't rightly know. It's a long time till then, and I reckon we'll have to wait and see what happens."

Aimee kissed the soft brown cheek, comforted by the familiar smell of cinnamon and spice. "Don't be sad, Damama. I'll look after you when we get to France."

"I'm sure you will, little miss."

"We'll be happy, won't we, like we were at home?"

"We sure as hell will! I promise we'll have fun even if it does rain every day."

Aimee went to sleep that night happy with the promise. But Damama lay awake, wondering, apprehensively, what the future would bring; listening as the night watch called a clear night, a calm sea and "all's well."

# BOOK II

## Journey To A
## Golden City

# Chapter 8

*Aimee and Damama's journey lasted six weeks.*
Mercifully, for the time of year, the sea remained calm and
the captain pronounced himself well pleased with their
progress.

The only excitement of the voyage came when, on approaching the French coast, the lookout spotted an English
frigate near the Bordeaux Light. One of the passengers became so excited at the possibility of pursuit by a ship of
France's archrival that he fell overboard and had to be recovered with great difficulty.

Customs and health officials arrived before the pilot
could come aboard at St. Nazaire and a four-day quaran-
tine was imposed despite the good health of crew and passengers. The captain sighed with relief that the officers had
not made the delay longer. He was carrying a cargo of rum,
sugar, molasses, limes, tamarinds and coconuts. "My con-
signment will be safe. They don't care about our cargoes,"
he confided to Aimee. "They tend to decide on the quaran-
tine period according to how officious they feel that day!
Sometimes, our holds stink like catfish by the time we dock."

At last, they were free to proceed up the Loire toward the port of Nantes. In the early dawn, Aimee stood with Damama watching the passing scene. The coast was dotted with lighthouses standing like white sentinels on jagged black rocks so treacherous that the sea seemed compelled to rise ever higher, foaming and lashing against them. The landscape on either side of the estuary was strangely pallid, pale green fields, pale yellow marsh iris, black and white cows, gray rivers and peasants working to bring in the last of the apple harvest. Apples were stacked in small mountains at intervals along the way, waiting to be turned into cider and potent apple brandy. Villages of somber gray stood near châteaux of granite with black slate roofs. Church spires pierced low milky clouds and arched bridges spanned beige rivers of muddy water. Small birds flew by crying a startling welcome from the colorless countryside. The sky was creamy white, the air soft and hazy. The scene lacked the life and the dazzling gaiety of flower island.

Aimee wondered where the sun was as she and Damama stood silently waiting for the moment of disembarkation. She had never felt so depressed in her life. Two nuns in white and gray met them and ushered them past officials on the quayside to a waiting gig. The nuns had rosy cheeks and happy smiles and Damama was temporarily reassured. She listened as Aimee chatted politely with her new acquaintances.

"Where is the sun today?"

"It's almost winter, my dear. In France, we don't have sunshine in wintertime."

"What is wintertime?"

"Oh! I forgot that you know nothing of our seasons. Well, winter is the cold time of the year. People here call these the black months, when wind and rain and snow and ice come upon us. It makes our hands and feet cold and we have to take care not to catch a chill. In the islands of the southern hemisphere the climate is almost always the same. But here, we have four quite different periods of the year. Reverend Mother will explain all about such things when she meets you."

First they passed gleaming white salt flats on the approach to the city center, then gabled houses of white and green, brown and cream, and endless streets of dull gray stone terraces. Aimee saw bread sellers, chair menders and dogcatchers. They passed a flower market in the main square where even the flower colors echoed the sallow countryside, in pale pinks, soft blues and subdued lilacs.

She heard a town crier calling the hour and saw in the distance a slave ship approaching the harbor, its decks full of naked blacks clad in tiny aprons to preserve the onlookers' modesty. The city had impressive arcades of black iron and white marble and coffeehouses full of laughing men. The ladies of the town appeared haughty and unsmiling. Their husbands had grown rich from the ebony trade and bought themselves mistresses on the outskirts of town or in princely villas on the Ile Feydeau. This made the townswomen bitter and jealous. But Aimee knew nothing of their chagrin. She saw only wealth, order and rigid social structure, colorless sky and untinted terrain.

Finally, they came to open countryside and a road sign indicated Goulaine. A canal of pale muddy water flowed parallel to the road and, just beyond, an old horse plodded along, dragging a cart full of noisy peasant folk on their way to work. In a village near the convent, a goose market was in progress, and ruddy-faced farmers inspected hundreds of waggling, cackling, fluffy white yellow-beaked birds. Aimee was half thrilled, half appalled by the strangeness of what she saw. France was as unlike flower island as butter from beeswax.

Suddenly, as they rounded a bend, the great wall of the convent loomed ahead. Aimee peered at the entrance gate fitted with spiked iron grids, wooden slats and shutters that hid all but the eyes of the nun who answered their call. The door opened to admit them. Then, with a hollow, metallic echo, it slammed on the outside world and they stepped into the obligatory silence of the convent compound.

In the days that followed, Aimee met her fellow pupils and was shown round by the Mother Superior. She learned the intricacies of the ancient building and soon identified the forge and refectory, cloisters and rere-dorter, cellarium, scriptorium and herbarium. She liked best the fish pond where carp with pouting pescatorial mouths lazed in green gloom waiting to be eaten on days of penance. Mother

Superior was a keen advocate of self-sufficiency and her word was law in the convent.

Aimee was given a cell-like room next to Damama's and told that this room would be hers until she left the convent in three years' time. She looked round at white walls, white covers and a brown carved wood cross and outside to pale landscape and misty autumn sky. Suddenly, she felt very tired. She sat on the bed, thinking of Pointe Royale and bright green parrots that squawked on red flower branches deep in the forest. A robin came to her sill, cocking his head and hoping for food, and she gave it the crumbs of her last sugar biscuit. Each day, it returned to remind her that new friends appear in the most unlikely places.

Damama went into a deep decline when she saw the harsh stone interior with its steeply carved staircase, sepia tapestries and tower-high ceilings. Her eyes glazed in horror at the tiny cell, a little taller than herself and only twice her width! She sat on the narrow bed, looking longingly out to the fields. Then she jumped up to wave enthusiastically to a farmer plowing on the other side of the wall. The farmer stared in amazement at the sight of a brown-faced giantess waving a red silk parasol from the stone sill of the convent. But he waved back, smiling broadly. Damama beamed as she estimated the drop from her window. That farmer looked like a strong fellow. He might prove very useful when loneliness became too stifling for her female appetites.

Mother Superior called Aimee to formally welcome her after she had settled to the routine of the convent.

"Are you well, child?"

"Yes, Reverend Mother."

"But you are very pale."

"It's cold and without the sun my skin turns white."

"In springtime the sun will return; have no fear."

"When will spring come?"

"In six months, perhaps sooner."

Aimee sighed. Six months was half a year. Half a year without seeing the sun! She felt tears well in her eyes and she looked down so the kindly woman would not see her distress.

"Beginning tomorrow, you will commence your lessons, child. You will follow a course of religion, writing, illumination of manuscripts and household management with a little cookery, music, quilting and embroidery. If you wish, you may also learn a language."

"I would like that, Reverend Mother."

"Which language would you prefer?"

"English if I may," Aimee replied with sudden enthusiasm.

"English! Why English?"

"Because Monsieur Armande, our chef, told me that half the world speaks English and so I wish to speak it too. I have already had some lessons from an English gentleman in Martinique."

"How very astute. Well, I shall arrange it, of course. From next week you will have an English tutor. Is there anything else you wish to learn?"

"I would like to play the mandolin and to make medicine for sick people."

"Very well. I shall see that your wishes are fulfilled. You will rise each morning at five-thirty and spend an hour in silent prayer. Breakfast is at seven, and matins a half hour later. Your first lesson will be at eight and you will finish your last formal class before luncheon at one. In the afternoon, you may join the sewing or embroidery class and on certain days you may work with Sister Thérèse in the dispensary so you can learn about your medicines."

"And what must Damama do?"

"Your Da is free to come and go as she pleases. If she wishes, she may also join in the afternoon activities. If she prefers an outdoor activity, I'm sure Sister Emmanuelle would be happy to have some assistance in the garden."

Damama looked relieved that she was not going to be given a timetable. She smiled politely at Mother Superior before allowing her mind to wander back to thoughts of Monsieur Armande.

"At seven bells, which is four-thirty, we have vespers, and supper is at six. Have you any questions?"

"Yes, Reverend Mother. When can I go out with Damama?"

"You will be allowed one outing of one day per term and one outing of half a day per month. We are generous in this order with free time. In some convents the pupils are allowed out only once a year!"

Aimee returned to her room with Damama, smiling imp-ishly at her nurse's stricken face.

"Allowed out once a year! What did that holy mean, d'you reckon?"

"Just that, Damama. They only go out once a year in some convent schools."

"I never heard of such a thing. That Monsieur Charles sure as hell knew what he was sendin' us to. I reckon we might have been best off at Macouba. Least I could have kept him under my control if he hadn't gone and got him-self buried under the avalanche! Oh Lord! Just look out there, gray sky and gray water and gray birds and the people got gray hair and skins like monkeys' backsides!"

Aimee settled into the routine after a few weeks. She draped her bed with one of Mama's best dresses, a bright pink silk covered in paillettes of pearl and tiny diamanté droplets. On the walls she hung taut satin ribbons and on the ribbons she pinned some of Mama's most beautiful jewelry. At night, in the moonlight, the gems gleamed richly bright like stars.

Damama went to town and bought herself a new red bedspread, a bright red dressing gown and a new red silk parasol with a heavy ebony handle. She filled the small cell with bright flowers from the flower market and pur-chased a parrot called Percy from a river captain who lived near the port. Within a month, she had friends in the town. Within two months, she had persuaded a restaurateur in the Rue Crebillon to give her free meals on visits to the city with Aimee. She had also found a spice shop, a pet shop, an underwear *midinette* who made wonderful red drawers and a bordello where a party was thrown every Thursday for all who wished to attend. She was almost happy except for the weather. Every day it rained and as it rained, Damama stood at the window cursing, "Damned disobedi-ent weather! Dammit!" The parrot soon learned to echo her sentiments.

Bells rang for prayer every hour on the hour and on Sun-days the sound of city carillons was deafening. Aimee began to look forward to her trips away from the convent with a fierce longing. She was so homesick that she found it im-possible to control her tears. Time seemed to make little

110

difference to this condition and she continued to pine for the wide-open spaces of her island home.

After three months, Damama began to worry about Aimee's loss of vivacity and the thinning down of her already fragile figure. The convent served rich, fine meals, each course provided from its own self-sufficient community. Only sugar, coffee, spices and condiments came from the city, and wine from a nearby vineyard. Everything else, from altar bread to succulent lamb, was raised, grown, fished, picked, plucked or spun in the silent enclosure. But Aimee could not eat. She longed to go home.

At Christmas, she wept openly for hours on end. Presents from new friends and patient teachers did nothing to console her. Damama's gift of banana bread and a new "trembling" pearl brooch released floods of tears and distressing memories and Aimee ran to her room, sobbing inconsolably throughout the night. Mother Superior called on her and assured her that when spring came she would feel better. She needed only some sunshine to warm her and make her happy again. Others continued the theme and Aimee began to equate spring with salvation and a return to the golden, happy days of times past.

At long last, the trees bloomed and pale green fields were dotted with the pink and white of pear and apple. The sky was faintly blue and a watery sun shone like silver. Aimee was appalled. Was this all that had been promised? Was this the French idea of sunshine? Summer turned to autumn and she learned that in France, the seasons were little different. The wind always blew from seaward. The sun shone but it had no heat and little color and always, unexpectedly, the rains came, lashing the coast and battering carefully planted garden flowers to a soggy, broken pulp.

As time passed, Aimee retreated into a dream world all her own and rarely spoke, except to Damama. To Damama she confided all her sadness, her fears and her bitter unhappiness.

"What am I going to do, Damama?"

"You just got to settle, little miss."

"I *can't* settle."

"You can if you have to," the wise woman told her.

"But you don't understand!" Aimee stood, looking out at the rain.

"I understand you need a education and this is where you have to get it. Till that's all finished we can't go home."

"Couldn't we run away?"

"Where to?"

"To Paris . . . or we could ask a captain to take us back to Martinique."

"Then where would we live?"

"With Aunt Tascher and Cousin Rose, of course."

"Your aunt's got barely enough money to put her own troubles right, let alone have us tied round her neck to bring her down."

At the beginning of the second winter, Aimee began to have nightmares. She screamed like a lost soul, waking all the convent till finally, Mother Superior was forced to be firm.

"I called you to see me, my child, because I am worried about you."

"Yes, Reverend Mother."

"You are still having bad dreams, I hear?"

"Yes, Reverend Mother."

"You have been with us now for well over one year. The teachers like you. Your fellow pupils adore you and I also like you very much. You have with you your own Da—none of the others have been permitted such a luxury—and you are allowed out to the city frequently with her. But you have never settled with us. You pine and cry and refuse your food and now you torment us all every night with your screams."

"I'm sorry, Reverend Mother, I'm truly sorry."

"Sorry is not enough, my dear child."

Aimee clenched her fists and struggled with tears as the nun continued.

"If you allow yourself to become one of those foolish people who long all their days to be something they cannot be, to own something they cannot own, or go somewhere they cannot go, you are a fool!"

The Mother Superior looked closely to see what effect her words were having. "I do not like to have fools in my convent, and I do not really think that you are one. Now let us discuss the problem, which is that you do not like France, and why not?"

"The sun rarely shines, Reverend Mother. It's so cold and I miss all the beautiful, colorful places of my own land."

"Did you see the yellow poppies last summer?"

"No, Reverend Mother."

"Did you see the marigolds and the red roses and the wonderful lilacs in Sister Emmanuelle's garden?"

"No, Reverend Mother, I didn't."

"Have you seen the squirrel that nests in the oak tree or smelled the pines in the forest of Les Moulins?"

Aimee fell silent.

"There are hares and otters and badgers in our woods. They are not so brightly colored as your animals, I must admit, but most of them are a good deal more friendly!"

"Yes, Reverend Mother, I know, but . . ."

"Our flowers are softly shaded to match our countryside. Wild garlic is white, willow herb is pink, sea holly is gray and forget-me-nots are deep blue. These are the colors of *our* countryside, my child, and I assure you they are no less beautiful than yours. Yours would seem only gaudy and brash in the delicate landscape of the Vendée."

Aimee looked at the nun through her tears.

"You must stop comparing, my child. Learn to appreciate every flower, every town, every person you meet in life for the love and the beauty and the fascination they can give you. If you find things deficient because they are not exactly like things on your flower island you will do many beautiful objects a terrible injustice."

"Oh, what am I to do, Reverend Mother? I'm so unhappy."

"You must decide immediately to be happy."

Aimee looked at her in bewilderment. The nun stood, looking down, eyes shining in a pale, vibrant face.

"If it is cold, shake your head and defy the cold! You have warm clothing and good boots and your stomach is full of good food, so what does it matter if the day is cold? Are you a baby that you flinch from it? If the sun shines less golden than the sun in Martinique, appreciate it for what it is. Look around you and see the beauty of this place. Never forget your home, my child, simply add this to the many places you will visit in your life. Accept them all for what they are. There is no escape from here, not for some time, and when you know there is no escape you must either settle or go mad . . . the choice is yours."

"I shall try to be happy, Reverend Mother."

"God's blessing on you, my child. From today, you will grow up and you *will* be happy."

Aimee told Damama all that Mother Superior had said. Then she went to bed and slept a dreamless sleep for the first time in many months.

In the morning, Aimee woke to the sound of a speckled thrush song. She rose and watched a skein of white geese flying across a pale gray sky. Autumn leaves swirled in the stony courtyard and a burnished copper-leafed creeper brightened ancient stone walls. Sister Emmanuelle was carrying a pannier of tomatoes to the kitchen; a novice stood with a yellow bowl, picking rosemary in the tiny walled *potager*. Smell of smoky autumn drifted in through the window as Damama arrived with her breakfast.

While sipping coffee and eating sweet yellow brioche, Aimee thought of her interview with Mother Superior . . . "When you know there is no escape, you must either settle or go mad." From that moment on, Aimee began to relax and accept life behind the gray stone walls. After a while, she was almost happy. She wrote on the first day of each month to Rose, and received in return many letters written in her cousin's childish scrawl, telling her of life on flower island. Rose often enclosed pressed flowers and handmade feather bookmarkers. Monsieur Armande always sent his respects to Damama and sometimes a letter came in his ornately precise hand.

Gradually, childhood memories relaxed their hold and became a beautiful montage of reminiscence to be cherished always.

One day, a letter arrived from Rose that caused Aimee great excitement.

My Dear Aimee:

I have such news for you. I am promised to be married and my husband will be Alexandre de

Beauharnais. Imagine, I shall be a Vicomtesse! It's such a story, Aimee, really romantic, I think. What do you think?

At first, the Vicomte requested the hand of my younger sister, but Mama said she was too young to leave home. So, I shall go to Paris to be married. I do so hope to see you before you return to Martinique so I can tell you all my secrets. Do you feel any better about living in a convent? Learning is such a bore, isn't it?

Everyone here on flower island is preparing for Vaval. When I go to watch the processions I shall think of you and wish you were here at my side. Monsieur Armande sends Damama his best wishes and I send her mine, too. We still miss you both very much.

Mama asked me to ask you to send her the new shipping catalogs for the autumn. Perhaps you can send Damama to collect them from the Maritime Office in Nantes.

Oh, Aimee, I am so very excited about my future! I don't know how I shall control myself until I get to France. Write at once and tell me your news. Don't delay, because you are the only person I want to share my special thoughts with.

As always, your loving cousin,
Rose

## Chapter 9

*Aimee was almost sixteen, at last, and looking* forward to going home to her flower island in the autumn of the year. Damama had made her new clothes and bonnets and prepared her for a regal return to their homeland. In midsummer, however, their plans were ruined by a letter Mother Superior received from Aimee's guardian, Monsieur Lautrec.

Most Reverend Mother:

As you know, my ward, Aimee Dubuq de Rivery, is due to return to Martinique on the 30th September of this year. I regret to inform you that I have been forced to review this arrangement and now must ask that you continue to guard her in the safety of the convent, as any attempt to cross the ocean in these troubled times would be folly. In the last three months alone eighteen ships sailing from France to these islands have been sunk or severely damaged by the English. I am told no cargo is safe on the

seas and even American traders are keeping clear of
our waters, as the English gunners are no respecters
of their flag and many innocent souls have been
consigned to the deep. Under the circumstances, I
feel I cannot sanction Aimee's return until I can
guarantee her safe passage. I enclose a further draft
to cover fees and subsistence and request that you
break this most unwelcome news in the most saga-
cious way possible, so as not to distress the dear child.
Please convey my warmest good wishes to her and
her Da.

> My respects to you,
> Charles Lautrec

Aimee wept when she heard the news. But Mother
Superior was ready with a proposal of her own.

"My child, would you answer a question for me?"

"Of course, Reverend Mother."

"We have grown fond of you in the three years you have
been with us. Now you are almost sixteen and your education is complete. Would you care to teach some of our
young children in this period of waiting before you return
home? They would greatly benefit from your knowledge
and education."

"I would like that very much, Reverend Mother," Aimee
said cheerily.

"I have arranged some new courses which you may
care to consider. You could learn the guitar and the dulcimer and also take lessons in Italian. With your ability to
assimilate languages at great speed, you will be an accomplished linguist; your dreams of travel will be easy
to fulfill."

"Thank you, Reverend Mother."

"One other thing, my child. I have here a letter which I
urgently need to send to Vannes. I intend, if you are willing, to give it to you to deliver. You may have leave of
absence to carry out this commission on my behalf."

Aimee stared in disbelief at this unexpected offer.

"One of the sisters could take it or I could hire a messenger, but the contents are so confidential and our sisters
so overworked that I hesitate to disrupt their routine."

"I would be honored to deliver your letter, Reverend Mother."

"Thank you, my child. A carriage will be waiting for you and your Da in the morning. On your return you must tell me all you have seen in that ancient city. I was born in Vannes and I think of it often. You will stay at Les Alizés in the Rue Faubourg St. Brieuc. It is a house of our order where sisters stay when they travel through the city en route for Mont St. Michel."

"Thank you, Reverend Mother. I must go and tell Damama the news."

Aimee ran like the wind upstairs to Damama's room. Damama beamed mightily and ran round packing and ironing and singing and slapping her thighs.

"Well, I'll be darned!" she laughed. "That holy sure as hell knows her stuff. She's done this as a favor, little miss. I hope you gave her a *big* kiss."

Aimee wondered if a big kiss would have been in order for such a supremely serene character as Mother Superior.

They departed at dawn on a misty morning, the silence pierced by the sound of foghorns in the distant bay and Damama's parrot shouting "damned disobedient weather" as they drove through the convent gate. Empty fields bordered empty roads until they reached Savenay, where they paused for breakfast and a change of horses. Damama was delighted to be free and Aimee ecstatic to be going somewhere new. She sang happily during most of the journey.

Damama looked at Aimee, marveling that she was now grown-up in all but one respect. And she was more beautiful by the week. They chattered and pointed out new sights to one another as the carriage churned up dust on the narrow coast road. On the beach below, children hunted for crabs and sea urchins. In the bay, sardine boats departed, bright sails billowing in the breeze. In quaint country villages, those with nothing better to do shot crossbows at wooden birds or jousted with wooden dummies in a dangerous game of quinlaine. Summer pleasure boats dotted the blue bay as holiday crowds jostled in the narrow streets of coastal towns.

They spent a night in the black and white hospice, where

kindly sisters served them a rich supper of cotriade, guinea fowl and crepes stuffed with apricot puree. Damama sampled all the cheeses on the tray and drank liqueur from every bottle on the table. She pronounced the kamok perfection, the Cointreau delicious, the prunelle exotic and the noyau magnificent. Then she swayed upstairs to bed with dreamy eyes and uncertain feet, leaving Aimee to amuse the nuns with stories of her Da's legendary appetite and her ability to catch iguanas. The nuns laughed outrageously till after midnight. Aimee went to bed smiling at their disobedience of the early curfew bell.

Despite the hour, Aimee found sleep impossible. A curlew called in the estuary, a tawny owl screeched in the barn and mice clattered inside the walls like legions of tiny clog dancers. Wild roses pushed through the window from the wall outside, scenting balmy night air with subtle sweetness, and in the distance, she heard the sound of a man singing.

In the oppressive warmth of the night, she writhed in an agony of longing, aware that her body was growing more and more impatient. She got up and examined herself in the moon's reflection in the open windowpane. She was still slim, though taller than before, but now her breasts were full and round and pushing forward, longing to be touched. Her hair fell like a silver curtain over her shoulders and down her back, covering her nakedness with its shimmering strands. She stood for a moment at the open window, holding lace curtains in either hand and staring at the moon, unaware that in the courtyard of the adjoining house, a young man watched with bright eyes and a curious smile. When she closed the curtains, he played a love song on his guitar and sang, softly, secretly, wondering all the while if the beautiful creature from the convent window was still awake and aware of him.

Aimee lay, listening to the words of the song and trying to decide if the singer had seen her naked. The thought inflamed her so she burned with desire. Finally, overcome by curiosity, she ran to the window and peeped through the curtains. But the moon kept the young man's secret and she saw only a white shirt, elaborately frilled at neck and wrist, and a curly head bent low over the guitar.

She rose at daybreak, impatient to be off, unable to settle

to peaceful thoughts for the pounding of her racing pulse. She heard the watchman's trumpet calling workers from their beds and the rattle of chains being removed from street corners as curfew ended and a new day began.

On their return trip, Aimee and Damama had almost reached Muzillac when a cry echoed in the silence of early morning.

*"Arrêtez, mesdames et messieurs!"*

Damama stuck her head out of the window in astonishment and saw an elegant gentleman on a snow-white horse. Plumed hat raised, velvet jacket immaculately gold-embossed, he was as handsome a fellow as she had seen.

She called out in a loud voice, "Young fellow, what are you doin'? What are your intentions, sir?"

"My intentions, madame? Have no fear. Come, Rigaud, follow me."

Damama realized at once that their coachman was in the fellow's employ. They were led down a narrow lane to a long, low farmhouse and Damama was deposited with Rigaud with instructions to be quiet or he would slit her throat! She watched the carriage disappear down the lane and prayed that Aimee would survive whatever that young man had in mind. She turned to her captor, weighing him from head to toe. He was short and stocky with a grizzled head and twinkling brown eyes.

"Now what am I supposed to do, sir?"

"Nothing, madame, until tomorrow. Tomorrow you and your lady will be free to go your way."

"Tomorrow! But little miss is due back at her convent *tonight!*"

"She will not be there, madame."

"Oh Lord! That holy'll have my skin for this."

"You can tell her the horse slipped, the wheel broke— whatever you like. I assume you can lie?"

Damama muttered under her breath as she walked inside the house. She looked round and saw a stove of black iron, scrupulously clean, with a pot of rabbit stew bubbling temptingly. A pine fire burned in the hearth and bunches of sage suspended from the ceiling scented the air with the sweet smell of home. She was almost happy at the astonishing incident. Then she remembered Aimee.

"What's happenin' to little miss, sir?"

"She has been kidnapped by Monsieur Duval."

"Why? We got no money to give him."

"He does not want money, madame. He wants *her*."

"Oh Lord! But she's a innocent child and only fifteen. She's not even a *real* lady yet. What's she gonna do all alone and not knowin' what's happenin'? And how am I gonna get her a good match after all this jiggerin' around? French husbands want virgins for their wives."

"A little pucker water will suffice. Most men don't know a virgin from a dungeon, madame."

Damama laughed, despite herself. Little miss had developed her female appetites long ago, that was for sure. Lately, Aimee had been absentminded and given to blushing at her own thoughts. Sometimes she could not sleep and sometimes she walked the night like a caged tiger. Perhaps young Monsieur Duval was just what little miss needed. Damama fanned her burning neck with a piece of rice paper.

"Who is he then, this Duval?"

"He's a highwayman, madame. He robs coaches between Nantes and Mont St. Michel and he has become very rich in the process. They hanged his great-grandfather at Tyburn. Some say he was more loved by more women than any other man in England."

"England! Do you mean that fellow's a *Englishman*?" Damama asked.

"No, madame, have no fear, he's a true Breton. Now, let's eat and be merry. Forget your charge, there's nothing to be done, and you and I have other business to attend to."

His eyes twinkled, but Damama sat, nonplussed at this turn of events. The man was strong, his face kind, and his friend, young Duval, had the look of a gentleman despite his unlawful profession. She remembered the anxiety in his eyes when he first saw Aimee and the momentary flash of delight in little miss's. Damama decided to accept the inevitable.

Aimee found excitement made breathing difficult as her carriage rattled along the rough road. It stopped within sight of the sea outside a rustic cottage with a garden of colorful flowers and heavy bent fruit trees. The frilled white cuff appeared at the window as Duval bowed graciously and helped her down. Aimee sniffed the smell of hay and lavender on his hair, which was black and curly and unpowdered. His eyes were pure violet, ringed with long lashes, and they seemed to smile even when he was serious.

"What is your name, mademoiselle?"

"I am Aimee Dubuq de Rivery, sir."

"You aren't French?"

"I am Creole, from Martinique."

He ushered her through a rose-arched door to a whitewashed room that was almost empty except for a fourposter covered in crusty white lace. Logs sizzled in the hearth and a pot-au-feu bubbled in a black caldron. In the corner, an old table bedecked with red roses was set for two.

"This is my secret place, little Creole."

"Who are you, sir?"

"Forgive me, my name is Duval, Dominic Duval. I am a highwayman and I intend to rob you."

Aimee felt her face burning, her heart thumping. She fanned herself quickly as she tried to think what to do. "I live at the Convent of Our Lady of Nantes, sir, and I am due back there this evening. Where is my Da, what have you done to her?"

"Rigaud will feed her and then entertain her royally."

"And what now? Am I your prisoner?"

"First, we shall have lunch. Then I intend to adore you."

"Sir!"

"There's no escape and you want none, so don't turn prim with me, young lady. Be happy, you are a beautiful woman and I'm a man who appreciates beauty. You have much to learn, I imagine, and I shall be an excellent teacher."

Removing her bonnet and gloves, Aimee sat down in the old wooden rocker. Outside, gulls called to seaward and a foghorn sounded in the bay. A summer mist fell, enveloping the house in a secret gray shroud, giving the landscape ethereal unreality. Aimee wondered if she should try to escape or if she really wanted to. She watched as Duval took off his jacket and strode purposefully round preparing their meal.

She felt hungry. So, reluctantly, she sat down at the table and waited to be fed. The young man's skin was bronzed and firm, his gaze direct, challenging and intensely flattering. As Aimee ate, she began to tremble and he teased her, but they both enjoyed the wild turkey stew and the fine champagne.

"I stole this beautiful wine from the Duc d'Orléans. It has been waiting for someone like you to come to honor it with your loveliness. Why are you trembling?"

"I'm afraid, sir."

"Of me?"

"Yes."

"Why?"

"Because I know nothing of men, and if you use me I will *never* be able to marry. You will have ruined my life, sir. I shall end by being a *mistress*!"

"Nonsense! I shall make you happy as a queen."

"You don't understand."

"Of course I do. There are many ways of simulating that which is lost. Ask your Da. She looks like a lady who knows more than is good for her."

"You're impertinent, sir. Damama is a good woman and I adore her."

"Eat your fruit and stop pretending indignation. I'm thirty years old and I've had a hundred women—maybe more—but I have never had one as lovely as you."

In late afternoon, Duval walked with Aimee along the beach and gave her a silver-pink shell. They picked pears and apricots in the orchard until she began to shiver in the chill evening air. Duval put his velvet jacket over her shoulders and they ran back to the cottage. Then, in the twilight glow from the open fire, he undressed and stood naked before her. Aimee watched as he turned down the bed and plumped the pillows. He unbuttoned her dress, laughing as her limbs shook with such ferocity that her teeth chattered. He kissed her cheeks reassuringly, asking questions that made her blush furiously. He toasted her with the last of the champagne, content to embark on a night of love without fear of unfortunate consequence.

"Remember last night when you stood naked at your window and I watched?"

"You are no gentleman, Dominic Duval!"

124

"Do you remember?"

"Yes, I remember. But I did not know you were there."

"What were you thinking about?"

"I was wishing I could go to sleep and wishing I could feel calm, the way I used to feel when I was a child. Perhaps I was also longing for love, though I know it is forbidden a lady."

"My God, you're honest! Take care, little Creole, or I'll fall madly in love with you."

He kissed her neck as he removed her necklace, her shoulders as he slipped down her heavy silk dress. He untied her boots and kissed her feet, continuing to unbutton and untie till he slipped off her bodice and drawers in one swift movement like a magician. Gently, he tasted her breasts and pushed her back on the bed so he could proceed to invade all her secret places.

Aimee thought the room seemed suddenly warmer, the flower scent heavier and the throbbing of her body even fiercer. She stroked his arms and slid her hands round his broad back, kissing his ears and sniffing the sweet scent of his hair. Duval laughed and teased as he titillated and tormented till she longed for him to make her feel all she needed so desperately to feel. For a moment, she opened her eyes and saw him poised astride her thighs in that final moment of anticipation. Then she closed her eyes, screaming in pain and ecstasy as his heat and hers intermingled. Back and forth he rocked till her body turned to flame and she heard herself cry out again and again as she pulled her captor toward her. She tried to tell him all the beautiful things she was feeling but she could barely speak.

Suddenly, she felt an overpowering ecstasy that made her body arch, her breath shudder, her limbs collapse in exquisite exhaustion. She lay breathless and trembling, smiling at the wonder of what had happened to her. Duval sat back, nursing her in his arms.

"Your husband will be a lucky one someday."

"I am ruined, sir!"

"But you enjoyed your ruination, didn't you?"

"Yes, I'm a sinful woman, there's no doubt of it."

"Nonsense! You're a real woman. You know, little Creole, there are two kinds of women, marble ones and chili pepper ones and you are not one of the marble ones!"

"I am a very sinful woman. What ever will happen to me now? I can't imagine what Damama will say when she knows, and Reverend Mother. Oh! *Mon Dieu!* Say a prayer that Mama was not watching from heaven!"

Duval laughed as he kissed her cheeks and said, "If you tell Reverend Mother, she'll die of apoplexy. Your Da will laugh and congratulate you, if I know anything. She's a lusty woman, that one. I only hope she doesn't kill Rigaud with her demands. As for your mama, well, everyone knows that in heaven folk see only what makes them happy."

They made love all night till Aimee's limbs felt like lead and her heart felt like gossamer. She laughed and sang and learned all Duval could teach her till pink dawn came softly over the horizon and it was time to go. Sadly, reluctantly, she washed as he watched and dressed with his help. They walked hand in hand to the carriage, pausing for a moment to say goodbye.

"I shall always remember you, little Creole. You will never forget me because I was your first lover and ladies remember that for the rest of their lives."

"Shall we ever meet again, sir?"

"I don't know about the future. Last night it was safe for us to take our pleasures but another time it might be too risky. I adore you and I would not wish to place you in a situation of shame and despair."

"But shall I *never* see you again?"

"Rigaud and I are often in Nantes. We stay at the Jolly Fisherman. Your Da will know of it. Now I must take you back to the road. Rigaud and your nurse are in the farmhouse down the lane. Kiss me and say goodbye, little Creole."

"Goodbye, Dominic Duval."

Aimee looked close to tears.

When they arrived at Rigaud's house and picked up Damama, she looked all of ten years younger. Rigaud cursed as he stumbled over stones in the garden, stubbing his toe on the gatepost.

"You look tired, Rigaud. Don't tell me you didn't sleep well?" Duvall asked.

"Sleep well? I didn't sleep at all!"

126

"Be quiet, sir, you're bein' impolite talkin' of such private matters!" Damama said.

"And you, madame, are an unmerciful she-devil!"

Damama climbed in the carriage and looked out of the window. She asked no questions. It was plain from the dreamy look in Aimee's eyes that she had had a very good night.

They arrived at the convent in the early evening and Damama told Mother Superior of their "accident," lying royally about a broken carriage wheel. Aimee retired to bed early to dream of her lover.

She never discussed Dominic Duval and all that happened in the cottage on the beach. She felt the need to keep that episode as her own precious secret. In days of loneliness or boredom and on dark wintry nights, she dreamed of him. And when spring came she wished he would come and take her away forever to his cottage by the sea.

But life continued calm and orderly. Only Aimee had changed, blossoming with the heady, sweet fire of her Creole soul.

# Chapter 10

*Aimee had written to tell Rose of her exciting* experience with the highwayman. Now, she waited, eagerly, to hear from her dearest friend about life in the elegant French capital. Sadly, they had not, as yet, been able to meet. Rose's ship had been forced by gales to dock at Quimper instead of Nantes and she had proceeded directly to Paris to meet her new husband. Aimee had heard nothing from Rose since the marriage and had been worried that her cousin was having difficulty settling in Paris. At last, a letter arrived and Aimee read, greatly dismayed by the contents.

My dear Aimee:

Forgive me for being so tardy in replying to your exciting letter. You are a naughty little minx but I love you dearly and hope you enjoyed your adventure with the wicked Dominic Duval. Have you met him again? Do write and tell me all about it. I am not very happy at the moment, I'm afraid, probably because I had expected so much of Paris and even more of matrimony.

Alexandre is exceedingly aggravated that I am not learned. He makes me have lessons in history and geography every week and a hundred times a day tells me that I must say say *round*, not *wownd*, but you know how we Creoles have difficulty with our *r*'s. He has made me so nervous, laughing and mocking me about my accent in front of all his fancy society friends, that I am almost too frightened to leave the house. What do you think of this, Aimee, don't you think it's rude to criticize a wife in front of all Paris?

Now, no more grumbling. The best news I leave to the last. I am going to have a child. Write at once and tell me your congratulations. I am longing to tell Alexandre because I feel sure he will be pleased, but yesterday he went away without a word of warning and I don't know where he is. That's how it is, Aimee. He's not exactly a gentleman by our standards, no matter how elevated his birth. I don't know when he will return but I feel sure he will be pleased with me. Anyway, the most important thing is that I am well. If Mama can get away during my last months, I know she will come here for the delivery. If she can, I shall be very well pleased, as I'm afraid to be alone at such an important time. Now, what else have I to tell you?

Paris is full of China blue silk and bonnets have become taller and tilted to the back of the head. I have bought so many new clothes I shall have to have new armoires to hold them all. When you come to Paris, I shall take you shopping to the very best shops and show you such things your eyes will fall out on the roadway! Please thank Damama for her note and thank you also for the lovely drawings of the countryside around your convent. It looks very peaceful and pretty but no place is as lovely as flower island, is it?

I shall write again as soon as Alexandre comes home and tell you how delighted he is with the news.

As always, your loving cousin,
Rose

Aimee soon learned all that Sister Thérèse could teach her of medicine, dispensing drafts and making antidotes for every known poison. Despite her misadventure en route home from Vannes, Aimee was permitted to travel from time to time for visits to nearby cities with Damama. Each time she returned to thrill the nuns with long recitals on the social scene and the latest fashions in dress and furniture. Her descriptions were further enhanced by thick illustrated catalogs from leading emporiums and fashion houses.

Damama never failed to be surprised by the effect Aimee had on these holy ladies of the silent enclosure. Their pale faces glowed, as their eyes scrutinized what she showed them. Even Sister Isabelle, the cook, made such dinners to celebrate Aimee's return that penance was in order for indulgence in the sin of gluttony.

Watching, one day, as Aimee enlivened her classes with merry songs and kindness to her small pupils, Damama was shocked to realize that this gray stone sanctuary had become their home. Walls, built high to keep out desecraters, had become for both a symbol of safety. Instead of feeling imprisoned, they felt a risk only when outside the enclosure.

As time passed, Aimee became adept at hiding her longing for home. Disagreements between France and England, rivalry on the high seas, robbery and extensive privateering still made the voyage too dangerous to contemplate. Eventually, she began to doubt that she would ever return to flower island. The sisters were so kind and so anxious to make her days happy that she was reluctant to distress them by appearing eager to leave the convent. She had come to love them and knew that leaving would be almost as painful as leaving her friends on flower island had been so many years before.

Aimee was now fully a woman, beautiful, vibrant and lonely for the warmth and sensuous excitement of her island home. Often, she sat looking out of her window and wondering why Dominic Duval never returned to woo her. Then she smiled, recalling the only time she had seen him since their meeting at the cottage by the sea. She had been visiting the Jolly Fisherman, a cafe in the Cours Cambronne. Duval had been there with a group of cronies and a couple of brightly dressed city strumpets who obviously adored him. One of the girls had been cheeky, mocking Aimee in a loud voice when Duval bowed low to make room for her to pass. Aimee had suffered the girl's taunts in silence. Then, as they left, the strumpet grabbed her hat and paraded around the terrace in mocking mimicry of the fine lady's style. Damama was speechless with rage, but Aimee tipped a bottle of jalap into the strumpet's coffee and disdainfully retired to her coach leaving the girl agape at her contempt. Aimee laughed, recalling Damama's stricken face.

"Why did you leave that trash with your pretty pink hat, little miss?"

"I dosed her coffee with the new bottle of jalap Reverend Mother asked me to buy!"

"You little minx! That was pretty quick thinkin'."

"With luck she'll get home before it takes her. If not, she might need my hat!"

Damama had roared loud and long at the very thought of the strumpet's discomfort. Only desperate entreaties had stopped her from telling the nuns such a capital story over supper!

As Aimee's birthday treat, the Mother Superior decided to allow her to visit Châtillon-sur-Chalaronne to witness the astonishing Montgolfier brothers, who could fly in balloons. Aimee would take some of her young class and Sisters Bernadette and Béatrice would take a party of older girls. The journey to Lyons would take at least a week and the party would stay in the Convent of the Immaculate Conception at Thoissey. Aimee and Damama were delighted at the prospect of a new adventure. They packed carefully and Aimee gave her class strict instructions on how to behave on their first long and arduous journey.

A few weeks before their departure, the Mother Superior received a note from Aimee's guardian saying that he had decided to book tickets for her return in May . . . "The seas are somewhat calmer and the hostilities over. Aimee cannot remain with you forever." Mother Superior was at once delighted and alarmed. Life would be less bright without the beautiful young lady they had all come to adore. She broke the news to Aimee after lunch on the eve of her departure for Chatillon.

Aimee sat silent and pensive. Finally, she spoke in a subdued voice.

"I expected to be jubilant at the news, Reverend Mother. Sometimes what I think I want does not please me and what I know is not good for me does. I believe I'm growing into a very contrary woman!"

"Not at all. You long to go home but you now have a second home here in the convent. It will be sad for you to leave so many people who love you."

Aimee felt close to tears.

"I think sometimes, Reverend Mother, that I don't really know what I want!"

"What we want is not important. What will be will be, my child. Now, go and tell Damama that she's going home. She, at least, will be ecstatic at the news!"

Aimee wandered upstairs, struggling to bring something back from the recesses of her mind. What we want is not important, what will be, will be. Where had she heard that before? Who had used those words wisely, resignedly, long ago? Then she remembered the seer on the dusty road near Pointe Royale. What was it Euphemia had said? Rose would marry and her husband would be taken from her. At least Rose had married and now lived far away in Paris, or wherever her husband's military career took him. He had not been taken away from her, though from Rose's letters Aimee knew she was unhappy. She sighed, knowing she had been right in her fears that she and Rose would never meet again. Though they were in the same country, fate had conspired to keep them apart. Now, Rose's life was with her husband and it was impossible to plan meetings, as she never knew how long she would stay in one place or where she would next be sent.

Aimee mulled over the seer's words. Cousin Rose had

certainly not become an empress and surely it was unlikely she ever would! As for her own prophecy, Aimee had crossed the sea, but she had not been taken to a land far away. She would soon be returning to flower island, that was certain. She had even seen the tickets. The old seer was wrong.

Aimee smiled at her reflection in the mirror. Tomorrow would be the start of an adventure. She was looking forward to seeing gentlemen flying like birds. She broke the news of their return to Damama, who sang loud and long and shouted happily to her parrot, "We're goin' home, little bird, you hear me?" The parrot looked out of the window, screeching at the damned disobedient weather.

They arrived, after a tiring journey lasting eight days, at the convent at Thoissey. They were given a sparse dinner and shown silently to their rooms. Aimee was awed by the severity of the order. Even the marble statues in bare hallways wore cotton skirts lest they offend the sisters' frail dignity. Aimee was appalled by the frugality of the place and the sad, silent faces of the nuns. How lucky she had been with her own convent. How very lucky! Life could have been very unpleasant in the long years of her stay in Nantes.

By early the next morning, the field was crowded with hundreds of people, children, horses and military personnel. Hussars rubbed shoulders with clerics, and whores in gilded coaches watched the excitement from distant prime positions. The two balloonists were papermakers from Annonay and Aimee thought them the bravest men she had ever seen. Both were dark with splendid moustaches and they wore caps instead of wigs and tight breeches with long, knitted woolen scarves.

May sunshine lit a blue sky and cherry trees showered pink petals on excited onlookers. A great cheer rang out as the vast green and white balloon rose into the sky. The balloonists raised their caps to acknowledge rapturous applause. Little children cried, dogs barked and a young man in military school uniform saluted smartly and shouted, *"Magnifique! Vive les Montgolfiers! Vive la France!"*

Surprised by his strange accent, Aimee turned and saw a youth of about fourteen, slightly built and sallow with burning eyes and a commanding mien that made him stand out from the rest of the crowd. She smiled politely, wondering if he were Italian or Swiss and what he was doing here, obviously far from home. The young man surveyed her shyly. His eyes sparkled but he was uncertain whether it would be mannerly to speak to such an exquisite lady. He followed curiously behind, stopping when she stopped, walking when she walked, never taking his eyes from her long silver hair.

Finally, Aimee came to a halt and turned to face him.

"Are you following me, sir?"

"Forgive me, milady."

"Are you foreign? Your accent is very strange."

"Your accent also is very strange, milady."

Aimee paused, slightly taken aback by his cheek.

"I am a *française créole* from the island of Martinique."

"And I am Corsican. My name is Bonaparte, Napoleon Bonaparte, at your service, milady."

"I am Aimee Dubuq de Rivery, sir. Are you in school near here?"

"I have a place at the military academy at Brienne."

"So, you intend to be a soldier?"

"Yes. And I intend to advance myself with the greatest speed."

"Soon, you'll be a general then?" Aimee teased. But she saw Bonaparte was in deadly earnest about his career. The young man blushed furiously under her scrutiny.

"Do you live near here, milady?"

"No, I've come from far away in Nantes with some children from the convent where I live. Soon, I'll be returning to my home in Martinique. I should have returned four years ago but the seas have been too dangerous."

"I wish you safe passage. The seas are still dangerous and I don't care for them myself. One can never tell what a wave will do next."

"The English are more dangerous than the waves, sir."

"Someday I shall destroy them for you."

Aimee wondered if he were mad. But then she saw that he was smiling. She looked closely at the sensuous mouth and the dark eyes that pierced her soul.

"How old are you, Monsieur Bonaparte?"

"I am fourteen, milady, almost fifteen."

"I wish you good luck in your military career, sir."

"Thank you. I shall not forget you. This is the first time I have ever walked out with a lady."

Aimee smiled happily and pinned a wild rose to his collar.

"And I shall not forget you, Monsieur Bonaparte. Good day to you, sir."

She walked daintily away, smiling at his blushing cheeks. Bonaparte watched her thoughtfully, fingering the sweet-smelling flower and vowing to keep it forever. He had heard stories about ladies of Creole origin. Men in the barracks swore they were addictive . . . He rubbed his chin, frowning at his trembling fingers. On the way out of the field he thought of the wide, wanton blue eyes, the pretty pearl teeth, the bobbing silver ringlets under a straw bonnet bedecked with red poppies. Someday, he would find out about those Creole ladies, but not till he was at least a general and could truly afford one.

That night, Aimee thought of the young man with the burning eyes. "I shall not forget you, Monsieur Bonaparte," she had said. Curiously, she felt she would not, though she couldn't define his attraction. Something in his manner had compelled all her attention, that was all she knew. She fell asleep, dreaming of striped green balloons floating lazily in a cloudless blue sky over a field of golden buttercups. It had been such a beautiful sight. She wished, longingly, that she could have met the two brave explorers of the unknown. Someday, with luck, she would marry a man as brave and as fearless as the Montgolfiers and live forever safe in his protection.

When she returned to the convent, Aimee settled into a final few days of peaceful routine. She slept long hours and studied favorite maps in the convent library. She watched Sister Gabrielle spinning the fine wool used to make vestments, and Sister Marie-Mont plaiting hemp for the soles of the nuns' shoes, and Sister Emmanuelle staking black currant bushes and spraying apples with soapy water. Each was a scene familiar and idyllic and would remain with her long after she had left the silent sanctuary. How peaceful and friendly it was!

On the day before her departure, Mother Superior gave Aimee an illuminated book as a souvenir of her stay with the order. Each nun had contributed something to its beautiful pages. Finely tinted and illustrated, it recalled the very scenes that had caused Aimee so much distress in the early days after her arrival. Pale apple orchards, brown rivers, yellow marsh iris, hazy autumn landscapes and the goose market at Goulaine. Now, she would treasure it as a memento of growing up and learning patience, tolerance and love. Sister Thérèse in the dispensary also gave her a book, elaborately tooled and gilded, with recipes for every potion known for every sickness suffered. "Someday you may need it," she said.

On the day of departure, all the children and every nun in the order gathered silently in the courtyard. Aimee kissed the children and dried their tears, then shook hands with each nun. Damama saw that Aimee was greatly distressed at the end of the brief ceremony.

As they drove through the gates, Aimee looked back, briefly, at a dozen hands raised in farewell and a dozen white coifs bowed in sadness. She heard the children weeping and found her own eyes wet with tears, her chest tight with emotion. Then the great gate closed with the hollow, metallic rasp that had become so familiar. The gray years were over.

Damama was silent as they drove toward the city. Mother Superior sat tight-lipped, sad-eyed, saying her rosary. They passed farmers on their way to market and pilgrims en route for Rennes to beg pardons of the bishop. As they clattered over the cobblestones of the city center, Aimee wondered how to say goodbye to the saintly lady who had taught her so affectionately and so wisely. She wiped her eyes, wishing the sad day was over.

The journey was soon over. They spotted the brig, *La Trouvaille*, small but well coppered and brightly hung. Mother Superior said goodbye to Damama and then turned to Aimee.

"I wish you Godspeed, my child, and a good, happy life."

"Thank you, Reverend Mother. Thank you for all you have taught me. Say a prayer for our safe passage."

"We shall all be praying for your early arrival. Oh, I

almost forgot. This came for you just before we left the convent. I think it's from your Cousin Rose."

Aimee took an elaborately written envelope and put it in her muff. Then, she shook hands and followed Damama up the gangplank.

As the ship's hooter sounded, she paused and, looking back, saw that the Mother Superior was weeping. Aimee ran back and threw her arms around the thin frame, kissing the pale face, and weeping herself, said, "Don't cry, Reverend Mother. Remember that I love you very much and I will write to tell you that I arrived safely."

"Thank you, my child, and God bless you."

Then, she was gone. Within the hour, the ship sailed under a blue sky with a fresh wind. Aimee stood on deck as they drifted once again down the Loire, past pale green fields full of black and white cows and muddy rivers under gray stone bridges. As they reached the mouth of the estuary, she saw a figure on horseback riding along the towpath that paralleled the river. Duval urged his horse up a steep incline and then raised his feathered hat, in silent salute. Aimee burst into tears as the white horse and the frilly white cuffs vanished into the mist of time remembered.

# Chapter 11

*Aimee read Rose's letter soon after the ship* sailed. Tears filled her eyes as she learned of the haughty husband who was so distressing her precious friend. Aimee bit her lip, vowing to horsewhip Alexandre de Beauharnais if ever she met him.

My dear Aimee:

Thank you for your letter. I enjoyed the part about Napoleon Bonaparte, the military student. From the sound of him, he will become a man that ladies love, bossy and overbearing and full of his own importance! What fools we are for falling in love with such gentlemen, but I must admit he sounded a very interesting character.

I am sorry that I must write another sad letter, but life is almost intolerable here. Alexandre returned for a few days and then went away again and I have not seen him since. Oh, Aimee, I've made such a horrified discovery, Alexandre has a mistress. A low woman who comes from Martinique, called Marie-Françoise Laure. Her relations live near Basse-Pointe and Mama says they owe money everywhere! Alexandre is undoubtedly besotted with her because he had the cheek to compare us to my face. I'm so afraid that he'll leave me. Men always leave me, as Papa did; that is my fate.

But I'm not going to think about that again for a while. I am his wife and he cannot just dispense with me, can he? When you return to Martinique, will you send me some clove pomanders. This house is very damp and I plan to put the pomanders everywhere so the smell will remind me of home. Isn't French weather awful? For three weeks it has done nothing but rain. Really, Aimee, before I came here I had never even heard of places where it could rain for more than a day. Can you write quickly and tell me what you think I should do about Alexandre? Men are usually so fond of me so I cannot understand my husband's impatience. Tell me what you think I can do to improve myself in his eyes. I am pretty, aren't I? Please write soon so I can follow your instructions. I wait eagerly for your reply.

> As always, your loving cousin,
> Rose

*La Trouvaille* seemed larger once they were aboard than it had appeared from the quayside. A fast sailing vessel, armed with an eighteen-pounder on a pivot amidships and four six-pounders with muskets and pistols, its cargo was demijohns of French brandy and barrels of wine for the islands and South America.

The captain was a rugged Breton called Le Pennec. Aimee smiled as he was introduced, secretly amused by the primitive Breton custom of choosing names from working titles or a person's most striking characteristic. She hoped it boded well for the long journey that the captain's most noteworthy trait was his obstinacy!

After an excellent dinner Aimee and Damama took a brief tour of the vesssel by moonlight. The ship was elegantly fitted with mahogany doors and woodwork, its brass parts shiny from careful polishing, every inch of the decks scrubbed clean. Their cabin was large and airy with curtains and covers of the finest rose damask. Aimee slept soundly, content to be on her way home at last.

Damama woke first the following morning, hungry as a hunter and puzzled by the bright pink of the sky. She racked her brain to remember what that meant but she had forgotten everything her sea captain friend had taught her.

They made their way to the passenger dining room for breakfast of steaming coffee and puffy white rolls with apricot jam. They were introduced to fellow passengers and learned that the distinguished middle-aged gentleman traveling alone was Dr. Kerjean, from St. Malo. The doctor was en route for America, restlessly seeking new fields to conquer far away from painful memories and the familiar streets of his hometown, which, since the death of his beloved wife, only reminded him of his loss.

The other passengers were the Le Tocquer sisters, Ariane and Eloise, whose father was a hatter in Le Croisic. The ladies were twins, aged about thirty, unmarried and unappealing, with pale faces, fluttering hands and simpering ways that irritated others. Damama watched, silently, thinking they needed a long session with Dominic Duval. But with their flat white faces it was unlikely such a discerning gentleman would do them the honor!

The remaining passengers were Commander and Mrs. Colbert, a couple from the fishing port of Honfleur. Mrs. Colbert was English, originally from the county of Sussex, where she had spent happy childhood years. Her husband, who had just retired from the French Navy after a distinguished career, was a rugged-faced gentleman with a loud voice and a habit of falling asleep while his wife talked and awakening the moment she was silent. Mrs. Colbert took one look at Damama and adjourned to the other end of the table.

After breakfast, Aimee sat on deck, looking up at the rosy sky. Commander Colbert strode by with a worried look and a breezy greeting.

"Better go below, m'dear, there's going to be a dickens of a storm before long."

Aimee curtsied but remained where she was, waiting for Damama, who was telling Dr. Kerjean about her rheumatism.

"It was the rain that started it, sir. That darned rain just got into my poor bones and jiggled the joints so they stayed permanently entangled!"

"Commander Colbert has just told me there's going to be a storm," Aimee interrupted.

"He's probably right, mademoiselle. Sailors study the sky and a red morning means a difficult passage, so I'm told," the doctor said.

Damama disappeared below to eat another breakfast. She believed firmly in the principle of eating enough to give her insides plenty of work so they would have no time to be sick. Aimee sat with Dr. Kerjean, chattering about the convent and her hopes for her future on flower island. She looked closely at him, thinking how handsome he was. Gray eyes and sandy hair combined to make him lack color, but his hands were fine and long-fingered, his figure tall and slim. As they walked the deck he took her arm to help her down the stairway and Aimee enjoyed this small solicitude.

Kerjean wondered about his dazzling companion as her subtle magnolia perfume wafted by. The young lady had spent long years in a convent and yet there was something so sensuous and demanding in her body that any man would respond to her allure! He resolved to look after her during the long and arduous journey. Such an exquisite presence should be treated like a rare painting or a precious jewel. They began to talk of distant places, and seeing her avid interest, he told her of countries he had visited during his youthful adventures after medical school.

"And which country did you like best?" Aimee asked.

"Best? Well, let me see, I think I liked Greece and Turkey because they were so beautiful. The Greeks are hospitable and though the Turks can be cruel and barbarous, theirs is an astonishing civilization."

"And what of Italy?"

"The architecture of Italy is perfection and their museums magnificent. I almost walked my feet off in Rome. Italian women are very beautiful and gentle and I fell in

142

love frequently during my visit. There's no doubt that travel is a great educator."

"What did you learn from all those strange places?"

"I learned that each country has its own way of assessing people. In Russia, a man is judged by the quality of his furs, in Holland by the size and quality of his pipe! In Turkey they assess men by their wealth and their ability to comprehend Turkish deviousness!"

"And what of the French?"

"Ah, the French forget everything for love, even money. It's my opinion that every Frenchman has two parts, one devoted to love and the other to business, family and social affairs. As he grows older, the half that seeks love swallows the other half so in his middle years he thinks of nothing but *l'amour*."

Aimee laughed delightedly at his observations. She thought it more than likely that Dr. Kerjean had already reached the middle years when love became a delicious obsession.

In late afternoon, the wind rose to gale force and they heard Le Pennec cry, "Hand light sails, reef the topsail." Damama began to look worried when she overheard Commander Colbert telling his wife that they were already off course and far south of their correct bearing. Behind, in the distance, the Bordeaux Light flashed on its rocky headland. Ahead lay the Spanish coast and the open ocean.

During the night, the storm abated and the next morning the sea was calm, the air fresh and dolphins swam alongside in leaping, frolicking welcome. The passengers sat on deck, chatting happily of storms they had heard of and mysterious disappearances at sea. Aimee talked with Dr. Kerjean till the lunch bell sounded. In the evening, Commander Colbert entertained with stories of his career in the French Navy and the problems he had encountered in marrying an English lady. Mrs. Colbert sat glowering at Damama, her gentility gravely offended by being forced to share the only public room with a mulatto giantess.

As time passed, the weather improved and Captain Le Pennec was heard to voice his relief at their deliverance from the intolerable storms reported in recent weeks. At Lisbon, they took on water, fresh fruit and fish. Crew and passengers relaxed on the quayside in warm sunshine, unaware of what lay ahead.

That night, they were wakened by the loud roar of thunder and flashes of purple lightning. In Aimee's cabin, scent and bitters bottles fell from dresser to floor and cupboard doors flew open, clattering shut and flying open again as the ship rolled wildly in a roaring tempest. The situation seemed grave and for the first time in her life Damama was tempted to contemplate a few well-chosen prayers. They received instructions from the captain to remain in their cabins. The decks were forbidden and walking the corridors was too dangerous for the passengers.

At first light, they heard a terrible crash, followed by the tearing, splintering and scraping of broken wood. Dr. Kerjean arrived at their door, white-faced and agitated.

"What a night! I thought perhaps you might care for a drop of coffee?"

"What's happenin', sir? Are we going down?" Damama asked.

"I don't know, madame. I cannot reach the deck because they have locked all the doors, but Commander Colbert is up there with Le Pennec and Galloudec and if anyone can save us those three surely can."

"What was that awful noise I heard just before you arrived?"

"I fear it was the main-topmast but I cannot tell for certain."

Aimee looked out of the porthole. All around, great waves towered over the ship as it tossed like an acorn on angry water. Foam lashed the glass as the gale raged unabated. The ship seemed to be passing through a narrow valley of water and rocks appeared, ominously threatening. In the distance, Aimee saw the peak of a jagged mountain, dotted with low white houses.

"Is that land, Dr. Kerjean?"

"*Mon dieu!* I believe it's Gibraltar! We are most lamentably off course. I fear we have just passed through the strait."

Toward noon, the wind fell and the captain unlocked the doors so his passengers could take the air and survey the damage. The foremast had fallen, taking the main-topmast and bowsprit close to the knightheads. In falling, it had shattered the cookhouse, the lee gunwale and waist boards. The main-topmast had torn the mainsail to pieces and they heard Le Pennec giving urgent instructions to secure the mainmast. *La Trouvaille* was broken; only the seamanship of three great mariners had kept them from going down in the tumult.

After a hard morning's work, Captain Le Pennec addressed the passengers. "*Mesdames et messieurs*, as you can see, the ship is most severely damaged. To retard drifting I have retained the wreck of the foremast, bowsprit, sails and spars fast by the bowsprit shroud. If my calculations are correct, we shall drift to leeward not more than four miles per hour. Soon, we shall be able to disembark at Palma on the Spanish island of Mallorca. I shall then assess the full extent of the damage. On behalf of the owners of the ship I wish to extend my apologies for this inconvenience and congratulate you all on your courage. And to you, Commander Colbert, my respects, sir, and my grateful thanks for your invaluable assistance."

Lunch of cold meat and wet biscuits was served on deck. The passengers did not complain. They spent a warm afternoon watching the crew patch up damage sustained in the night, nailing tarred canvas and leather strips over the broken plank sheer and throwing two of the lee guns overboard to lighten the load. As dusk fell, it became clear that a small hole had been breached below the waterline. The ship's hold started to flood and the horizon appeared to tilt at an alarming angle as the vessel developed a list to starboard. The passengers began to pray that twinkling lights a short distance away were the lights of the island of their destination.

They were forced to spend the night alongside the harbor wall, unable to dock because the port was deserted. Le Pennec cursed loud and long. "Those damned Spaniards work less and sleep more than any nation on earth!" Male passengers were recruited to relieve the crew in pumping for dear life. The ladies sat stiffly upright on deck, afraid to go below in case rising waters took them by surprise. Finally, at first light, they stepped ashore into the welcoming arms of newly arrived port workers. Passengers and crew stood together, soaked to the skin, surveying the beige stone causeway of Palma de Mallorca.

Aimee looked around and saw a cathedral and palm-lined promenade backed by ornate houses many stories high with iron-grilled windows covered with geranium flowers. The scent of oleander and sweet pine wafting in the breeze reminded her of home, and the deep gold sun warmed even the coldest individual. Dark-eyed men surrounded her, bowing politely and speaking excitedly in an incomprehensible tongue. She was taken, along with the other passengers, to a portside office where the harbor master's wife dried their clothing and fed them a fine lunch of prawns, rice and chicken with red peppers.

Before dusk, it was ascertained that *La Trouvaille* could not proceed on her journey for many weeks. Captain Le Pennec informed his passengers that he had managed to arrange for them to continue their journey the following day on a Spanish ship bound for Martinique via the Canaries. Their luggage was forwarded to a small quayside hotel, and half dead with relief, Aimee and Damama settled for the night in a spotless white room.

Outside, a young man played guitar and a gypsy dancer called loudly for *propinas* as she rattled her castanets. Cicadas chirruped in umbrella pines and branches of purple bougainvillea framed the windowpane. Aimee looked out on deep blue sea and a dark orange sunset, her eyes filling with tears. Despite the delay and the horrors of the storm, she felt confident she would soon be home on flower island. She threw the young guitarist a flower and he blew her a kiss and sang a soft lullaby under her window till she fell dreamlessly asleep.

Aimee woke at dawn, ready and eager for the second part of the great journey home.

# Chapter 12

*The new ship, the* Isabellita, *flew the Spanish* flag. She was a strong brig carrying fifteen hundred barrels of wine. Her captain, Duarte, was an Andalusian from Seville, a military man and an expert navigator. Commander Colbert was delighted with the new captain and his meticulously drilled crew. The Le Tocquer twins giggled incessantly whenever the captain's dark eyes rested on them, and Damama wondered if this journey might put a little color in their cheeks after all.

They sailed from Palma on a sunny morning with a fine levanter billowing the sails. Pied porpoises accompanied them, gamboling in the deep blue sea, and a hundred gulls fluttered white wings only to disappear as land vanished from the distant horizon.

Captain Duarte entertained them during lunch telling them stories of military campaigns he had fought or heard of. Aimee's eyes widened as he told of Russian soldiers who died frozen to sentry posts in winter blizzards past all imagination. They died in this horrendous fashion rather than defy orders, Captain Duarte explained. Aimee was quite taken with the captain's story. That night, she spoke to Damama about it.

"Would you freeze to death at your sentry post, Damama?"

"Sure as hell no!"

"But you always taught *me* to be obedient."

"No, I didn't. I taught you not to be disobedient of my orders, cos I knew my orders were for your good, little miss. It's a different thing if you get ordered to go jump down a cliff or go drown yourself in the sea or freeze in the ice and snow like a idiot person! Those orders are not for your own good and a lady learns to know the difference."

Late in the morning on the following day, they saw a French sloop of war mounting twenty-two guns, its sails blown to ribbons. The captain frowned, imperceptibly, ordering full sail to speed them safely out of the Mediterranean. But the wind fell and their speed with it. Soon passengers began gathering on deck to pass the time in games of chess and rummy.

By early evening, a pleasant breeze had come up from the north and they saw Cartagena in the distance with its tall cathedral spire and dazzling white cottages. A slave trader passed with black men and women dancing on its deck to the incongruous strains of a banjo and native gourd drum. The smell from the slaver hit them forcibly and lady passengers retired below until the air had cleared in the balmy cool of evening.

After dinner, Aimee was strolling on deck with Dr. Kerjean when she heard the lookout cry, "Spanish flag to port." They ran to the rail and saw a lateen-rigged privateer flying the Spanish flag and apparently drifting, manned by one solitary sailor. Captain Duarte hailed the lonely mariner.

"¡Ole, amigo, que pasa?"

"Ayúdame, señor capitán. Los bandidos Africanos han venido y estoy solo aquí. ¡Ayúdame, por favor!"

Duarte ordered the *Isabellita* to come alongside to pick up the survivor. He strode the deck furiously cursing the African corsair pirates.

"Those accursed pirates are the menace of our coast. They have attacked that fellow's ship and left him the only

148

survivor. He must have been hiding or they would have taken him off to the slave markets of Algiers, where I'm told they sell white men as the American traders sell blacks."

Aimee watched from the rail as the *Isabellita* drew near the drifting ship. Suddenly, she heard the harsh swish of canvas as the Spanish flag fell to the privateer deck, revealing the yellow corsair flag underneath. Her heart thundered and she felt dreadfully afraid. She heard Dr. Kerjean call out to warn the captain, but Duarte had already seen his error. The old pirate trick of masquerading as a friendly vessel had worked yet again to the horror of the *Isabellita*'s terrified passengers.

Aimee looked at the corsair flag, emblazoned with a red sun and crossed swords. She heard the captain blow his whistle to signal pirate attack and saw the crew shoulder muskets and bandoliers in readiness to defend the ship. The mate shouted, "Swallow your valuables," to the ladies and Mrs. Colbert choked on her wedding ring and gold chain necklace.

Damama appeared at a run, breathless and sweating with excitement.

"We have been deceived, Damama. The captain thought the ship was a Spanish vessel because it flew the Spanish flag."

"That's no Spanish flag."

"They had covered their own with the Spanish colors."

"Oh Lord! Now what's gonna happen?"

Damama stood at Aimee's side watching as the men who had been hiding in the pirate ship appeared on its deck as if by magic. A score of them ran, nimble as monkeys, up the rigging in readiness for the leap that would commence the battle for possession of the *Isabellita*. Armed with sabers, bows and scimitars, they were a wild-eyed bunch of savages, chanting, shouting, threatening and making strange whooping screams to startle the opposition.

Dr. Kerjean took a musket from one of the crew and suggested that Aimee and Damama retire below immediately with the other ladies. But Aimee was adamant. She was going home to Martinique and if she and Damama had to fight for their right of passage they surely would!

149

Dr. Kerjean compromised by putting them in the wheel-house with a pistol apiece. The captain looked grim as he heard the dreaded corsair boarding chant. . . *"Mena pero! Mena pero! Mena pero!"*

Suddenly, men swung over the sides screaming like dervishes. Aimee heard Commander Colbert roaring, "Strike, you damned rascal!" She watched as the old man fought with sword and musket, but he was fearfully out-numbered. Then a black-bearded corsair picked him up and swung him overboard into the sea. They watched, in horror, as Dr. Kerjean was hit from behind with a steel pike and Captain Duarte fell, body flung open by a jagged broadsword. Damama fired her pistol and hit one of the invaders in the arm. Aimee fired hers, hitting only a sea-bird on the wing. She sat down and composed herself with a silent prayer as the Spanish crew continued to fight for their lives. All hell broke loose as men died and others screamed in triumph.

"Will they kill us when all this is over, Damama?"

"I reckon they'll sell us in the slave market like the captain said, little miss."

"We must behave with dignity."

"These kind of men aren't interested in dignity, only plunderin' and rapin' and doin' wicked actions. You sayin' your prayers, little miss?"

"Yes, Damama."

"God bless you, child, and God help us both."

At last, it was over. Deathly silence and the sound of a seabird's lament. The captain of the corsair ship, called the rais by his men, ordered a search of the *Isabellita*. Mrs. Colbert, the Le Tocquer twins and five remaining Spanish crewmen were brought up on deck, struggling violently. Aimee combed her hair, scented her cheeks and wrists and stepped out of the wheelhouse with Damama a few paces behind.

The rais, struck by her fearlessness and incredible beauty, wondered if she were a royal princess or a famous personage. Her dress of fine orange silk, her pearls and jewels were dazzlingly expensive. Her eyes seemed to see into his soul and he moistened his lips uncertainly. He looked over at Mrs. Colbert, shrieking and crying over her fate, and the two colorless Frenchwomen, cringing and sobbing with fear. Then he looked back at the defiant young woman, standing silently on the bridge, looking down and censuring him with her dignity. He had never seen such deportment in the face of danger. This woman was obviously very special, and should be taken immediately to the Dey of Algiers.

He ordered a signal to be made to another corsair ship nearby. Silently, out of the dusk, a black-rigged, darkly painted felucca appeared and its rais hailed the captor of the *Isabellita*. Within an hour, Aimee and Damama were transferred to the new ship. As she stepped from the *Isabellita*, Aimee saw the Le Tocquer twins being hauled over the shoulders of two laughing pirates from the invading ship. Screaming uncontrollably, they were obviously aware of their probable fate. Looking down, Aimee saw Captain Duarte lying dead and she glowered with intense loathing at the newly arrived corsair captain who bowed ostentatiously and gave her his own cabin for the remainder of the voyage. She listened as the two captains called to each other, and was able to discern that the invading rais was giving her own guardian instruction on where she must be taken.

She watched as the corsair crew methodically and swiftly stripped the *Isabellita* of her cargo, trimmings and valuables, stacking everything around the mast in readiness for transferring the booty to their own vessel. She almost laughed as two hefty pirates turned Mrs. Colbert upside down, slapping her back till she heaved loudly and spat up all the jewelry she had swallowed. Damama, resisting a smile, remained impassive as she guarded her charge.

The new captain, Rais Tebessa, was a man of many parts. Aimee was astonished to hear that like many corsair captains he could speak English, Spanish, French and Turkish as well as his own Barbary tongue which mixed Arabic with Portuguese. His manners were polite, his eyes cautious, his behavior proud and correct.

"Where are we bound, Rais Tebessa?" Aimee surprised herself by speaking with such directness.

"We are for Algiers, milady."

"And what then?"

"I do not know. Baba Mohammed Ben Osman, commander of Algiers, will decide what to do with you. The other women will be sold in the marketplace at Bou Ismail. The two young ones will fetch a good price but the old one will bring nothing. The French doctor, when he has recovered from his wound, will make a fortune once he has bought his freedom because in Africa we have few men who understand medicine."

"How long will the journey take?"

"Our ships are fast." Rais Tebessa paused and suddenly laughed out loud. "I'm surprised the Spanish captain fell for our old trick. He surely should have recognized a corsair."

"Captain Duarte was deceived because the crewman spoke Spanish perfectly, as a native would."

"Perhaps he *was* Spanish. They join us sometimes from the poor regions of the south. But we are all trained to speak English to the English, French to the French and Spanish to the Spanish. They fall for the deception, disbelieving the evidence of their eyes and obeying only their ears. They are fools!"

Aimee fumed at his vanity. But Rais Tebessa only smiled at her scorn.

"Whatever your feelings, milady, you must agree that we corsairs are clever. We have but fourteen small ships in Algeria and the total in all of Tripolitania is not more than sixty. Yet we hold the seas to ransom and every country fears us. We are men like no others. And now you will go and rest, so you can look your best tomorrow to meet the master of Algiers."

Damama could not sleep. She sat on her bed, fully clothed, wondering what in God's name they were going to do. Aimee also lay awake. In the middle of the night, they lit candles and talked in whispers about how they should act.

"You're lucky, little miss. They sent the others to the market, 'cept Dr. Kerjean and he'll be just fine once his head's all in one piece again. You must have struck that pirate fellow as special so they're keepin' you for their boss."

"I must wear my white dress tomorrow."

"That's right, little miss. Better make everyone think

you're a innocent child. Heathen folk have funny ways of dealin' with soiled doves!"

"But what shall I do if they give me to this commander of Algiers?"

"I'll get a bottle of pucker water and a bit of red colorin' and you scream like he was cuttin' you in half!"

"Will they let us stay together, Damama?" Aimee was almost pleading.

"I don't rightly know. I get the impression that if you say you want me they'll let me stay. I could be wrong, but that's how it seems."

Morning came, with a bright gold sun and a deep blue sky. Aimee dressed in dazzling white satin and wore diamonds in her hair, round her neck and dangling from her ears. Damama followed with her red silk parasol, Aimee's jewel box and her most precious belongings.

The harbor of Algiers was crowded. The town rose in tiers on a steep hillside of streets and close-packed, white cube houses. People in flowing robes, turbaned against the heat and mysteriously veiled, milled around the port area. The air was full of jasmine blossom and for a moment Aimee felt almost at home in the color and bustle and excitement of this new land.

In the distance, she saw pink minarets outlined against a cloudless sky and down on the beach, women dyeing wool in steaming black caldrons and hanging it out to dry on driftwood poles. Scarlet skeins blew in soft sea breeze and men returned from a night's fishing in lantern-hung boats. As they docked, the strange sounds of peasants bickering, carts clattering, snake charmers whistling and water carriers' copper cups rattling filled the air.

Aimee was carried on a litter through narrow dirty streets and crowded squares toward the palace of the Dey. The Dey owed allegiance to Turkey, though he ran his state as an independent entity. In Algiers, his word was law, his authority absolute. Damama had to run along behind the litter, puffing and blowing and swatting flies that settled on her sweating brown face.

Aimee's litter passed shops selling copper kettles, rugs, musical instruments and mysterious piles of seed pods. Dogs ran by the side, wild, mangy, sick and too tired to bark. In a square near the Dey's palace, a man sat selling oranges, lemons and watermelons from piles stacked against the shimmering white of the fortress walls. The sight reminded Aimee, most forcibly, of flower island. She wondered longingly if she would ever escape this strange city.

Women of the area were neither pretty nor ugly, simply hidden from sight under burnooses of fine cotton and cloudy black gauze. Men paused to stare uncomprehendingly at the sight of an exquisitely pale goddess, being carried by two black-toothed pirates and followed by a great brown giantess.

When they arrived at the fortress, Aimee was led through shady white corridors to an inner courtyard with a splashing fountain. A strange green-tailed bird strutted on the intricately inlaid marble floor and an elderly man sat on an opal-studded throne watching her approach. His shrewd, wily eyes twinkled as they came face to face.

Aimee curtsied daintily, while observing him fearlessly. She saw a lined, worn face with glinting black eyes and a snow-white beard that reached his waist. His clothes were of the finest cotton, startlingly white and flowing far behind. His fingers were bedecked with heavy gold rings and around his neck he wore a gold fish with emerald eyes on a chain of symbolic letters.

The old man remained silent as he examined the huge black woman who accompanied this vision of loveliness. Truly, they were an astonishing pair! He rose from the jeweled throne and Aimee was surprised to see that he was as tall as Damama though fragile in appearance.

The Dey looked down at Aimee and said, in carefully enunciated French, "Welcome, dear lady, to Algiers."

"Thank you, sir."

"My most sincere apologies for all that has happened to you. But we poor Algerians have our lives to live and we must find money where we can."

Damama looked at the lavishly jeweled throne and snorted loudly.

"And now you must tell me all about yourself and this lady who accompanies you on your travels," the old man said with a smile, but his eyes remained watchful and wary.

The green bird spread its tail, displaying astonishing

154

plumage spotted with blue, black and silvery green. Aimee's eyes grew wide at the unexpected parade.

"Have no fear, dear lady. Like me, my peacock is vain. He is simply trying to impress you."

Aimee smiled, despite herself. The Dey clapped his hands and a servant appeared with mint tea and a brass tray of sweetmeats. Cushions of fine silk velvet were brought for them to sit on as they sampled their first taste of Africa. Aimee told the Dey her name, her origins, her hopes for the future and of her home on the island of Martinique. He listened, patiently, digesting the news and assessing this most valuable bounty.

Ben Osman was seventy and wise with the wisdom of his great age. His mind was both quick and devious and as Aimee spoke, he formulated a plan for his own advancement and for the security of his waning years.

"So you see, sir, I was on my way home when your pirates delayed me most grievously!"

"Forgive me, dear lady. I am sad that you should have been so inconvenienced."

"What are you going to do with me, sir? And what of Damama?"

"Your Da will remain with you, naturally."

"And what of me?"

"First, you must rest and recover from the ordeal and the shock of your capture. I shall give orders that you are to be treated like a princess, and as my honored guest. Then you will see some of our city and learn a little about us."

"But will you send me home someday, sir?"

"Dear lady, your looks are such that my men will already have spoken of you to everyone they meet. The wind has ears in these parts and it would bode ill for me with my master if I let you go without at least letting him appreciate his new property."

"Your master, sir! But who is he? We were told that you were master of Algiers."

"As indeed I am."

"Then who is your master?"

"The Sultan lives far away in a jeweled city. He worships beauty and would be most offended if I were to deprive him of the loveliest thing I have ever seen."

155

"I don't understand, sir. I don't understand what you are saying."

"You will, dear lady. In time all will be clear. But now, you must rest and soon you will see our city. Then, I shall send a teacher to instruct you in the language of my master. When the time comes for your departure, it will be easier if you can tell him your thoughts and amuse him with your chatter."

"And what language will I learn, sir?"

"Turkish, of course. My master is the Sultan Abdul Hamid, Emperor of the True Believers, Shadow of Allah upon Earth, Master of Masters, chosen among the chosen."

Aimee bowed her head, struggling to keep control of her feelings in the light of this stunning revelation. The old man watched her intently, surprised that she did not weep.

Damama's heart thumped and she felt a strange emptiness. She realized that they were never going home to flower island. She looked furiously at the silent old man with the half-smiling face and announced, "You are a wicked person, sir! You intend to deprive this young lady of ever returnin' to her home to see her own people. You can smile and act fancy but you are a wicked person, sir, wicked and bad!"

"Madame, I am Mohammed Ben Osman, commander of Algiers, and your life has been spared only because of the whim of this beautiful young lady. As for your comments, perhaps you are right, perhaps not. One thing is certain, when I have fitted out a ship suitable to convey her to the city of Constantinople, your mistress will be sent as a gift to my master, the Sultan."

"If you were half a gentleman, sir, you'd stop smilin' when you pronounce such a sentence!"

"We Arabs are like that, madame. We always kill with a smile."

He walked to the door, pausing to speak to Aimee. "I trust your quarters will please you, dear lady. I shall dine with you each day so you can tell me all you have learned from your teachers. May I wish you a convivial stay in Algiers. And now, ladies, I beg your leave."

He bowed regally and disappeared through the arched door, followed by the peacock. Aimee was left staring at the fountain and thinking of what Mother Superior had taught her . . . "When you know there is no escape you must either settle or go mad." She looked around, at high white walls and the red-cloaked, white-turbaned guards. Then she followed the servant to her new quarters.

# Chapter 13

*Aimee had spent three months in captivity, and* she felt sure she would soon be sent to the omnipotent Turk. The Dey had enjoyed her stay, teaching her all he knew of the ways of her new master, the customs of his country and the strange etiquette of the harem. He had realized after a few days that this was no ordinary woman. Aimee Dubuq de Rivery was a woman of great culture and good breeding, humorous, ingenious, stubborn and special.

The beautiful creature had learned quickly the basics of the Sultan's language and appeared to know more of Ben Osman's own city from tours and lectures than most of his own officers. Ben Osman had come to look forward to his evenings with Aimee and Damama. In the weeks of their captivity, he had lost a fortune playing cards with Damama, but he still could not figure out how she cheated.

Aimee had been given lavish jewelry and exquisite new clothes, embroidered by seamstresses from the oasis of Bou Saada. Once she had persuaded Ben Osman to give her money to buy medicine, herbs, marriage candles and other things from the bazaar and fine shops in the city. With the money, she had attempted to bribe her guards. But they had only laughed and reported her actions to her wily captor.

Ben Osman was highly amused. What spirit the Creole had, attempting to buy the palace guards right under their master's nose! He did not bother to scold her. Instead, he gave her a magnificent pearl necklace and boasted that the guards of his fortress were incorruptible, because dishonesty was rewarded by death and because they were corsairs and specially favored men. Aimee grew almost fond of the old man, and Damama was delighted with their progress. If Ben Osman lost a few more hands at the card table she reckoned she would have enough money to buy a ship and engage a crew to take them home to flower island. Every day, she practiced her sleight of hand with all the desperation of an unwilling captive.

As time passed, they grew accustomed to the sound of the muezzin calling the faithful to prayer and were less daunted by the maze of corridors in their exotic prison. Aimee found the climate relaxing, the red sun comforting, the soft green of her splendid suite soothing. Sometimes, as patterned walls reflected sunlight like an undulating emerald sea, she remembered flower island and the words of the old seer. Still, she prayed for the prophecy to be wrong, but now she was certain that her assessment of Euphemia's abilities had been grievously inaccurate.

Damama began to grow fat on the tasty dishes that appeared at all hours to tempt her. She washed down flower-garnished platters of tiny octopus with Boukha distilled from figs and dreamed sweet fantasies each night after a heavy meal of meat stew and her favorite thibarine. Watched closely by their guards, they visited the gardens of Bouzarea, where ancient jacarandas grew near prickly acacia and scented jasmine bowers of sensuous abandon. They explored narrow winding alleys in the medina, learning to identify strange smells of ginger, honey, pyrethrum and eucalyptus that filled the air and tickled the nostrils. Damama showed great patience with merchants in the casbah, buying quantities of nutmeg, incense and a stiff white paste that someone told her cured wilting masculinities when mixed with orange blossom honey.

"At my age, I might start needin' something to ginger up my female appetite. Once that goes to sleep, little miss, a woman might as well just sit down and die!"

"But that is for men, Damama!"

"If it works for them it'll work for me."

They saw a native wedding procession with a bride resplendent on a white camel. And gradually, they came to accept the strange sights and sounds of the city, brass beaters hammering, peddlers calling, tattooists chattering to keep patients from feeling their sharp needles. Curiously, they felt more at home in this alien community than they had ever felt in the misty gray landscape of the Vendée. Still, Aimee began to wonder how much longer they would be held in kindly imprisonment.

One morning, she was summoned to the sunlit courtyard and asked to wait for Ben Osman. The old man appeared, followed by the haughty peacock. He greeted her, as servants brought refreshments. Then he presented her with a special gift.

"This is for you, dear lady, to wear on arrival in Constantinople. You will dazzle them with your loveliness and your splendor."

"Am I to leave soon, sir?"

"You will be gone tomorrow, at dawn."

Aimee took the sparkling diadem with showering diamond cascades and placed it on her head. Ben Osman clapped his hands and a mirror was brought so she could admire her beauty. The old man smiled at the delight in her eyes. Women were all the same, luxuriating in the power of their loveliness! This one would learn how to use it to her own best advantage, of that there was no doubt.

"I have had a ship fitted for your journey. The upperworks have been gilded and the interior upholstered in the finest silk. The sails were sewn by the women of Bou Saada to match the color of your eyes. Her captain is Rais Tebessa, whom you already know. Here is a letter to give to my master when you are presented. I have no doubt that he will be greatly pleased with you."

"And when he has used me, will he send me back to Martinique?"

The old man, startled by her honesty, softly replied, "No one knows the Sultan's mind, dear lady. And perhaps you

161

do not know your own. Here, in Algiers, you are my captive, but you have been happy, have you not? Perhaps in the golden city you will also be happy."

Aimee sat quietly surveying the exquisite diadem and wondering why her heart felt so heavy, her soul empty of emotion. It was as though the sadness of this enforced imprisonment had dulled normal feeling. The shock of what had happened at sea had deadened her ability to think, plan and hope for a happy future and killed her desire to do anything about the gravity of her situation. Looking up, she saw that Ben Osman was about to depart.

As he reached the arch leading to his private quarters, he paused briefly and said, "Tonight we shall have dinner together and no doubt your Da will rob me of another fortune. What a cheat she is, the very best I ever encountered. Allah himself would envy her! In case I should forget in the pleasantry of the evening, I should warn you of one danger in your new life in Constantinople."

Aimee listened anxiously.

"The Sultan Abdul Hamid is old, fifty-eight years at least. He is a wise, kind man of great culture and learning. He has been gravely saddened by the character of his eldest son and heir, the Prince Selim. The young man thinks of nothing but books and learning. He is quiet and unwilling to improve his combat skills and he has always refused to have anything to do with the women of the harem. Some say he witnessed atrocities in the abortionist's quarters as a small child but I don't know if that is true. One thing is certain, his attitude has caused him to be viewed with great disappointment by his father, and disdain by one who is more powerful in that city than is right and proper."

"Who is that, sir?"

"I refer to the chief warlord, Korba-Khan. You have been taught of the warlords and of their rebelliousness and encroachment on my master's power. Korba-Khan is their leader and you must take care to avoid him, dear lady. He is an evil man who kills for his amusement, poisons for his pleasure and burns down the city every time he is displeased. His ambition has no bounds. Some say he wishes to rule the Empire!"

"Will I ever meet this man?"

"No doubt he will come to the harbor to meet you. The

head eunuch, who has charge of liaison between the Sultan and the ladies of the harem, will be there also to escort you to the Sultan."

"How will I know the evil Korba-Khan?"

"You will know him, dear lady! The aura of Korba-Khan's evil strikes like a blow to the head. I myself met him only once and I have never forgotten the horror of that moment."

Aimee stood, silently appealing to his pity. Could Ben Osman be persuaded to let her go? Could he even be tempted to keep her here, safe in his white fortress? The old man took her hand, smiling as though he read her thoughts.

"Enough of this! I am quite sure that you will succeed in the jeweled kingdom as none have before. Remember my advice: trust no one, talk little and listen. And always remember that nothing is secret in the silent city. Unlike my soldiers, many there are corrupt and the warlords destroy those who appear to have influence with the Sultan. There will be some in the city of the seraglio who love you and wish to serve you. Value them and keep their names known only to yourself. Till this evening then, dear lady."

Ben Osman swept out and Aimee was left alone, shivering despite the intense heat of the sun. She called for Damama and told her of the conversation with the Dey. Damama looked tired and, suddenly, almost old. Throwing her arms round Damama's neck, Aimee kissed her and said, "What would I do without you, Damama?"

"You're old enough now to do pretty good by yourself, little miss. I've taught you all I know."

"Don't say that."

"I'm tired by all these excitin' happenin's. My brain buzzes like a bumblebee all night so I can't sleep. I'm nearing fifty now, little miss. Time for a bit of peaceful retirement."

"You'll feel better soon. If I please the Sultan he'll be kind to us and give us a good life."

Damama turned to look out to sea and Aimee saw white hairs among the frizzy brown curls as she stroked Damama's neck. They walked through dazzling white corridors to their suite and Aimee ordered lemon tea and a plate of amlul. Damama munched happily and after a few minutes fell asleep until the golden bell called them to dinner. That night, Damama thought of Monsieur Armande and blew him a kiss from her far-distant prison. They would never meet again, that was certain. But perhaps Monsieur Armande would remember her and they would be together someday in a happier world.

Dawn came, golden bright on the horizon. Aimee looked out over the squat white dwellings of the city at guards in scarlet uniforms and tall white turbans, chattering excitedly and pointing out to sea. Smells of fenugreek and sandalwood filled the air and in the distance she heard the sound of chanting men. As her eyes scanned the harbor area, a ship approached, ornate blue sails billowing, lustrous golden prow shimmering as it dipped in azure sea. Her heart began to thunder, and she called Damama to show her the vessel that would take them to their mysterious destination.

"Oh Lord! Just look at that. Did you ever see such a sight? It looks like somethin' out of a dream."

"Do you think we'll ever go home, Damama?"

"I'm beginnin' to think not, little miss. I reckon you'll have to make the best of what lies ahead. I've prayed for you and thought all around the problem, but we're gonna have to accept that they're sendin' us farther and farther away from home and there's no one to take us back."

"We're together, at least."

"And I'll look after you till my strength gives out."

"You once told me you wouldn't die till I was as big as you!"

"I must have been exaggeratin' a little! If you ever grow big as me no one'll want you to go anywhere with them. Men are powerful frightened of ladies bigger than themselves."

They said goodbye to the Dey and were taken on silk-draped litters through streets seen first on the day of their arrival. Rais Tebessa was waiting, tall, handsome and commanding, to welcome them to the spectacular vessel that would take them away. Aimee was enthralled by the luxurious ship. She swept aboard, noting delightedly that the crewmen, filthy on most ships, were wearing uniforms of blue and gold with cockaded hats and shimmering tunics.

She waved goodbye to the old man on the parapet of his hilltop fortress as a conch shell horn heralded their departure.

In the early evening, they passed peasants in lantern-hung boats fishing for alaccia. And as the sun set deep red over the beehives of Médenine, Aimee smelled the tempting aroma of pigeon pie and peppery meat stew. She took Damama's arm and they went below to dress for dinner.

Later that night, Aimee heard the distant cry of wild boar, cheetah and wildcat. Then, as darkness came, the sounds of land faded and there was nothing but the splash of waves as the ship sailed on. Soon, the oscillating heat of the African coastline was only a memory.

As days passed, Aimee began to feel unwell. At night, her body burned and her hair felt wet as though covered in dew. Damama administered soothing tisanes, sure the illness was caused by nothing more serious than Aimee's nervous condition. Sometimes, when she felt well enough, Aimee walked on deck, comforting Damama about their future and encouraging her to cheerfulness. But all too soon the burning fever would return, forcing her to remain in her cabin, weak and sick and unable to move.

They paused, briefly, at Catania to take on water and fruit and later docked again at the beautiful Greek island of Crete. The whole town turned out to gaze in astonished admiration at the magnificent vessel and its regal passenger. As they sailed away musicians played a Greek goodbye on bouzoukis and tiny flutes and peasants lined jagged hillsides above the port, waving caps, scarves and shawls, anxious to be remembered with affection by one so favored by the gods.

Aimee watched as the ship pulled away. How strange and unreal everything had become. Already people were treating her as someone apart from themselves. She sighed, perturbed that life could never be as it once had been, as she had planned it in the home-loving arena of her mind. Life, if she were to survive at all, would be spent within the seraglio, the secret place within the city of Constantinople.

Damama soon seemed more cheerful. She had taken the peasant homage in her stride, waving her red silk parasol happily until the hospitable villagers of the tiny island

165

were no longer visible. Days of emptiness at sea were relieved by beautiful food and fine wine. Each evening, musicians played and sang for their amusement and Rais Tebessa told tales of the exploits of Algerian corsairs. Damama and Aimee passed the nights with stories and favorite memories of times long past—catching iguanas, going fishing and watching the carnival in St. Pierre. Sometimes, they talked of Cousin Rose, who, all alone in Paris, was still trying to find happiness.

One day, right before the midday meal as Aimee was walking on deck she saw the fabled city on the skyline. The previously deserted sea was suddenly busy with the ships of all nations, traders from the East, French sloops from Marseilles, galleys from Hammamet and Zarzis and strangely decorated caïques that Aimee assumed to be the transport of this strange country. The skyline was breathtaking and different from anything she had ever seen before. Aimee stood at the ship's rail, scrutinizing the scene. Dark cypresses grew in ever decreasing circles near gilded mosques and the towering gold parapets of fairy-tale palaces. Pavilions, finely decorated in pink and gold, walls intricately inlaid with mirror and shimmering mother-of-pearl, lined the shore, reflecting the pure periwinkle of distant sea vistas.

"Those are the pleasure houses where rich men take their forbidden women and they are called the Sweet Waters of Asia," Rais Tebessa told them. He smiled as Aimee blushed under his admiring gaze. Many times, during the voyage, he had damned the orders of Ben Osman that forbade him to touch this beautiful creature. She was, surely, the most desirable woman he had ever seen.

Aimee heard the monotonous thud of drums as they approached the harbor. She had not slept for three nights and now, in the heavily jeweled dress, felt hot as a furnace, her heart palpitating like a frightened bird. She prayed, fervently, that she would not faint before the omnipotent warlord's gaze. For some reason, the sound of the drums filled her with horror. "They sound like the drums played before an execution."

"They probably are. The Turks love executions and have them often on the Sultan's orders or those of the chief warlord, Korba-Khan," Tebessa explained.

Aimee shuddered and went below. There, Damama fussed over her hair and dress, loading her with jewels and wishing her every blessing in heaven.

"Won't be long now, little miss. We're dockin' already and I can see them tyin' the ropes. There's a procession waitin' for you and dozens of fellows in odd clothin' standin' all around the quayside. What a sight it is! Oh Lord! What a occasion."

"I don't like the sound of those drums, Damama."

"Don't listen to them, little miss. They're only drums. They don't mean a thing. I used to dance like a dervish to the drums at carnival time, remember?"

"Those were happy drums; these are drums of death."

Aimee pinched her cheeks to bring back the color. Then she went up on deck and told Rais Tebessa she was ready to be presented.

As she stepped ashore, a fanfare of trumpets sounded. She walked slowly along a narrow jetty, lined with warlord guards. As she passed, some caught their breath, overwhelmed by her beauty and dignity.

Rais Tebessa caught her arm briefly to make her pause.

"Milady, the man approaching is Korba-Khan, the chief warlord of my master, the Sultan. Behind him is the head eunuch, who is the most powerful man in the harem. Have no fear of him, he will adore you."

Aimee looked down the avenue of guards. Some wore loose jackets and leather boots of yellow or blue. Some had towering plumed headdresses and all sported long, stringy moustaches that fell like spiders' legs to their chests. A man approached, tall and slim, with a cloak of bird of paradise plumes and a face so white it appeared deathly as a cadaver. For a moment, their eyes met and Aimee shuddered, unable to control her revulsion at the obscene thin-lipped mouth and gleaming insane eyes, black, wet and empty as a bottomless pit.

The Khan motioned with long-nailed fingers for Aimee to follow. She felt her chest constrict with fear but she walked obediently behind him. Korba-Khan preceded a short man, fat as a pregnant sow, with dark skin and gleaming green eyes. This was the head eunuch, the Sultan's trusted emissary. The eunuch wore flowing flowered silk and a tall white turban covered in jewels, feathers

167

and miscellaneous insignia. Aimee caught his eye, grateful for the faint smile, the encouraging nod.

Damama walked behind the procession, observing the scene with something approaching awe. She thought, wryly, that she had never seen so many men so colorfully and astonishingly dressed in her life. What a spectacle! And all this for her beloved little miss!

As the procession moved forward slowly, Aimee kept her eyes on the flowing paradise-plumed cloak of the warlord. At the central gate of the city of the seraglio, they paused and Aimee saw that an execution was about to take place. The victim, a young man with a handsome face and sad eyes, looked calmly at her as though he accepted his sad fate. Aimee looked away before she heard the swish of the executioner's ax and the procession moved on. The executioner impaled the severed head on an iron railing spike above the city wall and its sightless eyes stared out tragically over the crowd. Shivering in horror, Aimee noticed that on all the spikes of the iron railing there were heads of others who had perished by the executioner's hand. The young victim's head took its place beside blackened rotting skulls of those long dead.

Korba-Khan looked round, curious to see the effect of this gruesome spectacle on the new arrival. He stepped proudly forward to face her, fanning himself with a monkey fur fan. As he towered above her, black strands of the harsh pelt caught her cheeks, but Aimee did not flinch.

The Khan spoke in a high-pitched, piercing voice. "Now, infidel, remember what you have seen and know that my word is law. I am Korba-Khan and I *must* be obeyed. Against me there is nothing you can do. Those who anger me die, as that young man died, on the executioner's block."

Aimee stared at him, full of anger, confusion and horror. She felt suddenly reckless and was happy to see his face change as she answered with a Creole curse.

"I can do nothing against a murderer like you, but my God is more powerful than any mortal man and if he chooses, he can devour your soul for the barbarous way you live. From this moment, you are cursed, your strength will wane, your health fail and your power crumble, and someday, my God will see the end of you and your kind."

The Khan drew his sword, his face a mask of anger, lips curling in fury.

"Will you kill me also?" Aimee asked. "Surely not! I am a gift to your master and he would not think kindly of the presumption!"

The Khan tingled at her insults. The infidel had cursed and humiliated him before his men. He would see her dead before the month was out. Aimee stood very still, aware that she had been foolish and that she had disobeyed Ben Osman's command to take care when she met the cruel warlord. But she felt better for her stand against him. Men like the chief warlord ruled by fear and only a show of courage sufficed to intimidate them. She shook her head, wondering if he would have her murdered before her presentation to the Sultan.

"You have made an enemy, infidel. When you are dying I shall laugh from the highest tower in the city and send my dogs to foul your grave."

"Whether I live or die is not important. My God will devour your soul and all who have heard my prophecy will watch you wither and die in the slow tortures of hell!"

Damama beamed delightedly, enjoying the scene despite her apprehension. Little miss had made a mistake, she should have stayed quiet, but she was a fighter and not inclined to keep silent about things she didn't care for. The Khan turned and saw Damama's pride in the infidel's curses and hated her with a deep loathing from that moment on. The head eunuch adjusted his paunch, fanned his sweating face and resisted the temptation to applaud the newcomer's courage. What a creature! What eyes and what a turn of phrase. If only he could think of such curses! Devour his soul indeed! He bowed to her, green eyes sparkling with affection. Damama took Aimee's arm to shield her, aware that every inch of the girl's slim body was trembling.

Korba-Khan, insane with fury at her affectionate action, took a whip from the horse master and set upon Damama with furious movements. The first blow cut her fine dress, exposing coffee skin running with blood. The Khan continued the beating, laughing insanely in wild enjoyment. Damama flinched but did not fall until a great blow hit her head, cutting her scalp and making blood pour down her face like a scarlet waterfall. The Khan smiled, savoring her agony and licking his lips in sensual ecstasy. Damama fell to her knees, trying in vain to staunch the bleeding.

Aimee felt the sun hot on her damp hair and heard onlookers muttering at Damama's punishment. She longed to go to the help of her dear friend, but her legs felt like lead and the throbbing vibrations of her heart confused and frightened her. Despite a great effort not to, Aimee fell, unconscious, at Damama's side. No one moved to help her and there was a deathly silence, broken only by the buzzing of flies.

The Khan was delighted at Aimee's collapse. He muttered contentedly to himself as the eunuch had the young woman carried into the enclosure. He was greatly relieved that the infidel was weak and no more than a woman. She spoke well but obviously her words meant nothing. He eyed Damama, dabbing at her eyes and trying to see her way through gushing red blood.

"You, servant woman! Take care what you do while you are here in the city of the seraglio. Your mistress has made a great and powerful enemy today."

"And you, sir, have made a enemy too!"

The Khan threw his head back and laughed at her humiliation. "Look at yourself! You are a weak woman and no threat to a warlord of Ottoman."

"I am descended from the warriors of a far island, sir, and someday I'll make you regret what you've done to me."

"Get out of my sight before I kill you!"

Damama limped painfully after the procession, looking about her wonderingly. The beautiful city of Constantinople lay across the water, spanned by a silver bridge, and here on a green headland, overlooking the sea, the city of the Sultan's seraglio lay hidden behind walls fifty feet high. The Dey had told them that ten thousand people lived within the walls, some never moving from the innermost core of its complex design. Everywhere there were walls, tall, forbidding, heavily guarded walls, and within the enclosure more walls, more gates and heavily locked compounds. Damama wondered if anyone would help her with her wounds. She looked around, sadly, aware that escape from such a citadel would be impossible.

The head eunuch approached, fanning himself violently, eyes swiveling to make sure they were not observed.

"Follow me, madame. Dear me, what a day! Take my arm if you please."

"Where's my mistress, sir?"

"She has been taken to the quarters of my friend, the Circassian, mother of the Prince Selim, heir of Ottoman."

"And what's gonna happen to me?"

"You are her nurse, are you not?"

"I am, sir, always was, always will be."

"Follow me, madame, and don't be afraid. I am your friend. You must come quickly before the madman returns."

Damama watched the waggling buttocks, the rolling stomach, and followed obediently. What kind of fellow was this, with his funny voice, his conspiratorial air and his dancing green eyes? Damama had never seen anything quite like the Sultan's head eunuch. He walked alongside Damama, nervously guiding the procession through the first courtyard and finally through the central gates of the palace.

"How many of these gates are there?" asked Damama.

"Many, madame. They are designed to keep out those who are not welcome."

"Or to keep us all in!"

"That too, madame. I fear it will be many months before you can find your way around the city of the Sultan's seraglio."

They passed armed guards at the central gate and walked for what seemed an eternity before reaching further guards at the Gate of Felicity. In the third courtyard, the eunuch led her past the throne room and the royal library and toward the heart of the city of the seraglio, the inner core of royal apartments, suites, gardens and the mysterious harem and selamlik quarters. Damama began to feel faint as she dragged herself along behind the eunuch.

"These are my quarters and behind them lies the harem. Your mistress is in the quarters of the Circassian. That is her garden; isn't it beautiful?"

171

Scent of lavender, hibiscus and oleander reminded Damama of the odors of flower island. Looking up, she saw a beautiful, voluptuous woman watching from a high window, as she followed the eunuch up a white stairway and entered the golden labyrinth.

The sight took her breath away. Ceilings shimmered with gold leaf, walls dazzled with brightly inlaid tiled patterns of flowers, birds and mysterious geometric designs. Nubian slaves waved fans of ostrich plumes to cool the heavily scented air and at every door on the ornate landing, girls chatted with friends, servants and female musicians.

As Damama passed, there was astonished silence. She began to feel faint and sat down on the soft cushions in the Circassian's suite, to listen as the eunuch explained the situation. The queenly Circassian smiled and explained to the eunuch that her personal physician was with Aimee. Damama examined the woman carefully. The Circassian was gravely beautiful and seemed concerned. Pale-skinned with violet eyes and a wide red mouth, her face was framed by shiny black hair plaited in thick ropes to frame her beauty. She was dressed entirely in crimson gauze dotted with diamonds, feet and nails stained with henna, wrists covered in strings of fine black pearls. Damama thought she had never seen such an exotic sight. She struggled to greet the woman in a polite fashion, despite her infirmities, as the Circassian welcomed her.

"I am the Circassian. Please don't trouble to rise. Your injuries have made you weak."

"Madame, I am most honored to make your acquaintance. I am Damama, nurse of Mademoiselle Aimee Dubuq de Rivery."

"Aimee is in the next room. I fear she is suffering from a sickness caught during her days in Africa. I have seen this illness only once before and it is very trying. She will sleep and wake many times before she is well again and often she will be confused and delirious with fever. No doubt Korba-Khan wishes her never to wake, but we shall take care of her and make her well again."

"Little miss is strong as a ox, madame."

"I hope so and I hope her God is as strong as she says."

"How did you hear about that?"

172

"In this place, news travels very fast, madame. Now, let me salve your wounds."

The Circassian's fingers were light as gossamer and Damama relaxed, happy to be in her care. Suddenly, she felt weary and tired of all the stress and strain of the past months. She longed to sleep and to feel safe again. The Circassian looked at her respectfully. The lady from the far island was a giant and strong as any warlord. A normal person would have been unconscious after the first whiplash, but this one had defied even Korba-Khan's cruelty. The Circassian put soothing herbs and healing oils on the harsh red wounds and wrapped cotton strips round Damama's head and body till she was barely recognizable. Then they returned to the receiving room.

"What shall you wear now you are here, Madame Damama?"

"Wear?"

"Your dress is torn. It must be thrown away."

"This is my best dress, madame. I'm real fond of it and I don't like to throw it away. As for wearin', well, I've a case full of my clothes somewhere about."

"I shall send a servant to find it."

"Thank you kindly, madame."

They talked until evening and Damama began to like her new friend. As the sun set, she went to look at Aimee, still in a fevered sleep. Poor child! Damama wiped a tear from her eyes. Too much had happened in her young life in the past few months. Now she would remain unconscious until her body was good and ready for all it had to experience.

Damama lay on a cushion-covered dais, thinking of all she had learned from the Circassian. The city of the seraglio was nothing but a prison surrounded by high walls and armed guards. The warlords were the police of the city of Constantinople and of the seraglio. They fought the wars of the Sultan and policed his border territories. The Khan was powerful and ambitious, some said, for the rule of Ottoman. One thing was certain, the Sultan could not be without his warlords. But they had power as no others. They could even depose the Sultan and replace him with their own appointed puppet. Damama pondered the vexing question of Korba-Khan until long into the night.

Aimee remained in a coma for many days. The Sultan was impatient for news of his gift but no one could wake her. The head eunuch went each day to see her in the Circassian's quarters. Sometimes, he played a flute in the hope that some distant corner of her troubled mind would wake to welcome sweet music. As time passed, he began to look forward to these visits. Green eyes flashing, he waddled to the beauty's side, determined to protect this new treasure forever. Sometimes Damama sat with him, watching him wonderingly and making him blush with her questions.

"How come you're allowed in this harem place, sir? The Circassian told me no men can enter the women's inner quarters."

"But I am not as other men, madame."

"Why not?"

The eunuch's eyes rolled and he begged Damama to ask the information of his friend, the Circassian. Damama watched him suspiciously. Perhaps he was a he-whore like Monsieur Charles. She considered the puzzle and decided that he was not in that mold at all. She beamed, showing all her teeth, pleased to see him turn scarlet under her scrutiny.

The Circassian also tended Aimee lovingly. Here at last was the ally she had prayed for, one exquisite enough to wield power as few could in the secret pavilions of the seraglio. She prayed each night that dawn would break in the soul of the beautiful creature and that she would wake refreshed from her long withdrawal from consciousness.


The Sultan's eldest son, Prince Selim, had witnessed Aimee's arrival from his own quarters in the silent city. He had shuddered at the execution and sympathized with the new arrival and her astonishing companion. He was well aware that the execution had been arranged by Korba-Khan to frighten and intimidate the Sultan's new lady and he was angry that her first day should have been so soiled by the warlord's obsession with power.

Selim was twenty, still frail from poison administered to him in childhood by his mother's rival, The Venetian. The poison had caused a long illness and he had never quite recovered from the shock of its insidious contamination. Selim cared nothing for the lazy-eyed concubines of the harem. He was lonely, longing for someone to whom he could confide his secrets, praying for a friend who would tell him tales of worlds far away from the stifling secrecy of the silent city. His servants talked excitedly of the beautiful one's illness. One said, "She has been asleep for three days. Perhaps she will sleep forever?"

At last, Selim could contain his curiosity no longer. As the city slept, he stole to the silk-hung room within his mother's suite and approached the beautiful French lady. He sat by the bed, watching her until pink dawn came over the horizon. Then he stole silently away. Each night, in great secrecy, he stayed, guarding the beautiful one, looking in astonished admiration at fine creamy skin, silver hair and roselike lips. Sometimes, he touched her fingers or stroked her shoulders. And after a time, he talked to her, telling her things he had never told anyone before.

One night, something stirred within Selim and he bent to kiss Aimee's cheek. Then he sat back, conscious that his heart was beating wildly, his breath racing like strong wine through a weary chest. As dawn came, he kissed her gently again and again. How soft she was, how elegant and wonderful, as different from the heavy-hipped houris of the harem as a gazelle from a jackal.

As always, Selim walked stealthily back to his own quarters, still savoring the magnolia sweetness of her skin. All day and every day he sat looking out to sea and thinking of her. Soon, he realized, with alarm, that he was in love with her. The beautiful one had wakened in him feeling she had thought dead or at least forever dormant. He paced the room, longing for the night and his next meeting with his sleeping love.

The head eunuch kept silent about these nocturnal visits. It was enough that he knew of them from Damama, who remained hidden behind the silk curtains of Aimee's room each night, listening to all that was going on. The eunuch was surprised and happy for the young man, but puzzled and distressed at the likely outcome of the heir's secret passion.

The girl was a gift to the Sultan. She could be given to no one else. The eunuch sighed. Why was life always so

175

complicated? He sat in his quarters, listening to larks singing in the perfumed gardens. Then he ate a whole plateful of almond sweetmeats while he tried to decide what to do about the latest conundrum.

A nightingale flew to the sill, singing a pretty song. And far away, in the center of the silent city, a woman played an old love song. Selim arrived for his nightly vigil, delighted to be with his loved one again. He held her hand and stroked her arm and from time to time told her his secrets. He began to wish she could stay asleep forever. This was the first time he had touched a woman, the first time he had ever smelled a woman's skin. He realized with something of a shock that he should try to achieve her respect and appear imposing in her eyes if ever she woke. He resolved to do something about his appearance immediately.

But Aimee slept on, unaware of all that was happening around her.

# Chapter 14

*Aimee awoke in a state of great confusion. Her* eyes, unaccustomed to sudden sunlight, watered, obliterating vision. She sat up slowly, looking toward the light, and finally focused on a white arched window inlaid with pink tulip-shaped tiles. Outside the window, blue poppies bobbed in the breeze and bees buzzed, unaware of her scrutiny. She heard water splashing in a fountain below and the sound of a woman singing.

She looked round the room, wonderingly. The arched ceiling shimmered with gold leaf. The walls mimicked a garden, with rows of tulips in every shade of red from rose to scarlet, coral to vermilion depicted in intricately cut tiles. Cool green leaves trailed upward to the shimmering ceiling and in a wall niche water jars of solid gold studded with emeralds dazzled her eyes. Her head began to ache with an alarming throb. She lay back, wondering where she was and how long she had been here. For a moment, she felt certain she had died and was in a colorful Illyria. Then she pinched her thigh and rustled the fine silk of her robe and knew she was alive.

She was lying on a raised sleeping platform at one end of a long room. The ground, covered in silk carpets patterned with a hundred strange designs, was strewn with velvet cushions tasseled in silver. Cushions also banked her head and supported her body and by her side a bowl overflowed with luscious red plums, purple grapes and scented lemons with shiny green leaves. But Aimee felt no hunger, only a great curiosity. She wiped sweat from her face and closed her eyes, briefly. When she opened them again she caught sight of Damama's red silk parasol leaning against the wall. She smiled, happily. Everything would be well if Damama was near. She tried to call out but her throat was parched and she was too weak to fetch water from the jeweled pitcher.

She shuddered as memory began to filter back. She had arrived in this barbarian country and collapsed from her illness as the warlord Korba-Khan horsewhipped Damama. She covered her face, remembering rotting heads on city railings and the sadistic warlord's hideous laugh. She fell asleep within minutes until the blue poppies closed their petals in the inky darkness of night.

Aimee awoke again just after midnight. The young man at her side saw the long lashes flicker and held his breath as blue eyes opened and looked up at him. From childhood, he had been taught that blue eyes were a sign of evil. He shivered with fear and then melted as Aimee smiled. She stayed absolutely still, afraid to ask the name of this lustrous-eyed man sitting so admiringly at her side. Pale-skinned and ebony-bearded, he had a startlingly intent gaze. His turban was fine pink silk with an egret cockade, his robes sapphire blue encrusted with pearls and amethysts. She noted that his face was gleaming with inner excitement and that he was a most handsome and intriguing person. As she spoke, her heart fluttered with excitement.

"Where am I?"

"Have no fear, you are in my mother's quarters."

"Who is your mother?"

"My mother is the Circassian. She has been tending you in the days of your illness."

"I don't understand."

Puzzled by his deference, Aimee examined the stranger

178

again. His bearing and splendid clothes forbade that he could be a servant. His manner indicated regal command, but he was too young to be the Sultan and too shy to be an important public figure. She wondered how he came to be in the women's quarters. Ben Osman had taught her that in the tradition of the secret city this could not happen. She remained calm, though greatly puzzled by the handsome young man's presence.

"But where am I?" she persisted.

"This is the seraglio of the Sultan Abdul Hamid. The seraglio is a secret place across the water from the capital, Constantinople. You might say it is a city within the city. Do you remember nothing of your arrival?"

"I remember a man with black eyes and long whiskers like tarantula legs, and I remember him whipping my nurse, Damama."

"Madame Damama is safe, beautiful one. She also is here in my mother's suite. And you have been sick for many days. But soon you will be completely recovered and able to join your nurse," the prince assured her.

Aimee began to tremble from shock and relief. The young man watched anxiously.

"Are you distressed?"

"Of course I'm distressed."

"Why?"

"If I told you, you wouldn't understand."

"Yes I would. I'm very learned and I understand everything."

"You are a Turk, sir, and no Turk could understand the thoughts of a French milady."

Selim sat pensively looking at his hands and longing to touch her. He thought of all the hideous happenings of childhood, the bitter rivalry, the intrigue and his first sight of the Bosporus so full of floating corpses that no one had eaten fish from its waters for a year! The beautiful one was right. Probably his countrymen had a barbarian reputation in the cultured salons of Europe. He sighed wearily, resigned to her condemnation.

Selim had lived a lonely life of contemplation and quiet study, trying desperately to remain alive by skirting the treachery of the warlords and the ambition of his mother's deadly rival, the Venetian. Mustapha, the Venetian's son, was the Sultan's only other male child and his mother longed for him to succeed. For more than a decade, she had plotted, untiringly, for Mustapha's future glory and she would never cease in her endeavors. Selim shrugged. No wonder this beautiful creature despised such a monstrous place and all its scheming inhabitants.

Aimee watched him cautiously and regretted her sharp reply. How handsome he was, how sensitive. The lustrous eyes glowed with awakening sensuality and Aimee began to feel a great need for his affection. She longed to touch his pale strong hands, to kiss the silken beard. She inhaled the musky fragrance of his skin, closing her eyes so he could not read her thoughts.

After a short silence, Selim spoke. "Perhaps you were right to think badly of our ways. But if you told me why you were so unhappy, I would understand."

"Are you so different from your countrymen?"

"Yes, I am not like anyone else in the city of the seraglio. And I, too, know what it is to be unhappy."

He saw tears in the blue eyes and took her hand, stroking it gently, desperately anxious to know how to comfort her.

"Please don't cry, beautiful one. It hurts me to see you so."

"I was going home when pirates from Algiers took our ship. Now I shall never see my flower island again!"

"You will have a home here and everything you desire will be given you."

"But this is not my home, sir."

"I understand that it is not your real home, but Constantinople can be a lovely place to live. The sun shines almost every day and there are flowers in the royal gardens with a thousand perfumes. If my father loves you, you will have jewels and riches like no other woman in Asia."

"What is your name, sir?"

"I am Selim, eldest son of the Sultan Abdul Hamid."

"Why are you here with me in the middle of the night? I was told that the ladies of the Sultan's harem never receive gentlemen."

"They don't, it is absolutely forbidden. But I have been here every night for almost a week. I came out of curiosity, then I stayed to talk with you and to tell you my secrets."

"I didn't hear what you said."

"That is why I told you," Selim replied softly.

"What else did you say?"

Selim blushed furiously and Aimee smiled encouragingly, adoring his reticence.

"I told you you were beautiful and many other things it would not be proper to repeat now you are awake."

"Are you married?"

"No, I am not. I could have four wives and a hundred concubines, but no one will ever die in the abortionist's quarters as a result of my excess. I shall never have a harem. When I become Sultan I intend to send all the women away to the old harem on the banks of the Bosporus."

"But you could have a wife someday, surely?"

"I don't care for any of the ladies I have seen."

"Why not?"

"In the harem, the ladies have bad teeth because they eat too many sweetmeats, and they gossip all day about nothing at all. They are stupid and vicious and sometimes very dangerous. I have never yet made love to a woman and I don't know if I can. My mother says I was made for learning, not loving, and probably she is right."

Aimee took his hand and raised it to her lips. She closed her eyes and listened to the harsh rasp of his breath as he watched her. She decided that Selim was too innocent to know what he needed. She smiled, aware of her strange situation and how it could be changed by this most impressionable learner in the art of love. She kissed his hand gently, feeling her heart pounding excitedly in her chest as she smelled his skin.

"In the morning, if I wake, what will happen to me?"

"They will prepare you in the weeks ahead for your presentation to my father, the Sultan Abdul Hamid."

"How shall I be prepared?"

"They will teach you our religion and more of our language and you will be put into the quarters of each of the most experienced ladies of the harem. They, in turn, will teach you all they know."

"And then?"

"When you are ready, they will show you the golden path to the Sultan's quarters and you will pleasure him."

"And when shall *we* meet again?"

"Probably we shall not."

"Don't be foolish!"

"I am not foolish. I told you I am very learned. I never visit the harem, and as I said, the seraglio is a great city. When you have been here many months, it may be permitted for you to visit within the walls accompanied by the eunuchs. But I doubt that you will ever see me again during my father's lifetime."

"I was told your father disapproves of you?"

"Who said that?"

"Ben Osman, the master of Algiers," Aimee answered.

"His tongue is too long by far!"

"Is it true?"

"Yes, it's true. My father loves me, but he is greatly disappointed in the man I have become."

"Why?"

"He wanted a son like himself, as all men do. Instead, he has me. I disdain the harem; I am neither brave nor bold; I cannot even stand in my armor. I never laugh and I spend all my days in study of those things near to my heart. In other words, in every way I am unlike him."

For a moment, Aimee was pensive. Then she asked, "What do you study?"

"I learn about places I shall never see, birds I shall never hear and people I shall never have the opportunity to meet."

"I can tell you about flower island if it would please you."

Aimee then told Selim of green parrots, jade lizards and masked ladies in carnival processions. She explained her family history and described La Maison du Midi in such detail that Selim could imagine it as clearly as though he stood in the silk-cotton trees around the green lawn. Selim listened intently as Aimee told all about the sad history of Cousin Rose. How she longed to hear of her cousin's life in Paris! Selim was upset to see the beautiful one so worried and he vowed to lighten her sadness.

After a moment, she smiled and recounted Damama's way of catching iguanas by whistling till the lizard fell

182

asleep and rolled off his high tree branch into her waiting arms.

Selim laughed and laughed and Aimee felt happy for the first time in many weeks. She told him the story of Monsieur Charles and how he had locked her in her room without food or water.

"But," she continued, "Damama had the pantry and cellar keys and we ate a lovely dinner and drank champagne because we knew a secret passageway to the pantry!"

"And what happened to Monsieur Charles?"

"Oh, he fainted from hunger. By the next day he had to admit defeat and beg us to come out."

Selim laughed even more, wiping his eyes and covering his face with his hands in utter confusion at the continued jollification.

"I'm sorry to laugh so, you must think me an idiot. But I'm not used to such stories and they please me greatly."

"I like it when you laugh."

"Tell me more of flower island," Selim urged.

"It's almost dawn. If you stay they'll find you here."

"You're right, I must leave. Please say nothing of my visit, not even to my dearest mother."

"If you like, I can pretend to be asleep all day and you can come and see me again tomorrow night. But you must bring something for me to eat. I'm feeling a bit hungry."

"I shall bring a beautiful basket of food," Selim assured her as he rushed away, flushed with excitement at having a new and secret friend.

All day he paced his apartments, wondering if she would be awake when he arrived. He collapsed, prostrated on a cushioned dais because he had forgotten to ask what she wished to eat. Why had he not questioned her? Her smiles had bemused his mind and made his brain turn to jelly! He knew nothing of her taste and had no way of finding out what he wanted to know. Cursing his stupidity, he rushed to the royal library to read all he could on French cuisine.

By early evening he was ready. He had had the finest basket prepared and filled with food suitable for a lady from France. He put the basket into a solid gold box and carried it carefully to Aimee's room.

Aimee was lying, eyes closed, hands folded on her chest.

She smelled of magnolia and her hair shone in the moonlight like a silver river. As Selim opened the box, the scent of honey-roast chicken and marbled larks' eggs reached her hungry senses and she sprang up, falling on the food with utter delight.

"How clever of you to think of a picnic. What is this?"

"We call them ladies' thighs. They're made of honey and nuts."

"I love them. In Martinique we have picnics in the afternoon on the beach or in the orchid glade. Creole ladies love picnics."

"There, you see, we have one thing in common."

For a moment, Aimee looked at him coldly. Then she said quietly, with dignity, "I could never have anything in common with you. Your world is not my world and I don't wish ever to adopt your ways."

Stung by her animosity, Selim sat humbly watching her. After a moment, Aimee was furious with herself for hurting him. Why, when she liked him so much, did she treat him so harshly? Puzzled by her own stupidity, she looked at him and smiled trying to reassure him. She felt the same throbbing in her inner core as she had felt in the moments of their first meeting. Could she be in love? She blinked, anxiously, at the thought. If she fell in love here she would never escape and return to flower island. She must definitely *not* fall in love! She stroked the soft hands and edged closer to him, longing for him to touch her.

Selim was young, innocent and crestfallen. He had done nothing to hurt her. He was, in every way, trying to please. She kissed his hands gently, controlling her desire to kiss him the way he really needed to be kissed.

Aimee apologized. "That was rude and unkind. Please forgive me. I don't know why I'm so irritable."

"There is nothing to forgive."

"Will you be my friend, Selim?"

"For always, until I die."

"I'll be loyal to you if you'll be a real friend. Do you understand what loyalty is?"

"Yes, I understand, but here no one is loyal except my mother and my father. Believe no one, beautiful one, trust no one while you are here. People in the city of the seraglio pursue their ambitions and think of nothing else."

184

"But if you are loyal to me and to your mother and I am loyal to you both, we are stronger than the others, are we not? We are three, four if you count Damama."

"Perhaps it is true, but my mother knows nothing of my visits."

Amiee smiled. She had talked with Damama, secretly, during the day and knew that the Circassian and the head eunuch both knew of Selim's nocturnal visits.

"Can you fight, Selim?"

"No, I never learned the martial arts. My father wished it, but I was not interested."

"All Frenchmen can use the sword. They're strong and very daring and sometimes they fight duels for love."

"I intend to learn now that I'm older. We have the very finest instructors in Turkey."

"Are you strong enough to fight?"

"No, not yet, but I'm going to be strong. I've sent for a doctor from Pergamum."

"Are you ill?"

"No, I just wish to be more than I am."

"Why?"

"I have decided that the time has come for me to learn many things. Until recently, I buried myself in books, so my body is unpleasing. Now, I wish to be more impressive."

"But why?"

Selim hesitated, uncertain how to explain his sudden change of mind.

Aimee smiled knowingly, longing to throw her arms around him and suffocate him with love. "But you are handsome and very kind."

"I am handsome? Are you sure?"

"Of course I'm sure. Your hair is like silk and though your skin is pale, it is fine and strong. You need to expose yourself to the sun and select a diet that will make you healthy."

"Will you write down what I should eat to grow stronger?" Selim asked, encouraged by her concern.

Aimee wrote down a list of foods to be eaten and foods to be avoided. She told him all she had learned about drugs and herbs and how to cure illness. The prince listened, awed by her very presence. Surely there had never been anyone like her in the city of the seraglio.

Aimee lay back, her naked body loosely wrapped in almond silk, with every fiber of her soul longing for Selim's touch. She watched as he ate the last of the quail pie and drank most of the sherbet he'd brought. Aware of her scrutiny, Selim tried desperately to inhibit urges, strange urges, that seemed suddenly to strangle his self-control.

Taking her hand, he looked gravely down at her. His words were serious. "This is the last time I shall come to see you, beautiful one. Soon they will know you are well and it could be dangerous for my mother if it were thought she had condoned our meetings."

"We'll meet again, though. I know we will."

"I think not," the prince replied sadly.

"We have a saying on flower island that the will finds the way. *I* will find a way," Aimee promised.

"And *I* will find a way to help you contact your Cousin Rose. I'm sure I can arrange for you to receive her letters and she yours." Selim knew this would please the beautiful one.

Aimee was overcome with joy to think that she might once again hear from her cousin. She sat thinking of Selim's words and wondering if he really could arrange such an amazing and forbidden correspondence.

The prince kissed her hand, but Aimee said, "Now we are true friends and we should kiss properly. Shouldn't we?"

He blushed furiously. But not wishing to appear gauche, he nodded politely and said, "Of course, beautiful one."

He had never kissed a woman except for gentle brotherly kisses bestowed on Aimee during her long sleep. He looked uncertain, then kissed her first on one cheek then on the other. Aimee took his head between her hands, kissing his mouth, at first gently, then exploring the unfamiliar scent of sandalwood on his skin. She heard a small gasp escape him but she continued to press against his body, hugging the breath from him and inflaming his sleeping spirit.

Selim felt soft skin under his hands and a warm wetness on his lips. She kissed his cheeks, his neck, his forehead

186

and then settled again on his mouth. He began to feel urges he had never known and struggled in confusion to reclaim his breath. Quietly, Aimee lay back, taking his hand in hers. She felt her heart pounding loudly as she watched his reaction. Sadly, Selim arose and walked to the window, picked a blue poppy and gave it to her with a resigned smile.

"My father has royal luck!"

"But you are my friend, Selim. Do you love me?"

"I know nothing of love."

"Do you want me?"

"I do but my father will have you. A gift to the Sultan can only be given to the Sultan or by him."

"Why?"

"Because that is the custom."

"Customs are made to be changed, bent or ignored if they are rules and customs against our wishes."

Selim fell silent and in the distance a cock crowed, signaling the dawn. They stood together, looking out at a fiery sun rising over the horizon. Aimee drew him toward her and kissed him again, swaying to and fro with intense longing. Alarmed, she knew that she was in love. Was it possible in two short meetings? She forgot reason and snuggled close to his shoulder. He held her face and kissed her again.

"I love you, beautiful one. Forgive my presumption, but I wish that you know my feelings. I love you and I always will." He picked up the golden box and shook her hand solemnly. "Goodbye, beautiful one. My prayers will be for your happiness."

"In France we say *au revoir*, not goodbye."

"What does it mean?"

"It means 'till we meet again' . . . Selim?"

"Yes."

"I wish you to know my feelings also."

Aimee paused for a moment, then said, "I love you. I *love* you."

Selim ran back to his quarters, tears rolling down his cheeks. He locked the door and buried himself in his private chamber sobbing with all the pent-up emotion of one who fears to hope. Finally, he slept, restlessly, tossing as his mind dreamed tempting visions of his own beautiful love. He could barely believe what had happened. He loved her and she loved him. What could be done? Was Allah so cruel? The only woman he could ever love would never be his. He remembered her determination . . . "I will find a way." He prayed, earnestly, that she could.

At noon, he woke and called for the sword master and the cook of his private kitchen. He ordered a new menu from the cook and lessons in gymnastics and swordsmanship from the sword master. The cook eyed the list, protesting that he could not find all the items in the city of the seraglio.

But Selim was insistent. "Then steal them or send a ship to find them or get the gardeners to grow them! I intend to be strong and I will be strong. I want no excuses or opposition."

The cook rushed away, astonished that his young master had so mysteriously acquired a sense of command. The sword master said nothing. He went immediately to the Sultan and reported every detail of the strange conversation.

At that same moment, Aimee and Damama were discussing the secret evening meetings.

"He's in love with me, Damama, and I *love* him. Is it possible after only two meetings?"

"It's possible after only half a hour!"

"He's so kind and gentle, and he makes me shiver when he looks at me so my knees turn to water and my heart thumps like a brass gong."

"I reckon he doesn't know much. I don't think he's had much experience with his masculine appetites until now. Gentlemen who start late usually get goin' pretty quick, though, and I reckon he'll be mad wantin' you by now."

"Are you feeling better, Damama?"

"I'm just fine, little miss, just fine."

"What do you think of the city of the seraglio?"

"It's very peculiar. They have some odd happenin's here, I can tell you. They have messengers that can't talk, eunuchs that can't operate like gentlemen cos someone cut their masculinities off and two hundred pretty things just sittin' around wonderin' what to do about their female feelin's! You should hear the things they say, turns the air blue as the ocean, I'll tell you. The other day, one of them

188

grabbed a halberdier in the courtyard and tried to *force* him to satisfy her! Oh Lord! He ran away shoutin' for his life. It's another world, that's what it is, it's not natural, all this restrainin' the appetites."

"What do you think of the Circassian?"

"She's a good woman and very wise. You two will be very good friends, of that I'm sure."

But Aimee was not happy. She sighed and said, "Where will it all end, Damama?"

"I don't rightly know, little miss. But we're together and despite all the peculiarities of the place I reckon we can get by. Just needs a little climatizin' to, like hurricanes and seein' elephantiasis for the first time!"

"Shall we ever escape?"

"I'm not sure you really want to, little miss, now that you're in love with that young fellow."

There was a knock on the chamber door and the Circassian entered regally. Aimee curtsied to the exquisitely bedecked vision.

"You've been very ill, Aimee."

"Yes, madame."

"Korba-Khan had great hopes you would die, but Damama and I have kept you well. Allah be praised."

Aimee smiled, delighted with her new friend.

"Today, if you feel strong enough, I shall show you the harem and you can meet some of your new companions."

"Am I to stay with you in your quarters, madame?"

"For the moment, but when you are fully recovered you'll be taken to the harem so the Ketkhuda can supervise your training. They surely will change your name and then your religion because that is the custom."

"But I am a Catholic, and I intend to die a Catholic!"

"They will change your religion and instruct you in the ways of this place. They will also teach you how to please the Sultan."

"In France we don't teach what comes from the heart!"

The Circassian listened in amazement. Either this fiery child would end by controlling the whole city or she would lose her head within the week.

"I came here when I was nine, Aimee. I am now almost forty and within a short distance of the greatest power a woman can know in this kingdom. If you are wise you also can know power because you are more beautiful than anyone I have ever seen in the harem. Your stay began with a calamity and you made an enemy of the chief warlord. You would do well to be cautious of what you say until you are sure of your position here."

"I want only to be with Damama. I'm not interested in the city and the intrigues of those who want power, and I do not intend to become part of it."

"You will never go home, Aimee," the woman said softly.

"Why?"

"Because no one leaves the city of the seraglio alive, except the very old or the very sick. And perhaps you will not really wish to escape?"

Aimee sat, despondently looking out over the garden in the courtyard. Jasmine trailed the walls, flame flowers nodded near lupins, lavender and mysterious amaryllis. A slave sat in the sun, working an ancient press to extract essence of geranium for the Circassian's perfume. And on the gilded spire of a nearby roof, a bird sang, rippling and trilling a dazzling cadenza. Aimee sighed. The color, smell and sound of birdsong reminded her of her island home. But now the Circassian sought to convince her that she would never go home. Her eyes filled with tears. The desire for flower island fought her need for love. Her head began to ache with confusion. She looked at the Circassian, surprised to see that she was smiling, almost mockingly.

"You'll settle someday and perhaps then we can be friends."

"I'm your friend now, madame."

"Do you give your friendship so easily?"

"No, but I know I am your friend."

"And how do you know that?"

"I cannot tell you my reason but I am your friend."

The Circassian was pleased. She had been told of her son's visits by Damama. At first she had been astonished, then delighted that at last Selim had found someone for whom he cared even though the object of his longing was doomed never to be his. She left Aimee then happy in the knowledge that her beautiful protégée was able to keep a secret when required. In time, she felt sure, Aimee would realize, that only with each other's help could they hope to be safe from the warlords and their ally, the Venetian.

Later, Aimee talked over the matter of escape with Damama until far into the darkness of the night.

"Escape! I reckon it's just impossible, little miss. I can't even find my way from the harem to the Circassian's suite. Take a year to get to know little bits of the buildin' and a lifetime to find our way to the exit and then we'd get stopped by the guards."

"What *can* we do?"

"Best see what they have in mind and then make our plans."

"I don't even know if I want to go home! All I know is that I want to be with Selim. If I can't be with him I want to go home."

"Doesn't matter what you want, you'll be given to the Sultan and that's that!"

"Then I'll make *him* give me to Selim. Oh, Damama! What a wonderful idea! I'll make the Sultan give me as a gift to his son."

"He'd never do it."

"Why not? He's too old to know what to do with me!"

Damama sighed. Oh Lord! What a child, determined to have her own way as always. Get the Sultan to give her to his son indeed. Damama prayed Aimee's head would not hang from the plane tree before the month was out.

After a week, Aimee was removed from the Circassian's suite and taken to the harem. She was renamed Blue Poppy because of her habit of picking the frail flowers that grew in such profusion in the gardens of the inner courtyards. The odalisques were frantic with curiosity about the new arrival.

"Where is France?"

"Are French gentlemen handsome?"

"Are their penises big or small and how often do they use them?"

Aimee was appalled by their directness and furious at their attentions in the ornate bathing chamber. First, she was oiled and pummeled by virgins who lived in cavernous dwellings under the harem floor. Then her toes were painted with brown henna paste that left patterns on smooth white

191

skin. Hair from most private places was removed with a paste of arsenic, lime and water as watching concubines giggled, delighted at Aimee's chagrin.

"Don't fidget, Blue Poppy. If the cream gets on your skin, your skin will fall off!"

The girls sat eating sweets, drinking iced tamarind juice and discussing Aimee's private parts and general demeanor as though she was not present. Sometimes she answered their questions and sometimes she grew tired of their curiosity and sat listlessly ignoring them.

"How did you make your hair silver?"

"I was born this way."

"Blue eyes are a sign of the evil one. Did you know that?"

"Then you'd better stay away from me, I might eat you!"

"The Sultan prefers dark women, like the Circassian. He was so fond of her in the old days that he had a heart attack and his doctors forbade him to see her for three months."

"Does he still love her?"

"Who knows? No one knows what the Sultan thinks. The Circassian's old now, at least forty, and no one wants an old woman to love."

Suddenly bored with the topic at hand, one of the women said, "Let's paint her face. She needs more color."

"What now?" Aimee cried.

"This is kohl and ground gold mixed with honey. We're going to make you irresistible, Blue Poppy. Close your eyes while we paint the lids . . . Bring a mirror so she can see how beautiful she is . . . and be careful, French girls have tender eyes . . . Now you've made them water! . . . Idiot!"

Everyday the women of the harem bathed and gossiped, did each other's hair and painted each other's bodies. Aimee lay watching the strange scene and wondering what Damama was doing. The Circassian, kind as always, had requested Damama as one of her personal retinue, reassuring Aimee that her nurse would be returned to her immediately if she were chosen to visit the Sultan. Aimee missed Damama's jolly presence and her loyal ways. Sadly, she waited, weighing those around who could be friends in the future and those who would obviously be enemies.

One day, she met the Venetian, mother of Selim's rival,

Mustapha. The woman was tiny as a doll with wide gray eyes and curly brown hair hung with pearls and shards of coral. She had a golden laugh and an angel's smile and she assured Aimee of her lifelong friendship the moment they met.

"We must be friends, you and I. I can speak French, so we can tell each other secrets and no one will understand. You know, of course, that my son will someday be Sultan. The true heir, Prince Selim, is a weakling and an idiot; some say he's quite mad. But no matter, he won't survive his father. When my son, Mustapha, is Sultan, you, *petite française*, will be our ally, won't you?"

Aimee smiled sweetly, placating the woman without answering the question. That night, she thought of the conversation and remembered the Venetian's words: ". . . no matter, he won't survive his father." If the ambitious one had her way no one would live who opposed her diabolical schemes. Aimee resolved to tread warily for her own safety in this den of duplicity.

Sometimes, for want of something to do, Aimee tried to count the ladies of the harem, but when she reached two hundred she stopped, appalled at the very thought that they all belonged to one man. She began to dislike the Sultan intensely without having seen him. Some of the women were beautiful, some were scheming bitches longing only to catch the royal eye. Once they had visited the Sultan, they were promoted and given new suites, jewels, slaves and the infinite prestige of being a chosen one. Some were permitted to have the Sultan's child. Some were not. Many died or were maimed in the abortionist's quarters. Aimee fell silent at the thought of that horrendous place. Every night, she prayed for success in her plan to persuade the Sultan to give her to his son. Every moment of every day she collected information about the old man that might help her in her impossible scheme.

Each evening, she ran along coral patterned corridors toward the Circassian's suite and chatted with Damama in the doorway of the Sultan's menagerie. Damama gave her interesting news gleaned from the head eunuch or anyone else she could bombard with questions. Often Aimee asked her advice on problems of the day, and always she was

193

happy to see the tall figure in the long brown dress clattering down the marble corridors.

"It's a very peculiar place here, little miss. You know what I heard today?"

"Tell me."

"Well, one of the Sultan's ancestors had three hundred children! Imagine what masculine appetites *he* must have had. The present Sultan's past it! The Circassian says he can't do it any more. He just likes dreamin' of ladies he can't rightly cope with due to his advancin' age."

"Then I do have a chance!"

"I don't know about that, little miss. Everyone says he keeps what he owns. He's as possessive as a magpie."

"But he *will* give me to Selim. I just know it."

"Best not to count on it too hard, little miss."

"I shall have my way, Damama. I intend to be happy here and I shall only be happy if I can be Selim's. I wanted to ask you what I should do about my religion. They're instructing me in their ways and they insist that I become a Moslem!"

"You just agree with them and smile sweet as honey. Long as you want to be a Catholic you are one, whatever these heathens say!"

"There's no priest to confess me."

"Well, you get down on your knees and whisper your confession to God. He'll listen cos he understands we haven't any choice in what we do, seein' as how we're locked in by these kidnappin' Turks."

"Have you heard anything of Selim?"

"Only that he spends all his days learnin'. The Sultan is disappointed in him cos he wanted a man that liked huntin' and fightin' and exercisin' his masculinity, but they say Selim doesn't even know he's got one, poor boy! I reckon they're wrong. I think he's just discovered it. Lord be praised."

"When I'm his I shall live just as I lived in Martinique. I shall pretend I'm in France and have my furniture sent from the *magasins du Louvre*."

"Oh Lord! You do have an imagination!" Damama chuckled to herself.

"I shall go out once in a while and drink champagne and no one will stop me. I didn't ask to come here, Damama, and I intend to make the best of it if I have luck with the Sultan."

"You'll need more than luck, little miss! There's all kinds of rules and traditions in this place. They got so many rules they forget what livin' is all about. They have rules for the silliest things like which slave has to serve the sherbet and which slave removes the tray! You've been given to the Sultan and he can do what he wants with you. You'd best talk real pretty if you're chosen to meet him. Men need to be told what you want before they start worryin' about their own desires."

"I know what I want," Aimee insisted.

"You always did!"

"I love you, Damama."

"And I love you, little miss. Perhaps if you get on well with the Sultan you can ask him if we can have a couple of brass beds. I can't get used to sleepin' on the floor. Any fool knows that rats and beetles start runnin' around at night. I never feel safe on the floor!"

Aimee lay thinking, dreaming that night. She prayed fervently that she and Selim would be together, lovers at peace with the world. She thought of Damama's caution . . . "Best not to count on it too hard, little miss." She smiled. For her, someday everything would be allowed!

The head eunuch was delighted with Aimee's progress. Each day he arrived to compliment her on her excellent understanding of life in the seraglio.

"Mademoiselle Blue Poppy, how are you today? I see you are more beautiful than ever. Oh, how jealous my naughty girls have become! If you don't guard yourself, I swear someone will poison you. Last month they were busy dyeing their hair black like the Circassian's. Now, they are bleaching themselves to death and already one of them has gone bald! Oh, dear me, what a time I have. I am a martyr, a true martyr. No one knows my pain."

"Damama has been looking for you, sir."

"Why?"

"I don't know, she said she wanted to see you."

"A charming lady, but rather persistent. She is very curious about the intricacies of my physique! Was she married in Martinique?"

"No, but she had many friends and one special one, Monsieur Armande, our chef."

"I think she needs a man to boss. I had best find someone for her or she'll make my life a misery."

"Damama never makes anyone miserable!"

"Of course not, my dear, she just makes me nervous . . . *very* nervous, in fact. Sometimes she appears to be looking clean through my clothing!"

Aimee liked the eunuch. She told him all her thoughts on the silent city and he laughed outrageously at her observations.

"How wicked and critical you are of all we try to do," he noted. "My master, the sultan, will either laugh till his beard falls out or throw you into the Bosporus! He's fifty-nine years old and has never been insulted in his life. Who knows how it will affect him!"

The eunuch rushed away, humming happily. Today, the harem would be searched. Cucumbers had been stolen from a storeroom and so many were missing it was obvious the ladies of the harem had been appropriating them for their own use. The eunuch sighed. The Sultan was old and past his physical powers. The ladies of the harem, desperate with boredom, had begun attacking the halberdiers and stealing anything they could find to satisfy their longing. Traders took great risks, providing rubber dildos in return for precious jewels offered by high-ranking hasekis and kadines. And when the traders failed to deliver, the fruit stalls were raided!

The eunuch threw his hands in the air. What a life! They would scream and shout and call him foul names and be wicked for weeks after the search. But what could he do? He had his orders. The Sultan's spies had insisted the ladies' games be curtailed immediately. Perhaps he would ask the imperial physician to make opium pills to lull the most restless troublemakers to sleep for a few days.

Aimee was apprenticed in turn to the treasurer, the water pourer, the mistress of the sherbet, the jewel keeper and the mistress of the harem, known as the ketkhuda. She learned the finer points of court etiquette and watched odalisques performing marvelously lascivious dances in the harem. She was taught to use pessaries of bezoar, ginger, musk and amber and learned the manner of love in this so submissive society. Aimee reserved her judgment on the love instruction, feeling, instinctively, that such things could not be taught. She had followed Damama's advice and pretended to accept the suras of the Koran, repeating the ultimate lesson, fervently, for fear of the consequences of disobedience. She heard herself say, "There is no God but Allah and Mohammed is his prophet," and saw the instructor smile. Now she was one of them. In the silence of the night, in the privacy of her own room, she assured God the Father, the Son and the Holy Ghost that she still belonged to him whatever circumstances forced her to say!

In an attempt to help Aimee, one of the women in the harem warned her, solemnly, that she must pretend not to notice if the Sultan failed to raise his masculinity. That evening, she met Damama, who exploded with laughter at the quaint advice.

"That is what she told me, Damama, but how could I pretend not to notice such an obvious calamity!"

"I don't know, I'm sure. If his masculinity's shrivelin' up there's nothin' to be done and he'll know it better than anyone. I reckon it's best not to get to the point where you have to make any such observation! Masculinities are very disobedient objects, specially in old gentlemen, past their best. You just sing to the poor fellow and play your mandolin or make him some of that medicine you keep givin' to the head eunuch to send him to sleep after dinner."

In the early morning, Aimee took her mandolin from the wall and sang softly, in a light, clear voice, smiling to herself at Damama's funny ideas. How clever the woman was and how precious! She played a lively tune of carnival time in Martinique and sang a Creole love song.

Below, in his private garden, Selim listened to the sweet voice. It was many weeks since he had seen the beautiful one and he grew lonely and despondent without her. He shrugged his shoulders and walked to the sword master's quarters. For an hour, he practiced under the master's watchful eye. With every thrust, every parry, he imagined himself ridding his adored one of her loathsome enemy, Korba-Khan.

The sword master marveled at the change in Selim. The new diet was obviously working and Selim's decision to expose his skin to the sun had given him a most favorable ap-

pearance. At the beginning of the lessons, the prince's hands
had bruised and bled but nothing deterred him from his in-
tention to become a great swordsman. He wanted a manly
physique and ability to equal that of the finest in the Empire. The sword master was of the opinion that if he continued to work with such dedication, Selim might well
achieve his wish. Overwhelmed by curiosity at the change
that had come over the heir to Ottoman, the sword master
continued to report his observations to the Sultan.

The warlord Korba-Khan heard of the lessons and was
amused. The pitiful specimen of weakness had finally decided to pretend he was a man capable of assuming the
Sultan's crown. Korba-Khan smiled as he fed a devil plant
with scarlet butterflies. The plant was black with lumines-
cent batlike green eyes and trailing black tendrils like the
Khan's arachnoid moustache. Red wings fluttered as its
mouth opened to devour the butterflies greedily. The
Khan watched delightedly. How beautiful it was. How
beautiful and how deadly.

He sat by the window, watching the happenings in the
busy first enclosure. Halberdiers ran by wheeling long
carts of felled tree trunks ferried on caramoussals from the
Black Sea. The imperial baker was taking the air, fanning
his face with a white cloth as slaves filled his storehouse
with goods from other merchantmen. Porters passed with
bananas from Alanya, dates from Egypt, oranges from
Fethiye and butter packed in oxhides from Moldavia.
Others came loaded with rolls of brocade from Brusa and
bales of cotton sent, no doubt, by the wily Ben Osman
from ransacked Mediterranean traders. The warlord flicked
a wasp from his face and stepped out into the sunlight.

The plane tree was hung with a dozen dead heads, others
stared down from the spikes of the city railings. The executioner's fountain was freshly red with blood washed from
his death-stained arms. The warlord strode over to the fountain and peered into its rosy waters, smiling exultantly.
Today was a fine day, a day greatly to his liking.
Bloodied water splashed over the fountain edge, staining
the dusty white floor of the enclosure.

The warlord thought again of Selim's lessons and
laughed. Sword-fighting lessons indeed! It would take
more than that weakling to usurp the strength of

Korba-Khan. Mustapha would be Sultan and no one would prevent it! He called for a servant to bring him a pretty new boy.

Inside the palace, life went on. Aimee recited her midday prayers. An astronomer, summoned by the Sultan, prayed for the accuracy of his predictions. Selim looked down from his window in the Rose Pavilion, noting every detail of the distant busy scene. And somewhere in the mazelike labyrinth, Damama adventured, twirling her red silk parasol. Before long, she was a popular figure in the innermost courtyard. Merchants invited her to coffee, dressmakers encouraged her to buy and the Sultan's horse master fell madly in love with her.

further punishment, he ordered half rations for a month for the rest of the recalcitrant force.

Genis Khan sat in his quarters looking at his own

# Chapter 15

*At last the day came for Aimee's presentation to* the Sublimity. The Mistress of the Harem woke her and took her to the head eunuch, who gave her final instructions on how to behave in the presence of the Sultan. Aimee was bathed, cleansed, painted and dressed in dazzling white. In the Circassian's quarters Aimee looked at herself in a long gold-framed mirror. She shimmered with diamonds. Her bodice was jeweled and her trousers made of fine white silk richly embroidered with a design of the favorite blue poppies. Her fingers were covered with expensive rings and mysterious lucky charms. And round her neck, she wore the angel's face amulet given her by Monsieur Armande. She fingered it lovingly, reassured by the happy memories it recalled.

She hugged Damama and asked her advice. "Oh, Damama, I just don't know what to do when I meet the Sultan."

"You'll do nothin'. You just be yourself and don't stare too hard at the poor old fellow."

"But I don't wish to go to him. I have prayed he won't choose me."

"Never mind what you wish. He'll be useful, if you play your cards right. You just stand there nice and quiet and leave all the decidin' to him."

Aimee decided that Damama was right. She must consider the situation after her presentation. Perhaps she would be lucky, perhaps the Sultan would not even care for her. Her fear of his power and insistent demands was at odds with her plan to manipulate him into giving her to his son. She walked to the presentation chamber in a state of apprehension and confusion.

Odalisques were lined in two columns on either side of a room that was richly decorated from floor to ceiling with gold filigree. A fountain tinkled at one end and at the other an ornate golden throne awaited the Padishah of the Faithful. Aimee took her place in the middle of the line, conscious that she was smaller, slimmer and less painted than the other newcomers. A bell rang and the head eunuch appeared, resplendent in scarlet satin, face solemn, green eyes for once serious and stern.

"Behold the Sultan, long live the Sultan!"

Aimee was shocked to see that the Sultan was a small, slim man with a beard obviously dyed a startling blue-black. The hair roots were as white as his pasty face. The Sultan caught her eye and, smiling graciously, inclined his head imperceptibly toward her. Turbaned in rose brocade, tunic heavily ornamented with pailletes of opal and rose diamond, he presented a figure of bizarre opulence. Aimee remained rooted to the spot, astonished by the small figure's regal demeanor.

Slaves arrived with refreshments and the other girls began to eat and drink and dance, showing off enthusiastically for the old man on the golden throne. Aimee sat alone and apart, wondering how long they would be inspected by an old fossil, obviously far too senile to be able to satisfy even his curiosity!

She was startled by the head eunuch whispering in her ear, "Mademoiselle Blue Poppy, you may now kiss the cushion."

As she had been taught, Aimee walked forward and kissed the silk cushion at the foot of the old man's chair.

When she looked up at him, he smiled knowingly as though they shared a secret known to no other. Aimee was curiously deflated by his urbanity. She returned to her quarters followed by the exultant head eunuch.

"I *knew* he would choose you. Oh, how lucky we are. The Circassian will be so happy. Tonight, Mademoiselle Blue Poppy, you will tread the golden path to the Sultan's quarters."

"No! I won't!"

"What?"

"I said no, I won't."

"What do you mean? 'No' is not allowed in the Sultan's seraglio. I'm not going to lose my head for one of your naughty whims!"

"I shall not go to see him. He is old and withered and I don't wish to be mistress of a senile gentleman. It's disgusting to think of such a thing."

"Dear me. I have my tribulations, I am a true martyr! My ancestors must have sinned greatly to persecute me so. Now listen, Mademoiselle Blue Poppy, the Sultan wants you. Perhaps he will even make you one of his wives. If you have his son you may even become Sultane Valideh of this land someday and you cannot be more powerful than that."

"I will not go to see him. You can hang my head on your plane tree, but I will not go!"

"Oh, what a day! You're enough to make me forget I adore you!"

The eunuch rushed away, past the treasury and the suite of the kadines to the Circassian's quarters. He arrived redfaced and sweating, waving his fan of ostrich plumes and sinking into the cushioned recess with a dramatic sigh.

"She'll be the death of us all!"

"What has happened?" the woman asked calmly.

"Mademoiselle Blue Poppy was presented and the Sublimity chose her, as you said he would. When I told her to prepare herself for the golden path to his quarters tonight she refused! *Refused!*"

The eunuch fanned desperately as tears rolled down his face. "First an invasion of cucumbers and now this, a chosen one who says no! She told me they could have her head for their plane tree but she will not go to him."

"What is her objection to the Sultan?"

"She says he is too old. She says it's disgusting to think of such a union. Oh, what a naughty girl she is, whatever shall I do? All is lost, my dearest friend, all is lost."

"Send for Damama!"

"The Circassian paced the room as she awaited Damama's arrival. The old lady came, beaming happily, unaware of the astonishing disturbance.

"Madame Damama, my dear friend."

"Milady."

"There's a little trouble, I'm afraid. Perhaps you could help us. Aimee has been chosen by the Sultan as we expected. But she has refused to go to him because he is too old!"

At this, Damama threw her head back and laughed loud and long.

"She told the eunuch that they can put her head on the plane tree but she will not go. What ever shall I do? I depend on her to please the Sultan. If she does, he will believe her when she tells him of the Venetian's plot to put Mustapha on the the throne."

"Little miss isn't too concerned about all these plots, madame. She just wants her own way, always did!"

"She will never go home, Damama. She must remain here all her life and it is best that she stays in a position of power. But she appears to be totally uninterested in protecting herself."

"She'd like to go home, madame, but she has other plans now she'd like a lot better," Damama replied.

"What can I do to convince her that she *must* see the Sultan? For years I've prayed for someone like Aimee to come along. With her help I can be Sultane Valideh and we can all live in peace with my son on the throne. But if Selim dies then we too shall die. Mustapha would throw us all in the Bosporus if he became Sultan."

Damama's eyes rolled at the prospect and she thought carefully for a few moments. Finally, she said, "Can you guarantee that I can be returned to little miss if she goes to see the Sultan?"

"Of course, anything."

"I'd best go and talk to her."

Damama rushed to Aimee's room and, closing the door

behind her, said, "I've heard about the commotion you caused. You did very well, little miss!"

Aimee stared uncomprehendingly.

"You've got yourself into a good bargainin' position, that's for sure."

"I don't understand."

"You must ask for me to be returned to you and for your own apartments and servants and jewels and anythin' else you fancy."

"I just want to be with Selim. If I can't I want to go home!"

"They won't let us go home, little miss. You have to use this moment to get everythin' we need for our comfort."

"I won't go to see him, Damama!"

"Yes, you will. Don't start bein' disobedient now!"

"You're against me, too. Oh, what have I done to deserve such a life!" Aimee cried.

"Against you! You say that? You just remember you're not too big to get put across my knee and given a good thrashin'."

"You've never given me a thrashing."

"No, but I might, someday, if I get the inclination."

They laughed and held hands and Damama kissed the velvet soft cheeks.

"Little miss, if he's so old, he dyes his hair and has a body frail as a willow branch, he can't do anythin'. So what's the problem?"

"I don't know if I could let him touch me without being sick!"

"Then don't let him touch you. Talk to him, tell him so many things he laughs till he falls over and doesn't know if it's Tuesday or Sunday. You know how to do that! Once you've charmed him, he'll let us be together and you'll have his ear. It's *very* important, you know that."

Aimee thought for a while, looking out on the crowded seaway.

Damama continued, "Once he's crazy about you, you let him know what you want. I've told you a thousand times you must get him to give you to that boy of his. Then you'll have a baby and he'll be the proudest old fellow in the whole of Turkey."

Aimee sighed. Was it really possible to persuade the Sul-

tan to give up what he most desired? She looked at Damama with eyes full of bewilderment. If she went to the
Sultan, Damama could return to her and they would be together forever. If she pleased the old man perhaps he really
would give her to her beloved Selim.

She made her decision. "Call the head eunuch and tell
him I've changed my mind. I will go to the Sultan."

The eunuch arrived with a slave carrying a tray of fresh
lime juice and Aimee's favorite almond sweets. She looked
out over the poppy garden to the Bosporus. A French ship
approached the harbor and soon gilded caïques deposited
passengers on the shore below the city wall. Damama
watched Aimee's inner struggle and wondered what she was
thinking. Perhaps she was dreaming of the home she
would never see again or about Cousin Rose, whose life
was now so separate from her own. Perhaps she was discovering the agonies of impossible love.

Damama brushed the silver hair as Aimee informed the
eunuch of her decision. "I shall go to see the Sultan."

The eunuch beamed and threw his arms round Damama.

"Madame, what influence you have! Thank you most sin-
cerely."

Damama coughed and looked out of the window.

"Mademoiselle Blue Poppy, I assure you, you will *not*
regret your decision."

At dusk, Aimee was carried on a silver litter to the Sultan's suite. She knew now why they called this long, un-
windowed, silent corridor the golden road. Ceiling, walls
and floor were covered with ornate patterns of delicate design. At intervals, strange symbols were outlined in heavy
turquoise stones and delicately cut sapphire motifs. The
whole area shimmered mysteriously in the torchlight glow.
Outside the door of the Sultan's suite heavily armed
guards stood, eyes unwavering, impervious to her presence.
Aimee's heart began to thunder and she longed to dissolve
into a thousand tears. She counted the weeks since she had
seen Selim and remembered what she had told him . . . "I
will find a way." She was now near the one man who could
give her her heart's desire. She prayed, fervently, for God's
help.

She was led into a room that was draped with feather-
light scarlet silk. Instead of cut tile-patterns, the walls

were studded with rubies and inlaid with mother-of-pearl. Aimee stood surveying a solid silver couch with pillars like cathedral spires. She walked to the window and looked out on a private garden of scented plants and climbing shrubs trained over a solid silver pergola. She almost laughed at the ostentation. Behind her, a door closed. Aimee turned to see the Sultan. He was smiling, relaxed and to her surprise spoke perfect French.

"You're surprised at my linguistic ability?"

"I'm delighted, sir."

"Sit down and tell me about yourself."

Aimee sat on silk cushions in the window seat overlooking the garden. The old man took his place nearby.

"I understand you were unhappy at the prospect of visiting me—why?"

Aimee blushed furiously and wondered what to say. After a brief struggle she decided to tell the truth.

"In my country, sir, it is considered undesirable for a a lady of my age to be involved with a man of yours."

"An honest woman! Can it be true? We Turks are indirect, you know. The truth tends to jar our ears. But after a lifetime of being lied to I'm not sure I don't find your censure amusing! What else do you not like about me?"

"I don't care for the way you dye your beard to make yourself appear younger. It isn't dignified. The Sultan is omnipotent whatever the color of his hair."

The old man threw back his head and laughed till his eyes watered, and announced, "You'll do me a power of good. I'm tired of the lily-livered weasels they keep sending me. They pretend I'm everything I know I'm not any more! They treat me like an imbecile and I may be old but I'm not stupid or childish."

"You're still a most distinguished gentleman, sir."

"I'm that and I'm wiser than everyone in the city except my son, Selim. But I am no longer the man I was. I am no longer able to do all I would like to do, though I pretend I can."

"Why do you pretend?"

"Because if I appear senile the warlords may decide to hang my head on their tree!"

"They wouldn't dare!"

"Oh, they would. Six of my predecessors were killed or

deposed by the warlords and no one is safe from their willfulness. They know I grow old and tired because no children have been born to me for many years."

Aimee felt sudden sympathy for the old man. She smiled reassuringly, wishing she knew how to make him happy.

"Now, tell me what you have done to my son?" the Sultan asked suddenly.

Aimee was thunderstruck by the question.

"There are messengers and spies in the harem and all over the city of the seraglio. *My* spies. One of them picked up a rumor and you have just confirmed it by your reaction to my question."

Aimee struggled to speak, chest constricting in fear and uncertainty.

"Don't be afraid, I'm not angry, only curious. Please explain what has caused the astonishing change in Prince Selim."

"I think he is in love, sir."

"Allah be praised! He is his father's son after all."

"Selim told me that we would never meet again because I would be given to you. I told him I would find a way."

"And will you?"

"With your help I may."

"You wish me to give you to Selim?"

Aimee smiled but remained silent.

"What have you in mind, my clever little tigress?"

"You have no children from recent times and this makes you unhappy because it signals your senility to the warlords."

Stuck by her cunning, the old man replied, "Continue."

"Your son has never shown an interest in the ladies of the harem and that also has made you unhappy."

"It has indeed!"

"If you, in your omnipotence, could contrive a way to change both those unhappy situations the problem would be solved in secrecy and only we three need know."

The old man paced the floor, tugging at his beard and muttering to himself.

"Did the Circassian put you up to this?" he demanded.

"No, she asked only that I seek your help in protecting Selim from the Venetian's friend, Korba-Khan."

"The Venetian's son is an idiot, quite mad, always has been."

"The warlords have selected him as their candidate for succession. They intend to make him a puppet ruler," Aimee disclosed.

"Impossible!"

"They plan to kill Prince Selim."

"The fools. They will never attain their evil goals!"

"They would not hesitate to have their way."

"I don't want to talk about them. Tell me how we can arrange the matter of your liaison with my son Selim."

"I am a woman, sir. I cannot form a plan. You must do that."

"But how?"

"The Circassian told me that secrecy is the obsession of the Sultan. No doubt you will find a way to arrange the matter."

"I can do anything."

"I'm sure you can. And I admire you as a special person even if you do dye your hair!"

The Sultan smiled. She was clever, this silver child of France. He would think over the conundrum tomorrow when he was not so dazzled by her presence. Aimee offered to play her mandolin and the Sultan listened happily as she sang songs from flower island. She told him stories of childhood, of Damama, Monsieur Armande and the sisters in the convent at Nantes. She detailed her observations of Monsieur Ben Osman, master of Algiers, and the Sultan laughed as he had not laughed in years.

"I saw your nurse from my window. She chases the head eunuch all over the seraglio till he screams for mercy. What does she want of him?"

"She is curious about his 'disabilities.' "

"She needs a man?"

"She has strong female appetites."

"I shall arrange for her to meet the captain of the guard. Why does she always carry a red parasol?"

"Damama loves her parasol, sir. I don't know why, but she has always carried it."

"She's a strong woman and I hear she has your ear. I must be kind to her so she won't come chastising me. I hear that protocol is of little interest to the lady!"

Aimee visited the Sultan many times in the days that followed. No one knew that they only sat, talking, joking and learning all they could of each other. No one knew that the Blue Poppy was anything but a new and favored lover of the great ruler. The Sultan began to feel impatient for her visits. He had sent for maps of flower island and of the area of France where Aimee had stayed so long in the convent. He had also prepared a small surprise for Damama and now waited with all the excitement of a young man to present it to her charge.

Aimee arrived on the litter borne by four black eunuchs. She kissed the thin cheeks and hugged the shapeless shoulders and then stared in amazement at the gift he handed her for Damama.

"How beautiful. What ever will Damama say? Surely she'll scream like a banshee!"

"She will say I'm the best inventor of presents she has ever known."

"The *very* best."

Aimee held out the gift to examine it. It was a replica of Damama's red silk parasol, but this one was quite different from the original. The handle and spines were of solid gold, the canopy of silk encrusted with rubies that made its weight so great she could barely lift it. Aimee sat stroking the parasol lovingly, marveling as it caught the light and glittered regally in opulent splendor.

She ran and threw her arms around the Sultan's neck, kissing him resoundingly till he sat down panting to pour himself a cool drink. She wiped his face with a scented cloth and he caught the flowery perfume of her skin. For a brief moment, he was sure she had bewitched him. He smiled resignedly, aware that he was infatuated by the exotic creature.

They ate dinner together, chatting happily as servants passed like silent phantoms back and forth. Sea scorpion soup, partridge caught by the Sultan's huntsmen, bowls of yogurt with cucumber and garlic, hot pastries of spinach and chopped lamb's brains. The *pièce de résistance* made the Sultan's eyes shine with delight. A fairy-tale castle topped with a head modeled meticulously in sugar to look like his beloved Blue Poppy. He sprang to his feet, clapping his hands and calling for the sugar modeler to come and be personally complimented.

When he had rested from his overindulgence, the Sultan asked Aimee to follow him. He led her through the garden of scented vervain to a locked room opposite his own bed-chamber.

"The rooms that surround this garden are all my private suite. This one was used in past times as a storeroom for my clothes. I have had it transformed for your use."

Aimee gasped as torches revealed a chamber flagged in lapis lazuli and viridian malachite, walls embossed with blue poppies and waving green leaves of cerulean sapphire and cut stone studded with emeralds. The ceiling was draped with sea-blue silk. The bedposts were solid gold inlaid with the same stones and jewels as the walls, and silk hangings drifted to and fro from its tall pillars in the cool evening breeze.

"This, my little tigress, is for you and your lover, my son, Selim."

Aimee stood, marveling at the exquisite workmanship of the room.

"You and I shall meet for an hour as we have been meeting. I shall continue to enjoy your conversation and your wit *and* your insults! Then you will go to my son and perhaps we shall all be delighted at the result. No one will ever suspect because no one has access to these rooms except through my receiving room."

Aimee hugged him and kissed his cheeks, eyes full of tears at the splendid gift. "I love the room. You're so clever and so kind."

"I am envious, and furious that age robs me of what I most desire. But I'm a realist. For a decade I have prayed to Allah that something would release Selim's imprisoned soul. Now you have come and he is changing every day. He tries so hard to become the man he believes you need that I almost pity him. Don't look at me like that. I am only human, little tigress. I might forget what you wish and make a fool of myself in your eyes!"

Aimee smiled happily and asked, "Will Selim come to-night?"

"No, he will come tomorrow. He knows nothing yet of our arrangement. I intend to send for him tomorrow evening after we have talked and tell him I have a present for him. I hope he doesn't collapse when he sees you! I hope he can manage you. His ignorance of women knows no bounds. But no doubt you will assist him in his moment of need?"

Aimee spent the next day in a state of incredible excitement. She told Damama her secret and together they laughed and plotted for the success of the night's mission.

"If he's too shy to touch me I'll teach him the calenda."

"That'll start him running around like a Christmas turkey!"

"You must borrow the Circassian's musicians and have them outside the wall at nine o'clock. If you hear me clapping the rhythm, start them playing the beat."

"I'll be there, don't you worry. I might even try a few steps myself!"

Aimee called on the head eunuch in the cool of evening with a bottle of honey and opium for his cough. The eunuch drank a drop, smacking his lips as he drained the bottle.

"You must only drink one spoon of your medicine, not the whole bottle!" Aimee said in alarm.

"I love it. It gives me such *beautiful* dreams!"

"It contains ether and opium and I assure you you'll fall asleep forever if you keep taking it in such large quantities."

"Are you happy, Mademoiselle Blue Poppy?" he asked, changing the subject.

"I am almost happy and soon I shall be very happy."

The eunuch wondered why Aimee was so pleased with life, why her eyes were shining in anticipation of her meeting with the Sultan. Only a short time ago, she had been screaming that she did not wish to meet such an old man. Now, everything had changed. The eunuch shook his head, thinking there was no accounting for the unpredictability of women. He looked in his book after her departure and consulted the dates of her visits to the Sublimity. Every night, for almost a month, she had been in the Sultan's presence. Soon, she would be with child and promoted to being the new favorite. He ran off to discuss her change of attitude with his friend, the Circassian, as soon as Aimee left.

212

Aimee arrived in the royal suite that evening trembling with excitement at the prospect of seeing Selim again. The old man poured rosewater cordial to cool her and chatted amiably, watching every move until Aimee was less agitated. He told her of his problems, his worries, and listened intently as Aimee told him all she had learned of the Venetian's plans for her son, Mustapha.

"It's true she is ambitious, but by the time I die Selim will be strong enough to manage his own affairs," the Sultan said.

"How can you be so sure?"

"He has changed so suddenly. He eats a new diet and drinks only spring water and every day he exposes his skin to the sun. He tries so valiantly at his lessons in gymnastics and swordsmanship that the master has begun to applaud him. If Selim can accomplish so much in a few months, what can he achieve in the years that lie ahead?"

"I'm happy for you and for your son."

"Happy? I'm thrilled by all that has happened. Soon, he will be more than a match for any opponent. I have plans about how to deal with the warlords. I must talk to my son about them."

"Couldn't you banish them to Cappadocia?"

"No, that would be impossible. When the warlords are displeased they burn the city and hundreds die, roasted like pheasants in their wooden houses. I must at all costs protect the people."

"But you are the Sultan and you are master of Ottoman, are you not?"

"No ruler is master of his fate unless he controls the army. My ancestors lost control of the warlords many centuries ago. Now, who can tell where their power will end?"

"You should form a new army and make them your own!"

The Sultan paused, surprised at the suggestion. What a thought! What a woman! A new army indeed. If only he were younger he would do just that. He continued to chat for an hour, delighted by Aimee's wisdom and provoked to admiration by her spirit. As dusk came, he led her with a conspiratorial smile to the tiny love nest he had lovingly arranged for his son's use.

"I shall send my son to you when he arrives. Be happy, little tigress, and tell no one our secret."

Aimee waited, listening as leaves gently tapped against carved window screens. She heard voices and the sound of the Sultan clapping his hands. She lay down, spreading the blue silk skirt in a circle round her body. Then she closed her eyes and pretended to be asleep. When Selim came through the door he would remember how she had looked on their first meeting. After a while, she dozed peacefully.

Selim was puzzled by his father's summons. The Sultan's color was high and he seemed greatly excited. Selim was flattered by his father's approval of his new ways and more confident manner but he sat uneasily, waiting to know why he had really been called to the imperial presence.

"Are those new clothes?"

"Yes, I have ordered many new clothes. My arms are much thicker because of the exercise I take and I think I have been careless of my dress for too long."

"Blue suits you well."

"I love this color. It reminds me of . . ."

"The sea and the sky and blue-violet eyes."

Selim was silent. What was his father leading to? What had the wily old fox planned for this unusual evening? He was surprised when the Sultan handed him a rusty iron key.

"Your present is over there, in the room that used to be my clothes store."

"Ask the servant to bring it, Father. The night is chilly and I don't care for walking in the garden."

"Go and see for yourself! It can't be carried by a servant. It's too precious."

Selim was overcome by curiosity. The Sultan loved buying presents and the Circassian swore he had a talent for knowing the heart's desire of those he loved. Selim walked through the scented garden, shivering in the evening air. As he put the key in the door, he was surprised to find it unlocked. Puzzled, he walked inside.

Torches flickered, illuminating jeweled walls and magnificent floors covered in rare silk carpets. The solid gold bed of his ancestor, the Sultan Suleiman, stood in the center of the room, and around its posts, curtains of hazy blue undulated in the gentle evening breeze. Impatient to know what was happening, Selim threw the curtains aside and saw his own beautiful one lying, arms crossed, eyes closed, fast asleep.

Selim closed his eyes, conscious of blood pounding through his temples like a fierce mountain stream. Was she a witch or a she-devil? The soothsayer had insisted that Aimee had the evil eye! How had she persuaded the Sultan to give up what he most wanted? Selim began to feel dizzy with apprehension. Aimee woke and kissed him delightedly.

"Are you well pleased with your surprise?" she whispered.

"I must return to my quarters. I am not well."

"This is your room and I must look after you when you are not well."

"I am confused, beautiful one. I don't wish to talk with you. I need time to think about what has happened."

Realizing that he was afraid and confused, Aimee explained patiently about her discussions with the Sultan and the arrangements made in great secrecy that would be good for the old man's image, good for his son's happiness and good for her own future. A child would stop rumors of Abdul Hamid's fading virility and imminent senility. A male child would someday be Sultan of Ottoman and in the far distant future on the day of his accession, Aimee would be Sultane Valideh, the most powerful woman in the Empire.

"You are a calculating woman, beautiful one."

"No. I am a cautious one. I plan for my safety and for the safety of those I love."

Selim thought for a moment. Then he kissed her gently. "It's a very good plan but it has one fault."

"What's that?"

"I am the error of it."

"Why?"

"I want to love you but I don't know how. I've read all the books in the erotic library but nothing makes my body stir. I fear the illnesses of my childhood have made me incapable of accomplishing all I long to achieve."

Aimee took off Selim's shoes and placed his tunic on the carved chest under the window. She brought him a robe of fine muslin and told him to change his other clothing.

"You're too shocked and tired to want me tonight so

215

we'll talk and laugh like we used to do when you came to visit me secretly."

Selim fumbled with the fastenings and Aimee smiled as he turned away to hide his body. They lay together on the jeweled bed, wrapped in fine mohair covers, and she told him of the slaves of flower island, of sugar plantations and of a special dance, the forbidden calenda.

"I love dancing! Sometimes I call a lute player to come to my quarters to play for me and I dance for hours alone."

"Then I'll teach you the calenda and we'll laugh the way Damama and I used to laugh whenever we watched it."

Unsuspecting, Selim stepped happily from the bed to await her instructions. He was greatly relieved that the beautiful one had not insisted on his trying to make love to her. He knew how the ladies of the harem were trained and he shuddered at the thought of such calculating ministrations. Aimee smiled gaily, delighted that she had arranged for Damama to bring musicians to the outer wall. She began to demonstrate the basic steps of the erotic dance.

"First, we are far apart, then we move, like this, toward each other . . . That's right . . . You have a good style, I think you're a natural dancer."

Selim tripped back and forth as Aimee hummed the simple refrain and clapped the insistent beat. On the other side of the high wall, Damama heard the handclaps and gave the signal to the musicians to start the gently throbbing beat.

"Now, as the drum beats more quickly, we go back and forth, faster and faster. Isn't this fun? Damama used to love the calenda, she's a truly great dancer . . ."

Selim beamed, throwing his head back as exertion made sweat pour down his neck. After a few minutes, the beat changed yet again to a fevered, pounding pulse. He began to feel uneasy at his own reactions. Body damp from inner excitement, he opened his eyes and saw Aimee demonstrating the final sequence of this astonishing dance. Arms raised above her head, Aimee stood rotating her hips back and forth, back and forth until he felt dizzy at the sight

216

of her contortions. She spoke gaily, ignoring his glazed eyes.

"In the final part of the dance, when we come toward each other, we gently brush our lower regions. That's right . . . Now repeat that a little harder. The slaves on flower island call this knocking on the door! That's very good, push forward with your hips, make them undulate to the rhythm of the drums. You *must* keep beating to the rhythm of the drums, faster, faster."

The drummers pounded passionately to a feverish finale. Selim felt strange changes in his body as he pushed back and forth, back and forth against the thin silk of Aimee's robe. At last, it was over. He sat down abruptly, dismayed at the obvious changes in his body. Aimee laughed merrily, throwing herself down on the bed and pretending not to notice his discomfort. She thought of Dominic Duval and thanked her stars that she had been lucky enough to learn how to lead her loved one to happiness.

"You must be exhausted, we'll lie quietly now and perhaps . . ."

"No! I don't wish to lie quietly. That dance has made my head whirl."

"And mine, it always does."

"I feel dizzy."

"Don't worry, it will pass. Hold me tight, I'm a little cold. The nights are so sharp in your country."

"Next time we come here I shall order a charcoal tendour."

"Your hands are warm. Put them over me or I'll catch a chill and cough every night instead of sleep."

Selim felt hard nipples under thin silk and a ripple running through Aimee's body as she shivered at his side.

"What are you thinking about, Selim?"

"I'm thinking I long to be a man."

"Then you can. Whatever you wish you can do."

"If only you are right."

Aimee smiled at his chagrin, well aware that he had no idea how to start all he so wanted to accomplish.

She wrapped long, slim legs around his body and lowered herself gently onto him. Hopeful of convincing the innocent one of her lost virginity, she cried out, startling him for a brief moment. Then, she descended with rapturous, blissful cries of complete abandon. Suddenly, Selim came to life. He threw off the robe and lifted hers over her head, hurling it to the floor. He looked closely, wonderingly, at the naked creamy body, so elegant and luxurious and tantalizing. He tasted the pink buds of her breasts, murmuring words of admiration and avid desire. Aimee fell back so he could look down on her, surprised by the intensity of her own feelings and the strange impression of being complete for the first time in her life.

Caught in the vise of her longing, Selim swayed, back and forth, round and round the silken bed. At last, with a great cry of ecstasy, he lost himself rapturously in her throbbing body.

Across the scented garden, the Sultan listened in astonishment. Only half an hour ago the poor boy had been ignorant! Now he was shouting like a dervish in ecstasy. The Sultan retired discreetly to his bedchamber. That little French vixen would teach his son all he needed to know and more besides. Praise be to Allah, it would work out as they planned.

Damama led the musicians from the other side of the wall back to the Circassian's quarters. Then she retired to her own room, beaming knowingly in her mirror, showing her teeth, clapping her hands and slapping her thighs as she complimented herself on all the worldly knowledge she had been able to impart to her precious charge.

Damama lay, in the still of the night, staring at the ceiling. With luck, in a little while, they would be quartered together and she could have a brass bed so she wouldn't creak from every aching joint. She heard the muezzin calling the last call of the night. The sound broke her train of thought and she called back to him loudly, "Quiet out there! There's folk tryin' to sleep in this damned prison!"

In the secret room, the lovers spent hours of delicious exploration, moments of calm affection and seconds of precious ecstasy, in a night never to be forgotten. At dawn, Aimee rose and returned to the Sultan's quarters to be taken back to the harem by waiting eunuchs with the silver litter.

Selim lay alone, lovingly touching the bedcovers, picking up a jewel fallen from Aimee's hair and smiling at his thoughts. What had she said? "You are the lover *all* women dream of . . ." He watched the rising sun and thought of her. A peacock shrieked in the outer court-yard, fanning its tail proudly for all to see. Selim rose and washed himself in the pearl-inlaid bathing chamber, sing-ing and marveling at the memory of his glorious first night of love. He was a man! A man with a beautiful lover of his own. He would never love anyone but her. He put on his robes and passed through the garden to greet his father.

"I ordered food for you, I felt sure you'd be hungry!" the Sultan said.

"I am a man, Father, as you are. I can love and fight and dare things I never thought possible."

"And you can think a hundred times better than all of us. I am very proud of you, my son. Someday, you'll be a ruler to be remembered."

Tears of joy ran down Selim's face. Until recently, life had been lonely, full of strange fears, doubts and the hideous, haunting memories of childhood. Now this sprite from a far island had come like a magic charm to change everything.

Servants entered with bowls filled to overflowing with figs, grapes and walnuts. Others followed with pastry, cof-fee and rose-leaf conserve. Selim was famished. He ordered a wild duck pie and a compote of peaches. He chattered like a child of lessons he planned to take, schemes he was formulating and dreams he longed to discuss. His father sat back, watching him happily, deeply at peace with his son for the first time since the days of his early childhood.

Aimee was sleepy. Damama, noting her languour, asked no questions. It was obvious that her charge was far away in the romantic world of true love. The head eunuch arrived to take coffee, peering into Aimee's face and as-sessing her exhaustion.

"Mademoiselle Blue Poppy, you are *tired*."

"Course she's tired! It's hard work bein' a Sultan's fancy woman."

"Come, follow me, I have a surprise for you both. After you, Madame Damama."

The eunuch sidled along the wall, keeping one eye on Damama. Aimee followed, yawning sleepily.

"Your new quarters are ready. The Sultan ordered that you were to have everything you desire. I was informed this morning by the Ketkhuda that all the arrangements are complete and everything is as I instructed. All that you wish has been granted. You're a lucky child, Mademoiselle Blue Poppy."

"How about the beds!" Damama asked.

"Those are here also, Madame Damama."

Damama rushed along the corridor, chortling joyously. The eunuch opened a heavily carved door and presented his tribute. Aimee looked around, delighted by what she saw. She ran through the hallway to a receiving room, bedroom, private bathing chamber and kitchen. On the opposite side of the receiving room she found a room for Damama with its own small bathing chamber. In both bedrooms, large brass bedsteads were hung with silk curtains and covered with counterpanes elaborately encrusted with pearls. The walls of each room were decorated skillfully, intricately in colors Aimee loved, coral, rose, violet and gold. And outside, in her own personal garden, a gazebo of gilded cedarwood was painted with scenes of her island home.

Aimee examined the garden house with feverish delight. The flowers in her own garden were all blue, poppies, lilies, lavender and spiky meadow grass, their scent intense and heady. She sat down, overwhelmed by all that was happening.

"Thank you for what you've done. It's really beautiful."

"I only carried out the Sultan's orders, to be truthful."

"Where's Damama?" Aimee asked as she looked around.

"I think Madame has gone to sleep on her new bed. She was complaining bitterly yesterday that she hadn't slept properly since her arrival in the city of the seraglio. She'll probably sleep all day!"

Aimee ran to Damama's room and looked down, lovingly, at the sleeping figure. The eunuch stood by beaming proudly.

"Shall I stay here always?" Aimee asked him.

"Perhaps."

"Why do you say perhaps? Why would I have to move?"

"If you become powerful you would have quarters in another part of the harem. The Sultane Valideh's quarters are far from here."

"I prefer these rooms to any I've seen."

"Well, you surely will stay for many years, and if I know you, you'll live where you wish!"

"I can see the sea and the land that runs by the side of the bridge."

"I've ordered your special herb pots to be brought to you and now I need a favor *please*."

"Of course, anything."

"Some more cough syrup for my sore chest."

"Have you drunk all the medicine in that big bottle I made for you?"

"My cough plagued me in the night. I didn't drink it all at once."

Aimee sighed, patiently.

"I'll make you some more in the morning."

The eunuch left, fanning himself contentedly. He went straight to the Circassian's suite to tell her that her protégée was now settled in the quarters adjacent to her own. They chatted for an hour, debating whether the God of the French mademoiselle could really devour the Khan's black soul.

# Chapter 16

*As weeks passed, Aimee settled to life as the* Sultan's captive. Each night, she was taken down the golden road to amuse him with funny stories, songs and insulting banter that lifted his depression and made him feel young again. Each night, after an hour with the Sultan, she hurried through the scented garden to the jeweled boudoir to await Selim's arrival.

During the day, she occupied herself with Damama or visited the Circassian for delicious lunch parties and an hour of scandalous gossip. Damama had begun to explore the city of the seraglio, and unable to control her wanderings, the head eunuch decided to allow her total freedom. Damama tramped for miles around the walled passages of the vast complex, discovering new places, faces and facts of which she was previously unaware. She saw the kitchens where a thousand cooks prepared food for the occupants of the secret city. She became acquainted with a one-eyed blacksmith who spoke fluent French from days long past when he was a captive of the French army of the interior. Her best friend, however, was called Haya. The woman lived in the first courtyard with her husband, who was one of the Sultan's gardeners. The Khan had killed her three sons for no reason except his own sadistic pleasure and Haya longed for revenge. Damama enlisted her willing help and the old lady began to watch the Khan's quarters. Each day, Damama visited Haya and learned who had called on the Khan, when and for how long. Damama was well satisfied with her small but faithful army of spies and she reported all her findings to Aimee. They gradually pieced together the form of the Khan's days and the details of his most frequent contacts within the seraglio.

Sometimes Aimee hated the city of the seraglio. She had no opportunity to see Selim except when the Sultan summoned her to his apartment. They could never do the things lovers enjoyed together, walking in the garden, visiting the city, attending parties or meeting friends and interesting visitors. Life in the secret city was life in a golden prison, meetings confined to the dazzling bedroom chamber and perfumed private gardens. But Aimee was happy. Selim was inventive and intuitive of her moods, loving her when she needed love, talking when she longed to chatter. He was even arranging for her gifts and notes to be sent, via the diplomatic pouch, to her cousin in far-off France. There was no doubt in Aimee's mind that Selim was the only man she could ever love, but she still hated the confining strictures of her new homeland.

When the night was clear and the nightingales sang in the trees, Aimee longed to go adventuring along riverbanks and far away to the mysterious city seen only in the distance. Instead, she ate dinner with Selim from a solid gold table, as though they were the only customers in an exclusive restaurant. Often, they made plans until the small hours, drawing imaginary new homes, small palaces, and going through Aimee's catalogs of French furniture. Claustrophobic closeness, far from being boring, drew them nearer and nearer until the two thought as one and acted in mutual harmony. Aimee fell more deeply in love each day, relinquishing her desire to return to flower island in return for Selim's devotion. He was her adored lover and she needed him as much as he needed her. Could she ever abandon him to his fate? Even if rescue came, Aimee knew she would never leave him. The city of the Sultan's seraglio would be home forever.

One night, Aimee was chattering away to the Sultan when her vision clouded and she fell against him half conscious, half confused.

The Sultan leapt up and called to a servant, "Bring water, ice and hot towels."

"I am well again, sir. Forgive me; I have been feeling weak for some days. Perhaps I have a chill?"

The Sultan rang a bell and summoned his son. Aimee lay quietly on the Sultan's couch, wishing the room would stop revolving before her eyes. Selim arrived, wide-eyed and anxious, and the Sultan whispered to him, calming his trembling hands. The young man kneeled at Aimee's side.

"Beautiful one, tell me you feel better."

"I am quite well, just a little dizzy. Perhaps I ate something disagreeable."

The Sultan gave Aimee iced water and covered her feet with hot towels. Within minutes, she fell asleep, unaware of the two anxious watchers.

"I am sure she is with child. She eats pineapple and clover honey as though she could eat every pineapple in the hothouse! For a month or more the dish has been her mania."

"What are we to do, Father?"

"Nothing. Having children is easy for women. I've fathered fifty of them and I never worry. I stay calm, quite calm. Dear me, if she has a son I shall build her a private yali and line it with diamonds! It's fearfully hot tonight, isn't it?"

"It's quite cool, Father, but you are very hot and I think overexcited."

"Imagine it! My son's first child. I shall give her her choice from the imperial treasures and behead everyone who displeases her."

"What shall we do now, though?" Selim interrupted. "She is not well. Look, her face is ghastly pale. Forget your plans and tell me how we can help her."

"You're right, I was carried away. Call the guard and

send him for the imperial physician and ask the head eunuch to bring the Circassian. She always knows what is required."

Aimee woke in her own quarters. Damama was fanning her face with an osprey fan and the Circassian stood looking down at her, smiling happily. Aimee eyed the flowing red robes, the ornate jeweled turban and ruby-sprigged shawl. How beautiful the woman was and how welcome a visitor!

"Are you better, my dear?"

"Yes, madame. I am much less dizzy than before."

"You are to have a baby."

Aimee began to weep, tears of happiness and sadness at a secret impossible to share. She longed to rush to Selim, to make plans and tell everyone in sight that she and her beloved were to have their first child.

"The Sultan had to retire. In his excitement, he fell and sprained his wrist. I have never seen him so excited!" the Circassian told Aimee.

"Is he ill?"

"No, by noon he'll be as always, but he's old and not used to such excitement."

"And Selim?"

The Circassian watched Aimee closely and said, "My son is in my quarters. He asked if he could wait until I was sure you had recovered. No doubt he wishes to take the news to his father."

"Tell him I am very well and I will . . ." Aimee broke off, aware that she had almost revealed what she most needed to hide, that she would be seeing Selim again the following evening. "I will be completely recovered by the evening."

The Circassian smiled. Aimee, she thought, was an inefficient liar. There was obviously more to the situation than she had at first imagined. She returned to her quarters, recalling the Sultan's exultation and excitement as he told of his plans for a summer garden, a sea palace, a treasure trove of jewelry to be given to the exquisite French lady. He had never proved so highly delighted at the prospect of his own offspring!

Selim, pale-faced, trembling with anxiety, came then, pleading for news of his dear friend.

The Circassian hugged her son reassuringly. "Aimee is well and happy. By tomorrow she will be completely recovered."

"Are you sure, Mother?"

"I am quite sure. In the early days of a woman's first confinement she is often sickly and faint. We must take care of Aimee. She is valuable to all of us."

Selim lowered his eyes, afraid of his mother's scrutiny. He was unhappy with the duplicity and reluctant to deceive one he loved so dearly. He looked at the wise, beautiful face, stroking the petal-soft cheeks.

"Mother, there is something I think I must tell you. I cannot keep you in ignorance of the true situation."

"Tell me nothing, my son. I think I know what you wish to reveal."

Selim smiled with relief as he held the pale silky hands. They talked and walked around his mother's garden and then he went silently back to his own suite. He looked out on the dark waters of the bay, aware that his mother's wisdom and understanding would support his most earnest endeavors.

Aimee woke at dawn, longing to see the sunrise. Damama arrived with fruit, coffee, almond rolls and rose-petal jam. She carried the tray to the window seat and lifted Aimee as though she were a small child, setting her down on velvet cushions. Then she opened the shutters and covered Aimee with a mohair blanket.

"Are you feelin' better, little miss?"

"I'm feeling marvelous, Damama."

"You'd best let the Sultan know that you'll be havin' your son in your own quarters. I've inspected the arrangements in the harem and you're not gonna get involved with any Turkish jiggerypokery!"

"Why not?"

"They have a chair that you sit on fully clothed like you were going to a party and you drop the child, when it comes, into a little pot under the chair. A most disgustin' procedure! I told the head eunuch he could stuff his chair right . . ."

"Damama!"

"I'll look after you, like always, little miss."

"Have you ever delivered a baby, Damama?"

"Course I have. My sister Dinabelle had fourteen and I started helpin' her when I was ten! There's nothin' I don't know about babies comin' into the world."

"They'll try to make me go to the harem. It's the custom that the birth of a possible heir to the throne must be witnessed."

"Then we'll get witnesses, but we'll not go to the harem."

"I'll be too weak to fight with them by that time."

"Fight! There'll be no fightin'. *I* shall tell them what you want and they'll all do what they're told!"

Aimee settled down to months of waiting. The Sultan and his son saw her when they wished in the secrecy of the special suite and as time passed the three grew close, learning the peace of total trust. During the daytime, Aimee entertained the Circassian and the head eunuch in her suite, listening to their problems, supporting their endeavors and forging bonds strong enough to last a lifetime.

The Sultan lessened his son's wild fears and tried to still his own pounding heart. Stay calm, he advised a dozen times a day. Stay calm! If only *he* could! Every night he wondered if he would wake up grandfather of his beloved son's first child. If it was a boy he would throw such a celebration they would talk of it for decades. The Sultan sucked an opium pill, muttering praise to Allah for its calming balm.

Leaves turned gold in the gardens, giving way in early springtime to lemon blossom, lilac and then to the luxurious blooms of summer.

Finally, one morning, Aimee woke in the early hours filled with a strange cramp that made her nauseous. She woke Damama as dawn came, red gold over the horizon, and they made ready for the delivery.

The Venetian arrived, informed by her spies that the long-awaited event was imminent. The Circassian followed, alarmed at her enemy's presence.

The Venetian immediately tried to reassure Aimee. "Have no fear. I want to help you, *petite française*. At a time like this a woman needs friends around her."

"I need no one but Damama and the Circassian."

"And who will witness the child's birth? You *must* be

confined in the harem. I've already sent for the imperial physician."

"I need only my friends, and I do not wish to go to the harem."

"Are we to be deceived by a strange child smuggled in to claim rights not properly his? This birth must be officially witnessed."

"You get out of this room now!" bellowed Damama.

Aghast, the Venetian replied, "Do you allow a servant to speak to me so?"

"The birth is gonna be witnessed by the Circassian and others approved by milady. You had best go away pretty fast or I'll forget my good manners and throw you clean through the window."

"I intend to stay. The birth *must* be witnessed."

The head eunuch spoke up from the doorway. "I shall witness the birth, madame. Now return to your quarters. I am in charge of these proceedings."

The Venetian disappeared muttering under her breath as the eunuch walked in, fanning himself and bowing haughtily. As the door closed, he sat down suddenly, mopping his brow and cursing furiously. "That bitch of a mangy dog's litter has already sent her spies to Korba-Khan's quarters to inform him! I came the moment I heard, Blue Poppy."

"Thank you, my dear friend," Aimee replied.

"I shall stay in the receiving room with the Circassian until the birth is imminent. My eunuchs are outside so no one will disturb you and I've sent for the Sultan's personal guard to make sure we are all safe. My eunuchs will take the imperial physician to the Sultan's quarters when he arrives. He can wait there in case he is needed."

Sun burned on deep blue sea as Damama stroked the pale hands and wiped the sweating brow. The eunuch retired, discreetly, to read in Aimee's receiving room as the Circassian made tisanes and cooling poultices in the tiny kitchen. At nine-thirty, they heard Aimee cry out softly. The eunuch began to tremble violently. He paced the floor, muttering quietly to himself, "Dear me, what a performance. Why can children not arrive *easily* like cholera and the spotted sickness!" Aimee cried out again. The eunuch began to shake with a nervous ague and the Circassian

229

found herself comforting him with large doses of his favorite medicine.

Damama worked quietly, encouraging, directing, soothing, rushing back and forth, feet clattering on the marble floor. The eunuch decided to go to the kitchen to look for almond sweetmeats to comfort his strained nerves. He passed through the bedroom at the very moment of birth and saw that the child was a boy.

Letting out a cry of delight, he fell prostrate on his face. "Allah be praised, we have a son! Allah most wise, our thanks for this child. Oh, how lucky we are, how very lucky!"

He rose, weeping unashamedly, and threw his arms round the Circassian. "Madame, my dear friend, I am *so* happy for you and for myself and for all who hope for peace in our time."

He bent over the tiny baby, tears dropping on its hands. "Mashallah! Mashallah, little prince. I must go and inform the Sultan immediately."

"Do you know where my son is?" the Circassian asked.

"The Prince Selim is below, madame, in the blue garden, praying."

The Circassian met his eyes. The eunuch touched a finger to his lips in the sign of eternal silence as the baby cried its first cry. Below in the garden, Selim wiped tears of relief from tired eyes. It was over. He paced the narrow paths praying for the safety of his beautiful lover. After a while, he looked up and saw his mother smiling down at him. He ran to the balcony and she told him that Aimee and her son were strong and well. He went immediately to his father's quarters and together they gave thanks in the Sultan's private mosque.

"We shall call him Mahmoud," the Sultan announced.

"So be it, Father."

"When the beautiful one is awake we shall go and see the babe, and when she is well again we shall have a celebration such as we have not had in decades, not since you were born!"

"Oh, Father, I long to see her."

"You will, my son. I have arranged everything in great secrecy."

Extra guards were posted outside the corridors leading

to the Circassian's and Aimee's adjacent suites. Other favorites in the same area were moved immediately to new quarters in distant parts of the golden honeycomb. No one could enter and no one leave the entrance doors at either end of the long corridor without passing the Sultan's personal guard.

In great secrecy, during the months of Aimee's confinement, the Sultan had brought builders from Moldavia to construct a spiral staircase from the storage room at the side of his own suite to the Circassian's quarters above. He revealed his secret to Selim and they climbed the stairway and walked together to Aimee's suite in the twilight of a midsummer evening. No one could witness their arrival. No one knew of the stairway and the guards were safely outside the corridor doors.

Aimee was asleep, her son at her side. Damama was waiting, patiently, forewarned of the Sublimity's arrival by the Circassian.

Awaking to find Selim looking down at her, Aimee said, "He looks just like his father."

"We shall call him Mahmoud, if you approve, beautiful one."

The Sultan stepped forward, picked up the child and walked to the window.

"Mashallah, little one. That is your city, Mahmoud. Someday it will be yours to do with as you will."

The Sultan closed his eyes, deeply touched by the occasion, as he held the tiny bundle close to his heart. Then he returned the baby to its mother and left as silently as he had come. In a city of spies and protective secrecy, father and son had achieved the impossible. They had kept their secret.

At dawn, a fearful discord filled the air and Aimee woke to the sound of her son crying. Damama was pacing the room, shouting out of the window from time to time.

"What on earth is that noise, Damama?"

"I don't know. I've sent for the Circassian's servant to tell us what's goin' on. Shut up out there, you noisy bezums! Don't you know the baby's sleepin'!"

The servant arrived and informed them that the warlords were striking their copper mess caldrons as a sign of great displeasure.

"They will burn the city across the water as they always do when they are furious!" the servant told them.

"Why are they furious?"

"They asked for concessions as a celebration. The Sultan gave permission for a great celebration but denied the warlords their concessions. They have no right to make such a din, they do not know their place!"

"If I had my way they'd be makin' that noise in hell within the hour!" Damama said.

"Please try to stop them. I can't stand it much longer," Aimee pleaded.

"They will bang their drums until they are ready to burn the city. Milady, no one can stop them. They have always done this and they always will. Time changes nothing in the city of the seraglio."

Aimee began to sob, her exhausted body racked with tension, her mind confused by the barbarous customs of her new home. The sound of the beating of the warlords' kazans continued as ten thousand angry men surrounded the city walls battering hollow copper caldrons. The cacophony continued until Aimee screamed in torment and Damama was forced to give her a sedative.

The head eunuch arrived, determined to soothe away her fears. "They are burning the city now, Mademoiselle Blue Poppy. A couple of hundred of the wooden houses will vanish. Then they will rape and pillage and plunder like the barbarians they are. Oh, if only *I* were Sultan I'd have their heads for my lawn!"

"Quite right, those buzzards need seein' to pretty quick," Damama agreed.

Aimee covered her baby's face as the faint smell of burning filtered through the window. Damama locked the shutters and they waited, silently praying for the tumult to cease. At nightfall, silence returned. The warlords' revolt was over. In the concourse of the warlords' courtyard the soldiers laughed, swinging sabers and giving fantastic accounts of their exploits during the day. They had shown the Sultan their disapproval of the infidel and her son.

By the next dawn, the leaders of the revolt had been arrested. By noon, their heads joined others on the plane tree in the first courtyard. The Sultan was furious. As a further punishment, he ordered half rations for a month for the rest of the recalcitrant force.

Korba-Khan sat in his quarters looking at his own souvenir of the revolt. He smiled grimly at a child's bonnet, for he had impaled a dead boy on the city wall for all to see. Someday, he would do the same with the infidel's son. He looked in the mirror and noted for the first time a strange yellow tint to his skin. Greatly alarmed, he sent for a doctor and then retired to his room to curse Aimee Dubuq de Rivery. If only she were dead, he would be well again! She had cursed him and told him her God would devour his soul. Korba-Khan looked anxiously in the mirror. Surely his skin couldn't be changing color?

He sent for the Venetian's servant and one of her faithful mute dwarfs. He gave the most explicit instructions on a matter of the greatest urgency. The mute's eyes shone with malevolent glee as he ran on crooked legs back to his mistress with the warlord's instructions.

For many weeks the Sultan and his son were engrossed in preparations for the celebration. A thousand nightingales had been imported, ten thousand sugar blossoms made in the imperial kitchens and a bower of spun pink sugar erected in the sugar maker's kitchens to rival anything ever seen in all of Europe and Asia. Jugglers, fiddlers, dancers and magicians were ready, camped on the outskirts of the city, and a troop of French actors arrived from Marseilles to perform especially in honor of the new prince and the beautiful one. Extra flowers, imported from Moldavia and Bessarabia, graced the courtyards, and a sea of blue poppies bobbed merrily in the royal enclosure.

The awaited day dawned a crisp autumn gold with a clear blue sky. At noon, a fanfare of trumpets sounded and the Noble Guard marched into the Sultan's courtyard taking their places behind his personal guard. Below, on the road outside the great wall, the warlords appeared resplendent in lynx-edged jackets and bright leather boots. White eunuchs preceded the black eunuchs in ceremonial procession and ambassadors to Constantinople arrived, bedecked in scarlet and gold.

Another fanfare ordered the procession to commence,

and mounted horsemen led a parade presented by the trade guilds of Constantinople. The Sultan beamed as the Seamen's Guild enacted a sea battle on a float hung with deep blue silk. The crowd shuddered as the Executioners' Guild displayed instruments of torture. Children laughed as pastry cooks offered fresh cakes, and veiled ladies stared wide-eyed at stuffed animals in the taxidermists' display. Lion keepers marched by, leading their beasts on ornamental gold chains. The lions yawned, ferocity controlled by handfuls of meat well dosed with opium. Dolphins, sea lions and sea cows appeared in tanks on the fishermen's float and five thousand beggars ran by ragged, wild-eyed, one-armed, blind, halt and lame from the quarrelsome Beggars' Guild of the great city.

The Sultan lifted the baby over his head, acknowledging the crowd's cheers, and roared approval with a regal nod. And in a window overlooking the imperial enclosure, Aimee prayed for Mahmoud's safety. She heard the Sultan order the feast to begin and soon Damama arrived back with the tiny bundle. Mahmoud was asleep, unaware of the jubilation his presence had caused. Below, the enclosure swayed and the crowd struggled to see all that was happening. The Sultan bestowed gold coins on favored subjects before he disappeared back to his royal quarters.

Later in the day, Aimee took her place in the great hall with Damama, the Circassian and the women of the harem to watch a performance by the visiting French players. Tall screens had been erected and draped in brocade to hide the occupants from the actors. Each woman cut a small vantage hole and watched the stage, giggling and making rude comments as the actors struggled to please their unseen audience. At the end of the play, the actors were ushered out and magnificently rewarded. Then they were taken to the port and dispatched hastily back to Marseilles.

Aimee returned to her quarters with Damama, delighted with all she had seen. Damama was strangely silent. The leading actor had been such a fine fellow that she had fancied exploring his masculine potential. But as the afternoon wore on she had felt a little sleepy and she realized for the first time that her female appetites had begun to wane. The idea depressed her enormously and she went straight to bed.

She was lying in the big brass bed when Aimee came to find out what was wrong.

Looking down at her beloved nurse, Aimee said, "You look sad, Damama."

"I'm gettin' old, that's what."

"How do you know you're getting old?"

"I thought that big fellow in the play looked good enough to eat. Then I started feelin' sleepy and forgot all about him. It's old age, little miss. My life is over, my female appetites have gone to sleep!"

"We all lose our appetites someday, Damama. It doesn't mean we're old and useless."

"I wonder what Monsieur Armande's doin'. I keep wishin' I could see him again. Sometimes, I think of him all day and all night and all day again."

"As soon as we can we'll write to him."

Damama looked out of her window at the busy seaway and said nothing.

"Damama?"

"Yes, little miss?"

"I still need you. And now you have another child who needs you more than I ever did. If your female appetites have gone to sleep you're still the best nurse in the whole world and I want Mahmoud to benefit from all you can teach him. You just have a good sleep and make up your mind that you're going to live to be a hundred so you can take care of him until he's as tall as you!"

Damama lay thinking. Live to be a hundred, indeed! She smiled suddenly. She might do just that.

The next day, the Venetian's mute dwarf arrived with a gift of sweetmeats for the Blue Poppy. Aimee was astonished at the kind gesture and ashamed of herself for having been so hostile to the Circassian's rival. She took the gift, smiling politely at the misshapen creature prancing back to the door, but started when Damama called to the mute before he could leave the room.

"Come here, you little buzzard, and eat one of these fancy contrivances," the black giantess commanded.

The creature's eyes rolled and he made strange noises in his throat.

"You hear me, come here and eat one of these things!"

With surprising speed, Damama ran to the door, grasping the dwarf as he turned to run. She swung him like a crumpled doll on the floor at Aimee's feet. The Circassian arrived, disturbed by the commotion, as Damama stuffed two of the sugary confections from the gift box into the dwarf's mouth. Then she bent low to watch his reaction. The mute spat the sugar on the floor. The Circassian watched, eyes hard, heart pounding. Aimee sat quite still, as though mesmerized by the grotesque scene. Before they could move, the mute ran for the window and leapt, arms outstretched, to the ground. They leaned out to watch his flight but he had fallen awkwardly and was lying, neck broken, deformed legs alarmingly spread-eagled like a dead animal.

"Were the sweetmeats poisoned?" Aimee gasped.

"Obviously they were. I told you, my dear, the Venetian uses poison as others use sugar!" the Circassian said with a shudder.

"Damama?"

"Yes, little miss?"

"How did you know what she had done?"

"The Khan sent for the Venetian's mute the other day. I know cos Haya and her daughters watch his quarters for me."

"I don't want to believe all this."

"Don't worry, little miss. I intend to look after you like I promised your mama I would and that's just what I'll do."

The three friends talked until the small hours and Aimee explained to the Circassian that she intended to educate her son in the French style. He would not be tended by surrogates in the harem. He would not be pampered, spoiled and doted upon. He would eat food cooked by Damama or his mother and nothing else. Mahmoud would be permitted to go out only with the Circassian, his mother or a member of the Sultan's personal guard. The Circassian nodded, relieved at Aimee's caution. The French mademoiselle had finally learned the perils of this most dangerous place.

That night, Aimee crept to the ruby-studded cradle and bent to watch the sleeping child. How beautiful he was,

236

how fragile and precious. She lifted him in her arms and kissing him gently said, "We must take care of you, little one. They want to kill you, but I shall look after you and love you forever." She looked down at the solid gold cradle, its jewels glowing in silver moonlight, and thought how lovely life would be in the seraglio if it were not for the terrible ambition of its occupants.

Celebrations of the young prince's birth continued for three days. On the second day, Aimee received gifts from the Sultan that thrilled and astonished her. Rubies like thrush eggs in a box of inlaid lapis, chessmen of ebony and cut tortoiseshell, ivory carvings and a necklace of swinging, glittering diamonds elaborate as a French chandelier. Aimee was entranced as box after box appeared with the compliments of her adoring "husband." The Sultan sent messages that she would be taken to see her new yali on the far edge of the seraglio grounds as soon as she felt strong enough. Aimee was thrilled at the prospect of having her own summer home away from the curiosity and animosity of the harem. Perhaps she would send for furniture from famous emporiums of France. Perhaps, for a brief moment, she would pretend she was back on flower island. She waited impatiently to regain her strength so she could visit the palace-in-miniature.

In the next room, Damama dusted the ruby parasol. Since the evening she had received it, it had stood against the wall of her bedroom unused and untouched. The jewels and heavy gold handle awed and intimidated her. Damama had never seen such a work of art. She began to practice secretly for her first visit to the new summer home. She would take her jeweled parasol with her and surprise little miss with her fancy ways. She staggered under its great weight, grinning at her stylish reflection in the mirror. What a perfect sight she was, an almost perfect sight. She waved the umbrella back and forth and then lay down to rest to recover from the muscle-pulling strain.

On the third day of the celebration, the head eunuch brought two final presents. Aimee opened them, examined them and burst into tears. The first was an ormolu clock decorated with fine champlevé enamel work. The box in which it lay bore a gold-embossed label, R. Dugret, Horloger Royal, 26 Place de la Concorde, Paris. Aimee thought of all the times she had complained to Selim that she had no idea of the time. The seraglio had no clocks, the hour traditionally recorded by the cry of the muezzin. Tears rolled down her face as she unwrapped the second heavy parcel. Its cumbersome shape, when opened, revealed an enormous book, part encyclopedia, part gazeteer, part fashion and furniture catalog and part gossip writing on the current French social scene. Aimee dried her eyes and examined the extraordinary volume more closely. She realized it was many separate books bound together between a specially illuminated cover. On the flyleaf Selim had written "For my beautiful one, to read when passing the lonely hours until we can be together . . . always."

She touched the book lovingly, entranced by its fascinating pages. She ran to Damama and they looked more closely at her present, laughing, crying and dancing with delight.

"Oh, Damama, I love him a thousand gold louis!"

"I'm glad you do, little miss."

"The first time I met him I was just kind, though I like him very much and pitied him because he was so pale and shy. But then I fell in love with him and now I think he's the kindest, cleverest man in the world. If he died I should jump in the sea!"

"Stop thinkin' of such dreadful things! You'll jump nowhere, you've got your own little prince to look after!"

"I'm so lucky, Damama. So very lucky."

"We'll not have a easy time, little miss. We've enough enemies to make a army."

"I know, but we'll be together, won't we, Damama?" Aimee kissed her cheeks and they sat together poring over the mammoth volume.

Night came and with it, the sound of silence. Wrestlers, jugglers, gypsies and strolling players dispersed and the occupants of the city of the seraglio slept.

Far away, in wild country outside the great wall, a jackal lay in wait for a wildcat. The cat screamed as the jackal pounced; and its mate, hearing the alarm, ran like the wind to its aid. Sounds of grim conflict raged and far away the jackal lay dying. The wildcats ran stealthily to safety away from their attacker.

Korba-Khan lay in his quarters listening to the distant sounds of the night. A jackal and a wildcat? The jackal would triumph because a jackal was always stronger than a cat. The cry of the cat rent the air and the answering cry of her mate, fiercely growling. Then, there was silence. The Khan frowned. The jackal seemed ominously subdued. The wildcats continued to communicate until their cries faded into obscurity. The Khan was displeased. The strong one had been no match for the weak united.

# BOOK III

*Friends
and Enemies*

# Chapter 17

*A letter arrived for Aimee, her first for so many* years. She saw it, lying in a solid gold box, delivered by Selim's most trusted servant, Ahmin. Her heart began to flutter as she took the violet envelope and saw Rose's childish scrawl. As soon as the servant disappeared, she read the letter voraciously, pleased that Selim had kept his promise to help her contact her dear cousin.

My dear Aimee:

Today, a man came to my door and said he was from the residence of the Turkish ambassador. He showed credentials which seemed in order and asked me to write a letter to you. Oh, my dear, can you really be alive after all these years? Your guardian, Monsieur Lautrec, made inquiries everywhere after your ship disappeared but he could find no news of where you had gone. Everyone in Martinique believed you dead, except me. I have always longed and waited for you to contact me again. The gentleman refused to say where you were living but I am assuming that you are in his country, Turkey. Please write, if you can, and tell me you are well and happy.

I have two children now, Aimee, their names are Eugène and Hortense. Recently I sent them to stay with friends in the country because these are troubled times in France. Alexandre, my husband, was taken into custody to answer questions the other day. Goodness knows I don't understand why, but it seems, lately, that being an aristocrat is a crime as grave as stealing and being a murderer. Anyway, the children are safe so I am not too worried. If Alexandre is not released very soon, I intend to take my family back to Martinique. We can wait there until all these troubles are over, and it will be so lovely to be home again. Politics are a frightful bore, don't you think? I don't understand anything of what is going on.

When I hear from you, I shall send you a long letter and tell you *all* my news. Do you realize, Aimee, it's six years since I last wrote to you, but I still think of you every day. Please write to me very soon.

As always, your loving cousin,
Rose

The Sultan called for Aimee's son on his seventh birthday and showed him the burning houses of the city across the water.

"The warlords have set fire to the city again because they wish to show their displeasure at your existence. They do this every year and no one can stop them."

"Mama talks often about the warlords. She says you need them to fight on our far borders so you can't cut their heads off."

"How is your mama today?"

"She's not very well. Every time she hears the sound of the warlords' kazans she becomes so angry her head aches and Damama has to give her a tisane of camomile."

244

"And what do you think of this?"

"I shall kill them when I am a man."

"All of them?"

"Yes, every one. Mama says it's the only thing to do."

The Sultan looked down at the small, solemn face. Mahmoud resembled Selim, with luminous dark eyes and silken black hair, but his soul and spirit were those of his mother. The boy was already a tiger, too young to fight, too tender to hurt, but with a warrior's vengeance buried so deep that someday he would succeed in controlling the warlords where others had failed.

"Mustapha is back from the gray country, papa."

"How is he?"

"Mama says he's mad!"

"Why?"

"Because he stares so wildly and he never speaks. I think he's mad too. Last week he rode his horse through the selamlik and it trod on a slave and squashed him to death. Then he rode out of the city and tried to trample Damama."

"And what did Madame Damama do?" the old man asked, always eager to hear of Damama's exploits.

"She pulled him off his horse and hit him very hard on the head with her gold-handled umbrella."

The Sultan roared delightedly. "What a woman she is! If all French Creoles are like her and your mama they must be the greatest race in the universe."

After Mahmoud returned to his mother the Sultan sat thinking of what the child had said. He sighed. The Venetian's son was the very devil, quite the opposite of Selim. Where one had a dedicated desire for work, learning and peaceful pursuits, the other rode with the warlords, fighting on frontiers and behaving like a barbarian. The Venetian was proud of her son's eagerness for valor but even she feared the silent depths of his black soul. Mustapha's only true friend was Korba-Khan. The Khan loved him with a fanaticism that bordered on idolatry. Mustapha was his candidate for ultimate power. Mustapha loved violence, death and defilement as much as the Kahn did. The Khan lived for the day when he would see the infidel's head on the warlords' plane tree—the day when Mustapha would be crowned Sultan of Ottoman.

Aimee listened to the warlords' drums, writhing in an agony of despair. How long would it last? Would it ever end, this hideous defiance, this cruel persecution?

She told Damama of her meeting the previous day with the Khan, shuddering at the memory of their conversation. She had been wandering with an accompanying guard of eunuchs in the city of the seraglio. They had passed from the inner courtyard through the third court and the Gate of Felicity to the warlord's enclosure. For the first time since her arrival in Constantinople, Aimee had seen the plane tree and shivered again at the decaying heads of those who had displeased or disagreed with imperial omnipotence.

Korba-Khan had appeared at the door of his dwelling, beckoning her attention. Determined not to appear afraid, Aimee had followed despite the eunuchs' urgent entreaties. She had stood in the doorway of his cell, listening as he taunted her.

"Tomorrow is your son's birthday. I shall order my men to burn the city as I always do. You must be surprised to see me alive and well despite your curse."

Aimee observed the skeletal thinness of the man and his yellow skin. She saw the blueness of the Khan's nails and smelled the sickly odor of his foul breath. She said nothing, aware only of a strange feeling that she was being watched. She searched the room and saw the deadly black plant beloved by the warlord. Following her gaze, he took live red butterflies from a jar and fed the plant, smiling as Aimee recoiled in horror.

"This is a plant from Cathay. Natives there call it the flower of death or the devil's flower. See how greedily she eats these pretty butterflies. I have the plants brought especially for my pleasure. I am never without one of my greedy little companions."

Inner petals glowed green and two eyes watched, seeming to follow the Khan's every move. Aimee saw long black tendrils flick out and the flutter of red wings disappearing into a cavernous mouth. The Khan threw back his head and laughed his madman's laugh as she turned to leave, nauseated by the ugly sight.

"Tomorrow we shall burn the city and soon I shall burn your son and eat his fat legs for my dinner."

"Look in the mirror, Korba-Khan. Your skin is yellow

and your nails blue because your blood stagnates. Your breath stinks because your intestines are putrefying. You are a very sick man. My God works slowly and without mercy. He will not grànt you a speedy death because you are evil and the evil are made to suffer for many long years. You'll live until you cannot walk and are forced to crawl or be carried about your business. Then, at the very moment when you long most to continue, you'll breathe your last and be buried and forgótten!"

Aimee had turned on her heel and returned to her suite.

A second later, Korba-Khan stood looking in his glass. The infidel was right—his skin was decaying, his once strong body ached from an unknown malady that all the doctors of Pergamum could not assess. He lay on a couch, eyes closed, lips fervently mouthing crude curses . . . "May her eyes pour blood, may abscesses grow on her body and may she die in agony among rabid dogs and the scum of the earth . . ."

Aimee shuddered recalling the meeting. She glanced at Damama and thought immediately of her love. She ignored the white hair, the brown skin now faded to pale coffee. Damama's eyes still shone and her temper was as volatile as ever. But now she often felt tired and each afternoon she went to sleep on the big brass bed so she could be wide awake to entertain Aimee's friends during the evenings with favorite tales of flower island.

Damama thought about Aimee's story of her meeting with Korba-Khan. Each year on the young prince's birthday, Damama's heart filled with murderous loathing. But she waited, biding her time and hoping that someday things might change. If not, she felt sure the opportunity would arise to rid her beloved one of their most dangerous enemy.

They sat together looking from the windows to the road below. Peasants shouted insults to each other and Damama laughed at the quarreling men.

"Damned heathen Turks, all they like doin' apart from cuttin' off heads is shoutin' loud enough to be heard in Paris!"

Across the river, a Genoese tower drew Aimee's attention. In the Jewish section of Galata, mansions of stone and brick withstood all the warlords' evil destructiveness. Jewish traders had allied themselves with political and religious fugitives from other countries, Italians, Armenians, Greeks and Spaniards. They worked hard, feared no one and theirs was a lasting prosperity. Aimee watched, curiously, through her spyglass. The people of Galata dressed like Algerians in baggy trousers, tasseled hats and short, loose jackets. They smiled and laughed and shouted, enjoying their own noise in an area that was a hive of industry. Sailors, merchants, craftsmen, tradesmen vied with each other in a living bazaar that looked like a Western city but thought like an Eastern one.

Aimee looked longingly across at the place tradition decreed she could never visit. If only she could go out! If only she could walk free, far away from watchful eyes ever present in the city of the seraglio. She looked down on the silent courtyards, grimacing at their spy-ridden calm. She had learned, long ago, to control her longing for flower island. Mahmoud could never leave the seraglio and she could never leave him. Her adored Selim had used ingenious thought, a treasure house of jewelry and all his precious love to find ways to take her mind off the harsh longing for home. Aimee was deeply grateful for his thoughtfulness. As time passed, she loved him more, and waited, impatiently as always, for the nights when he would come secretly to visit her. But sometimes she prayed for a miracle. Sometimes, like the day of her meeting with Korba-Khan, the longing to escape was so powerful it hurt.

The Circassian arrived moments later to lunch with Aimee. Aimee looked at the older woman, trailing yards of exotic ruby-studded satin and showers of scented jasmine. Despite her sadness, the younger woman smiled and confided, "I was thinking of flower island."

"I can always tell when you think of home, Aimee."

Anxious to lift her spirits, Aimee called to Damama, "Where's Mahmoud?"

"Young prince is lunchin' with the Sultan, little miss. Ours is just about ready now. I'll bring it back," Damama answered as she left the chamber.

"Have your men reported any news, Madame?"

"None that we want to hear, Aimee. Mustapha has gone back to the front with the warlords. They say our army will be victorious and I'm told Korba-Khan plans to leave

248

twenty thousand men in the provinces and only ten thousand in the city of the seraglio. Oh, and one other thing! The Venetian saw the Sultan yesterday and made demands he would not entertain, so she threatened him and he had her removed to her quarters and locked in!"

"What did she want this time?"

"The usual recognition for *her* son, not yours. A post in some distant province for Mahmoud so her son can get his hands on the throne. I think she will plot to kill us all if she fails to attain her ends. I only wish the Sultan would see her for what she is—a most dangerous lady."

A Nubian slave arrived to play the baglama. The girl was pretty and talented and Aimee listened happily to the sweet music for a while. But she realized that no sounds were coming from the kitchen, and she went in search of Damama. But even the old spice room was empty.

"I don't understand. Where can Damama be?"

"She said she was going to bring back our lunch, didn't she?"

Aimee nodded. "She never disappears like that."

The Circassian helped Aimee prepare the food, enjoying the unaccustomed labor and comradeship it involved. Afterward, they lounged and picked from a meze of white beans, onions, fried liver, delicate pastries and heaped yellow rice. They were about to take coffee when Damama rushed in, feet clattering, arms waving wildly, voice roaring like a fish vendor. "Little miss, I have somethin' terrible to tell you. Oh, Lord, what a calamity!"

"Calm yourself, Damama."

"The Sultan's ill. I reckon they've gone and poisoned him."

"What are you talking about? You said you were going to the kitchen to make lunch. Where on earth have you been?"

"I was cooking lunch when I saw Korba-Khan in the distance takin' a walk with the Sultan's new food slave, that squintin'-eyed fellow from the Danube. Sight of them together sent shivers down my spine so I ran outside and followed them to the ice pits."

"The ice pits, what were they doing there?" Aimee asked.

"I don't know, but when Korba-Khan left he was laughin' like a hyena and that slave went and served lunch to the Sultan. Now they say the old fellow's sick and we'd better do somethin', little miss. Sure as hell they've poisoned him. I feel it in my bones."

The Circassian ran to the door and called the head eunuch.

"Madame, my dear lady, what can I do?" he asked as he came rushing in.

"You must give this message to the Sultan at once and bring Prince Mahmoud back to his mother."

"Is something wrong?"

"The Sultan's new food slave has been seen in the ice pits with Korba-Khan!"

The eunuch rushed away, teeth chattering in agitation. He reached the Sublimity's quarters and was informed that the Sultan was asleep. The little prince was nowhere to be found. The eunuch called the head of the Sultan's guard.

"Where is Prince Mahmoud?" he demanded.

"The Sultan felt sick after his lunch. He now rests in his bedchamber. The food slave was sent to return the prince to you so you could return him to his mother."

"But I have not seen him! Dear me, what a disaster. I am a martyr, sir, a true martyr."

The eunuch rushed away, muttering wildly, fat rolls undulating, arms swinging at his side. He reached Aimee's quarters and reported his findings to the Circassian, who immediately called the guard. Minutes later, the eunuchs brought the captain of the guard to her quarters. Unaccustomed to entering the women's quarters, he blushed furiously and appeared uncertain how to react to receiving orders from a member of the Sultan's female household.

"Hussein Pasha, Prince Mahmoud has vanished. He took lunch with his father, the Sultan, but the Sultan was taken ill and now rests in his quarters. The new food slave was told to return the prince to the head eunuch, but Mahmoud has not been seen. The food slave *was* seen, however, in the ice pits talking with Korba-Khan."

"I shall search the Khan's quarters immediately."

He turned to his aide and ordered him to call the Noble Guard to assist in the search.

"The warlord will not permit you to enter his quarters," the Circassian warned him.

"I take my orders from the Sultan, not the warlord, milady."

Aimee watched as the captain disappeared. She felt dizzy and sick, her head like lead, her knees like water. She went quietly to her room to lie down, silently praying for her son's safety. Fury buzzed in Damama's head at the cruelty and treachery of this secret place. She thought of the Khan and fervently wished him dead. She paced the room cursing him loudly, then she went to comfort Aimee and found her weeping. The Circassian returned to her own suite to pray for the child's safe return.

Mahmoud followed the new food slave through an underground passage from the ice pits to the courtyard of the Divan. Blinking in strong sunlight as they emerged, he followed the slave happily as they hurried through the second enclosure. He was thinking of the wonderful secret passage he had just been shown. Tomorrow, he would tell his Uncle Selim of the new route. Selim had shown him every known passage within the walls, but even he did not know of the one from the ice pits.

Mahmoud hesitated as he saw Korba-Khan emerge from his quarters. Uncertain what to do, but aware that a prince of the royal blood must not show fear, he wondered what his mother would say if she knew where he was. Aimee had expressly forbidden her son ever to speak to the evil one and Mahmoud loved her far too much to disobey. As he considered what course of action to take, the food slave lifted him in the air and bundled him through the Khan's door.

The door slammed and the boy picked himself up from the floor. The warlord was waiting for Mahmoud and was surprised to see that he was calm and unafraid. The Khan examined Mahmoud with curiosity. The infidel's son was tall for his age, slim and fine-boned like his mother. The Khan walked round, slowly assessing his prey.

Mahmoud knew he was in grave danger. He debated whether to shout and scream for help. But he knew the warlord's dwelling was surrounded by the quarters of his own men and traders' houses and shops. No one would help the son of the infidel for fear of Korba-Khan. He wondered if the Khan intended to put him in a sack and throw him in the Bosporus and he remembered Damama's story of the big snake and the little mongoose. He waited, quietly, thankful that he had been taking lessons in the ancient martial arts of Cathay from his uncle's skillful instructor, Nsai. Nsai had taught Mahmoud that a young boy could overpower a grown man if he became master of the art of silent combat. Mahmoud hoped Nsai was right. Soon he would have the opportunity to test the old man's assumption.

Mahmoud brightened as he watched Korba-Khan pacing the room. The Khan's face was yellow and his breath stank of decay. Perhaps he was dying? Mahmoud smiled happily at the thought. The Khan sat down, furious at the calm, happy face. He motioned the boy to approach.

"I am Korba-Khan."

"I know."

"And you are the son of the infidel."

"I am the son of Aimee Dubuq de Rivery and the Sultan Abdul Hamid."

"That is untrue, but unimportant. If you wish to think you are the Sultan's son you can remain an ignorant fool."

Mahmoud frowned, uncertain of the Khan's meaning.

"Do you know why I brought you here, boy?"

"No."

"No, *my lord!*"

The Khan's black eyes glittered as he took the jar of trapped butterflies and fed them to his devil plant. Mahmoud watched, disgusted by the cruel sight. His heart began to pound inside his narrow chest but he stood firm and returned the Khan's gaze unflinchingly.

"You know a slave from Cathay called Chang?"

"Yes, I play with him and the son of Hussein Pasha."

"Chang's father, Nsai, cannot speak. You know why, I'm sure?"

"He can't speak because *you* cut out his tongue!" the prince replied defiantly.

"And he has no fingers. Do you know why?"

"Because *you* cut them off!"

"Do you know why I cut them off?"

"No."

"I cut them off because it pleasured me to do so."

"Nsai can still fight in the ancient way of the warriors

252

of Cathay even without his fingers," Mahmoud said as he continued to return the Khan's gaze.

"In a moment, I shall cut your tongue out and send it to your mother. Then I shall cut off your fingers and send them as a small souvenir of her son."

Mahmoud watched every move of the Khan's hands.

"Then I shall throw you in the sea and sleep easier in my bed because the loss of you will kill your mother."

"You cannot kill me. Many people saw me come here. The Sultan, my father, will have your head for the plane tree."

"The Sultan will never have my head. I am Korba-Khan, chief of the warlords, and *I* rule this kingdom. My men dictate what the Sultan may do, because without us he is nothing. Without us he would lose his Empire and die in chaos and anarchy."

The Khan drew his dagger and advanced on the boy. Mahmoud prepared for the attack, circling warily as he had been taught to do. As the Khan grasped his shoulder, the boy twisted his body away, raising his leg in a kick that caught the Khan's spine a resounding blow. The warlord stumbled and Mahmoud whirled like lightning, kicking again and catching the Khan's groin. The warlord stooped, momentarily, in agony and the boy kicked desperately with all his force, breaking the Khan's jaw.

The warlord fell, striking his head on the stone floor. He lay, arms widespread, face contorted in painful immobility.

Mahmoud listened to the silence and the sound of a fly buzzing. He looked toward the window at the evil black plant. Then he climbed on a chair and pulled it from its pot, snapping the stalk until black tendrils disintegrated on the dusty floor. He was stamping its watchful face into the ground when he heard the sound of marching men. He ran to the door and into the arms of Hussein Pasha. Then he burst into a flood of tears and wept as though his heart would break.

Hussein Pasha saw the warlord lying unconscious on the floor, his mouth agape, his jaw out of alignment. He took Mahmoud's hand firmly in his own and walked with him past the dreaded plane tree into the second courtyard.

"What happened, little prince?" he asked finally.

"The Khan ordered the Sultan's new food servant to bring me to him. I didn't know of this; the servant told me only that Mama had a surprise for me. He took me through a secret passageway to the Khan's quarters. I'll show it to you tomorrow."

"Then?"

"The Khan said he had cut out Nsai's tongue for his own pleasure. He kept laughing a horrible laugh and I felt a bit sick. He fed butterflies to a black plant and it ate them! I didn't cry, though, Hussein Pasha. I didn't even let him see how frightened I was."

"You're a great little warrior."

"Korba-Khan took his dagger and said he was going to cut off my fingers and send them to Mama. Nsai had been teaching us a special way of fighting. We learned that a child can overpower a grown man if he masters the martial arts of Cathay and it's true! I must go and tell Uncle Selim! He's learning the fighting art too. What do you think Mama will say, Hussein Pasha?"

"First she will cry, then she will laugh, then she will throw a celebration for you, little prince."

Damama roared till tears ran down her face. She hugged Aimee delightedly and congratulated Mahmoud till he hid his face from her admiring gaze. Aimee wept, then she laughed, then she decided to throw a party for her son. She held him close, stroking his hair and telling him how much she loved him. After a while, Mahmoud disappeared with Damama to find the special ingredients for a celebration cake covered in sugared violets, his favorite sweet. Aimee lay on the silken bed thinking how much she loved the boy and how she wished fervently she could spend every hour of the day with his father.

Selim, too, heard the news and summoned Mahmoud to his quarters.

"I've sent for Chang and his father, Nsai. I intend to promote Nsai to the rank of my personal gardener. He and his wife will come to live in a special house in my gardens and Nsai will continue to instruct us both in his special way of fighting."

"Are you pleased with me, Uncle?"

"I am more than pleased with you, Mahmoud. I have a very special present to show you."

Mahmoud ran along by Selim's side, exclaiming, "Show me quickly!"

"There . . ."

The boy saw nothing but an empty room next to his uncle's receiving chamber. He stood quietly surveying a vast stone fireplace inscribed with signs designed to keep away the evil eye.

"What should I see?"

"Nothing, because there is nothing to see!"

"Are you joking? Is there really no present?"

"Follow me, Mahmoud, if you dare . . ."

Selim stepped up inside the chimney. The boy followed eagerly behind. Once above the hearth, a staircase was revealed and a narrow dark passageway.

"If you continue straight up there the wall ladder leads to the roof. Remember that in case you ever have to escape with your mama."

"And the little passage, where does that lead?"

"Follow me, carefully, and you'll see," Selim bade.

They crawled on all fours, through total darkness, emerging triumphantly from the storage cupboard in Aimee's bedroom.

She was resting, half asleep, but leapt up, eyes wide, heart thumping, at the appearance of her unexpected visitors. "What on earth are you doing?"

"This is my present from Uncle Selim, Mama."

"Present?"

"A secret stairway to the roof and a passage to your room. We must use it if ever danger comes."

"I've been working for two years on the stairway, beautiful one. I wish you could see my handiwork."

"Then I shall."

"No, you cannot, you'll dirty yourself."

"If we're to use it in emergency, I'd better know where I must go. Lead the way, Mahmoud, show me what I must do."

Mahmoud led her back along the dark passage and down the stairway to the empty room next to Selim's receiving room. They emerged, dusty but delighted, returning to Aimee's suite by the same route.

Damama was in the bedroom, hanging silk gossamer dresses in a gilded wall-robe as they stepped out covered in dust from the cupboard. She stared, openmouthed, at the new arrivals. "Oh Lord! Now what? Folk startin' to come out of the damned walls!"

"It's a secret place, Damama. Uncle Selim made it for us."

"There's more secret passages in this city, little prince, than there are real ones. I don't know, a body can't do anythin' without gettin' frightened clean to death."

Aimee and Damama ate dinner that evening with the Circassian. They toasted Mahmoud's miraculous escape from Korba-Khan's clutches and talked merrily until the last call of the muezzin. But their happiness was short-lived. As they were about to retire, news came that the Sultan was dying. He wished to see Selim and the Circassian immediately.

In the small hours of the morning, the Circassian returned sadly to her quarters, where Aimee was waiting. She drank a rose-leaf tisane as Aimee helped her undress.

"If the Sultan is alive in the morning, he asks to see you and Mahmoud."

"Is he very ill? He seemed so well yesterday."

"He's old and his heart is tired but I think Madame Damama is right. The food slave surely poisoned him with a slow-acting draft."

Aimee could not sleep. She thought, with horror, how suddenly death came in the silent city and how much she owed to the wisdom and support of the dying man. She remembered his delight on first meeting, his eager presentation of the secret room where she and Selim became lovers. Abdul Hamid had protected them, encouraging their love and being an adoring father to his son, Selim. She sighed.

If the Sultan died, the Circassian would become Sultane Valideh and Selim would be crowned Padishah of the Faithful. Would the warlords accept him? Would they know peace at last and live as a happy and contented family? She longed for Selim, missing his presence and the loving touch of his hands.

Before dawn, Aimee dressed and prepared her son for his last visit to the man he called father.

The head eunuch appeared as the sun rose. "Hurry, Mademoiselle Blue Poppy, the Sultan waits for you and he will not last the hour."

They ran together down the golden road.

Aimee looked at the Sultan's face, so wise and tolerant. His eyes showed sadness at parting, and his voice, sometimes strong, sometimes fading into the oblivion of exhaustion, quivered as he greeted her and Mahmoud.

"How pleased I am to see you, little tigress, and you, my son. Kiss me. There's a good boy."

Mahmoud kissed the Sultan's hand and his cheek and sat on the silken couch playing with the fringed covers.

"I must be ill! You've not told me how awful I look today."

Aimee smiled at the memory of the insults of earlier days which had so amused the old man.

"In those days there was much to criticize because you dyed your hair and painted your cheeks. Now you have the courage to look as old as you really are!"

"That's right, make me die laughing. No one ever treated me so. It's been a most glorious experience."

Aimee recounted, in detail, Mahmoud's adventures of the previous day. And the Sultan hugged the child to his chest as they sat quietly talking together.

"Korba-Khan will try again, you know," the Sultan warned.

"Is he to remain free?"

"There were no witnesses to his treachery and if Selim began his reign by beheading the chief warlord he wouldn't continue for a week! They would see him dead and Mustapha on the throne. You must be patient. In time, Selim will form a new army as you suggested and then he can overpower the warlords. But without an army one man can do nothing. Mahmoud?"

"Yes, Father."

"You know I am dying?"

"Yes, Father."

"When I am dead, your Uncle Selim, will take my place as Sultan and also as your father. You must obey and love him as though he were your *real* father. Tell me you understand and that you promise to obey."

Mahmoud's eyes filled with tears.

"I already love my uncle as though he were my father and I will always obey him. When I grow up I shall fight at his side and kill all the warlords so they never upset us again!"

The Sultan smiled contentedly, closing his eyes in peace. Within seconds, the sound of labored breathing ceased.

# Chapter 18

*Aimee received another letter from Rose shortly*
before Selim's accession. This time, it was written in nearly
illegible writing on plain, cheap white paper. Aimee wondered what on earth was happening to make Rose so
nervous she could barely write. And why was she writing
on what looked like the inside of a cheap paper bag?

Dearest Aimee:

This is a very short letter because I am in prison.
Alexandre is dead, murdered by this bloodthirsty
mob of ruffians. I cannot tell you what they are
doing to the aristocrats because it is too terrible. My
children are safe, thank God. But I don't know if I
will ever see the light of day again. I would like to
tell you everything that has happened to me but I
have only this small piece of paper begged from a
fellow prisoner and I am so nervous I can barely
write. In France, there is a revolution. It's all too
horrible for words and if I did not believe Eu-

phemia's prophecy I should die of fright a dozen times a day.

Yesterday, a new head of the Army of the Interior was appointed. His name is Barras and he called me in for questioning. I put on my best white muslin, thinking I might as well die looking pretty as looking awful. I made my way to his office trembling like an aspen. You cannot imagine what an oaf he is, fat as a Christmas goose and just as greasy. He made unmentionable suggestions to me till I cried like a waterfall, then he told me to give him an answer by Saturday, that's tomorrow. I have been trying, desperately, to decide if freedom is worth doing what he wanted me to do. I shall think about it again later as it's too upsetting to dwell on just now.

Aimee, I am sending this letter via a brave friend who comes to the gates of the exercise yard and risks everything carrying messages for me. If you can write, please send your letter to my house in St. Germaine. Pray for me. I need everything to help me make my decision.

> As always, your loving cousin,
> Rose

In the dawn of a golden day, Selim was proclaimed Sultan and Emperor of the True Believers. He immediately ordered all the childless members of the harem to be retired to the women's quarters of the Old Harem on the banks of the Bosporus. Those with young children were permitted to remain in the harem so their offspring could be educated in the imperial school.

Aimee wondered what Selim's accession would mean to their relationship. Would he still love her and see her often as in the days of his father's reign, or would he fear a scandal and the roar of the warlords' drums? That night, Selim came to her through the secret passageway.

He reassured her that nothing would alter, calming her fears and soothing all doubts about the future. "Nothing will change, except that I shall be Sultan instead of my father's heir. I have many plans for us and for Madame Damama."

"Tell me about them."

"Would you have me waste the night talking? Well, I see you would! First, I intend to build you a beautiful yali on the banks of the sea, and then a secret route by which we can visit the city together."

"But now you are the Sultan . . ."

"I am still Selim, I have not changed at all. Did you think I would become a different man the day after my father's death?"

"I wondered if you would fear a great scandal. I have a son that the people believe is the son of Abdul Hamid. If I visit you or you come to me the warlords will know of it and perhaps they will realize that Mahmoud is the son of Selim, not of the Sultan who has just died." Aimee was trembling.

"Beautiful one, we cannot live our lives according to what the warlords will think."

"I love you, Selim."

"And I you, and soon, when my plans for my country are complete, you will have no need to fear the warlords."

"Will you send them away?"

"No, but I intend to limit their power."

"How?" she asked.

"Leave my work to me and I shall do everything I can to keep you safe and happy. Now, stop asking questions and tell me you adore me."

Selim smothered her face with kisses, making Aimee forget all she had feared. Selim loved her, of that she was sure. She told herself he would find a way to deal with the cruel warlords.

Selim immediately initiated many changes within the palace.

As a precautionary move, the Venetian was isolated in new quarters inaccessible from other parts of the innermost sections of the city of the seraglio, except through the quarters of the head eunuch. Hussein Pasha was given the honor of being made a member of the Sultan's personal household.

The Pasha of Rustchuk, a childhood friend of Selim's,

was promoted to general of the frontier forces. He was a fiery man, seven feet tall and full of laughter, banter and rude imaginings. His women friends were legion, his valor undisputed even by his enemies and he had always worshiped the learning and sensitivity of the new Sultan. The Pasha was convinced that with Selim's accession, Turkey would again be great, no longer corrupt, no longer controlled by harridans in the harem and the threat of the warlords. As he took the oath of allegiance, the Pasha of Rustchuk wept tears of fervent patriotism.

If Aimee was awed by the genial giant, Damama was stunned. She watched his vast frame lumber through the golden corridors and disappear along the city wall with excitement.

"He's a good-lookin' fellow, that Pasha of Rustchuk. If I was ten years younger I might have given him a bit of trouble."

"He asked who you were. Selim told me," Aimee said.

"Did he now?" Damama asked with curiosity. "And what did Selim tell him?"

"He said you were a lady from the far islands of the southern ocean and that your ancestors were warriors. He wants to meet you, Damama."

"How old is he then?"

"I don't know. He must be older than Selim. Perhaps forty."

"Well, I just might take him and show him a few things around this place that he never even heard of. He looks to me like he could fight an octopus all on his own. You never know when we might need him real bad."

The Pasha finally met Damama on one of his trips to the secret city, and expressed a determination to familiarize himself with its three great sections. On one of his walking tours with Damama, he stood outside Korba-Khan's quarters and bellowed to his guard, "This is the chief warlord's dwelling. Mark it well and let him know you watch him every hour of the day!"

Inside, Korba-Khan lay suffering still from his injuries, unable to reply. Damama beamed ecstatically, slapping her thighs and encouraging the Pasha in a loud voice. "Follow me, sir. I'll show you a place you never dreamed possible. I only discovered it myself the other day."

"You're a fine woman, madame of the far islands. How many husbands have you annihilated?"

"I didn't trouble with husbands, sir. Husbands get the habit of curlin' up and smokin' their pipes and forgettin' their marital duties. But I enjoyed the company of many excellent gentlemen in my younger days. Now I'm fifty-eight years old and I'm too old to think of such excitin' things!"

"The twinkle in your eye says you're lying, madame."

Damama blushed furiously. She looked him up and down, winked and hit him a great blow with her gold umbrella. The Pasha's laugh resounded through the seraglio. Far away, watching from her window, Aimee burst into peals of laughter and threw herself on her bed. The Pasha of Rustchuk was probably the first man Damama had ever met in all her life that she had been able to look up to! The two made a fine pair of giants.

A few weeks later, the Pasha departed for his home in the provinces. The Sultan stood outlined against vivid blue sky, waving a last goodbye as his friend disappeared into the far-distant landscape. Selim was sad. With his good friend around, the city of the seraglio seemed safe and even hospitable. But now the warlords began again to plot and debate how best to rid themselves of their unwelcome ruler.

But as time passed, peace reigned, and on sunlit afternoons Aimee and Damama picnicked in the yali on the shores of the Bosporus. Cedarwood walls, carved like delicate lace, formed the facade, and a gilded roof shone in the sun. Inside, everything was in the French style, ordered from the catalogs Aimee had kept from years long past. In moments of loneliness, she read the leather-bound book Selim had given her until she had memorized its out-of-date contents. In the summer palace, she imagined she was in France, queening it over her own exclusive salon. In the long warm months of summer, fear, treachery and the warlords' loathing seemed as far distant as her home on flower island.

Damama had long complained about the lack of liquid refreshment in the city of the seraglio. Cordials and sherbets were too sweet for her taste and both she and Aimee longed to take wine with their meals. But wine was forbidden and for years they had contented themselves with tisanes and iced lime juice cordial. Then, one day, Damama came home triumphantly bearing a case of the finest French champagne.

"Where on earth did you get that?" Aimee asked.

"I acquired it, little miss."

"But *where* did you acquire it?"

"Well, I met a fellow who works in a bawdy house in the Galata district and I told him I was just burnin' for a drink of French champagne and he brought this for me."

Aimee thought for a few moments as Damama shifted uneasily and pretended to look out of the window.

"And what did you give him in return?"

Eyes rolling, mouth pursing, Damama tried desperately to avoid the question.

"Damama?"

"Well, you know the carts that arrive with silk from Brusa and fine velvet from Lord knows where. They put them in the first courtyard and then unload them into the stores."

"Yes."

"One of them disappeared."

"You stole it!"

"I accidentally let it get took. He's bringin' another case next week and a dozen more on the first of the month. It's old age, little miss. My poor old bones ache somethin' terrible for a drink of fine champagne."

Damama beamed winningly and Aimee kissed her cheek reassuringly.

"You're a scoundrel; nothing but a scoundrel!"

"But I'm a useful scoundrel, you've got to agree. To your good health and happiness, little miss. God bless you!"

Damama tried the wine and smacking her lips tried it again. Uncertain as to its "quality," she drank a few glasses to absorb the flavor and then opened another bottle and drank that too. Then she retired, singing loudly, to the hammock under the tamarisk tree. The sun shone warm and golden as she swung lazily back and forth, dreaming of Monsieur Armande and catching iguanas on flower island. Within minutes she was sound asleep, snoring loudly.

Aimee welcomed Selim to the lunch table and offered him a sample of the surprise gift.

"Try this and tell me if you like it."

"How can I drink it when bubbles go up my nose? What is it? I don't care for it at all."

"Drink it first, and then say you don't care for it."

"I'm not sure what I think. It's most peculiar!"

"Try a little more, and then tell me what you think," she coaxed.

"It's very good for the thirst."

"Some more?"

"What is it?"

"This is the finest French champagne."

"Alcohol is forbidden by my religion! Would you turn me into an infidel?"

"No, of course not. I'll drink the rest. I shouldn't have offered it to you."

"No, I want to finish it."

"Why?"

"Because if you drink it it cannot be evil. I hope Damama will like it. Where is she?"

"She's asleep on the tree hammock. Can't you hear her snoring?"

"Is that what it is? Only giant people make noises like that. When the Pasha of Rustchuk snores they say it can be heard in the city across the water!"

"The champagne made her drowsy. Sometimes it does," Aimee explained.

"Women have weak heads."

"Would you like some more?"

"Of course. It has no effect on me."

An hour later, when Selim tried to rise to walk with with Aimee in the cool of the evening, his knees wobbled and his eyes closed and opened and closed again. He felt confused and uncertain of what was happening.

"Is the room shaking, beautiful one?"

"No, of course not."

"I've been poisoned. Call the imperial physician immediately!"

"You haven't been poisoned, Selim, the champagne has made you drowsy, that's all."

"I'd best lie down."

"I'll help you undress."

The sound of a bouzouki tinkling in the outer courtyard

provoked Aimee to a hip-swinging dance. She threw her clothes on the pink marble floor, laughing merrily as Selim sat watching, senses dulled by the fine wine into unaccustomed passivity. Aimee jumped on the bed, undulating above him, amused by his confusion as she threw her clothes on his bewildered face.

"I think I can see two of you!"

"Then you'd better love both of me, hadn't you?"

"You're a wicked woman."

"No, I'm enticing. All *créoles françaises* are enticing!"

He grasped the creamy thighs, pushing her head on the bed as her hips whirled provocatively before him. He felt strangely distant from the proceedings as he explored her secret places and provoked her to ecstasy. Aimee sighed, deeply content, as he touched her sensuously, sinuously with increasing urgency and curiosity. Who would have thought the timid young man of years past would have grown into such a wonderful lover?

Hours passed and sunset came to calm waters. Aimee lay peacefully asleep, dreaming of days of love and nights of intense feeling in the scented boudoirs of the summer palace.

The Sultan sat, half bemused, half aware, looking down on her. What a new world she had opened for him. He sighed, delighted with her, as always. Tomorrow, he would send for a hundred cases of the sparkling wine that she loved. He would ask her how best it should be stored and perhaps he would build a special secret cupboard in which to keep it. He thought of his religion and sighed. He wanted what she wanted whether it disobeyed the stringent rulings of his religion or not. Sharing was exciting and nothing seemed important enough to prevent the joy of being one.

Each day they walked arm in arm in the garden. After lunch they played with Mahmoud, praising his gift for languages and his ready wit. Sometimes, Damama showed them card games, cheating expertly as always and winning a fortune from the hapless pair. Aimee was so happy in the peace of the summer palace that she wished, fervently, that she could remain in its isolation forever. But autumn came and the harsh chill of winter and soon they were back, overlooking the blue garden.

In the winter months Aimee surprised everyone by asking for a French dancing master. Hilarious evenings were spent with Damama, Mahmoud and the Circassian, learning the intricacies of new and fashionable French dances. In the Sultan's occasional absences, Aimee spent her time embroidering pillows, making tisanes, jams and pickles in the Creole style and telling Mahmoud stories of valorous French knights. It was her constant emphasis on the superiority of Frenchmen that provoked her first quarrel with Selim.

It was springtime; pear and peach blossoms scented city air with subtle sweetness and newborn lambs gamboled by their mother's side in fields outside the city wall. Aimee was telling Mahmoud of the day in Lyons when she had seen two brave Frenchmen fly in balloons. Selim walked out of the room, furiously jealous. Aimee ran after him, shocked to see him angry for the first time.

"Selim! Why are you so angry?"

"I am sick of hearing you tell Mahmoud of great Frenchmen! He has become a completely French child, there is nothing of my country about him. He's my son, too, you know, and someday he will be Sultan of Ottoman, not King of France!"

"What should I tell him about?"

"Some of my ancestors were great men. Some of them were conquerors of half the world. Why can you not tell of their valor and distinction?"

"The only distinction your ancestors ever had was that they perfected the art of cutting off heads!"

For a moment, there was deathly silence. Damama stared in alarm and disappeared to her room.

But Selim turned to Aimee, icily shattering her composure by saying, "That is no longer correct, beautiful one. *Your* country now has that distinction. They have perfected a machine that cuts off heads more quickly and more efficiently than anything my ancestors ever dreamed of. They call it a guillotine, and I'm told by our spies they intend to use it to cut off the head of every aristocrat in France who opposes them, including the King's."

Aimee collapsed, face ashen, hands trembling. "What are you saying, Selim?"

"It's true, beautiful one. I am desolated but it is true.

Some time ago the mob stormed the Bastille and ever since France has been in turmoil. The people are dissatisfied, hungry and overtaxed. They believe the King is responsible so they are going to try him and some say they will have his head. Many feel that thousands will die before this is over."

"On what basis will they kill?"

"Only the highborn will suffer."

Aimee thought of Cousin Rose, lonely, forsaken but eminently well-connected. She began to tremble violently.

"I wish to go to my room."

"I love you. Please forgive me for being so cruel."

"Go away! What can you do for me and for those I love and can never see again? What can you ever do for me?"

"I can die for you," he replied slowly.

Aimee looked at the earnest face and kissed the silky hands. "This is our first quarrel."

"We should celebrate our survival, beautiful one."

"With champagne?"

"And a thousand kisses. Say that you know I love you and have always loved you. I'm so sorry to have distressed you. I was never going to mention the problems of your country."

In the night, Aimee rose as Selim lay sleeping. She looked out over the rooftops and listened, but the city was silent as a tomb. Only the gentle lapping of sea on shoreline relieved the intense emptiness. She watched until dawn came, a bird sang and cooks rushed to their kitchens to make breakfast for the hungry occupants of the city of the seraglio. Weary and anguished, she made her way to the pantry, where Damama was preparing a tray laden with yogurt, white cheese, olives and wild sage jam. She sniffed new bread and scented coffee and hugged her nurse as they talked in whispers, not wishing to wake the household.

"Damama, they are cutting off the heads of all the aristocrats in France. They have imprisoned the King and Selim says they will kill him. Whatever can we do for Rose? If she is still in prison, does it mean that they will cut off her head also? Oh, *mon dieu!* Whatever can we do?"

"We can't do a thing, little miss. But if I know anythin' Rose'll find someone to look after her. Are you sure Selim is right? I never heard of such a thing. Sounds more like what happens here than in France. After all, the French are a civilized race, not barbarians like these jiggers."

"Selim's spies have reported it. They say a machine has been invented that cuts off heads. It is called a guillotine."

Damama shuddered at the thought. "I'm sure as hell gettin' old. When I was young such happenin's didn't exist and I'm real glad they didn't. Now, here's your breakfast. Where do you want to eat it?"

"Under the window."

"Still wantin' to go out?"

"I always want to go out."

"I could take you. We could go by the secret passageway that Mahmoud showed us through the ice pits. It comes out on the other side of the city wall."

"They'd know and I'd be punished, or worse, you would!"

"Selim wouldn't punish you!"

"I couldn't go unless he said I could."

"Oh Lord! What a woman; one minute you're goin' crazy cos you can't go out, next minute you're all obedient and docile."

"I'm not docile!"

"I know you're not and you just remember it. If you want to go out, go!"

"Women don't leave the harem and the inner courtyard in Turkey, Damama. I'm lucky to be allowed out into the third and second courts of the seraglio."

"You are not women. You are Aimee Dubuq de Rivery and you do what you want, always have, always will. You had your baby how you wanted to. You brought him up to be a good French boy just how we planned. You've done everythin' you wanted, so why stop now!"

A messenger arrived with a note for the Sultan. Damama greeted him graciously and asked him to wait in the Circassian's quarters. Selim dressed at once and went to his mother's suite. Hussein Pasha was waiting with an urgent dispatch.

"My Lord, spies working for the Pasha of Rustchuk have captured one of the messengers of the warlord Korba-Khan. He was carrying instructions for Mustapha, who is on his way back from Ankara."

"What were the instructions?"

"They were to tell Mustapha to attack the seraglio to-night, sir. I believe they intend to usurp the throne and kill you."

"How many men can I rely on?"

"One hundred and fifty, perhaps more."

"And the warlords?"

"Twenty thousands are in the provinces and ten thousand on the Russian front. In the city of the seraglio and the center of the capital there are about ten thousand."

"Send a messenger to the Pasha of Rustchuk and tell him that I need his help."

Selim had made arrangements that in the event of trouble in the seraglio, he would control the entire water supply. Within a few days, the warlords' wells would run dry and to drink from the river would be certain death. He had also purchased new arms and ammunition from France, loading new equipment in the storerooms of the Sultan's pavilion and moving staff formerly quartered there to other parts of the building. Now, only Aimee, Mahmoud, the Circassian and Damama lived in the tower of the Rose Pavilion. Selim looked out at blue waters outside his window and wondered if the new war machines from his secret and revolutionary foundry could be made ready in time to save their lives.

"I had hoped we would never need all I have prepared," Selim mused. "Now, go and bring the loyal men to the royal enclosure, quarter them in the former servants' building and use my father's old kitchens for their provisioning. The new arms store is next to the menagerie. Here is the key; see you guard it well. Hussein Pasha, I have one other surprise."

"Sir."

"I have built a cannon foundry and brought in French engineers to make new war machines. Unfortunately, they are not ready yet and neither are my new ships, so we must try to do our best with what we have."

"You've done well, sir. Be confident that what you have told me will remain a secret. We can only pray to Allah that the Pasha will come to our assistance."

The attack did not come that night, though the silent watchers were ready in the quadrangle of the Rose Pavilion. Some slept, some talked and the Sultan donned his armor.

In the twilight, before dawn, Damama prepared food and filled water jars to be stored in Selim's secret passage. Every few minutes she ran anxiously to see if the warlords were advancing, cursing Korba-Khan and his followers with Creole maledictions. Aimee waited at her window, praying for the arrival of the Pasha of Rustchuk. She had great faith in the giant and his devout loyalty to Selim.

A red dawn came and with it the sound of the shuffle of soldiers' feet, the metallic murmur of armor. As the warlords surrounded the Sultan's enclosure, intoning their marching chant—Kerim-Allah-Rahim-Allah—Aimee saw that they were led by Mustapha, the Sultan's half brother. The madman waved his sword and urged Selim to surrender peaceably.

Meanwhile the Pasha of Rustchuk had arrived, and quietly led his men to the Rose Pavilion by the underground passage from outside the seraglio wall. Silently, they took their places and set into position the new light cannon from the Sultan's arms store. By first light, three thousand men were ready to defend the royal enclosure, training their cannon outward on the warlords. Aimee withdrew to the secret passageway as the first booming shots rang out. Damama beamed. The Pasha had done what no one expected. He had come to their aid, silently, secretly, by the hidden route from outside the city wall that she had once shown him.

The Khan had anticipated an attack by the main gate, and he prepared to attack, unaware of the Pasha's presence. Warlords surrounded the Rose Pavilion, their depleted numbers thinly spread around the vast enclosure. The Pasha's men prayed for victory, content that they had only a small area to defend.

Within an hour the warlords were scattered, felled by cannon shot and the Pasha's deadly archers. Some fled to wild country at the far reaches of the city limits, some were killed by the archers or captured and imprisoned. For hours the battle raged, walls shook and the Pasha roared encouragement like an angry lion. At Selim's side, he defied the warlords, decimating their number with careful strategy and incredible courage.

Inside the passageway, Damama swore she would kiss the Pasha of Rustchuk till his head wobbled off his shoulders. Aimee sang songs of flower island to comfort them all.

Suddenly, Mahmoud tapped her shoulder gently. "Listen, Mama. I believe it's all over."

They listened and heard nothing. Then, gradually, they discerned the sound of the wounded moaning, the dying calling for their sons. Aimee emerged from the passageway and heard the Pasha roaring outside her window, "Is everyone safe up there?"

She remained behind the gilded window screens and called to him, "We owe you our lives, sir."

She heard the Pasha ride away and the sound of his conversation with Selim.

"How many are dead?" Selim asked.

"Of ours, my lord, only about fifty. Of the warlords, ha! We reduced their numbers a bit. They began with ten thousand; now about two thousand are dead."

"We've been lucky, my good friend," Selim declared.

"We stayed firing from behind the walls of the Rose Pavilion as you ordered. My archers did the rest."

Mustapha disappeared and the Venetian remained locked in her quarters, fearful of her fate. Despite Aimee's entreaties, Selim would not punish her. The Venetian continued, as months passed, to send messages via her faithful mutes to the warlord Korba-Khan. The warlords had suffered heavier losses than had at first been estimated. A month after the uprising, only five thousand remained in and around the city, and Korba-Khan was forced to send for reinforcements from the front line. In due course, another five thousand soldiers returned from frontier duty to strengthen the Khan's hold over the city.

Selim poured money into the cannon foundry, the naval school and the building of a secret regimental training academy under the aegis of the Pasha of Rustchuk. The warlords sent spies to the recruiting centers and, from time to time, tried to infiltrate the elite new ranks. Each time, the Pasha sent the hapless spies' heads back on a silver salver. On sightless faces he pinned the message: "Remember, Korba Khan, the Pasha of Rustchuk can *smell* a warlord!"

For a time, there was peace and deceptive calm.

# Chapter 19

*Some time later, Aimee received another secret* letter from Rose, in Paris. The mood of this letter was very different from that of the first, and Aimee was relieved to know that Rose was deliriously happy.

My dear Aimee:

What a long time since I last wrote! You cannot imagine what has happened in my life. In a thousand years, I warrant you could not guess. When I was released from prison, Barras kept me like a pet dog for a few weeks and then tired of me. As usual, he wished to get rid of me and he passed me on to a young man you have met, Napoleon Bonaparte. Bonaparte is marvelous and I love him dearly. He asked me to marry him every day for a year but I said no, because the spring of my life is past and I did not know if I could preserve his ardent love which amounts to mania. Well, I never intended to marry him but Hortense and Eugène pleaded so prettily that I said yes and now I am the wife of Napoleon Bonaparte. I am older than he is, of course, but nothing matters because he adores me and says he will stay with me forever.

Only one thing troubles me now and that is his absences. He is forever away fighting and he cannot understand that I am not at all interested in war. Soon, we shall be moving from this pretty house in the Rue Chantereine to a veritable palace called Malmaison. The gardens are magnificent and Bonaparte has promised to bring me shrubs and plants from all over the globe. He keeps his promises, Aimee, and I feel sure that this time my luck will hold and the only man I have ever truly loved will stay at my side forever. His family hates me, by the way, and they are worse than Monsieur Charles and his retinue, the very worst, cattiest little group you could imagine. But I don't care! Bonaparte swears he will be Emperor of France before long and that his sisters will have to carry my train at the coronation. What fun, don't you think, Aimee?

Probably, it's only a dream but I enjoy pretending that Euphemia's prophecy has come true and you will be Sultana of Turkey and I Empress of France. I'm sending you some pressed flowers and all the catalogs, also some fashion talk on the latest trends in everything of interest to a lady. Thank you for your gift, I was overwhelmed by the sight of such jewels and had to go to rest for an hour until I could recover my wits sufficiently to examine them. Aimee, this is the jolliest letter you will ever receive from me because today I am the happiest woman in the world.

As always, your loving cousin,
Rose

Postscript: Napoleon Bonaparte says Rose is a good name for a serving wench but an improper name for an aristocrat. He has changed my name and rechristened me "Josephine," which he thinks a very fine name for a lady. Isn't he an amusing fellow?

During the time of peace that followed the Pasha of Rustchuk's victory, Mahmoud grew strong and confident, loved by his mother, his true father and the ever doting Damama.

To celebrate Mahmoud's birthday, the Sultan gave him a string of pure white horses and a personal stable with grooms, guards and every luxury befitting his rank as heir to the throne of Ottoman. Mahmoud was so excited that he rushed to tell his mother the good news. He found her sitting by the window, longingly watching the distant scene. Something despairing in her attitude made him pause. He watched for a moment, then ran to her, throwing his arms around her neck and kissing her joyfully.

"Mama, why are you sad?"

"I've been in the seraglio for many years, Mahmoud, and in all that time I've never been outside the city walls. When I was young like you I ran free and went fishing with Damama or shopping in St. Pierre. And all my life, until I came here, I could go where I wanted, when I wanted, with whom I wanted."

"I love you so much, so much," the prince comforted.

"I'm sick of being a prisoner. I want to go out and see the bazaars and the quarter of Galata. I want to ride in the countryside and breathe fresh air."

"Damama said she'll take you. And I could come along! We could pretend to be peasants and dirty our faces so no one would know us," he ventured.

Aimee looked down on the eager face and kissed the olive cheeks. "You're the best son in all the world and for you I'd happily be a prisoner forever. But sometimes I just long to be free again. You must ignore my grumblings, Mahmoud. Women can be very silly," she said cheerily.

"You are never silly, Mama." But he could not forget the uneasy face, the soulful eyes. He gave his mother a hurried kiss and ran in search of Damama. Running anxiously toward her, Mahmoud said excitedly, "Mama is unhappy. She wants to go outside!"

"I know she does. She been wantin' it for years."

"Oh, what can we do, Damama?" The young prince was overcome with concern.

"I reckon you'll have to have a talk with your uncle and get him to let her go out on a little excursion."

"He'll say no," he replied sadly.

"If you tell him your mama'll get sick as a old lady with spotted fever he'll let her go out. After all, she might die of unhappiness bein' trapped like this for the rest of her life."

"I'll go at once. Don't tell Mama where I am or she'll be disappointed if I fail."

"I won't tell her a thing, little prince. You just do your best for her and make sure he says *I* can go too. It's my job to protect your mama."

Mahmoud thought carefully for a moment and asked, "You're getting a bit old now, Damama. Can you still protect Mama?"

"I shall protect her till I get so old I shrivel up and die."

"I love you, Damama. Tell me I shall be lucky with Uncle Selim."

"You can't fail, little prince."

Mahmoud arrived in the middle of Selim's lunch. He approached the gilded table, smiling winningly at the Sultan.

"Uncle, I have a very serious problem I would like to discuss with you."

Selim looked down and thought how like his mother the boy was, not in looks or color but in the depth of his feelings and the determination of his manner. He stroked the silky dark hair as he drew Mahmoud toward him.

"Tell me your problem then."

"Mama is sad today, I think she has been crying."

"Why? Is she ill?" Selim asked anxiously.

"No, she's not ill."

"Allah be praised. You troubled me."

"She wants to go out in the city across the water and she cannot."

Selim looked at the child sadly.

"Mama has never been outside the city of the seraglio. That is why she is so upset."

"And she can never leave, Mahmoud."

"But I have been everywhere with you. I've visited the gray country and the training ground of the Nizam Djedid at Rustchuk. I've seen the caravan route from Lycaonia and the buffalo in the rivers of Cappadocia. I tell Mama all about my travels but it's not the same. *She* wants

276

to feel free to go to the market or the bazaar. I don't know what to do with her."

"She cannot go out!" Selim insisted.

"Why not?"

"Because with her hair and her eyes she would cause a sensation and everyone would follow her."

"We could cover her with veils and a big black cloak."

"And who would guard her?"

"You could release Hussein Pasha to go. He wouldn't mind."

"I cannot ask him to do that! We already make a hundred concessions to the beautiful one, living like Frenchmen at her instigation, drinking champagne and ignoring our traditions. Allah will turn on us like a tiger someday! Women do *not* go out. Forget the matter, Mahmoud."

"But it's not fair!"

"It is the custom."

"It's the custom for Turkish ladies, Uncle. But Mama is a *créole française* and she isn't like our women. You've put her in a cage like the one our princes used to live in before Father's day. Now she longs to be free. I think her heart will break and she'll die if she doesn't go out. Oh, whatever will I do without her?"

Selim leapt up and paced the room. "Have I not enough trouble without this?"

"You told me to tell you if Mama was ever unhappy. Now you tell me you don't wish to know."

"I cannot bear to think of her sad."

"You love Mama, don't you?"

Selim looked curiously at his son's anxious face.

"What makes you say that, Mahmoud?"

"I know you love her but you don't love her as much as I do. When I'm Sultan I shall take her out. I don't care for tradition; it's nothing but a nuisance!"

Mahmoud ran away and hid for an hour in his favorite secret place in the dense branches of a weeping willow tree. Then he returned to his mother's suite and played in the corner of her room with his new silver trumpet.

That evening Selim arrived for dinner and Aimee greeted him happily, unaware of the tension between her two men. Mahmoud frowned across the table from time to time, declining to play any of his favorite games with

Selim after dinner. As dusk came, Damama carried silk carpets to the garden and made strong coffee and luscious honey pastries. She paused, mouth gaping in astonishment as Selim made an announcement.

"Tomorrow, you are to go out, beautiful one."

Mahmoud ran to kiss his father and Aimee leapt up frantic with excitement. Barely able to believe her ears, she kissed Selim and thanked him for the extraordinary surprise.

"Where shall I go? I can't believe it, I truly can't believe it."

"You've been wanting to go out for a long time, I understand, so you can go to the city across the water. You'll see the capital of Constantinople and all its most interesting areas."

"Why are you doing this, Selim?"

"Because you are unhappy and I want only for you to be at peace with your life here in the seraglio. Don't look so worried. I've arranged everything personally."

Aimee flushed with shock and pleasure.

"Damama and Hussein Pasha will go with you. You are both to wear old clothing and be covered as our women are covered when they walk out. Hussein Pasha will be dressed as your servant and will follow a route which I have specially ordered for your interest."

"I'm amazed. No, I'm speechless!"

"You'll be interested in what you see, beautiful one. I know it will do you good. I hope you have a very memorable day."

"But what of tradition?"

"My dearest one, since you came to the city of the seraglio you have trampled on every tradition that exists. You changed my father's mind about everything. You brought up your son as a Frenchman. Your nurse adventures around the seraglio and interferes in everyone's quarters. Even the selamlik isn't sacred to her! Why, for your good, should I deny you this one last break with tradition!"

"I love your surprise."

"You must thank your son. He's a very persuasive young man."

Hours later, Aimee lay awake, thinking of her day of

precious freedom. How kind Selim was to be willing to set aside the traditions of a lifetime in order to make her happy.

At dawn, Aimee and Damama were led by a subterranean route to the path outside the seraglio wall. Donkeys waited to take the strange trio across the bridge to the narrow streets of the capital. Breathing deeply, Aimee luxuriated in the knowledge that the walls of the silent enclosure were far behind.

Damama sang loudly until Hussein Pasha begged her to be quiet. "We must take care, Madame Damama. Our ladies do not sing in the French manner."

Hussein Pasha sighed. What next? What further devotion would be required of him after this astonishing expedition? Then, he looked at Aimee's radiant face and his heart melted. How beautiful she was, hidden under gray gauze and the mysterious black cloak. Damama roared to her donkey and rode ahead, red silk parasol waving excitedly.

On the roadside, they saw men wrestling bears in booths and elderly lined faces smoking nargilehs in coffeehouses heavy with the smell of tumbeki. Aimee grimaced at mud and filth in deep potholes and rat-ridden alleyways. She asked a hundred questions as she trembled with sheer joy at the glorious feeling of freedom. Hussein Pasha rode on, happy to disobey the rules of a lifetime to please the exquisite milady.

They paused to buy sweets from a vendor and again to buy sherbet in a cypress-lined square. Smells of spice, ginger, cardamom and jasmine filled the air as they toured the colorful stalls in the noisy spice market. Aimee fingered the amulet Selim had given her against the evil eye, smiling at his fears, superstitions and innocent alarm at her departure. For Selim this was a great and unprecedented undertaking. For her and Damama, it was a brief return to normal life.

The passing scene was strangely exotic. Traders shouted, clients chattered, bells rang and everywhere men worked to make money. They ate lunch at a stall near the port, relishing simple dolmas and a stew of aubergine and parsley. Aimee bought pickled okra, onions and cucumber, delighted to have something uncontaminated by the warlords' loathing. For Mahmoud she selected crystallized apricots and figs and creamy peaches from the southern provinces. Damama carried her purchases, grumbling under her breath at the insanity of buying anything when they could have everything they wanted free.

At every corner, new vistas delighted Aimee's eager eyes. She paused to examine piles of pomegranates, melons, plums and pears; dancing fiddlers, tumblers and acrobats caught her eye. The tiny soup kitchens, where the poor of the city lined up to be fed bowls of steaming soup, threw Aimee off guard. Misery and poverty did exist away from the regal splendor and plenty of the city of the seraglio. Flies buzzed in the faces of small children as they played in slimy streets near the fetid cesspits of Galata. Cries of chestnut sellers, egg and summer fruit vendors and fishmongers surrounded by shrill-voiced women reminded her how intensely silent it was in the city of the seraglio and how different life was in that forbidden place. She thought how shabby the poor people looked and how rich and fat the merchants were.

She asked Hussein Pasha why there were so many tripe-stew sellers. Damama howled with laughter at the man's blushes, and told Aimee, "They eat tripe to absorb the liquor they drink in bawdy houses around the harbor, little miss. I know that cos Haya told me all about the habits of the gentlemen of this city!"

Hussein Pasha squirmed at Damama's knowledge, rushing ahead and praying Aimee would ask no more difficult questions. Aimee walked slowly on, savoring the smells of the busy city, oyster stew, melons, coffee and bruised fruit, sandalwood, rose oil and the sickly sweet odor of kif. She bought peaches, musk and amber to make a new drink she had discovered and rushed on, childishly delighted to be far away from the imprisoning walls of the silent city.

Finally, she began to feel tired and knew she could walk no more. It was time to return to the city of the seraglio. As they crossed the bridge, she heard newly familiar noises fading into the distance. She paused to look back sadly, wondering if she would ever come again to enjoy the bustle and hustle of this lively metropolis.

Damama took off her veils and breathed gratefully. "I

don't rightly know how women suffer these things, little miss. Damn near suffocatin' me, they were. Veils are just not healthy. You ought to get the Sultan to ban them!"

They followed Hussein Pasha through the subterranean passages, emerging safely in Aimee's suite.

During the evening, she recounted her adventures to Mahmoud and the Circassian. She told of the different people she had seen, Jews and Moors, Serbs and Berbers, Greeks and Phrygians, all working in warehouses and markets of the city. She described colorful scenes and loud arguments in the bazaar, recounting Damama's disapproval of her purchases.

She concluded merrily, "I believe the trip has made me want to go out again! Perhaps I'll ask if I can go every week."

Mahmoud stared in alarm. He stroked his mother's arm lovingly, persuasively, and said, "When I'm Sultan I shall take you out almost every week, Mama."

"Must I wait so long?"

Mahmoud looked to the Circassian for assistance. His grandmother smiled knowingly. "Selim was so disturbed at your absence, Aimee, and so fearful of your safety that he had to retire with a sick stomach. He threatened to throw Mahmoud and me into the Bosporus if you didn't return! I have never seen him so upset. I would hate to have to tell him you were going out again!"

Aimee laughed a golden laugh and Mahmoud rushed to her arms, reassured by her happy smile.

"Anyway, Mama, you *did* go out!"

"And you arranged it, little prince. You are undoubtedly the very best son any woman had since the world began."

Selim lay in his room giving thanks for Aimee's safe return. He tried to sleep but the night was humid and his body longed for her. His head still ached from the tension of the day and he dozed fitfully, wishing morning would come. At first light, when he felt better, he would rush to her room and kiss her a thousand times. They would eat breakfast with their son and talk of all Aimee had seen.

The curtains wafted and he smelled the familiar magnolia perfume.

"Who's there?"

"I'm a lady from the Sultan's harem, come to tempt him with my body."

"What is your name, mysterious lady?" he asked playfully.

"The Sultan calls me his beautiful one, the ladies of the harem call me Blue Poppy."

"I don't remember you. Come closer please."

Aimee moved to his side and he felt her naked flesh near his cheek. The heavy perfume intoxicated him as he tried to capture her. Like a phantom, she eluded him and he was obliged to get up and pursue her. In the garden, he caught her and they fell on silk carpets that served the imperial feet for evening strolls in scarlet sunset glow.

"Come inside, beautiful one."

"No."

"Why not?"

"I want to be loved in the garden," she teased.

"Wanton French monster, we'll catch a chill."

"Not if we keep warm. We must move quickly, like this, back and forth, faster and faster and faster. Oh, stay there, I don't want you ever to leave me."

She closed her eyes in ecstasy as Selim invaded her eager body. They loved and rested and loved again, laughing and talking and planning a lifetime of passionate delight. As dawn came, they ran inside to wash in the gilded bathchamber and the Sultan watched, wonderingly, as Aimee cleansed her body, undulating before him mischievously, till he forgot his ablutions and fell on her, drowning her cries in warm scented water.

# Chapter 20

*As time passed, Mahmoud began to show signs* of becoming a fine swordsman and an expert linguist. Selim walked the tightrope of the warlords' envy and increasing public displeasure. The people had expected to be happier, richer, less taxed and less burdened with the rigors of daily life on the accession of a new and energetic young Sultan. Instead, the recruitment of a new army had drained the imperial purse. Wars raged on every frontier diminishing the gold reserves and all the while the warlords spread rumors of an infidel who manipulated the Sultan with evil suggestions that would someday ruin the power of Ottoman.

The people had no faith in the warlords, who burned down their city whenever they were displeased. But they had never seen their Sultan. Unlike his predecessors, Selim remained aloof, fearful that his quiet personality would disappoint those accustomed to the bizarre opulence of his forefathers. Sadly, he chose to ignore Aimee's advice to reassure the anxious masses. He would guide his country without resorting to vulgar exhibition.

Aimee grew more beautiful with the years and Damama more adoring of her charge. Theirs was a joyful alliance of kindred souls with common interest bound by a lifetime's devotion. One day, when they were walking in the garden, Damama made a very important suggestion.

"Little miss, I reckon Mahmoud should be told about his father."

Aimee blinked, then she sat down, fanning her face with a lace fan.

"He's comin' to the age when he's jealous of Selim's attentions to you. Sometimes I reckon he feels it's not proper for the Sultan to be so affectionate with his father's lady."

"I'll do as you say, Damama. But what do you think he'll do? Will he hate me?"

"Hate you! Mahmoud loves you. He couldn't hate you if he tried."

Evening came. The violet and turquoise winter sky threatened storms and torrential rain as Mahmoud arrived in his mother's quarters to eat dinner with her.

"I have something I wish to tell you, Mahmoud."

"Why so solemn, Mama?"

"I'm not sure you're going to like what you hear. When I arrived in the city of the seraglio, I was sent to be trained in readiness for my presentation to the Sultan Abdul Hamid . . ."

"Mama?"

"Yes, Mahmoud."

"Say no more."

"I *must* tell you something! Please don't interrupt, this is difficult enough without you obstructing my thoughts."

"I already know what you wish to tell me, Mama," he said softly.

Aimee looked uncertainly at her son as he continued, "Some time ago, my father gave me a letter left by my grandfather, the Sultan Abdul Hamid. The letter was to be opened when I was ten and it explained many things and made me very happy. Father and I went out hunting to celebrate our introduction!"

Aimee threw her arms around the young man's neck. "Do you still love me then?"

"More than ever, Mama. And I love my father as much as I loved him when I thought he was my uncle."

"Oh, Mahmoud, you're just like Damama. There's nothing I can do to surprise you!"

They walked together in the blue garden, and Aimee paused to pick her favorite poppies, remembering, "When I first came here, the head eunuch called me Mademoiselle Blue Poppy."

"But now he calls you Madame Aimee out of respect and gazes into space every time you pass by. I think he adores you too much. You should discourage him, Mama."

Aimee smiled brightly and said, "Never mind about that. Tell me about your visit to Kusadasi."

"Father and I leave at first light tomorrow."

"You will take care, Mahmoud?"

"Of course, we always do. I'll bring you back a dozen lynx fur skins for your bedroom, Mama," he replied, anxious to please.

Aimee turned suddenly, aghast at the onset of the clamor of the warlords' kazans. "What now?" she despaired.

"Have you forgotten, Mama?" the prince said in subdued tones.

"Forgotten?"

"Tomorrow is my birthday. They'll burn down the city across the water and kill people, as they always do. They'll send the mutes to spy on us and apothecaries to poison us. All for nothing. Mama, please don't cry."

But it was too late. Aimee was weeping aloud when she said, "Sometimes I wish I were dead. I truly hate this place!"

"I promise to kill them when I am the Sultan. Please don't be sad; you cannot be sad on my birthday!"

Inside, the French clock chimed midnight and a wildcat cried outside the city wall, as mother and son walked back inside the heavily guarded royal enclosure. Mahmoud stayed with his mother until she slept. Then, he climbed up the secret stairway to the roof and stood looking down on the warlords' distant campfire. He closed his eyes, praying fervently to his mother's God for strength to banish the evil forces forever from his kingdom.

Someday, when he was a man, he would keep his promise.

In the privacy of her garden one morning, Aimee read Rose's latest letter, and grew angrier by the minute at its contents.

My dearest Aimee:

I'm sorry not to have written for so long. Your ambassador in Paris will have told you by now that I was crowned Empress of France at the side of my beloved Bonaparte. We were so happy and he swore a hundred times a day he could never live without me. But now, the glorious days of our love are over. Bonaparte has left me, as all men leave me, and my heart is broken. He claims he will make a settlement on me of three million francs a year and I shall be allowed to continue living at Malmaison. What a calamity for a lady—to be divorced! I am only glad Mama did not live to hear of it! What upsets me most of all is that I have been banished because I cannot provide an heir. Oh, Aimee, every day I look into the mirror and say, "I told you so." I knew I shouldn't have married him, but I wanted security and being a mistress is a most insecure situation.

Now I am alone, and you know how I hate loneliness. Every night I think of Bonaparte and pray he will come back, but in my heart I know he will not. Rumor has it he intends to marry an Austrian. How his family will gloat and how I will wish I could forget all the love he has given me, all the promises he has made, all the sadness he leaves behind. Do you know something, Aimee, Bonaparte still carries in his wallet the violets I gave him at our first meeting. And when we part, he still has to smother tears because he hates to go away from me and my children. Would you not think he still loves me? I'm so tired and dispirited that I cannot imagine what is in his mind. Please write me a letter very quickly and tell me you are still my very dearest friend.

As always, your loving cousin,
Rose

༺༺༺༺༺༺༺༺༺༺༺༺༺༺༺༺༺༺༺༺༺༺

# BOOK IV

*Sunset and
Silver Days*

# Chapter 21

*Sound of the muezzin calling the faithful to* prayer, hum of a dragonfly precariously perched on a blue poppy, hollow echo of silence as Aimee sat at her window, looking out on gilded minarets and leaden rooftops. Since the death of the Circassian, Aimee and Damama had drawn even closer. Aimee shared her love and her secrets with Mahmoud and his father, but she shared all her thoughts, hopes and fears with Damama. The old lady was still a force to be reckoned with. Her body was thin and leathery, her lined face dominated by big brown eyes that penetrated every situation with alarming speed. Her will and loyalty were undiminished and she adored Aimee with undying devotion.

Mahmoud had grown into a fine man, in looks a carbon copy of his father, in mind, customs and manner as French as his indomitable mother. At forty-three Aimee was still beautiful. Her silver hair, clear blue eyes and regal figure were known and respected by all who wanted peace and stability in the city of the seraglio. Her influence with the Sultan was known only to close and trusted friends—the head eunuch, Damama and the Pasha of Rustchuk.

Selim had also changed in this caldron of confusion and dissension. Wise and firm, he led his country bravely through the difficulties of passing time. The Russians were advancing yet again on the Turkish borders. And now the British fleet was approaching, summoned by the Venetian's allies. Their purpose, Selim knew, was to remove his French adviser, Napoleon's commander, Horace Sébastiani. Sébastiani had been in Constantinople for many weeks, supervising the Sultan's defensive strategy and assessing for him the precise power of the warlord force. The warlords were furious at his presence and greatly displeased at this show of friendship by the French dictator.

Earlier in the day, Sébastiani's lookouts had reported the British fleet to be refueling on the island of Límnos. Soon, the Sultan knew, they would come through the Dardanelles and try to cannon the city to submission. He went to Aimee's suite to tell her the latest news.

"Have you summoned Sébastiani?" she asked.

"He's on his way."

"He'll know what to do. Oh, my love, when will it end? Why can't you throw the Venetian and Mustapha in the Bosporus?"

"When you first came to Turkey you called us barbarians. Now you advocate all you so despised."

"I suppose I don't mean it. I don't know really. For over twenty years they've been a constant danger to us. Surely something must be done to prevent our living forever under their threat. Please think about it, Selim."

The next day, the British fleet appeared in sight of the golden city. But Sébastiani had not been idle. Warlords were deployed along the walls, citizens of the seraglio armed and every man able to stand was told to position himself so the British could see the strength of the opposition. And cannons ranged the battlements.

As dawn broke the British admiral heard the sound of a furious bombardment. He watched, resignedly, as the sea around his ship leapt with grapeshot and huge stone cannonballs. Looking up at the strategic perfection of the city walls, he saw hundreds of men appear, murderously armed with sabers, scimitars and shimmering yataghans.

The wind fell and the British ships barely moved. The admiral considered his position. His ships were now sitting targets for all the barbarians' wrath. He shuddered as a sail crashed down and men fell dead or hideously injured. Finally the English admiral gave the order to retreat. The Turks were no nation's ally! Why should he risk men of the British Navy to assist a bitter internal battle for power? As his ships sailed slowly away, a great cry of victory rose from the city. Warning shots and a deceptively strong show of force had been enough to intimidate the unenthusiastic aggressor. Sébastiani was proclaimed a hero. The people cheered and celebrated wildly. The Sultan was never more popular with his own.

News came of the imminent departure of the French general for his home in France. Korba-Khan gave word to the warlords that the long-awaited moment had come. At last, they would destroy the Sultan's new army. Men of the Nizam Djedid were still lodged in the city, celebrating the victory. Only their commander, the Pasha of Rustchuk, had returned immediately to his country home. The new commander of the Sultan's guard, Taiher Effendi, had been given leave to visit his dying father in a far province.

Korba-Khan nodded wisely. This was the moment; there would never be a better time. He ordered the warlords to act.

At midnight they moved, slaughtering sleeping soldiers of the new army; silently, swiftly they slit throats and plundered bodies. Arms from the new armory disappeared into the warlords' powder house. At first light, a special brigade entered the royal enclosure, overpowering the Sultan's personal guard, and took over the buildings of the Rose Pavilion.

Aimee was breakfasting with Mahmoud when Damama rushed in to warn her.

"Little miss! The warlords have taken the Sultan prisoner and locked him in his quarters!"

"Whatever are you saying?"

"Selim is imprisoned in his quarters! There are dead men all over the place and blood runnin' in the garden and the courtyard of the vine trellis. Oh Lord! This is a disaster. I reckon you'd best go hide in the passage. I'll do what I can to confuse them when they come for you."

Aimee refused to move.

A song thrush sang in the Judas tree as litter bearers arrived carrying Korba-Khan to witness the infidel's indignity.

Damama had disappeared swiftly to the kitchen when she heard the sound of marching men. She waited now, with bated breath, ear to the door, listening to the Khan's words.

"At last you are my prisoner."

"Run, Mama, I can fight them," Mahmoud screamed.

"I shall run nowhere. Put down your sword, Mahmoud, this is no time for fighting. The murderer would enjoy ordering his men to butcher you before my eyes."

"But not as much as I shall enjoy ordering them to kill *you!* I have lived through all the agonies of this long illness to see your head on the warlords' tree." The Khan's words were full of hatred.

"You'd better kill me quickly then, because from your pallor you may not be here in the morning."

"First you must see all I have worked for these many years to accomplish. Look down, infidel, and know the power of Korba-Khan. I am a dying man but still I am stronger than all the forces of the Sultan of Ottoman."

Aimee looked out of her window and saw bodies strewn about in the blue garden, the Sultan's courtyard and the parapet of the tower. Her heart pounded harshly in her chest. Was this how it would end? They were all dead— her loyal friends and the men Selim had waited so long to train. She struggled to appear calm, praying desperately that they had not already killed her adoring lover. Suddenly, she realized that Damama was nowhere to be seen. She looked round in confusion as Korba-Khan fell back on his litter, overwhelmed by the violence of his pain.

"Put them in the Sultan's quarters so they can discuss their fate. And guard them well. If they escape you'll all die!" the Khan ordered his men.

Aimee walked with her son to Selim's suite. She began to feel better as she approached the place she knew so well, the place from which, with luck, they could all escape.

She looked lovingly at the fireplace in the empty storeroom and thought of the secret stairway to the roof. Selim greeted her with a kiss and took them both through to his receiving room as the guards disappeared.

"I love you, Aimee Dubuq de Rivery."

"You've never called me that in all these years." Her voice was full of emotion.

"To me you have always been the beautiful one. Now, Mahmoud, we must plan what can be done."

"They took my sword, Father."

"I have swords hidden under the floor and others on the roof. They will surely wish to kill me first so they can proclaim Mustapha Sultan."

"Let's go to the roof now, Selim!" Aimee cried.

"No, beautiful one, this is no time for flight. We must wait to know if the Pasha's spies have informed him of our predicament. We could hide on the roof, but they have also surrounded the entire royal enclosure. There would be no escape and we would die of thirst or sunstroke within a few days."

As day turned to evening and summer sun to twilight chill, they ate dinner, trying to boost each other's morale. Uncertain of when the dreaded summons of death might come, they lapsed often into apprehensive silence. Then Mahmoud thought to ask his mother where Damama was.

"I don't know. One moment she was warning us and the next I noticed she'd gone. Perhaps she went to find help."

"She's very old now, Mama. You can't expect Damama to help us. She's probably hiding."

"Damama may be old, but she would never cower and hide," Aimee replied indignantly.

With that, the royal family resumed their meal in silence.

Damama remained, silently, in the kitchen storage cupboard until the warlord led his prisoners away. Fearful of discovery, she remained unmoving for an hour before creeping cautiously into the empty suite. She wrapped food in a kerchief and went to the secret passageway. Painfully, slowly, she dragged herself along the dark stairway and up to the roof. She looked down and saw that the warlords had occupied every building in the Sultan's enclosure and surrounded all the walls. There would be no way out through the corridors and passages she knew so well. She thought for a while and then descended again down the narrow staircase, returning to Aimee's suite.

At nightfall, she lowered herself through the spiral staircase from the Circassian's former suite to the unused storeroom below. She ran to the ice pits and through the long corridor, emerging in the second courtyard. Calmly ignoring the curfew, she untied a horse and led it through moonless darkness to the gate of the warlords' enclosure. Then she rode like the wind into the shielding blackness of the night.

A guard raised the alarm and men rode after her, spraying the air with arrows. But Damama had vanished. The guards had not even seen her. They remained unaware that the fugitive was the infidel's faithful servant.

The Pasha of Rustchuk was in the bath, soaping his great bulk and singing like the happy man he was. His new wife had just borne him a son and it was summer. Golden sun shone on parched landscape around his domain as he wrapped himself in a velvet robe and swept out to visit the new arrival. He was gurgling delightedly at the baby when Damama was led in by the guards of the Pasha's fortress.

"I'm Damama, nurse to the French milady."

"I remember you, of course. Look at my son, Madame Damama. Isn't he a perfect child?"

"He's real fine, sir," she replied, shifting nervously on her feet.

"Now, what can I do for you?"

"The warlords have captured the Sultan and imprisoned my mistress and Prince Mahmoud."

The Pasha leapt up, face ashen, eyes wild.

"Call the guard! Alert my men and be prepared to move out in one hour."

He rushed past Damama as a servant arrived with tea, cheese, bread and fig jam. Damama ate and soon fell asleep. She was snoring loudly when she became aware of the Pasha calling.

"Come, Madame Damama, I need your help," he said. "I intend to lead the main force through the central gate of the warlords' courtyard. We shall take them by surprise and reach the third gate before they can do anything to

296

stop us. I shall set my archers on anyone who opposes us and on those who attempt to escape. But you must lead some of my force through the underground passage to the Sultan's quarters. Are the prisoners together in the Sultan's suite?"

"They were, but Korba-Khan could have killed them by now. He's been waitin' for years for this moment."

"I'll eat that dung dog's liver for breakfast, mark my words."

"I don't need to mark your words, sir. Korba-Khan has seen his last sunrise!" Damama's vow was sealed in her heart long before, but now she pledged to see his death.

With a fierce cry the Pasha led his force through arid desert landscape. Three thousand brave warriors against eight thousand warlords was gravely uneven odds, but the Pasha galloped confidently ahead, soul ablaze with loyalty for his beloved master. For hours they rode until they reached the parched plains bordering the city walls. Damama was speechless with exhaustion and the Pasha saw she could barely move. He allowed her an hour's sleep in the twilight of a summer evening. Then he sent her with a hundred chosen men to enter the city by the underground route from outside the seraglio wall.

"I shall attack at first light. See the gates are open."

The captain of the chosen few bowed obeisance. Then he and his men followed Damama to the tunnel like silent shadows in the dark night.

Aimee walked arm in arm with Selim in the scented garden, recalling the first time he had come to see his father's "gift." They laughed like children and taking the old key from its hiding place, entered again the lapis-floored suite where love had ripened into lifelong devotion. Aimee snuggled against the tall figure, sniffing the sweet jasmine smell of his skin and gently stroking the lustrous beard.

The lovers lay, side by side, on the golden bed where they had first made love, talking and planning as though determined to ignore the hideous torture of waiting. Selim kissed her cheeks and ran his hands through the silvery hair.

"Mahmoud is a fine son, beautiful one. He's everything my father wanted me to be."

"You are everything your father hoped you'd be."

"Thanks to you. I wish I were a poet so I could tell you all I feel."

"You've shown me all you feel, so often. Words are only words. You've made me very happy despite the warlords and the horrors of life in the city of the seraglio. What more could any woman want?"

In the twilight, they made love, laughing as they had always laughed at irreverent jokes and stories of times long past when their passion had been less expert, their ardor less controlled.

In the cool of evening, they returned to Mahmoud, through the narrow paths of the scented garden. Mahmoud sat alone in the receiving room, reading his father's books and trying not to think of the morning and all it would bring.

They ate their dinner, lingering over delicacies as though they feared the meal's end. As they drank coffee, Aimee's face paled at the sound of marching men.

"They are here. Oh, why can we not escape? I'd rather die of sunstroke than have Korba-Khan kill you!"

"You must stay calm, beautiful one. I think they only wish to take me."

"I love you so much, Selim. I don't want to live without you," Aimee cried.

Warlord guards appeared with instructions to separate the captives. Aimee and Mahmoud walked proudly back to her suite, leaving Selim alone in his quarters. Selim protested that they must stay together, but Korba-Khan laughed his demonic laugh and confined the Sultan with harsh words. "You'll be less confident apart because you'll never know when I have killed the other."

Locks turned, bolts scraped and Aimee wept as she thought of Selim's last words . . . "Remember I love you, beautiful one. Remember that death means nothing to me because I shall always love you and wait for you to come to me." Was death so near? She lay on the silken bed, no longer sure of anything in this harsh, heathen land.

Mahmoud sat by his mother's side, trying to comfort her. "I brought a dagger, Mama, and some steel hooks in case we must escape through the window. My father will fight long and hard."

"I loved him, I always have loved him, but I never realized how much until I knew I might lose him."

"You've always loved him, Mama. It was very obvious to me as a child; that's why I was so jealous!"

"I don't want to live without him," Aimee said frantically.

"He'll survive, Mama. Try to rest and in the morning the Pasha of Rustchuk will come to help us."

Mahmoud looked out on dark blue sky. Surely Korba-Khan intended to kill his father, but when? He sighed as he watched Aimee tossing on the ornate bed. His mother was an innocent, trapped in a country she could never love by cruel circumstances beyond her control. He resolved to spoil her to death if they survived the next few days. As dawn came, he kneeled to pray for his father's safety.

Damama led the Pasha's men to unlock the city gates. Then she returned by the subterranean passage to the Sultan's quarters.

She found Selim praying in his private mosque and kneeled to pray with him. Then she stood at the rear of the chapel waiting for him to finish. When he rose, Damama asked what she should do. "The Pasha's comin' to the central gates at dawn. Some of his men are hidin' in the passages leadin' to little miss's quarters. Is the prince with his mother, sir?"

"He is."

"Shall I stay with you or return to little miss? And where do you want the Pasha's men?" Damama asked.

"You must hurry to her and tell her what is going to happen, and you must order the Pasha's men to stay and protect her."

For a moment, the Sultan paused. "Damama."

"Yes, sir!"

"When the Pasha of Rustchuk enters the seraglio and proceeds to the inner court, the Khan will send the dwarfs to murder me."

"I'll bring some of the Pasha's men to help you, sir."

"No! They *must* stay with Mahmoud and his mother.

I order you to make them stay with her." The Sultan was adamant.

"Yes, sir," she replied sadly.

"Tell the beautiful one that I will love her forever."

Damama felt a great lump rise in her throat and unaccustomed tears fill her eyes. She blew her nose hard and tried desperately to retain some semblance of dignity, but she was exhausted and suddenly feeling her great age. The Sultan took her arm gently and ushered her to the secret stairway. Suddenly, a great tumult broke with the sound of cannon firing, men screaming, hooves clattering on stone walls and marble courtyards.

"Go quickly, Damama, and tell the beautiful one to hide herself and my son."

"Goodbye, sir."

Damama stood tall, knowing the dreaded moment had come. Their eyes met for a brief moment, then she climbed slowly up the stairway inside the stone fireplace. As she reached the passage entrance, she heard the Sultan cry out and knew that the Khan's mutes had arrived.

Selim stood calmly facing his enemies, sword in either hand, one man against five grotesque puppets. The murderous ones cackled merrily, swinging silken cords that would end the Sultan's life. The Khan had offered a reward to the one who killed the infidel's adoring one. The dwarfs drew long daggers and slashed at Selim's legs. With wild cries they surrounded him but Selim was too fast and quickly killed Nesir, Mehmed and Faitthah, wounding Hadji Ali grievously in the chest. Triumphantly, he chased the last aggressor through the marble hall to the scented garden, unaware that members of the Khan's personal guard had entered the royal apartments and were watching the furious conflict with grudging admiration.

The dwarf, grunting with effort, backed the Sultan past the pond of silver fish to the marble pillars where the warlords watched. Selim wheeled, struggling violently and felling the nearest attackers. But he was outnumbered, a dozen to one. He ran, gravely wounded by a dagger in his back, to the tower and threw the writhing dwarf into the courtyard below. The warlords laughed as they surrounded him. Selim remained defiant as the daggers plunged.

As the Sultan died they cheered in triumph. Then the Kahn's guards threw his body down the steps into the scented garden, kicking and abusing it before sending one of their number to give the glad tidings to Korba-Khan.

Across the river, warlord patrols policed the narrow streets of Constantinople, unaware of the tumultuous happenings in the city of the seraglio.

Outside the city wall the Pasha of Rustchuk gave the order to charge the gate. They had reached the inner courtyard before the warlords were awake. Archers immobilized the guards and confined the treacherous force in their crowded barracks.

The Pasha ordered Korba-Khan to be brought to him and the warlord arrived on his litter as the giant roared for the traitors inside the Rose Pavilion to surrender and return the Sultan immediately to his rightful place. There was no answer from inside the silent courtyard. Nothing but the shrill cry of birds in the Sultan's menagerie. Far away, in the first courtyard, warlord captains were led, heavily chained, to underground dungeons to await their fate.

Outside the Rose Pavilion, Korba-Khan waited uneasily as the Pasha gave orders for the gate to be rammed. As the massive doors fell, the Sultan's murderers were revealed despoiling his mutilated body.

The Khan began to laugh, hysterically. "There is the pig, ready to be roasted!"

The Pasha fell to his knees, weeping like a child, oblivious of watchers and impervious to the Khan's evil smile. Mustapha appeared with his mother and the Khan struggled to sit up and welcome him in effusive tones of magnanimous greeting.

"My lord, Sultan of the Faithful!"

The Pasha of Rustchuk leapt up, grasping the madman by the throat and raising him higher and higher until he dangled from the giant's outstretched arms, legs swinging like a pendulum.

"No madman will reign here while I live."

The Venetian was led off to captivity by the Pasha's guard, and Korba-Khan watched helplessly while his beloved Mustapha was slowly strangled. They were startled by a cry from the roof of the royal pavilion.

"Let him go!"

The Pasha dropped the unconscious traitor as Mahmoud came down the outer stairway.

"My faithful friend, for the second time I have you to thank for my life."

"But milord, what of this murderer?"

"Mustapha will spend the rest of his life in the cage."

"He *must* die, milord. He has plotted the murder of the Sultan."

Mahmoud stood looking down on Selim's body. His eyes filled with tears and he turned away so no one could see his grief. He walked to the parapet and looked far out to sea, trying desperately to control the waves of grief that submerged his tired mind. Aimee stood watching the tragic scene from the rooftop of the secret passageway. She could not weep. She stared silently down, numbed by the horror of the scene.

After a while, Mahmoud returned to the Pasha and gave his first orders as Sultan of Turkey. "Call the executioner. You will watch your captains die, Korba-Khan. You are too ill to be slaughtered so you will remain in your quarters, never to leave them again."

Mahmoud then ordered the household servants to prepare for the celebration of his accession, and returned silently to his mother.

The Sultan's murderers died within the hour, their heads suspended on the warlords' plane tree. Branches ran with blood and the stench of death filled the city of the seraglio for many days.

On a fine summer evening cannon boomed and Prince Mahmoud was proclaimed Padishah of all Ottoman, Sultan of the Faithful.

# Chapter 22

*Once again Aimee sat staring out to sea. The* moment had come that she had planned and hoped for. Her son ruled the land and she was the omnipotent Sultane Valideh of the Turkish Empire. But it gave her no joy. She gazed out of the window, deaf to Damama's entreaties, her mind wandering to a scented world with a young man who had once brought her a picnic in the darkness of the night. She was still unable to shed tears, her emotions atrophied by agonizing shock. Nothing interested her, nothing challenged her to retrieve her sorely damaged spirit. She could think only of the beloved lover who had died to keep her safe.

A thousand tears drenched her soul but her eyes remained vacant as she watched the busy seaway. Echoes of happy days in the scented garden, burning nights of passion in the secret suite and cool afternoons in the imperial caïque cruising to the elegant privacy of their summer palace flittered like butterflies of doom through the defeated labyrinth of her mind. Nightingales sang as the sun set red gold on the horizon, but Aimee remained motionless, seeing nothing but the broken, beaten, bloody body the murderers had thrown, like a dead animal, into the marble courtyard.

Damama watched, her heart broken by the intensity of Aimee's grief. She stayed awake in the long dark nights that followed, knowing in her heart that the Khan would never give up his attempt to kill her mistress. He would try with his dying breath to destroy the hated enemy. Damama waited, silently, secretly, learning everything that went on in the city of the seraglio from friends, guards and the faithful Haya, who watched the Khan's quarters.

Damama looked in the mirror and saw an old face, wrinkled and lined and surrounded by fluffy white hair. She settled on the big brass bed and thought of happier days on flower island when Aimee was a pretty child, rushing through green undergrowth with arms full of flowers. They had been good days, happy days, full of lusty happenings and luscious tropical color. She wiped a tear from her eye at the memory. Damama was old and tired and ready to die. She muttered softly under her breath to reassure herself that she could still do what had to be done. "Age is nothin'. I'll still be ready when the time comes."

She had not long to wait. The head eunuch informed her that his spies had discovered large quantities of powder from the Sultan's arms store being ferried to Korba-Khan's quarters. No one had interfered with this strange traffic, but the Pasha of Rustchuk had been informed and the Sultan had ordered extra surveillance. In the dead of night, Damama crept to the courtyard of the warlords' camp and watched an amazing scene. Guards led Mustapha to the Khan's dwelling, standing sentinel as the two plotted. Damama cursed furiously. Mahmoud should have killed the lot of them, but he was determined to be a French gentleman and not the Turkish barbarian his mother might loathe. Damama thought wryly that someday he would discover the error of his ways. He was his father's son and someday he would be a Turk!

Damama knew what must be done. There must be no more vile infamy to torment little miss. It was time for the Khan to die. She fondled her gold-handled umbrella, swinging it a few times to give herself confidence. Then

304

she slipped through the darkness to the Khan's door. She reached up and took a flaming torch from the wall bracket outside the entrance and stepped into the interior like a dark phantom.

Startled by her sudden appearance, Korba-Khan screamed, but his guards were too far away to hear. They were drinking a bowl of soup and telling tales of their bravery to warlord friends around the campfire. Mustapha grasped a dagger from the wall, threatening Damama's life. She looked calmly at the pair, one mad, the other evil as the devil and trembling with fear. Korba-Khan lay unable to move, aware of a fanatic gleam in the old lady's eyes. Damama assessed the room, backing slowly toward a pile of crates and boxes of powder from the Sultan's arms store.

The Khan screamed shrilly, "Put out the torch or you'll kill us all."

"I like hearin' you scream, Korba-Khan. It does my old heart good!"

Mustapha darted behind her and tried to put a knife between her shoulders. Damama hit him roundly with the precious parasol and he fell, half stunned, to the ground.

"You remember tellin' the Sultan when he was a little boy that you cut out Nsai's tongue because it gave you pleasure?"

"Never mind that! Get out, you servant of a whore!"

"You also told him that you cut off Nsai's fingers because it gave you pleasure. Well, I reckon you beat me so I'll have the scars forever for the same reason. One thing is certain, sir, you're the most wicked person I have ever met!"

"Kill her, Mustapha! For the love of Allah, kill her."

Mustapha lunged toward Damama, but she turned quickly and plunged the burning torch in his face. His agonized screams brought the guards and soon the Khan's room was full of advancing menace. Damama smiled broadly, content for the first time in many weeks.

"I come here tonight, you murderin' swine, cos the time has come for you to stop tormentin' my mistress. I come here tonight to do somethin' to give me pleasure. The sacrifice is worth it just to see your cowardly face."

Damama thought of Aimee, crossed herself and whispered, "God bless you, little miss." Then she plunged the burning torch into the nearest box of powder. The explosion shook the very foundation of the warlords' courtyard.

The Pasha of Rustchuk sent messengers to find out what had happened, but nothing remained of the warlord's dwelling except stony rubble and a fierce fire. Only the solid gold umbrella, jeweled cover disintegrated, gold spines bent and discolored, revealed Damama's part in the gory happenings of the night. The Pasha bowed his head and paid tribute to the lady warrior from the far island.

The warlords, ranks greatly reduced, festered with loathing. Forays were made to destroy the barracks of the new army and all remaining equipment. Mahmoud was unperturbed. Months prior to his father's death, thirty thousand new men had been engaged, equipped and sent to a far distant province to be trained. The warlords knew nothing of this mammoth new undertaking. Even the Pasha of Rustchuk had been kept in ignorance of the secret battalion. Only Aimee dreamed of the day when they would end the warlords' infamous rule of terror.

She went each day to the courtyard of the warlords' campfire, looking fixedly at the spot where Damama had died. She placed Damama's old red silk parasol in her scented blue garden and looked down on it, able to feel the strong, loving presence still near. But she was lonely and heartbroken by all that had happened. Only grief remained, clouding her mind so nothing could penetrate her stillness.

Mahmoud began to despair of ever making her well again. Spring came, followed by humid summer, golden autumn and a winter of surprising chill. He racked his brain for a solution to his mother's grief. Then he remembered her comment about Korba-Khan . . . "He only lived so long because his hate kept him alive."

When Mahmoud had first read the letter that had just arrived from his mother's cousin Josephine, he had decided not to give it to her, in case it caused her further distress. But suddenly, he changed his mind. Taking it from his pocket, he reread its perfumed pages:

My dearest Aimee:

Please forgive me for not sending you news of my life, but I have been ill with distress about all that has happened. Bonaparte divorced me, as you know, then he changed his mind about letting me stay on at my beloved Malmaison. He said two empresses were too much in such a small area, meaning that I was living too near his new wife, the Austrian! I have been forced to take refuge in Normandy and the move so distressed me I have been living like a recluse and not even writing to you, my dear, because I could not concentrate enough to put pen to paper. Now, he is off on another campaign to Russia; no doubt he will return victorious as always. Some say he wishes to conquer the whole world.

Just before he left, he gave me permission to return to Paris, so here I am, well and relieved to be home. He does not visit me, except out of dire necessity. I once said he was not one to let love impede ambition and I have been proven right. I live alone, lonely and longing for death. Without him there is nothing . . .

Mahmoud placed the letter on Aimee's bed and retired early to his suite.

Aimee was bathing, memories of flower island filling her mind as she splashed in warm torrents of water. She smiled, wistfully, recalling the pretty pink room where Mama had let her play with ornate jewel boxes and the deep green glades near La Pagerie where Cousin Rose had grown up, unaware of all that lay ahead. For a brief moment, she fancied that she could see Rose again. How they would talk and what tales they would tell!

When she returned to her bedroom and saw the official dispatch and the letter on violet paper she felt at first that she had imagined it. But she grasped the document eagerly. Reading it, she felt for the first time in many months the rage that always came in defense of those she loved. She read the note on violet paper again and again . . . "he was not one to let love impede ambition."

Aimee rushed from her suite to Mahmoud's quarters, roaring like a virago.

"Mahmoud! Mahmoud, wake up! I must speak to you."

"Mama?"

"What is this? Why was I not told of this before?"

"You've been ill, Mama and interested in nothing," he explained.

"Well, I'm interested in this."

"Allah be praised, you're better at last." Mahmoud hugged the slim body.

"What can we do, Mahmoud?"

"Nothing, Mama. We shall wait and do what we can to obstruct that gentleman's ambition."

"He wishes to conquer the world!"

"No, Cousin Rose says he wishes to conquer Russia."

Aimee thought for a moment. For years war had raged on their frontiers with Russia, draining the Tsar's army and weakening their own.

"We must make peace with the Russians," Aimee announced.

"Why?"

"So the Tsar's forces can return to defend the interior."

"I agree."

"Please send messengers immediately to the Tsar."

"I sent them a week ago, Mama. Within a month a peace treaty will be signed. I promise."

"No one must be told, not even the Pasha of Rustchuk."

"You taught me a proverb from your island when I was small: 'in war you do not warn your enemy.' I've always remembered it. Napoleon Bonaparte will invade Russia imagining himself safe because most of the Tsar's forces are busy on the Turkish borders. He will discover his error too late."

"I hate him!"

"There's nothing to hate, Mama. Ambition will rob him of all the happiness he could have known. He will never be content because he has traded the only thing he truly loved for something he can never enjoy. He pursues the impossible like all madmen."

"I would like to write to Rose."

"You shall send her gifts and a note by special courier.

308

Oh, Mama, it's so wonderful to see the light in your eyes again."

Aimee returned to her quarters and prayed for the happiness of her cousin. The next day she sent a short note and gifts of spice, rare lily bulbs and a carved crystal bowl of sapphires from Samarkand. In the weeks that followed, she steadied herself and began, once again, to take an interest in the daily life of the seraglio.

In the heat of midsummer, the Venetian died, heartbroken that her allies were all vanquished, her son unmourned, her ambition forever unfulfilled. Aimee felt a great surge of relief at the passing of her last great enemy. She threw a party for Mahmoud, inviting the daughters of two of her women friends, ignoring protocol determinedly, as always.

After the guests departed, she walked with Mahmoud in the blue garden, chattering and urging him to tell her all his secrets. Then she served champagne for him and the head eunuch and the three sat reminiscing about times long past and friends happily remembered.

The eunuch had developed a taste for the fine frothy wine. He had even given up the opiate cough mixtures the more to enjoy this intoxicating enticement. He excused religious sanctions on the grounds of health. Mahmoud laughed as his mother clapped her hands gleefully at the eunuch's hypocrisy.

"I shall be sixty-five tomorrow, Madame Aimee. Who would wish to be such a great age? If it weren't for my medicine I should have been in the tomb long ago with all that I have suffered."

"Your medicine is very expensive!"

"Dear lady, don't mention the cost. What is money but a means to elysia!! Well, I must return to the harem. My naughty girls are now naughty old women and their daughters play tricks on me and call me rude names! I fear the young are not as they used to be. The modern world is no place for a martyr. Goodnight, my lord, goodnight, dearest lady. It was a *beautiful* party."

He waddled off.

Mahmoud turned to his mother, eager to share her happiness. "Mama, I have a small surprise for you."

"Tell me quickly then."

"It's time to go to our summer home."

"I don't want to go there now that your papa is dead. He designed everything in the yali and I see him in every room. I couldn't bear to be so sad again."

Mahmoud wrapped his arms around her neck, and said in agreement, "Now that I am Sultan, I shall need to stay close to my quarters. The warlords are always dangerous and I don't wish to leave them for a moment."

"Then we'll stay here for the hot months. We don't need to go to the summer palace," Aimee said.

"I have an idea which might please you, Mama. Are you very tired?"

"No, I'm not tired at all."

"Then come with me, there's something I can't wait to show you."

He led her through gilded passages to the Sultan's suite. Then through the scented garden to the room where she and Selim had first been lovers. Aimee was surprised to see that a door had been cut in one of the ornate walls. Mahmoud handed her a key.

"Are you surprised, Mama? Promise me you knew nothing of this."

"Of course I'm surprised. What mischief have you been up to?"

"No mischief, Mama, only a token of my love for you."

Aimee turned the key and emerged in an enclosed patio with a fountain. From the patio, a flower-covered pergola led to the sea. Behind lay the buildings of the Sultan's private enclosure. Aimee ran through the scented bower, emerging on the shore. She looked round, puzzled by the mystery. Then she saw a gazebo in the French style of lattice wood and curled white iron. She opened the door and cried out with delight. A single room padded with flowery silk awaited her pleasure, floor littered with velvet cushions, air scented by plants suspended from the ceiling. In the corner, a bluebird sang in a French gilded cage, and around the walls, on low shelves, lovingly arranged, she saw favorite books, shells and small paintings executed by her son in the years since early childhood.

"This is your new summer house, Mama. It's small; one room that is really a big padded bed with a roof and walls to hide you. I designed it myself."

310

"It's beautiful, truly beautiful."

"No one can reach this spot but me. When I'm busy you can come alone. But when I'm free, we'll have picnics here and you can tell me funny stories like you used to."

Aimee hugged him happily and he whirled her round like a small child.

A month later, on the Sultan's birthday, the warlords banged their drums and burned down the city across the river. Aimee wept. So, it would never change? The death of Korba-Khan and the accession of a new Sultan made no difference to the enmity of the vile force. She retired to bed, trembling with a fierce ague.

Mahmoud read reports on the progress of his new army and smiled. Soon they would be ready. Soon he could keep his promise. He rushed to Aimee's suite and found her weeping.

"Mama, please don't cry. I promised to destroy them, didn't I?"

"You were a child, you didn't understand what you said. No one will ever destroy the warlords."

"I shall, because I promised and you taught me always to keep my promises."

"I pray God will let me see the day."


Sometimes Aimee went out to the city accompanied by her son, both of them disguised as peasants. Mahmoud loved these adventures as much as his mother. He had noticed an exquisite creature in a high window above the main square. Surely, he thought, he was in love. He sent an emissary to find out about the beautiful lady. Aimee was delighted by his choice and waited as excitedly as he to know all about his first love.

Sometimes they ventured to the treasure caves of the city of the seraglio and made neat inventories of the palace treasures: Chinese porcelain, pearl-studded armor, ruby-wrought cradles and cornucopias. Aimee tried on out-landishly bejeweled hair decorations and solid gold helmets that fell on her shoulders, hiding her face completely.

On one special occasion, Mahmoud took her to the fortress of the Pasha of Rustchuk for the first trip she had ever had away from the city. At last, she saw the country-side of her adopted land. The trip, accomplished in great secrecy, gave the Pasha almost as much pleasure as it did his distinguished visitors. He excelled himself as a lavish host and showed Aimee all his treasures.

As time passed, Aimee was almost content. Only the daily fear of another warlord coup marred the idyllic autumn of her days. Mahmoud watched over her, adoring, trusting, confiding all he hoped to do. These, Aimee reflected, wistfully, were the golden years, the years she had fought for and won. She looked out on the sunlight sea of blue poppies and smiled. She would never see flower island again; now this dusky rose marble quadrangle was home. She looked down and saw Damama's red silk parasol, now faded, leaning against the ornate gold wall. The past was past. Only the future was important. She had only one more wish and her son had promised it would be granted.

In the warlords' courtyard, men sat polishing their great copper drums, unaware of what was in store.

Some weeks later a letter of effusive politeness arrived from Napoleon Bonaparte. The Sultan flushed with fury. Aimee read the letter twice and threw it on the ground.

"Imagine! The Corsican writes of eternal friendship between our two nations. The last time he did that he attacked Egypt within the week! Now what is he up to?"

"He has written this hoping that I will keep his enemies busy on our border territory because he needs my help in his attack on Russia. He suspects nothing about the treaty."

"How fortunate. But what will our people say when they know the terms you agreed with the Tsar in order to keep peace? We lost land, and the people love their land."

"The people don't care about the lost territory. They want peace more than anything after all these years of war."

"And the warlords?"

"The warlords want war. They will rebel against the treaty but I shall be ready."

"Why do they always want war?"

"Because in war they take booty. In war they earn vast monies from the imperial treasury and grow rich and powerful. Peace is death to a warlord."

In early summer, news came that Bonaparte had invaded Russia. Couriers from the Emperor began to converge on the city of the seraglio with messages, notes, personal eulogies and requests for audiences for his most important negotiators. Aimee was delighted.

"He still has no idea of the treaty!"

"I told you, Mama! He will be far into Russia before he learns of it and then it will be too late. By September, the Russian winter will come and freeze him and his great French army to the ground!"

Time proved the Sultan right and Aimee was content that family honor had been vindicated. The Corsican was exiled to an island off the Italian coast and surely that was the end of his ambitions! She sat in the flower-walled gazebo and wrote again to Cousin Rose, wondering why she had received no reply to recent communications.

In the city center, panic raged. Plague had been discovered in a poverty-stricken ghetto and it began to spread like wildfire. Bodies lay piled at the street corners, waiting to be burned by the collectors of the dead.

The warlords, still angry over what they felt were ignominious terms in the Russian peace treaty, longed for battle. They viewed the Sultan with increasing suspicion. He was an infidel, like his mother, cursed by her dominance. Mahmoud had changed the old order. He was known to despise tradition. Even his dress was not like that of his ancestors and it was rumored that he drank champagne imported in great quantities from his mother's country. The Sultan was a blasphemer and unworthy to rule. The warlords plotted their final battle, unaware that on the great plains of Kusadasi, in the valley of the Maeander, a new army prepared to march to the Sultan's orders.

Aimee gazed out her window as rain fell steadily. She felt hot despite the winter chill and shivered violently, covering herself with silk carpets and mohair shawls. She forbade her son to visit her in case she had caught the dreaded plague. But Mahmoud ignored her entreaties and stayed at her side, night after night.

Aimee began to cough, spitting blood and trying desperately to hide it from the agonized watcher. The doctors diagnosed a fatal lung complaint, but the Sultan prayed desperately that they were wrong.

The new army marched on toward the city.

# Chapter 23

To the Sultan Mahmoud of the Divine Port of Constantinople, most loved being on earth, father of his people:

Sire,

You asked me to report on the situation of Josephine Bonaparte, divorced wife of Napoleon Bonaparte. I am, therefore, most honorable sire, the bearer of ill tidings. Josephine Bonaparte is dead and has been so for some time. Some say she died of a broken heart but I consulted with her physician and he said she died after a chill and because she did not wish to live longer.

Bonaparte, the former Emperor, was exiled, but he returned to try to regain his position. Fortunately, he was unsuccessful. He was a most difficult gentleman, sire, an ambitious man whose ambition amounted, some say, to mania. They say he is now a broken man, that he cries out for her whom he rejected each night in his sleep. And wherever he goes, he carries a miniature of Josephine painted when they were still together. My spy also reports that the former Emperor walks round Malmaison at night, calling to her and fondling flowers she gave him long ago which are now most definitely dry as paper about to crumble to dust. Perhaps he is mad, sire. It is most unlikely that such a man will recover from all his unhappiness.

Most reverend sire, this is the news you asked and I regret its most unhappy content.

I am your most respectful subject,

Ahmed Talardi, Ambassador to Paris

Folding the letter, Mahmoud vowed to keep its contents from his mother.

Winter wind whined round the golden towers. A doctor from Pergamum looked down on his patient and knew she was dying. Aimee looked up, questioningly, then, seeing the sadness in his eyes, understood.

"Mahmoud? Please send for the Catholic priest."

"I have already sent a boat to bring him, Mama."

"I feel no pain. Why must I die before my time!"

Mahmoud smiled. Mama would rebel all the way to the gates of heaven! The doctor whispered softly in her ear and Aimee nodded, resignedly. Guards led the Catholic priest to her side even as the soldiers of the new army made camp outside the city walls, hidden from the warlords' scrutiny by the hills of Constantinople. The priest, puzzled by this astonishing summons, knelt at her side, intoning the absolution . . . "deinde, ego te absolvo a peccatis tuis, in nomine Patris et Filii et Spiritus Sanctus."

Aimee lay dreaming of flower island. She watched the priest depart and asked the doctor to leave her alone with her son.

Mahmoud lifted her from the bed and carried her to the window.

"Over there, Mama, beyond the great hills, our new army awaits the dawn. I shall keep my promise, have no fear. Every warlord has been summoned from the far provinces. They are all in the city awaiting my command. Tomorrow, I intend to provoke them into rebellion and trap them in the archery stadium where they are to have a meeting. They will die, Mama, my plan is perfect."

"I love you, Mahmoud; you never broke a promise. You've truly been the very best son in the world."

Aimee looked at the setting sun, shivering in the chill breeze of approaching night. Mahmoud carried her back to bed and she asked for Damama's red silk parasol. As the muezzin called the last prayer of the night, Aimee closed her eyes and remembered happy childhood days on flower island. She imagined she could hear the sound of slaves singing, parrots squawking, birds calling. As she lay quietly waiting, fireflies danced, frogs croaked and Damama appeared on the steps of La Maison du Midi, waiting to welcome her home. Aimee smiled happily as she saw her beloved Selim and Cousin Rose rushing to greet her . . .

They buried her in an imperial turbeh of black and gold. On the tomb, at her request, they placed Damama's red silk parasol and the engraved book given her by Selim. Mahmoud prostrated himself in prayer, asking that the road to paradise be scented with all the familiar smells of flower island and that his father would be happy again now he and his beautiful one were reunited.

At dawn, he rode out to the camp of the new army, bearing the imperial standard and the standard of the Prophet Mohammed. He visited the commanders and listened as they repeated the plan they had rehearsed for many months.

At midday, the new army surrounded Constantinople, blocking all exits and containing the warlords in the stadium where they were holding their meeting.

For two days battle raged. The warlords fought with desperation and great skill, but they were outnumbered and the new force had the element of surprise as well as a foolproof plan.

By sunset on the third day, twenty-five thousand warlords lay dead in the stadium or floating in the Bosporus. Their leaders hung from the plane tree like grotesque puppets for all to see and the blue waters of the bay turned red as bodies floated past the islands to the open sea.

Mahmoud watched the scene and knew that whatever his mother had taught him, he was Sultan of Ottoman and truly his father's son. In the tradition of his ancestors, death had been the reward of those who dared defy the imperial presence.

He donned his finest garments and made his way to the imperial turbeh. As night fell, he kneeled before the gold tomb and whispered gently to the listening spirits, "It is done, Mama. I kept my promise. You can sleep, forever, in peace . . ."

## ABOUT THE AUTHOR

Helene Thornton is an English writer who was educated at Elmslie and at the Sorbonne. In addition to English and French, she speaks Italian and Spanish. Her hobbies include painting, cooking, and collecting antique crucifixes. She has just completed her first screenplay and a historical novel set in Ireland during the potato famine. She is divorced, and has one daughter.

# FREE
# Fawcett Books Listing

There is Romance, Mystery, Suspense, and Adventure waiting for you inside the Fawcett Books Order Form. And it's yours to browse through and use to get all the books you've been wanting ... but possibly couldn't find in your bookstore.

This easy-to-use order form is divided into categories and contains over 1500 titles by your favorite authors.

So don't delay—take advantage of this special opportunity to increase your reading pleasure.

Just send us your name and address and 35¢ (to help defray postage and handling costs).

**FAWCETT BOOKS GROUP**
P.O. Box C730, 524 Myrtle Ave., Pratt Station, Brooklyn, N.Y. 11205

Name_____
(please print)

Address_____
City_____State_____Zip_____

Do you know someone who enjoys books? Just give us their names and addresses and we'll send them an order form too!

Name_____
Address_____
City_____State_____Zip_____

Name_____
Address_____
City_____State_____Zip_____